W9-BHK-502

THE
APOCALYPSE STONE

PETE EARLEY

○

TOR®

A TOM DOHERTY ASSOCIATES BOOK
NEW YORK

This is a work of fiction. All of the characters, organizations, and events portrayed in this novel are either products of the author's imagination or are used fictitiously.

THE APOCALYPSE STONE

Copyright © 2006 by Pete Earley

All rights reserved, including the right to reproduce this book, or portions thereof, in any form.

A Tor Book
Published by Tom Doherty Associates, LLC
175 Fifth Avenue
New York, NY 10010

www.tor.com

Tor® is a registered trademark of Tom Doherty Associates, LLC.

ISBN-13: 978-0-7653-4900-2
ISBN-10: 0-7653-4900-0

First Edition: June 2006
First Mass Market Edition: July 2007

Printed in the United States of America

0 9 8 7 6 5 4 3 2 1

For Patti Michele,
who believed I could

CAST OF MAJOR CHARACTERS

LESTER TIDWELL AMIL, rapper and murder suspect

FRANK ARNOLD, computer wunderkind

MAXINE ARNOLD, mother of murder victim

TAYLOR CAULDWELL, Virginia attorney general

PATTI DELANEY, defense attorney

THE REV. DR. DINO ANGELO GRASSO, biblical scholar

CHARLES MacDONALD, former detective

EVAN LeRUE SPENCER, Virginia circuit court judge

MELISSA VANDENVENDER, wealthy socialite

PART ONE
CURSED

○

I will give him a white stone, with a new name written on the stone which no one knows except him who received it.

The Book of Revelation, Chapter Two, Verse 17

1

PATRICK MCPHERSON WAS LOOKING AT THE TEN OF SPADES and seven of clubs, a total of seventeen in blackjack. He'd bet a thousand dollars. The dealer's up card was the ten of hearts.

"I think you've got another face card," McPherson told the dealer. "That'll give you twenty. So the only way I can win is if I can draw a four."

The gambler on McPherson's right snickered. The odds were against McPherson. Chances were, if he took a third card he'd bust. Just the same, he tapped a finger on top of his cards, signaling that he wanted another. The dealer slipped one from the red plastic shoe and flipped it over. It was a four. McPherson had hit twenty-one.

"How the hell did you know you were gonna draw a four?" the plump woman sitting on his left demanded. McPherson leaned close to her cheek, his eyes falling naturally downward into her bulging cleavage. *Why did housewives from Des Moines dress like whores when they came to Las Vegas?* he wondered.

"I can see the future," he whispered. "You're going to take another card and bust because it will be a queen."

She glanced at her cards and then at him. She had sixteen, a lousy hand. *Was he joking? No one could predict the future!* Ignoring his warning, she motioned for another card. It was a queen. She'd busted just like he'd predicted. But she didn't say anything. She suspected he was cheating or card counting and hoped, if she kept silent, that he would tell her his secret.

"You play a lot of blackjack?" she asked.

"No," he replied. "This is my first time."

She looked down into her purse, searching for a pack of cigarettes, and noticed his left hand, which he had kept hidden under the table.

"Oh my god!" she shrieked. "You're bleeding!"

The dealer paused. Everyone stared.

"No," he said calmly. "It's a birthmark on my palm. But sometimes it looks like blood." He jammed his left hand into the pocket of his tan cargo pants, and with his right hand, pushed every chip he owned to the woman. "Here, you take these."

"That's twenty thousand dollars!" she squealed. "Oh my god! Oh my god!"

McPherson moved away from the table quickly, exiting the casino through a row of clanging slot machines. *How do you hide a murder? Was his secret safe? Did it matter now, really? God knew. Judgment was being made. There would be no escape, no forgiveness, no last-minute reprieve. The biblical scriptures were clear about what God was demanding. "Leave immediately," the verses said. "Go to Sodom and Gomorrah, cities of great wickedness and debauchery. . . ."*

"Hello?"

The woman's voice interrupted his thoughts.

"The Federal Express driver picked up your package from the hotel a few hours ago," she said. "It should be delivered before noon tomorrow. Is there anything else I can help you with?"

"No," he answered, handing her five dollars. She hadn't done anything out of the ordinary for a hotel concierge, but in Las Vegas you tipped everyone. *It didn't matter. Money was no longer important.*

He walked to an elevator; at least, it would have been called an elevator in any other Las Vegas Strip resort. In the Luxor, it was called an "inclinator" because the hotel-casino was built in the shape of an Egyptian pyramid. Four inclinators traveled up and down its corners at a 39-degree incline. Entertainment architecture. He'd looked at the New York, New York casino, with its miniature Manhattan skyline facade, and briefly flirted with staying at the Paris resort, with its mock Eiffel Tower. But the pyramid shape of the Luxor, with its hollow center, best served his purpose. Earlier, he had eaten breakfast in the resort's Pyramid Café and had read on the restaurant's paper place mat that the Luxor's atrium was one of the largest in the world, big enough to hold nine Boeing 747 airplanes stacked on top of each other. It was perfect.

He pressed the inclinator's twenty-eighth-floor button, but before the doors closed, two couples and their gaggle of kids joined him. Cut-off shorts, bright yellow tube tops pulled snugly over fatty white flesh, orange Kmart fanny packs that jingled with each step, a T-shirt with the words "I'm with Stupid" printed on it. McPherson stood silently among them, listening to their twisted jumble of grammatically tortured sentences. Their words pounded inside his head. At Harvard Law, he had honed a talent. When he concentrated, he could actually see in his mind sentences that people were saying, complete with punctuation. During trials, it was useful, but in the inclinator it was maddening. *Wasted lives. Shallow dreams. Nobodies, going nowhere. Spending the pitiful three hundred dollars they had put aside for their vacation gambling. McPherson was not one of them and never had been. He was the third child born to Alfred Cumberland McPherson and Alice Chaucer Hayworth of Stamford, Connecticut. Old money. And plenty of it. He'd been born into the gene pool of America's upper crust, although the rich knew better than to acknowledge the existence of such a cultural hierarchy. Better for the minions to believe America was still a land of opportunity, a country where a peanut farmer from Georgia and a kid from an Arkansas trailer park could become president. They could, of course, but even after they'd moved into the White House, they still did not become one of them. Presidents made interesting dinner guests, but they were passers through, entertainment. You could study as much as you wished, but you would never master the social nuances and intricacies that McPherson's ilk knew. It was in their blood and breeding. No one in his family had ever engaged him in a casual conversation. Every word he uttered had been scrutinized and, if possible, used against him. His choice of clothes, his table manners, his diction, his ideas, his every thought and every action: all had been critiqued by a horde of nannies and tutors, as well as his siblings and parents and grandparents. After all, he was a McPherson. And that meant something. He had to be molded, else he might prove inferior. After Harvard, he'd joined one of Boston's oldest, most influential law firms. Where else would he have gone? He'd married the daughter of an equally old-money family. Whom else would he have chosen? He was forty-nine now. His hair, graying at the temples, gave him a dignified look. His life had seemed perfect. No, had been perfect. Absolutely perfect. A summer home in Martha's Vineyard, a studio apartment in Paris, a seven-figure income. Everything was on track. And then nine months ago, he had received an unsolicited package. A gift. Or so he'd thought. A joke. Or so he'd thought. In fact, it had been the beginning of the end. It is what had led him here.*

McPherson burst from the inclinator as soon as its doors opened. *Finally, silence. The typewriter in his mind stopped pecking.* Except for a discarded room service tray piled with dirty dishes, the hallway was empty. He hurried along the corridor until he reached its midway point. He stopped there and glanced over the waist-high wall that kept guests from tumbling into the atrium. From this perch, he could see a line of ticket holders twenty-eight floors below waiting patiently to enter an IMAX theater. Others had crowded around two life-size robotic camels whose computerized voices spewed out tidbits about the Luxor's amenities. Like miniatures, still others were sitting at tables in a ceiling-free fast food restaurant.

McPherson climbed over the wall and rested his heels on a two-inch-wide lip that ran along its base. He leaned forward into the atrium, his arms stretched back to grip the wall's top edge. *The package was gone. Now someone else would receive the gift. There was only one final task for him to perform. He had to pay for his sins. Atonement.*

He suddenly felt the urge to think of a happy event in his life. Something he could recall as he released his grip. It was difficult. But it finally came to him. *It was summer and it was hot. He was ten. Another boy, Michael, had been visiting his grandmother and the two families had arranged an introduction. The two boys became buddies, and one afternoon, they discovered an abandoned stone quarry a few miles outside Stamford. They'd stripped to their undershorts and jumped from the quarry's jagged ledges into the black, seemingly bottomless pool of cool water that had filled the angry scar left behind by dynamite and earth movers. After repeated jumps, they'd stretched out on the warm stone and let the July sun dry them as they chatted innocently about whose cannonball had made the biggest splash. It was Michael who had taught him how to do a swan dive. They had taken turns, springing from the ledge, stretching their arms wide at their sides, as if they were huge birds taking flight. McPherson had learned to squeeze his thighs tight, point his toes down and cock back his head, arch his back and look upward into the blinding afternoon sun. He would wait until the very last possible second— just before he was about to hit the water—before he tucked, entering the pool head first, his thin body causing barely a ripple.*

McPherson released his grip and his body fell forward. As he dropped into the resort's atrium, he stretched out his arms, squeezed his thighs tight, pointed his toes downward, cocked back his head and shoulders, and arched his back. He fell silently, his two-hundred-and-twenty-pound body slamming into a Formica-topped table six feet from the polished stainless-steel counter of the Luxor's McDonald's restaurant. He hit with such force that his body exploded, spewing bits of blood, bones, organs, and brain matter into the stunned diners' half-eaten Big Macs and supersize french fries.

He was free now. He'd paid for his sins.

2

AT AGE SEVENTY-TWO, THE REVEREND DINO ANGELO GRASSO certainly had enough seniority and political pull at the Catholic University of America, the only college in the United States with a charter directly from the Vatican, to be exempt from teaching an introductory theology class. But the Rev. Dr. Grasso, an internationally recognized expert in Old Testament studies and biblical translation, insisted on instructing at least one entry-level course each semester. He enjoyed interacting with first-year students because he found their religious naivete inspiring, and they in turn always voted his class their favorite first-year course. The fact that none of his students was absent from today's lecture did not surprise the cleric. The topic was miracles, specifically the Mystical Stigmata, and Grasso correctly assumed that his former students had spread word that this was not a lecture to miss. To an outsider visiting the campus, Grasso's popularity might have seemed odd. He was, by any description, a hideous-looking man. He had a hunched back and a pumpkin-shaped bald head that was so big it looked as if he would topple over if he leaned forward. He had a boxer's smashed nose, a distracting left eye that wandered uncontrollably, skin deeply pitted by acne, and too many yellow teeth crowded into his tiny mouth. Even though he bathed daily, there was a pungent odor about him and his breath reeked of onions. His right leg was two inches longer than his left, and he had been born with a useless left arm. It was as if God had chosen to experiment on his body, seeing how many physical disabilities one man could endure. Yet inside this grotesque frame was a brilliant and gentle man who welcomed each morning with enthusiasm.

There was nothing in the priest's past that would justify such cheerfulness. His parents had been ignorant laborers who had lived in squalor outside Cassino, an Italian city between Rome and Naples. He'd been the tenth of eleven children and his mother, upon seeing his deformities, had intended to suffocate him as she knew he would always be a financial burden to the family. But she had felt a pang of motherly guilt as she was lowering a pillow over his face and instead had elected to abandon him in front of a nearby Catholic monastery. Had she chosen any other sect of Franciscans, her newborn son would have been delivered to an orphanage in Naples run by nuns. But the monks in this particular friary believed that there were absolutely no coincidences in life, that every action was planned by God, and so they saw the arrival of an unwanted infant at their door as a sign that God wanted them to rear this child, as if he were a crippled bird that had fallen from a nest. Grasso had spent his boyhood toiling under the monks' stern rule. It had been a childhood filled with harsh tasks, perpetual prayer, denial of all pleasure, and constant correction with few signs of affection. What love Grasso had felt had come from his reading of the Holy Scriptures and his fervent belief that Jesus Christ was able to do what no human being seemed capable of doing: truly love him. By the time he was six, Grasso understood that he'd been an unwanted child and at night in his barren cubicle he would wonder if his parents' actions had been preordained by God as part of a divine master plan. Alone in his thoughts, he became convinced that God had created him for a specific task, that his parents had never really had any choice but to reject him. They had been moved by God's finger in a mysterious way. Likewise, his physical afflictions were tests meant to prepare him, and because there were so many for him to overcome, he deduced that the task that God was preparing for him had to be a monumental one.

As the years passed, Grasso worked diligently to prepare himself and waited patiently for God to show him the secret mission that only he would be able to accomplish. By the time he was a teenager, he had a powerful intellect. He could speak five languages fluently and read Latin and Greek. The monks arranged for him to move to Rome when he was nineteen, where he was assigned to work in a research position inside the Vatican's Secret Archives. It proved a perfect match: the church received the benefit of Grasso's superior intelligence while keeping him hidden from public view. Deep inside the archive's bowels, Grasso had pored over ancient manuscripts with such a passion that he often forgot what time it was and labored without pausing for days and nights. It was during this time that he had become proficient in Syriac and quickly mastered the Hebrew text of Sirach, the Wisdom of Ben Sira, and other ancient writings that biblical scholars consider elementary to understanding the origins of Christianity.

When he was twenty-one, Grasso had caused quite a stir among Vatican scholars by writing a research paper that questioned the legitimacy of the shrine to St. Anthony outside the Italian city of La Spezia. For centuries, devout pilgrims had traveled to the shrine to see a holy relic: a tiny piece of bone reportedly from the saint's foot. Nearly a hundred miracles had occurred at the shrine, and when Grasso visited it, he found its gates decorated with crutches discarded by healed cripples. Grasso's painstaking research showed that the bone housed in the shrine was not from Saint Anthony at all. Rather, it was from the skeletal remains of an Italian peasant whose bones had been unearthed and shattered into bits in the ninth century by a profit-seeking crook posing as a monk. The priest at La Spezia had spent nearly all of his impoverished rectory's funds to purchase the relic and had become convinced of its authenticity when a miracle had occurred three days after the bone was put on display. The terrified parents of a small unconscious boy had rushed inside the church carrying their son. He'd been digging in a field when he had fallen to the ground shaking uncontrollably. His parents assumed he'd unearthed a demon. The priest, clutching the relic, had called upon St. Anthony to cast out the devil and within seconds, the boy had awakened with no memory of what had happened. News of this exorcism swept across Italy, and with each retelling the legend grew. Grasso's research revealed that the boy had suffered an epileptic seizure and had come out of it quite naturally. His report was passed up the ranks to a panel of Vatican monsignors whose job was to review supernatural happenings. Almost three years after he had written his paper, Grasso received a letter from the panel thanking him for his impressive scholarship. Part of it read:

No dishonor is done to God by the continuance of an error which has been handed down in perfect good faith for many centuries. Devotions to relics, such as this bone, are often deeply rooted in the hearts of the peasantry, and we cannot simply sweep them away without some measure of scandal and popular disturbance, even if our scholarship shows them to be fraudulent. To create a sensation about this shrine, therefore, seems unwise. Hence, there is justification for our practice and the practice of the Holy See to allow the cult of certain doubtful ancient relics to continue.

Grasso's paper was locked in a section of the Secret Archives, where manuscripts that were deemed inappropriate for public distribution were kept.

Grasso had not complained. He believed in the wisdom of the Holy See. But the incident had caused him to wonder: *How many other miracles are fraudulent, how many other ancient relics are fabrications?* By his thirtieth birthday, he had experienced a crisis of faith, but then God had intervened. He had shown him a sign that erased all doubts. Grasso witnessed a miracle.

The old professor always began his lecture about the Mystical Stigmata by explaining the Vatican's official position on unexplained events. The gift of miracles, the church declared, had its roots in the First Epistle to the Corinthians when St. Paul wrote that the Holy Ghost had extended certain extraordinary powers to select believers. These were special gifts, bestowed only to a few, and in nearly all cases they were given so that God's chosen messengers could help others. In Greek, these powers were called *charismata,* or in the theological technical language, *gratiae gratis datae* (graces gratuitously given), to distinguish them from *gratiae gratum facientes* (grace given to a recipient for his own salvation).

Wanting to make certain that his students understood the difference, Grasso asked if anyone had a question. One student raised his hand: "Dr. Grasso, can a sinner or nonbeliever be given the power to perform miracles? I've seen these television evangelists claiming they heal people when it's clear to me that all they want is to get your money."

Grasso grinned. This is why he taught—the passage of knowledge from one generation to another. "You've asked an excellent question and one that our early church fathers hotly debated. The Holy See teaches that grace—*gratiae gratis datae*—can be bestowed by God to the just and to the unjust, but only rarely is it given to the unjust. This means that even sinners can perform miracles—yes—they can even have supernatural powers, but only if they use these powers for the good of others. Real miracles can never be performed by anyone as proof of his own personal sanctity. That would be a deception and derogatory to the sanctity of God."

"So," the student asked, obviously still confused, "can television evangelists heal people or not?"

"None of us knows why God chooses someone as His instrument, but if we look at the situation that surrounds these TV miracles, then perhaps we can tell if it is God's handiwork or some trickery. To what purpose are these television evangelists performing miracles? Is it for the glory of our Holy Father or is it for their own enrichment? Have they patterned themselves after Jesus Christ and are they living, as he did, a simple life, or are they riding in limousines, residing in grand houses, wearing expensive clothes? If so, then they have more in common with P. T. Barnum than our beloved Lord and Savior Jesus Christ."

Grasso had anticipated laughter but none came and it dawned on him that his students didn't recognize Barnum's name. *My, my,* he thought, *I am getting old.*

"Ask yourselves," he continued, "why would God give a sinner extraordinary powers—especially when there are so many true believers eagerly awaiting such a wonderful gift?"

For the next several minutes, Grasso recounted the church's doctrine regarding miracles, and then finally, he began the story that he knew they had been waiting to hear.

"When I was working at the Vatican, my colleague Father Petrocelli Zerilli and I were dispatched to Sicily to investigate a reported case of the Mystical Stigmata that had appeared in a teenage girl who lived in a tiny fishing village." The stigmata, Grasso explained, were wounds that had appeared many times throughout the centuries, most often in the hands, feet, side, or brow of extremely devout Christian believers. These wounds mimicked the cuts made on Jesus Christ when he was whipped, nailed to a cross, and crowned with a halo of thorns pushed onto his forehead. St. Francis of Assisi had been the first stigmatic recognized by the church, although hundreds of others claimed to have the wounds in the 1200s. The church had documented at least fifty cases of the stigmata in the nineteenth century. "There were so many proven cases that nonbelievers stopped doubting their existence and instead tried to explain them by using science," Grasso told his students. In Paris in 1901, Dr. Pierre Janet placed a copper shoe with a window in it over the foot of a stigmatic to ensure the wound was not self-inflicted. While the shoe made it impossible for anyone to touch the sore, Janet reported that it continued to increase in size on its own.

"When we arrived in the fishing village, we found the young girl so weak that she could not leave her bed, and when we examined her feet and hands, we saw nail punctures consistent with the stigmata. I remained skeptical, however, and thought her parents might have inflicted them to somehow profit from the attention," Grasso said. "To prevent self-mutilation, we moved the girl into the house of the local priest and Father Zerilli and I took turns maintaining an around-the-clock vigil at her bedside. We also cleaned the girl's wounds and wrapped bandages around them to see if basic medical aid would help the wounds heal."

Grasso paused. Every face in the classroom was locked on his. "Never once did we leave this girl alone," he continued. "We even tasted the soups brought to her by her mother to make certain they didn't contain some secret elixir. When the girl needed to use a bathroom, we helped her behind a screen, all the while, keeping her feet and hands in our sight. We went so far as to inspect her excrement and urine for some chemical explanation. After five days, we were absolutely convinced that she was not inflicting these wounds on herself nor was anyone hurting her. Despite our bandages and visits by medical doctors, the wounds refused to close. In fact, they became larger."

Again, Grasso paused to take a breath. No one in the class

was fidgeting. Every student was waiting eagerly for him to continue. "On the thirty-third day after the stigmata had first appeared, the girl slipped into a trance. Our first thoughts, of course, were that our beloved Lord and Savior Jesus Christ had been thirty-three years old when he was crucified. The girl's body began to shake so violently that we summoned a doctor, but there was nothing he could do to calm her. He gave her a series of sedatives, more than enough to have sent her into a deep sleep, yet she remained alert and wide awake. We could see that she was beginning to suffer extreme pain and we knew this was in keeping with the Mystical Stigmata. Suffering is an essential part because this miracle appears only in believers who have tremendous pity for our Lord and Savior Jesus Christ. A stigmatic literally participates with him in his sufferings, sorrows, and ultimately his death. This is how it must be because the wounds would be empty symbols, theatrical representations conducive to pride if the stigmatic didn't die."

In his telling of the story, Grasso himself appeared to have slipped into a trance. He was recalling the events with such vividness that it was as if he was seeing it all happen again before his own eyes. "While I was sitting at the girl's bedside praying, she began describing the last days of Christ. She was having a vision. You must remember that this girl, although devout, was uneducated. There was no possible way for her to have known the minute details. As she described Christ being tormented, I could see new physical wounds actually appear on her arms, forehead, and neck. When she said he was being whipped, her entire body shook and she screamed as the lashes hit her. Her cries were so piercing that Father Zerilli rushed in to see what was happening. The two of us sat on either side of her bed and watched as this girl assumed Christ's role. Her words stopped being descriptive and, instead, she began uttering words we knew from our biblical studies that Jesus, himself, had spoken. Finally, her fragile body shook violently one final time and then a burst of air came gushing from her lungs. Father Zerilli immediately listened for a heartbeat but the girl was dead. Of course, the local police were suspicious but they did not detain us. The town's constable, who was a nonbeliever, demanded an autopsy. The results showed that the girl had died from the exact same injuries that are caused by a crucifixion. The autopsy also revealed that the blood, which had oozed from her wounds, was actually not blood at all. Rather it was ordinary bodily fluids, but in the girl's case, they had pooled on the surface of the skin without explanation.

"To this day, I know of no scientific evidence that proves a human being can produce the stigmata purely by the power of their imagination, emotion, or even desire. Tests of deeply religious persons under hypnosis have failed to duplicate the stigmata, and while there are some diseases that might produce a bloody sweat, nothing in medicine nor psychology can explain the appearance of such wounds and the discharge that comes from them. This teenage girl had no history of hallucinations, no history of emotional turmoil, no history of mental illness. There was no physical way that she could have murdered herself by imagining that she was being crucified. No, my students, this was not something that happened in her head, but in her heart. She had literally died with Christ. I was there. I saw it happen."

The bell rang. The time was up. But no one stirred.

"Although my mind could not produce a rational explanation," Grasso said, "in my heart I knew I had witnessed a miracle. But for what end? Why had this young girl gone through Christ's suffering and agony? What was God's purpose?"

Grasso glanced at the clock above the exit. "This we will discuss during some later session," he said. "But for now, class is dismissed." He could hear a collective *ohhhhh* of disappointment. "I will leave you with one final thought," Grasso said. "As horrible as this girl's death might seem to you, I would've gladly exchanged lives with her. To have seen our Lord and Savior Jesus Christ, to have felt his wounds, to have been with him during the moment of his crucifixion, to have died with him. Yes, there was agony and suffering, but there was also in this girl's tortured face a joy I had never seen before or since. It was as if she had seen the face of God, and I would have given anything at that moment to have switched with her."

Grasso always was exhausted after he told the stigmatic story. By the time he had limped across campus to his tiny office, he had decided to skip his lunch and take an afternoon nap. His secretary, who rarely missed a meal, was already gone. But she had left his mail on his desk. Most of the stack was letters: an invitation to give a sermon, another to present a guest lecture. However, at the bottom was a large manilla envelope. Return Address: Coroner's Office, Clark County, Las Vegas, Nevada. Grasso didn't recall knowing anyone in Las Vegas. He removed a typewritten letter and smaller sealed envelope.

Dear Dr. Grasso,

I doubt if you will remember me, but twelve years ago I was a theology student at Catholic University and I heard your lecture about the teenage stigmatic in Sicily. After my first year, I left the university and entered medical school. Now I am the chief pathologist here. I am writing because of a puzzling case. I have enclosed several photographs in a sealed envelope for you to examine. I didn't know if your secretary opens your mail and they're rather gruesome.

A man, identified as Patrick McPherson, committed suicide by leaping into the atrium of a Strip casino. He hit with such impact that his body exploded. The man's wife confirmed that he had been suffering from some mental disorder. Sadly, for us suicides are rather routine. But when I examined this man's body, I found an unusual mark on his left hand. I think it was a stigmata.

I remember you telling us that a stigmatic doesn't always ooze blood, but a combination of chemicals from inside their body form a substance that resembles blood. I ran several tests and discovered this was not the case here. This man's mark was bleeding. I have no medical explanation for this. Initially, I suspected he might have burned or branded himself because it looked as if he had touched something that had blistered his skin. Yet there was no scar tissue that would indicate branding or self-mutilation.

I remember you telling us that the wounds of the stigmata duplicate the wounds of Jesus Christ. But there was only one wound on this man's body. There were no similar wounds in his right hand, feet, side, or on his forehead. The shape of the mark on his left hand also is not consistent with a nail puncture as you will see. (Photograph marked 3-A.)

My office is not pursuing this matter. To us, the case is a simple suicide. But I have been unable to forget the unusual mark on this man's palm. Is it possible that he was suffering from some sort of stigmata that has no connection to Jesus Christ? If not, why would he have only one mark? And why would he have been given the gift of the stigmata and then killed himself? I thought stigmatics were deeply religious persons who were emulating Christ's life. Isn't suicide still considered by the church to be a mortal sin?

The letter was signed "Dr. Paul Harris" and he was right: Grasso didn't remember him. There had been too many students over the years. Grasso opened the second envelope and several snapshots tumbled out. The first was of a man's severed arm. A yardstick had been placed beside the limb and someone had written along the picture's border: "Right hand to elbow." There was nothing unusual about the photo. It was the three other pictures that piqued Grasso's interest. "Photograph 2-A, left hand to shoulder" had been taken with McPherson's palm facing the camera. Grasso could see two bright red slashes on the left hand. A third photograph, marked 3-A, focused entirely on the palm. The red lines appeared to be fresh blood but they were not random cuts. Instead, they were in the shape of a cross. A fourth photograph made with a close-up lens revealed even more detail. It appeared that there was a human figure hanging on the cross. Fetching his magnifying glass, Grasso studied the picture. The red lines were so amazingly detailed that Grasso could make out the outline of a crown of thorns on the crucified figure's head. He put his magnifying glass on his desk. He'd never seen anything like this. What could it possibly mean?

3

CHARLOTTESVILLE, VIRGINIA

THE FED EX PACKAGE FROM LAS VEGAS ARRIVED AT THE THIRD-floor office of Judge Evan Spencer inside the Albemarle County Courthouse just before ten A.M., but his clerk, Alice Jackson, didn't recognize the sender's name so she had a sheriff's deputy take it to be X-rayed. Jackson, whom everyone called Miss Alice, was about to celebrate her fiftieth year working as the presiding judge's chief clerk, and she was not about to open a delivery from Sin City without making certain it didn't contain explosives. Miss Alice had long suspected that the Albemarle courthouse would become a terrorist's target. The city of Charlottesville was known as the capital of the cradle of Democracy, a fertile swath of central Virginia that had been the home of three presidents: Thomas Jefferson, James Madison, and James Monroe. Who better represented the federal government than these three patriots, all of whom had played key roles in forging it? As an avid member of the Albemarle County Historical Society, Miss Alice knew that Jefferson, Madison, and Monroe each had walked the same floors of the courthouse that she now walked, and she was going to do all that was in her power to protect that heritage.

Built in 1763, the courthouse sat on a slight hill in the middle of Court Square in what used to be the very center of town. Although it had gone through a number of expansions, the building retained its original colonial look. It had a redbrick facade, was two stories tall, and had four white Ionic columns and a portico at its front entrance. Its wooden front doors led visitors directly into a large courtroom. Three paintings decorated the walls. Jefferson's portrait hung directly behind the judge's chair. Madison and Monroe faced each other on the side walls. No other pictures were permitted. A chain with a large ring attached to it dangled down from the ceiling a few steps from the judge's seat. The chain was attached to an iron bell on the roof that was rung years ago to announce to the crowds waiting outside on the lawn that a jury had reached its verdict. Albemarle County had added a second redbrick building adjacent to the original courthouse. The sheriff's office and the commonwealth's attorney operated out of its basement. The first floor held the general court, where traffic tickets and other minor legal disputes were resolved. Marriage, divorce, and other public records could be found on the second floor in the county clerk's office. The third floor was where Judge Spencer's chambers were located and where Miss Alice, as the grande dame of the courthouse, ruled.

Miss Alice had a personal reason for feeling passionate about the courthouse. Her great-great-grandfather, Horatio Jackson, had died only a few paces from its front door during the Civil War. He had been under the command of Confederate Colonel John S. Mosby, the famed Gray Ghost, and was with him picking up supplies in Charlottesville when Union troops stormed unexpectedly into town. Mosby and Jackson fled as Union troops opened fire. Mosby escaped but Jackson was fatally shot and fell from his horse. Jackson had been a distant cousin to Confederate General Thomas "Stonewall" Jackson, who at the time was giving federal troops a bloody beating throughout the Shenandoah Valley, racking up victories in nearby Front Royal and Winchester. Miss Alice had inherited Horatio Jackson's Leech & Rigdon Confederate Army .36-caliber pistol, a rare artifact. It was kept on permanent display in a glass case just outside the door to Judge Spencer's office, along with Horatio's rebel cap and a leather pouch, which still held ammunition. Besides that Civil War exhibit, there were two stone monuments outside the courthouse that paid tribute to the Confederacy. A Rebel soldier armed with a rifle stood watch directly in front of the building. On either side of him were cannons. A larger monument of Stonewall riding his horse was on the western edge of the square.

For Miss Alice, it was hallowed ground.

Although none of Horatio Jackson's descendants had become wealthy or famous, Miss Alice never missed an opportunity to mention her dead ancestor or her distant kinship to Stonewall Jackson. Over the years, she had used both to stake her claim in Charlottesville's high society. She was currently the president of the Daughters of the Confederacy of Albemarle County and frequently appeared in newspaper photographs taken at various charity events.

Judge Spencer had inherited Miss Alice's services after he had been appointed by the Virginia General Assembly as a judge in the sixteenth Judicial Circuit. Although he would have gladly gotten rid of her if he could have. Spencer knew, however, that firing the feisty spinster would have hurt him politically, so he kept her as his chief clerk while at the same time maneuvering to reduce her responsibilities. Likewise, Miss Alice understood that bad-mouthing her boss was not politically savvy, so she presented to the public an overly polite demeanor and quietly watched for opportunities to undermine him. In the five years that had passed, neither had managed to do as much damage to the other as they had hoped.

Judge Spencer suspected that Miss Alice was secretly jealous of his social standing, which he considered ironic since he had not earned it but had married into both wealth and prestige. His wife was Ophelia Elizabeth Victoria VanDenvender, a member of one of the richest and oldest families in the state. The VanDenvenders traced their ancestry back to colonial times when King George II had awarded several thousands of acres to Sir Edward VanDenvender. By the time of the American Revolution, the VanDenvender family had become rich, thanks mainly to tobacco and lumber. Despite the family's political ties to English royalty, Edward's son, Augustus VanDenvender, had joined his neighbors in helping plot the revolution and afterward had greatly expanded his family's holdings. Each heir seemed to have a magical touch and the family fortune multiplied. Even after the Civil War, when other Southern plantation owners were ruined, the VanDenvenders not only survived but thrived. Because their holdings were still privately held, no one knew exactly how much wealth the family had, but there was more than enough for thirty descendants to live off plump trust funds. Spencer's wife, whom everyone called Melissa, was one of the younger heirs.

Spencer hadn't had a clue about Melissa's background when they first met. She had spent much of her childhood in a New England boarding school, so she had been as much a stranger to

Charlottesville as he had in 1972 when they both reported to the University of Virginia, known simply as "the University" by most Virginians. Melissa was an undergraduate student studying art history. Spencer had already completed his bachelor's degree at the University of Illinois and was entering law school. Melissa hadn't wanted anyone to know that she was a VanDenvender so she had enrolled under the last name Burroughs; it was her mother's maiden name and also the name of her favorite beat author, William S. Burroughs. At the time, Melissa was in what she later would describe as her "antiestablishment, dope-smoking, Jimi Hendrix, Janis Joplin, hippie phase." She was five years younger than Spencer and, although smart, didn't take her studies seriously. There was no need.

They had been brought together completely by chance. Her roommate, a reporter on the campus newspaper, *The Cavalier Daily,* had asked for help interviewing students at a Vietnam War protest. Melissa had spotted Spencer standing apart from the crowd. Most students were wearing T-shirts, denim jeans, and Jesus sandals, but he was dressed in an ironed white shirt, pressed trousers, and tan Hush Puppy loafers. He'd been horrified when she had approached him with an outstretched microphone attached to a bulky cassette recorder. She liked the challenge of badgering him into talking to her. One reason why he hadn't simply turned away was because she was wearing a white handkerchief halter top with a red peace symbol sewn on its front. Spencer, who had grown up in a tiny Illinois farm town, was not used to seeing women braless, and she had caught him twice staring at the outline of her nipples. During their brief exchange, Spencer told her that he was opposed to the Vietnam War, but didn't support antiwar demonstrations. His father was a World War II veteran and career Air Force officer who had been killed during a training accident. His mother still worked for the U.S. Postal Service, and Spencer believed the United States was the best nation in the world. His first priority was earning a law degree, he explained, and if students wanted to end the war, they needed to work through the proper political and legal channels to change the system from within.

"I feel confident," he had then added, "that Thomas Jefferson would have felt the same way I do."

It was his statement about Jefferson, which was published on the campus newspaper's front page the next day, that had caused a ruckus. At any other college, his quote might have passed unnoticed, but the University of Virginia had been founded by Jefferson in 1819, and despite the anti-establishment fervor sweeping campuses nationwide, Jefferson still retained saintlike status at the University. As William Howard Taft once noted, many in Charlottesville still spoke of "Mr. Jefferson" as if he were in the next room.

What would Jefferson have done about Vietnam?

Overnight, Spencer was thrust into the role of spokesman for the "responsible right" and was quickly dragged into a formal debate about the war, sponsored by the University's student government association. His opponent was a member of the radical Students for a Democratic Society who had driven down from Philadelphia. Spencer had stayed up all night practicing his arguments. But his SDS opponent, who was chosen to speak first, began the debate by chanting "Fuck the Establishment!" and within minutes two Charlottesville policemen had wrestled him to the floor. While he was being hauled to jail, Spencer had stumbled awkwardly through his own speech.

From the start, Spencer had been mesmerized by Melissa. But she had not felt the same about him. Instead, she considered him an "interesting project," a curiosity because he was so different from the well-polished sons of wealthy families whom she knew. Rather than being offended, Spencer had worked harder to charm her, and by the end of the first semester she surprised him by moving into the cramped attic apartment that he rented off campus.

Back then, there had been no hint of Melissa's hidden wealth. At Christmas, Spencer had worked as a department store Santa to earn enough to buy her a music box that played John Lennon's 1967 song "All You Need Is Love." She gave him a beaded peace necklace that she had made. It was only after Spencer had convinced Melissa to marry him, and she had shocked even herself by agreeing, that she had revealed her true last name. Shortly thereafter, Spencer had been hustled into the boardroom of Charlottesville's oldest law firm, Van-Denvender and Wythe, for a meeting with Melissa's father.

Spencer had been seated on one side of a huge mahogany table inside a posh conference room across from six VanDenvender family members who were being assisted by two accountants and three lawyers. For more than two hours, the VanDenvenders had grilled him about his grades, his childhood, his parents, his family history, his religious beliefs, his political views. They had demanded to know his professional and personal aspirations, and had even questioned him about girls whom he had dated in high school. All the while, they had referred to notes from a thick file compiled by a private detective. After Spencer had answered their questions, Melissa's father, Augustus VanDenvender VI, had bluntly told him what he could expect.

"You'll not get one damn cent of VanDenvender money!" the old man declared. While Spencer apparently had been found to be acceptable husband material, he would never become part of the VanDenvender dynasty nor would he ever be given access to its vast wealth. The shrewdest attorneys in the country would ensure that he could never file a successful legal claim against his in-laws or demand any of his future wife's holdings. In case of a divorce, he would walk away with only what he had brought with him into the marriage. If he and Melissa had children, they would be recognized as VanDenvender heirs but their shares would come only from those that Melissa already held and whatever shares she inherited from her parents. As part of a premarriage contract, he would have to sign a secrecy agreement that would prohibit him from revealing any of the family's financial dealings or making any public statements "that might be viewed by the general populace as demeaning, critical, or prurient" toward the VanDenvender name.

Evan Spencer had been twenty-three years old at the time and he hadn't given a damn about the VanDenvender family or its fortune. He had signed every document thrust before him in triplicate and had walked defiantly out the law office's front door. *Who needed their money?* He had naively thought that he and Melissa could live normal lives without the family meddling. The first hint that he was wrong had come later that same day when Melissa announced that she did not intend to take the name Spencer after they were married. "Lots of women are keeping their maiden names now," she shrugged. "Besides, why would I want to become a Spencer?"

His hopes for independence had been further dashed after he and Melissa wed. She refused to move away from Charlottesville and no local law firm wanted to hire him. The first question prospective employers asked was: "Why aren't you working for VanDenvender and Wythe?" If his own father-in-law would not give him a job, why should they? Spencer had briefly considered starting his own law practice but had just as quickly realized the futility of it. Melissa's flirtation with anonymity and poverty had ended, and she had no intention of living on a newlywed's budget. Her father had given her a thoroughbred horse as a wedding present and the cost of keeping it boarded was more than Spencer could afford on a struggling attorney's salary. The gift had been a calculated move by Melissa's father. He had immediately suggested that Melissa keep a substantial bank account of her own on the side so that she could afford the niceties that she was used to enjoying. With no other viable job prospects, Spencer had tucked his tail between his legs and gone to work for VanDenvender and Wythe. He became a skilled lawyer but that hadn't mattered. He was dismissed by most members of the Charlottesville bar association as simply VanDenvender's son-in-law.

While it had taken some time, Spencer had eventually proven himself. And then fate had intervened. In 1981, the general district court judge asked if Spencer would fill in for him during the summer. Spencer had been nervous but soon discovered that he had a knack for interpreting the law. In Virginia's two-tiered court system, minor traffic matters and legal disputes under fifteen thousand dollars are resolved in the general district court. As its only judge, Spencer heard a wide variety of complaints: disorderly conduct, possession of marijuana, assault and battery. He enjoyed it so much that when the summer ended, he let it be known that he was interested in a permanent appointment.

The local bar association—about two hundred attorneys—informally discussed his qualifications and, after much schmoozing by Spencer, agreed to recommend him. The bar presented his name to the politicians who represented Albemarle County in the Virginia General Assembly in Richmond. And after even more schmoozing by Spencer, the politicos passed his name on to a judicial committee that then officially nominated him for a vote before the entire General Assembly. It had rubber-stamped his appointment. Spencer wasn't certain what, if any, effect his status as Augustus VanDenvender IV's son-in-law had played. But he was proud that he had never asked his father-in-law to pull any strings.

If anything, Spencer had moved quickly to sever his ties with the law offices of VanDenvender and Wythe. He'd also dropped out of the clubs and social organizations that attorneys join as a way to meet potential clients when they are first starting out. He basked in this new independence. Midway through his six-year term, the Albemarle County Circuit Court judge in Charlottesville died from a heart attack and Spencer put out word that he wanted the job. It was a step up from general court. Once again, the schmoozing began and Spencer was appointed by the legislature to an eight-year term on the sixteenth Judicial Circuit bench. He was currently serving his second eight-year stint and had recently been chosen by the other five circuit judges as the presiding judge. For all practical purposes, Spencer was the law in Albemarle and its adjoining counties. He presided over all jury trials. There was only one judicial position higher than his and that was a seat on the Virginia Supreme Court. Getting there was Spencer's ultimate goal, but for now, he was content. Most of all, he felt free from the VanDenvender's leash. He was no longer known as Augustus VanDenvender VI's son-in-law. He was Evan Spencer, chief circuit court judge.

If anyone had doubted his independence, Spencer had proved his impartiality shortly after he was appointed. A county tax assessor had noticed during a routine audit that the Fox Run Country Club was operating a twenty-seven-hole golf course, but was only being assessed property tax for an eighteen-hole course. When the auditor raised the club's tax assessment, its board flew into a frenzy and filed an appeal. Judge Spencer heard the case. Augustus VanDenvender VI, who was one of the country club's directors, had bragged that his son-in-law would automatically rule in the club's favor. But Spencer hadn't. The incident had badly embarrassed Augustus, so much so that he had launched a behind-the-scenes effort to boot Spencer from the country club's rolls. It had been Melissa who had pointed out that Spencer had never actually been approved for membership. He'd been added only because he was married to her.

At this moment, Judge Evan Spencer was not thinking about his father-in-law, his wife, or the twenty-three years that they had been married. Dressed in his black judicial robe and sitting beneath Jefferson's portrait in the Albemarle County courtroom, Spencer was imagining what Patti Delaney, a young-looking forty-two-year-old defense attorney standing before him, would look like naked. Visualizing defense attorneys nude during a burglary trial was not something Spencer normally did. He'd always been sexually faithful to Melissa, although he wasn't certain his wife could make the same claim. The very rich, he had discovered, often act as if they are above the social mores that bind ordinary people. Spencer knew of several country club members whose wives had caught their husbands cheating. Yet that news rarely led to divorce. The matter had been smoothed over by what Spencer called "auto-gratification." The going price for sealing the lips of a college coed who worked as a waitress in the club's restaurant was a silver Audi TT convertible. The cost of smoothing things over with a wronged wife was higher-end: a Lexus or Mercedes. What wives paid for their indiscretions was not so obvious.

Spencer's faithfulness to Melissa had more to do with his own self-image than any strong moral feelings about fidelity. A circuit court judge was supposed to be honorable, law-abiding, trustworthy, wise, and not act as if he were a schoolboy gigolo.

"Your Honor!"

It was the commonwealth's assistant attorney Charles Bailey's raspy voice. Too many cigarettes and cups of coffee.

"The commonwealth is ready."

Spencer addressed Patti Delaney. "And the defense?"

She was digging through a badly worn black leather briefcase and appeared frazzled.

"Yes, uh, sure, I mean, yes sir, your honor."

Delaney was the newest lawyer to set up shop in Charlottesville, and lots of gossip about her had made its way through the courthouse. She had moved to town three months earlier from Grundy, Virginia, where she had spent two years teaching at the Appalachian School of Law, one of the state's lesser-known law schools. Before that she had practiced in Baltimore, Maryland, along with her husband. Rumor was that their marriage and law partnership had come to an abrupt end after Delaney came home unexpectedly from an out-of-town business trip and found her husband in bed with a male construction worker who, she later realized, had been taking an unusually long time remodeling their kitchen. The Charlottesville Bar Association had politely welcomed her, but there was an unspoken understanding among the city's lawyers that the county really didn't need any more attorneys, especially a Yankee, especially a Yankee woman. Since then, she had handled some wills, completed a few simple real estate settlements, and appeared in general district court. But this was her first time in the circuit court and her first jury trial in Albemarle County.

Spencer had noticed Delaney shortly after she had arrived in town. She was hard to miss. She had fiery red hair, green eyes, smooth ivory freckled skin. Although she was not stunningly beautiful like Melissa, who had always been model thin, permanently tanned, and immaculately groomed as only the rich can afford to be, Delaney had a robust outdoorsy look to her. He could easily visualize her joining a touch-football game after a Thanksgiving family dinner or going camping in a pup tent in the Blue Ridge Mountains—two activities that Melissa would never have considered. Attorney Delaney struck him as the sort of woman who was constantly trying to lose those extra five pounds that seemed to cling to her thighs.

But it wasn't her red hair or shape that made Delaney stick out. It was her choice in clothes. It was awful. At this moment, she was wearing a bright red Chinese silk jacket, decorated with millennium dragons in gold stitching, and a shiny black leather skirt. Her hair was in a bun with two chopsticks poking out from it. It was more waitress than defense attorney.

Spencer had arranged for Delaney to be assigned to this burglary case. She didn't know it, but he had telephoned a general district court judge who owed him a favor and suggested that Delaney be appointed. Although the Commonwealth didn't pay much to court-appointed attorneys, it was a way for her to break into criminal cases. Spencer wasn't completely certain why he had decided to help her—especially now. It had taken all of yesterday to get a jury impaneled, a torturously slow process in a routine burglary case, and Delaney was the cause. She was acting as if O.J. Simpson were on trial. At first, Spencer had found her painstaking examination of potential jurors amusing, but he'd soon grown weary of it.

Delaney's client was Rufus Johnson, a twenty-year-old accused of breaking into Hallman's Clothing Store, a men's clothing shop on the downtown mall. The Commonwealth had offered Delaney a deal in order to avoid the time and cost of a jury trial. In return for her client pleading guilty, prosecutors were prepared to recommend a three-year sentence with all but one year suspended. It was a generous offer. If convicted, Johnson faced five years. But Delaney had flatly rejected prosecutor Bailey's offer and proclaimed that she was going to prove that her client was innocent.

"What happened when you opened your store on the morning of March 22?" the gruff-voiced Bailey asked his first witness.

"I saw that someone had broken into the back of my store," Chris Hallman replied. "A window had been forced open. Lucky for me, the thief couldn't open the steel door that leads from our storeroom into our showroom. The only things in the back room were some boxes that contained last season's clothes and, you know, stuff that really hadn't sold that well, like a box of long-sleeve purple shirts with French cuffs."

"Can you describe what was stolen by the burglar?"

"I wrote out a detailed list for the police but you really don't need a copy of it."

"Why not?"

"Because the defendant over there is wearing one of the purple shirts with French cuffs that was stolen and those brown pants—they were stolen from the storeroom too!"

Spencer expected Delaney to object, but like everyone else in the room, she was preoccupied staring at her client's clothing.

"I can't see his feet," Hallman continued testifying, "but if he's wearing oxblood wingtips, then he stole them too!"

Spencer looked. Sure enough, Johnson was wearing oxblood wingtips.

"Judge," an embarrassed Delaney said, quickly rising from her chair, "may I have a short recess to confer with my client."

Spencer gave her fifteen minutes and when court reconvened, Delaney asked for permission to approach the bench. "I've spoken to my client and the commonwealth's attorney and the prosecution is still willing to offer my client a plea bargain," she said in a hushed voice. "So we'd like to withdraw our plea of not guilty and accept a three-year sentence with two years suspended."

"You understand, Ms. Delaney," Spencer replied, "that Mr. Bailey can only recommend a sentence. It's up to me to decide, and quite frankly, I'm tempted to give your client five years for sheer stupidity. Is he really wearing clothes he stole during the burglary?"

Delaney cleared her throat. "Your honor, I don't want to say anything that might incriminate my client, but my understanding is that, well, apparently, yes."

"Why would he be so dumb as to wear clothes that he had stolen?"

"Ah, your honor, ah, I'm afraid that's probably my fault," Delaney said. "I told him to wear something respectable. He said the stolen clothes were the only nice clothes he had."

Spencer fought back a smile. "I'll approve the plea bargain, but I want to see you in my chambers after we adjourn." Within minutes, Spencer had quickly dispatched the case, thanked and dismissed the jury, and retreated to his chambers. He'd just removed his black robe when Delaney arrived.

"Judge, I am so, so sorry about what happened," she began. "I didn't intend to waste the court's time. This is not the first impression I wanted to make."

"This case was a joke," he declared. "You should've pleaded it out to begin with."

"I'm really sorry. Everything today just went in the wrong direction, starting with my alarm not going off and there not being any hot water in my apartment and me not being able to find a place to park and . . ."

Spencer cut her short. He hated excuses and suspected that calamities were a routine part of her life. "Ms. Delaney," he replied, "my court is a serious place for serious attorneys. I can assure you that I take the law very, very seriously and I have a reputation for being a very serious judge. While today's escapade was amusing, it's not something that I will ever want to see in my courtroom again. Have I made myself clear?"

"Yes."

"Also," he continued, sounding very fatherly, "I expect lawyers who appear before me to dress appropriately."

"Judge," she replied, her voice bristling, "are you suggesting that I am not dressed appropriately to do my job? Is there a dress code in Albemarle County that I'm not aware of?"

Spencer suddenly realized that he was treading on thin ice. "Most women attorneys wear more conservative attire," he said. "I just thought I would mention it. You may go."

She slammed the chamber door behind her. "I'm a serious judge, this is a serious courtroom, I want everyone to be serious, serious, serious," she whispered. "Most women wear more conservative attire! Maybe I need to buy a Southern ball gown. What a pompous asshole!"

Moments later, Spencer stepped out from his chambers. "I'm leaving early today, Miss Alice," he announced. Her desk was directly outside his chambers. Miss Alice picked up a Federal Express package.

"I was just about to bring this in to you," she said. "The sheriff's office didn't find a bomb in here but what they did find is rather strange. Someone's sent you a rock."

"A rock?"

She handed him the box and he peered inside. He saw a white round stone about the size of a man's fist wrapped in clear plastic.

"Any letter or note?" he asked.

"None."

"Who sent it?"

"Patrick McPherson," Miss Alice said, reading the delivery label. "Someone you know?"

"Just put the package on my desk, please," he told her. He didn't volunteer an explanation. Why should he? Instead, he stepped out into the hallway and made his way to the stairs. *Patrick McPherson.* He hadn't heard that name or thought of him in years. McPherson had been one of Melissa's many suitors. He was from a wealthy Boston family. *Why had he sent him a rock?*

The air outside smelled fresh. It was fall, the leaves had started to turn. It was crisp but not yet cold enough for a jacket. Spencer gazed at the black Jaguar XK8 convertible in his parking spot. It had cost eighty-five thousand dollars with options and had been a reward to himself. Every penny had come from his own bank account. Melissa had been amused. Judges in Charlottesville, she told him, drove Lincolns or Cadillacs. If they were especially daring, they could drive a Mercedes, but a Jaguar sports car smacked of excess, irresponsibility, and a major midlife crisis. Spencer knew she was correct. That's why he had compromised and ordered black rather than the carnival red that had been his first choice. Black seemed more judicial. Sliding onto the car's leather seat, he turned the ignition and was backing up when he saw a flash of blue in the rearview mirror, heard the squealing of brakes, and then felt the impact of another car slamming into his. He turned and saw the oldest and most dilapidated-looking Saab that he had ever seen. Patti Delaney stepped out of it.

"It's you!" she stammered. "You okay?"

He didn't know what to say. She began looking in her purse for her insurance card as he inspected the crumpled rear panel of his Jaguar. He'd driven it fewer than fifty miles. It was going to be expensive to repair. The ancient Saab, meanwhile, had only a scratch on its front bumper.

"Miss Delaney," he asked, "are you trying to make a bad impression?"

"It's 'Ms.' and my insurance company will pay for the repairs. What kind of a car is that anyway?"

"A Jaguar. An XK8 sports car. A very expensive sports car."

"How nice," she said, unimpressed. "Well, that's why we

have insurance, isn't it?" She handed him her business card after writing the name of her insurance company and policy number on it. He slipped it into his pocket. "Well, aren't you going to give me your insurance information?" she asked.

"You hit me, remember? Besides your car doesn't look any worse than it already did."

"Excuse me, Judge Spencer, but you were backing out of that spot pretty fast and with that huge SUV parked next to you, I doubt you saw me coming. Anyway, under the Virginia statutes, I am entitled to it and I want it."

He didn't have any paper, so she handed him another one of her business cards and he jotted down his insurance information. He waited until Delaney had driven out of the parking lot before pulling onto High Street. "Jesus Christ!" he said, slapping his palm against the wheel. "What a bitch!"

Within a few minutes, he had escaped from the city and his mood lifted. He pulled onto the side of the road, tucked down the convertible's black top, and reinspected the damage. It really wasn't that bad. Returning to the highway, he pressed the car's accelerator and it lunged forward. *This was a feeling that women simply would never understand*, he thought. Melissa was correct. He *was* having a midlife crisis. He pressed the pedal harder. It was only a short drive from the outskirts of Charlottesville into the Blue Ridge Mountains and the rolling estate where Spencer and Melissa lived. He was going to take each curve as fast as he dared.

Melissa had been given the deed to VanDenvender Hall by her parents as a one-year wedding anniversary present. It was an imposing six-bedroom, seven-thousand-square-foot farmhouse constructed in 1856 on a one-thousand-acre estate that contained meadows awash in wildflowers, three mountain brooks, and miles of hardwood forests.

The main house was a traditional colonial made of red brick with a circular driveway and a tall portico supported by four white columns that protected guests from inclement weather. There were two badly worn limestone steps at the front of the house that rose from the ground and led nowhere. They were a holdover from the days when horses provided transportation. Carriages would pull up next to the steps so their passengers could exit gracefully. Melissa had made more than a few improvements to VanDenvender Hall. A swimming pool, hot tub, pool house, tennis court, guest cottage, and servants quarters had been added behind the main house. Other amenities included a four-car garage, workshop, and a stone stable built to accommodate as many as ten horses. Melissa had paid for the additions from her own personal funds.

For much of its existence, VanDenvender Hall had been a working farm so the house itself, while expansive, was not ornate. There were no outside decorations as were commonly found on the beaux arts estates of the Vanderbilts and the Belmonts. Although traditions were changing, in Virginia it was not the size of a man's castle that revealed his wealth, it was the number of acres and the quality of his horses that defined his social rank. Melissa adored thoroughbreds and kept a stable of six, including a three-year-old that had been sired by the winner of the 1998 Kentucky Derby. It was her favorite. She named him Little Thunder, and as Spencer pulled through the iron gate that led to VanDenvender Hall, he spotted Melissa riding the stallion across an adjoining meadow. He beeped the Jaguar's horn and as she turned the horse toward him, Melissa shot him a "come on" look. He gunned the Jaguar, sending crushed blue stone flying from behind its rear wheels. Then, he quickly braked to a stop. Accepting the challenge, Melissa positioned Little Thunder next to the sleek sports car and then sent her horse flying forward. Spencer counted slowly, in the spirit of fairness, and gave the beast a good twenty-second start. Then he jammed his foot down on the gas pedal, knowing the Jaguar could reach one hundred mph in seventeen seconds. It quickly zoomed past Little Thunder's sweating flanks. But the steed didn't slow down; instead it pushed itself harder with Melissa urging it on. Spencer eased up, intentionally slowing to let the horse gain ground, but just as they were about to reach VanDenvender Hall's circular driveway, he floored the Jaguar and then spun it to stop.

"Man triumphs!" he yelled.

Melissa turned Little Thunder toward the stables without comment.

"What, no prize for the victor?" Spencer called after her.

"Go take a shower," she replied.

With Melissa, that could be either a lead-in to a seduction or rejection. Spencer wasn't certain. Inside, he washed and while drying off glanced in the mirror at his own naked torso. He sucked in his stomach and flexed his arms in a muscle-man pose. He was six feet tall, weighed 180. His body wasn't well toned but for a forty-six-year-old man he seemed fit enough. He laid down naked on their bed and waited. She arrived twenty minutes later, sweating from having brushed Little Thunder. When she saw him, she closed their bedroom door and pretended alarm. "Oh my, I'm being robbed," she said coyly. "Someone has broken into my bedroom."

Years ago, Melissa had introduced games into their sex life. She liked to pretend that she was someone else—a cheer-leader about to be deflowered by the captain of the football team or a maid being ravished by her employer.

"Please steal whatever you want," she continued, "but don't rape me."

Spencer had a different scenario in mind.

"I'm not a burglar," he replied. "I'm a circuit court judge, a powerful, tyrannical judge, and you are a rebellious defense attorney, whom I am about to find in contempt of court."

Melissa took his cue. "Oh, Your Honor, what's wrong? Is there a problem with my legal briefs?" She pulled up her black sweater, revealing breasts and an abdomen still as firm as when they had first made love at the University. He'd al-ways suspected that one reason why she had not wanted chil-dren was because it might spoil her figure. She removed her riding boots, pants, and panties. She smelled of sweat and horse but he didn't care. Nor did he bother with foreplay. He was a judge, she was his victim. As he entered her, he thought about Patti Delaney and he became even more excited. Melissa responded by grinding her hips against him. "Oh, Your Honor," she groaned. With Patti Delaney's face planted firmly in his mind, Spencer pounded harder and wondered: *Who was Melissa imagining on top of her?*

Afterward, she went to shower, leaving him to wonder: *If you are imagining another woman when you're making love to your wife, are you guilty of adultery? If so, how many hus-bands could plead innocent?* He reviewed his life as if he were an accountant studying a ledger. He was married to a strikingly attractive woman who also happened to be fabulously wealthy. They lived in an estate assessed at $8.8 million. He drove a Jaguar XK8, albeit one that had a crumpled panel now. He and Melissa were in excellent health. They attended the best country club, ate at the finest restaurants, had all the right society friends. They lacked for nothing. He loved his job. He felt certain that his life was perfect. *Why then, was he thinking of Patti Delaney?*

"Hey, Your Honor," Melissa called from their bathroom. "You need to get ready. We're attending the Arnolds' dinner party tonight, remember?"

"Oh, Jesus, no!" he groaned. He rolled over and buried his face in her pillow. He could still smell her there. "Can't we not go?" he said, his voice muffled.

She stepped into their bedroom wearing a white Prada bathrobe, her hair wrapped in a towel. When she sat down at her makeup table, he noticed that her gown had gapped open and he could see the hint of a red nipple in the mirror's reflection. He marveled at just how beautiful she truly was. And then she shattered the moment by speaking.

"Don't be a shithead," she said, "and don't think for a moment that I'm going to ride to their party in your midlife crisis car."

4

MOST GUESTS AT THE ARNOLDS' FRIDAY NIGHT DINNER PARTY would have been embarrassed to arrive in an eight-year-old Ford Bronco. But one advantage of being a VanDenvender was that Melissa could drive any vehicle she wanted. She was already so rich that she had nothing to prove. If anything, driving a mud-caked SUV made her appear down-to-earth.

En route to the party, Spencer complained about the pompous crowd that usually attended these social outings.

"You can't even have a decent conversation about football," he griped. Elsewhere in Virginia on fall Friday nights, men were gathering around propane-fired grills flipping hamburgers, drinking beer, and arguing about the Washington Redskins. But no one in Charlottesville's moneyed crowd had ever felt the urge to break into a chorus of "Hail to the Redskins" while the after-dinner Fonseca Port was being poured. The only sport ever discussed was fox hunting but Spencer didn't consider it an actual sport.

Melissa had taken him on his first fox hunt shortly after they were married. The night before, she had schooled him about hunting etiquette. "You must say good morning to the Master of the Hunt as soon as you arrive; it's expected," she explained, "and only hunters who have earned their colors are permitted to ride in front."

"Colors?" he'd asked. "Is the Albemarle County Hunt Club a gang?"

"In its own way, it *is* a gang, a very elite one," she'd replied. "Colors are ribbons awarded to the most proficient riders. They're the highest honor the Master of the Hunt can give and usually take five or more years for a rider to earn. Of course, I earned mine in only two years. Because I have my colors, I will be riding at the front while you will be at the rear with the grooms."

"I can't ride next to you?"

"Not until you earn your colors, my dear. Some other quick pointers: Don't run your horse into the horse in front of you. Look out for red ribbons attached to the tails of horses—that means they kick. A green ribbon tied to a horse's tail means the rider is inexperienced. You'll have a green ribbon on your horse."

"This just keeps getting better and better," he said with sarcasm, something he had fallen into using frequently with her. "Do I have to wear an initiation beanie of some sort too?"

She ignored him. "Another rule: never talk to the hounds and don't talk to anyone when the hounds are near the horses because it distracts them."

"The riders, horses, or the hounds?"

"All of them!" she snapped. "And if you happen to fall or

be thrown off your horse and both of your feet touch the ground, you will be expected to deliver a bottle of premium whiskey to the Master of the Hunt after everyone returns to the stables, and if he chooses, he will require you to serenade the other hunters with a song."

"What about the secret handshake?"

"Why does everything have to be a joke with you?" she asked.

They had risen early on the morning of the hunt to dress. Melissa had bought Spencer a riding outfit that included a black bowler cap, black riding coat, canary yellow vest, canary breeches, and black boots. Only later would he realize that she had not given him the clothes out of affection, but because she had been worried that he might wear khakis and boat shoes. Melissa had looked stunning in her riding attire. She wore a black riding cap and black riding coat with two large black buttons sewn on the back and buttons bearing the Albemarle County Hunt Club's crest on the front. Her white vest had polished brass buttons and she wore buff breeches, black leather boots with black patent-leather tops, white string gloves, and blunt spurs, and she held a hunting crop in her left hand with a thong and cord nap. She had told Spencer that she was not allowed to use the crop unless she was specifically instructed by the Master of the Hunt, but it was part of the women's official uniform.

"Kinky," he'd quipped.

Just before the hunt began, Melissa had delivered her last set of instructions. "If you see a fox, point your horse's nose in the direction of the fox and take off your cap and point it at the fox too. That way, you will not distract the hounds. Of course, if the fox is far away, you may call out "holloa" followed by "tallyho," but only in that order. Please don't yell anything else."

"You mean like, 'There's the helpless little bugger, let's have the hounds tear him to shreds with their teeth while we all head back to the club for a jolly good cup of tea!' "

At that point, Melissa had turned her horse and ridden to a position next to her father and the Master of the Hunt. Spencer had had an exhausting and boring time. He rarely rode horses and he was stuck on a disagreeable one between two of Charlottesville's grande dames who complained incessantly about their husbands, the weather, their husbands, household help, and their husbands. As soon as the hunt had started, he'd lost sight of Melissa. Only later would he come to realize that their separateness that morning was a prelude of what was to come.

The valet at the Arnolds' dinner party had looked disappointed when Spencer tossed him the keys to Melissa's battered Bronco.

"Be sure to park it where it won't get dented," Spencer called out, but the valet hadn't gotten his smart-ass attempt at humor.

"This party might be less stuffy than you think," Melissa said. "I understand the Arnolds are eccentric. They're from California, you know."

Frank and Maxine Arnold were newcomers who had arrived in Charlottesville just eight months ago. In Albemarle County, everyone was a newcomer until several generations of their ancestors were buried in the local cemeteries. Frank was a Silicon Valley whiz kid identified as number eighteen in *Fortune* magazine's Richest Americans Under Age Forty list, with a personal net worth estimated at $450 million. A graduate of MIT, he had earned his fortune by designing an optical computer switch and then selling his company just before Internet technology stocks plunged. The Charlottesville Chamber of Commerce had hosted a welcome-to-town luncheon in his honor when he and his wife had first arrived, and after everyone had finished the meal of fried chicken, mashed potatoes, and green beans with peach cobbler for dessert, the guest of honor had been asked to explain his invention. "The evolution of the public Internet network is on a migration path," he had declared, "that began with adapting existing networks to deliver new services. My invention, the Arnold FNZ3600 Intelligent Optical Switch, is designed for smooth progress on this evolutionary path from today's traditional environments to the networks of tomorrow. Deploying the FNZ3600 as an alternative to digital cross-connect equipment in traditional networks substantially reduces operating expenses and allows optical light paths to deliver new managed-wave services over hybrid infrastructures."

Spencer had been absolutely certain that there wasn't a single person at the luncheon who had understood what Arnold had said or what his Arnold FNZ3600 Intelligent Optical Switch actually did. But there had been enthusiastic applause when he had finished speaking and everyone had seemed genuinely excited that Charlottesville had finally gotten its own miniature Bill Gates. Because the Arnolds spent much of their time commuting back and forth between Virginia and California, where they owned additional houses, few Charlottesville residents had become friends with them. The Arnolds had constructed a five-bedroom estate with twelve thousand square feet of living space on a hundred acres west of the city, and tonight's dinner party was serving two functions: Frank and Maxine were greeting their new neighbors and showing off their new house. The Arnolds had rejected the traditional multimillion-dollar older estates on the market and instead had built a two-story contemporary house that looked as if it belonged on a California hillside overlooking the beach or in a Palm Beach neighborhood, but not tucked between the honeysuckle bushes and dogwood trees of upland Virginia. It had a bright white exterior with an all-white tile roof and a white brick walkway. The second floor had eight porthole-shaped windows in a straight line across its front exterior and the main floor had two huge circular picture windows on each side of its white double entrance doors.

"My god," Melissa whispered as they approached the house. "This looks like a grounded ocean liner!"

Frank Arnold had loaded the interior with high-tech gadgetry. Two weeks before the party, Spencer and Melissa had received an embossed letter from the Arnolds asking them to fill out a Private Visitor Comfort Questionnaire and return it ASAP. It contained multiple-choice questions about such things as what sort of music and lighting they preferred. The letter explained that their preferences would be entered into the Arnolds' home computer system so each guest's visit could be personalized. "Don't be surprised if you enter a room and your favorite melody begins to play!" the note declared. Neither Spencer nor Melissa had filled out the form. Both thought the questions tacky. Despite this, as they stepped into the house's grand foyer,

a woman asked their names and handed them lapel pins with
blue flashing dots. The pins were personal identifiers—
monitoring devices that the house's computer used to track
them as they walked from one room to the next. Spencer dutifully clipped his pin to his jacket's lapel, but Melissa slipped
hers into his coat pocket. "Traitor," he said.

They were directed to a parlor on their left, which is where
the Arnolds were welcoming their guests. The parlor's floor
was made of white Italian marble and its walls were also
painted a brilliant white. There were five chrome and black
leather chairs in the parlor but not a single piece of furniture
beyond that. The only splash of color came from two paintings.

"Good evening, Judge," Frank Arnold said as Spencer and
Melissa approached. Arnold gripped Spencer's hand tight,
shook it, and then welcomed Melissa by kissing her cheek. As
Spencer leaned forward to give Maxine Arnold an obligatory
peck, she swung her right hand in front of his chest and gave
his arm a squeeze. Spencer was always aware whenever
someone other than Melissa touched him, especially women
whom he didn't know well, and he found her action curious.
He tried to study her without staring. She was at least ten
years younger than her husband, which would have made her
about twenty-nine. She had long, bleached blond hair that fell
almost to her waist and she was very tall. Spencer guessed she
was at least six feet one inch. He had always assumed wealthy
women in California had undergone cosmetic surgery because
of Hollywood's fixation with youth, beauty, and big breasts.
But Maxine Arnold clearly felt comfortable with her own thin
figure. Her small breasts were barely noticeable under the casual plum-colored cotton knit jacket and floor-length patterned dress that she was wearing. Yet Spencer found her
gauntness sexy. She had her high cheekbones and pouty lips.
Those lips, Spencer thought, could have earned her a small
fortune in the porno movie business. Frank Arnold was at
least six inches shorter than his wife and bull-like in build. He
was wearing tan poplin trousers, a button-down plaid shirt,
and Docksiders—much too casual for the host of a Charlottesville dinner party. Already nearly bald, he had pulled
what hair he still had back tight into a ponytail.

"You're not wearing your personal identifier," Arnold said to Melissa.

"Naughty, naughty me," she replied.

He waved to an employee who quickly handed him a new lapel pin, which he attached, without asking, to the Giorgio Armani sequined top that Melissa was wearing.

"You'll be missing out on a lot of fun if you don't wear this," he explained. "We've even got prizes when we give the house tour!"

"Oh, goodie, goodie!" she deadpanned.

Spencer glanced at the painting hanging behind the Arnolds. "That's a Georgia O'Keeffe isn't it?" he asked.

"Yes," Maxine Arnold said, obviously pleased that he had commented on it. "Do you know much about art, Judge?"

"My mother has painted all of her life and Melissa's degree from the University is in art history."

"This particular painting is called 'Black Hollyhock, Blue Larkspur' and was done in 1930," Maxine explained. "The other is called 'Bella Donna' and was done in 1939."

In typical O'Keeffe-style, both paintings only showed the open petals of flowers. "Black Hollyhock, Blue Larkspur" featured vibrant blues and purples. "Bella Donna" was mostly white with a bright green center.

"I selected Georgia O'Keeffe for this room because she once lived in Williamsburg, Virginia," Maxine continued. "I find her work intensely sexual although she always denied it was meant to be. The way that she peels the petals open always reminds me of a woman spreading her vulva."

Melissa, who had not commented, said: "They are excellent reproductions. Who painted them?"

Maxine glared at her. "They aren't copies. I've never really thought much of people who hire artists to imitate another artist's works."

"Oh, I assumed most of O'Keeffe's works were in museums," Spencer said, coming to his wife's defense.

"Many are but these are not." She slipped her hand through her husband's arm and said: "Frank bought them for me from private collectors because he knew I wanted them."

A beaming Frank Arnold led them outside to the rear of the

house where a hundred guests were mingling on the lawn underneath a huge purple and gold circus tent. Four-foot-long gold tassels dangled from the tent's corners. "The wine we're serving came from a little California vineyard we've just bought," he said. He plucked a Merlot from a server's silver tray and handed it to Melissa. "Wine is a new hobby of Maxine's," he continued.

Melissa took a sip. "It's a bit tannic for my tastes," she replied.

"Really," said Maxine, taking a sip from her own glass. "It seems delicious to me."

"You work out?" Arnold asked Spencer. "Jog, lift weights, that sort of thing?"

Melissa laughed.

"No," Spencer replied. "I don't have much time for going to a gym."

"You should make time," Arnold said. "Every morning, five A.M., I'm pumping iron."

"It's an obsession," Maxine added.

"That's right. In eighth grade I was puny," Frank Arnold continued. "Littlest kid in school, every bully picked on me. I hated it. So I completely remade myself by lifting weights. Twice a day, every day, I was at the YMCA. By graduation, I was the strongest kid in the entire school. I may have been known as a computer geek but I was the computer geek who could bench press three hundred and fifty."

Jacob Wheeler, the commonwealth's attorney in Charlottesville, and his wife, Florence, joined them.

"Wonderful party! Great party!" Wheeler gushed. "Hello, Judge," he said, reaching out to shake Spencer's hand. He nodded politely to Melissa. "Good evening, Mrs. VanDenvender." Spencer was used to people greeting him casually but always acting formal whenever they addressed his wife. It came with the VanDenvender name. "I heard that new lawyer in town made a complete ass out of herself today in your courtroom, Judge," Wheeler volunteered.

"Really," Frank Arnold said. He seemed genuinely interested. "I always enjoy stories about attorneys, especially when they are made to look like fools."

"Her name is Patti Delaney," Wheeler continued, "and she told her client to wear something nice, you know, decent clothes, to court. This idiot comes in wearing clothes that he had stolen during a burglary—the very one that he's on trial for! It turns out he was just following her instructions because she told him to dress up!"

Frank Arnold turned to Spencer and said: "Think there may be grounds for an appeal here since he was just following her orders?"

Spencer was trying to think of a witty reply but before he could answer, Wheeler said: "What really makes this even funnier is Patti Delaney is one of the nuttiest dressers you've ever seen. Some of her outfits look like they came out of a *Saturday Night Live* skit or *Star Wars*!"

One of the Arnolds' employees interrupted them and whispered in his boss's ear. Frank motioned to Maxine and they excused themselves, leaving Spencer and Melissa standing with the Wheelers. Although Spencer and Wheeler both worked in the courthouse, they traveled in very different social circles. Wheeler had campaigned for the job of commonwealth's attorney mainly because he was having a difficult time earning a living as a lawyer in private practice. At best, he was mediocre, and it hadn't taken local defense attorneys long to begin exploiting his weaknesses. Because he disliked trying cases, they were able to cut generous plea bargains for their clients. Strangely, his ineptitude worked to his advantage when it came to job security because few of his fellow practitioners wanted him replaced. He always ended up running for reelection without an opponent.

For several awkward moments, no one spoke and then Wheeler asked: "Hey Judge, you a Redskins fan?" Melissa nearly spilled her drink.

Frank and Maxine Arnold reappeared minutes later with a new guest in tow. Taylor Cauldwell was Virginia's Attorney General and, after the governor and lieutenant governor, the third most powerful elected official in the state. The Wheelers scampered over to greet him but Spencer and Melissa stayed put. They were not celebrity chasers.

"That woman really needs a new hairstyle," Melissa said.

"Florence Wheeler?"

"No, Maxine Arnold. She's too old to wear her hair like that. And too old to be that blond too." She took a sip of Merlot. "And this wine of hers tastes like shit." Melissa poured her drink onto the grass. "Do you find her sexy?"

Spencer knew better than to answer truthfully. "She squeezed my arm. I think she was checking my biceps," he said.

Melissa laughed. "They'll never fit in here despite his money. You can't buy class no matter how many fake Georgia O'Keeffes you own."

"She said they were authentic."

"Whatever."

Spencer glanced at his hosts. They were guiding Attorney General Cauldwell toward them.

"Of course, you know Judge Spencer and Mrs. VanDenvender," Arnold said.

"Know 'em?" Cauldwell replied. "Hell, I was in school with both of them. The judge is one of my closest, longtime friends. And Melissa, why you look as beautiful as when we were students and I was trying to win your heart away from this clever bastard."

Cauldwell kissed Melissa's cheek and for several minutes they exchanged polite chitchat. Then Cauldwell announced in a booming voice that he had to leave the party. "I'm needed back in Richmond because this Republican governor of ours has stuck his nose into that messy television newscaster's case."

Everyone knew what he was talking about because the newscaster case had been big news all week. Three years earlier, a television newsman in Washington, D.C., had suffered massive brain damage during an automobile accident. It had left him in what doctors called "a vegetative state." His family had decided a few days ago to remove his feeding tube, but when Governor George Anderson heard about their plans, he held a press conference to announce that he was going to court to stop them. Anderson claimed that removing the tube would be a deliberate act of murder.

"We've never had a governor intervene by filing suit like this," Cauldwell told the party crowd. "Of course, as the Commonwealth's attorney general, I'm stuck arguing the governor's case tomorrow before the Virginia Supreme Court even though, quite frankly, I'm in complete disagreement with him."

The *Washington Post* and other media had speculated that Governor Anderson's actions smelled of pure politics. Originally, Anderson had been elected as Virginia's lieutenant governor but midway through the term, the governor had suffered a fatal heart attack and Anderson had succeeded him. Virginia only allows its governors to serve a single four-year term. But because Anderson was filling a vacancy, the law permitted him to run for reelection. He recently had made several decisions that had outraged the ultraconservative sector of the Republican party. His unprecedented decision to intervene in the newscaster case was now being seen by pundits as a not too subtle effort to appease those right-wing conservatives.

"I personally think Governor Anderson has stuck his tittie in a ringer and it's just breaking my heart!" Cauldwell said sarcastically. He and Anderson were bitter political rivals.

As Cauldwell began saying his good-byes, he singled out Spencer and whispered, "I need to see you privately Monday morning. I'll have my secretary call Miss Alice to set up a time. I assume she's still there."

"Yes, she is," Spencer said through gritted teeth.

"Old bitch never will die, will she?" Cauldwell chuckled.

It took the attorney general another fifteen minutes before he actually left the party because he had to speak to every guest. As soon as he had gone, Arnold announced that dinner was ready.

"We thought we'd bring a bit of California casual to Virginia," he said, "so we're serving the food buffet style and it's Tex-Mex cuisine. We didn't assign seats so just sit where you want and enjoy."

A horde of guests stampeded to the front of the buffet as Spencer guided Melissa to an empty table away from the crowd.

"Would you like me to fetch another one of those delicious Merlots," he asked. "I understand it goes very well with a red bean burrito."

She rolled her eyes.

Their few seconds of quiet were interrupted by the Wheelers who returned carrying plates overflowing with food. "Isn't this great?" Wheeler declared, as he took a huge bite of a soft taco. "Everyone is speculating that Cauldwell is going to announce next week that he's running for governor. You're his friend, Judge, you heard anything?" Before Spencer could answer, Wheeler added, "I'm guessing he came here tonight to raise money. Beating Anderson isn't going to be easy, especially with all of his friends from up North—if you know what I mean." He took another big bite of taco and Spencer noticed that a piece of cheese had gotten stuck on Wheeler's double chin.

Anyone vaguely familiar with Virginia politics understood the phrase "up North." From the mid-1920s until the early 1970s, politics in the Commonwealth of Virginia had been dominated by one of the most powerful political machines in the nation. It was created by Democrat Harry Flood Byrd after he became Virginia's governor in 1926. His son, Harry Flood Byrd, Jr., later took its reins when he became a U.S. senator. For nearly five decades, no one was elected or appointed to a political post in Virginia without the Byrd machine's approval. Although the Byrds were not racists, the men behind them were all white and all rich. They included bankers, lawyers, businessmen, and gentlemen farmers. The machine was able to retain its political might because Virginia had a small electorate, strict voting laws, and a prejudicial poll tax. This guaranteed a low voter turnout that was easily controlled, and it effectively excluded blacks and most poor whites from the system. The machine's interests were intertwined with the interests of the Virginia Electric Power Company (VEPCO), the state's large banks, and the University of Virginia. What was good for them was deemed good for the general public. In Charlottesville, the VanDenvender family had been strong supporters of the Byrd machine, giving it juicy campaign contributions in return for dozens of special favors.

But in the early 1960s, the machine began to crumble. The reason: white flight. Racial unrest and riots in Washington, D.C., caused hundreds of thousands of federal workers to flee to the suburbs. Overnight, tiny Virginia towns that rimmed the capital began mushrooming. Northern Virginia residents had accounted for less than 6 percent of the vote in the 1950s. By 1975, they controlled 20 percent, and by 1990, more than 30 percent. At about this same time, Virginia's Tidewater area, which included the cities of Norfolk and Newport News, began to grow. These two demographic changes robbed Charlottesville and other rural towns in southern Virginia of their political stranglehold.

In the last election, the state's gubernatorial candidates had each made a one-day courtesy stop in Charlottesville but that was it. Rather than wasting their time in Albemarle County, which had a population of about ninety thousand, they focused on the more heavily populated D.C. suburbs up North. This snub had not gone unnoticed, especially in Charlottesville, especially by the VanDenvenders and their cronies, but there was little that anyone could do about it. Times were changing.

There was still one branch of state government where remnants of the Byrd machine could be found. During its heyday, only loyal Democrats had been appointed as Virginia judges, and while time had eaten away at those appointments, Democrats still controlled most of the 31 judicial circuits in the state and many of its 122 circuit courts.

"If anyone can find a way to defeat the governor," Spencer said, "it'll be Taylor Cauldwell. I'm sure you'all will recall that he was an underdog when he campaigned for attorney general."

Spencer decided to tell one of his favorite political stories. "The Virginia Bar Association was holding its annual meeting in Virginia Beach during the election," he began, "and it invited Cauldwell and his opponent, Max Masters, to debate one another. The turnout was huge. We had more than two thousand guests and most of them were attorneys and judges. Masters arrived an hour late. He never said why and everyone was irritated by the time he finally came strutting into the ballroom. Because the program was so far behind schedule, the moderator announced that he was going to skip the introduction of dignitaries and honored guests. And that's when Taylor Cauldwell leaped to his feet. He says 'This isn't right! The men and women in this room are the people who make certain justice is administered in Virginia.' And then Cauldwell began calling out names, actually picking people from the audience, introducing them and asking them on his own to stand up and be recognized. He'd say, 'I see Virginia Supreme Court Justice John Harrison sitting over there. Stand up, John.' And everyone would clap. Then he'd say, 'Why there is Charlie Johnson, the prosecutor in Farmville!' He was naming prosecutors from counties that most of us didn't even know were part of Virginia. It took nearly twenty minutes but no one objected and to this day I have never seen any politician duplicate that feat. There are more than a hundred judges in Virginia and he seemed to know every one of them by name and sight. I later asked him how he had memorized all that information and he told me that whenever he met someone he thought might be useful to him, he wrote their name on an index card and jotted down something personal about them. Maybe they had a dog named Fluffy or they were good at golf—just small details. Before the bar association meeting, he had gone through his cards, studied them, memorized those details. He told me: 'Spencer, never forget that the person you are about to meet may be the person who casts a vote that changes your destiny.' Max Masters thought he had the election in the bag but he'd underestimated Taylor Cauldwell. Never make that mistake."

Spencer was proud of his story but Melissa had heard it too many times. "Enough politics," she said dismissing him. "Why don't you go get us something to eat now, Spencer?" She turned toward Florence Wheeler, who had not uttered a word. "What a lovely dress," Melissa said. "Where did you find it?"

"JCPenney," she replied, thrilled at the compliment. "They were having a fabulous half-off sale."

As Spencer made his way to the serving line, he could hear Melissa questioning Florence Wheeler about her dress with what appeared to be genuine interest. Yet he knew that Melissa VanDenvender had never once set foot inside a Penney's store and never would. Like Taylor Cauldwell, she could be as charming as she wished when it served her purposes.

"If you are finished eating," Frank Arnold told his guests about a half hour later, "I'd like to make several introductions." Waiters wearing red, blue, and green Mexican ponchos and black sombreros decorated with threads of silver and gold braid were still delivering guests piña colada–favored ice cream along with two Mexican fiesta ball cookies—small balls of chocolate mixed with coffee and maraschino flavors—but Arnold had eaten his dinner and he never ate dessert. He was eager to get started. "I like to shake things up wherever we go," he proclaimed. "Change is good. So is controversy. Both help spark progress and that's what makes this country great. But enough of my sermons. This is a coming-out party of sorts for Maxine and me. We hope to spend more time in Virginia and we want to become someone you can count on if you need to run next door to borrow a cup of sugar or," and at this point he paused in his delivery, "should I say Grey Poupon." His guests laughed. "Most of you have met my lovely wife, Maxine," he said. He took her hand and she stood up next to him. "I'd like to now introduce our daughter, Cassie, whom I call Cookie." An eleven-year-old pixie with a freckle-covered face stood up next to her mother. She looked awkward in the bright orange and black Mexican party dress that she was wearing. Spencer guessed she was a tomboy more comfortable in a shirt, shorts, and tennis shoes. "Her nickname doesn't have anything to do with those cookies we just served you," Arnold said. "I call her Cookie because I was creating a way to prevent Web sites from sending cookies to personal computers when she was born."

Again, brief laughter. His daughter smiled, revealing a mouth filled with ceramic braces.

"There's another young person I want to introduce to you, a man whom my wife and I have taken into our home and are treating as if he were our own son," Arnold continued. "Lester, please stand up."

A muscular African-American man in his early twenties rose from a seat next to Cookie. He was wearing a bright red and white basketball jersey, with the number forty-four printed on it, over a white tee shirt. Gold earrings dangled from both ears and his head was covered with what looked like a white handkerchief tied tight. On top of it, he was wearing a red baseball hat turned sideways.

"This is Lester Amil, better known to his hip-hop home-boys as Click, Click, Four, Four. He's from the inner city in

Los Angeles and I originally hired him to work for me as a liaison. Not long ago, Maxine and I set up a charitable foundation called Get Plugged In, which helps inner city kids develop computer skills."

Someone began applauding but Arnold modestly waved them quiet.

"Please, please, this was not strictly a humanitarian gesture on my part," he explained. "At the time, I was looking for ways to get more people connected to the Internet so I could sell more of my company's optical switches!"

He paused, as if to collect his thoughts. "Maxine runs all of the charities that we have founded over the years, and she came to me after she had spent some time with Lester and told me what a marvelous and bright young man he was. When I began spending time with him—well—he became more than an employee, he became the son that I didn't have. He's now living with us while a tutor helps him prepare for his eventual entrance into college."

Again, someone began clapping and everyone joined in. This time, Arnold let them finish.

"You know, I'm going to take a real gamble here but that's the sort of man I am. I'm going to ask Lester if he will sing one of his hip-hop songs so you can hear what the young people of today are thinking."

Lester sauntered to the microphone and suddenly a thundering, primal beat came pulsating from speakers that earlier had been playing the greatest hits of Herb Alpert and The Tijuana Brass. Glasses on the tables began to shake because of the throbbing bass booms as Lester launched into his rhyme:

I'm draped in the latest street fashion that's been adapted to the
   runway/
now that trigger happy's marketable I like to entice gunplay/
`the smoke it rises from my open mouth like hollow skulls in slow
   motion/
I'm hypnotized inside the zone, I give rhythm to the ocean/
little interest in the hate you gave/
a shitty liquor drinker, send my body to an early grave/
some consider this inner-city nigger still a slave/

they might try to adapt, reevaluate or save/
teach me how to behave/
some bullshit if you ask me—you the ones who come from
    descendants who used to live in caves/
now you want to change places and paint faces/
white corporate America is racist/
the government is spending money on war games/ space stations/
    but nobody ever talks race relations until your daughter's
    caught on the front page naked and freebasing/
conspiracy theories and Freemasons/ it's all misunderstood
come through my neighborhood/ see the planet that I dwell
    within/
I'll take you through heaven and back to hell again/ young, pro-
    black, intelligent
my skin is melanin/ and to you this is a rebellious sin/
try to duplicate my essence, but you failed again/
you've got your scientists/
flirting with a delicate balance/
challenging Mother Nature murdering Africans with AIDS
    viruses/
It's widespread down to cloning human genome cell embryos/
to cloning stolen Nokia cell phones/ I'm well known for throwing
    elbows
trying to break codes/ I rest my heart behind a Kevlar vest/
so chrome never penetrates my chest/ relieve stress by smoking
    cess/
fuck trying to impress guests/ I'm wild like the West is/
with words and metaphors/ apex predator/ settle the score
Click, Click, Four, Four/ nevermore . . .

Lester Amil ended with a clenched black fist raised high. Arnold hurried forward and hugged him. "Wasn't that great?" Arnold beamed. "Wasn't that fabulous? Now it's time for the tour of our house." With his wife draped on his arm and Cookie and Lester falling behind him, Arnold weaved through the tables, completely ignoring the stunned looks on his guests' faces. Several couples rose and followed him into the house, but Melissa was not one of them.

"Let's go!" she said sharply. About a dozen other guests

joined her in walking toward the front of the house and the valets.

"How about our hosts?" Spencer asked. "The tour? The prizes? Saying good-bye? Thanking them for the evening? You know, Southern hospitality."

"Fuck 'em," Melissa replied. "That man insulted us. My god, Spencer, wake up! Didn't you listen to the words of that dreadful song. He couldn't have made his contempt for any of us more clear."

"I'm assuming Mr. and Mrs. Frank Arnold will not be asked to join the Albemarle County Hunt Club?" he replied. She shot him an angry look and didn't talk to him on the ride home.

Saturday proved uneventful until Spencer and Melissa went to dinner at their country club where they met several of Melissa's longtime friends and, together over cocktails, they verbally keelhauled the Arnolds. On Sunday morning, Spencer rose early and, armed with a cup of coffee and the hefty Sunday edition of the *Washington Post,* began leisurely reading the news. The front page contained two stories that mentioned Taylor Cauldwell. The first revealed that Cauldwell was about to "throw his hat into the Virginia governor's race" according to "informed sources close to Cauldwell who asked to remain anonymous." The *Post* was famous for writing stories based on confidential sources, a term that had always amused Spencer. As a circuit court judge, he had watched reporters and politicians for years, and he knew the dance that both played in scratching the others' backs. He suspected that Cauldwell himself was the source of the leaked *Post* story. He had offered the reporter an "exclusive" in return for the reporter promising to shield his identity— something the writer was happy to do since it made it appear as if he had made an investigative scoop. According to the news article, Cauldwell was contacting potential campaign contributors and asking them for donations for what could very well be the most costly gubernatorial race in the state's history. Spencer had just finished that article when Melissa entered the kitchen.

"Just reading about you," he said.

"In the *Post*?"

"Yes, it says Cauldwell is going to run for governor and he wants you to help finance his campaign. Well, it doesn't actually say your name, but Cauldwell told me at the Arnold fiasco that he wanted to speak to me privately tomorrow morning, no doubt to enlist my help in wringing some bucks from the great VanDenvender fortune."

"You're the one who wants to be on the state supreme court, darling," she replied. "How much do you think that will cost me?"

When he didn't respond, she announced matter-of-factly that she was spending the day riding Little Thunder. She abruptly finished her coffee and left. Since the older married couple who worked for them as a cook and gardener had Sundays off, Spencer found himself alone in VanDenvender Hall. He considered taking his Jaguar for a drive, but didn't want to give Melissa an excuse to needle him any further about a mid-life crisis, so he decided to fix himself a sandwich instead and continue reading the paper while eating brunch on the veranda.

The second story on the *Post*'s front page that mentioned Taylor Cauldwell was about the flap that Governor Anderson had caused when he intervened in the brain-damaged newscaster case. Cauldwell had argued on Saturday during a special hearing before the Virginia Supreme Court in favor of forcing the family to leave the newscaster's feeding tube in place. He'd claimed that a 1992 state law, which allowed the removal of nutrition from vegetative patients, didn't apply because the newsman was not dying. Removing the feeding tube amounted to euthanasia, he argued, which is illegal in Virginia. But the nine-member court had rejected his argument by ruling that the removal of the tube "merely permits the natural process of dying and therefore is not a mercy killing."

The newscaster succumbed four hours after the tube was removed. His widow had lashed out angrily at Governor Anderson afterward. "This was political grandstanding," she said. "The governor put us through sheer hell and I think an apology would be in order but I don't expect one!"

Spencer had just completed the story when he heard a *whooshing* sound and voices. He looked to his left and right, but didn't see anyone. Then he heard the noise again: *whoosh!*

and a shadow passed over him. He looked up, squinting to avoid the morning sun, and saw a bright green and red hot air balloon soaring some fifty feet directly above him. There were five people in its basket and one of them, a young girl, waved. He didn't recognize anyone until he heard the voice of Frank Arnold.

"Judge Spencer! Beautiful day for a ride! You should try it!"

Spencer waved back to the young girl—Cookie—as the balloon drifted across the meadow and trees of the VanDenvender estate. Off in the distance, Spencer saw Melissa riding Little Thunder, completely unaware that her privacy was about to be invaded.

What a pampered life! he thought.

It was raining Monday morning. Spencer overslept and arrived late at the Albemarle County Court House. Miss Alice was waiting with a handful of pink message slips. "The attorney general has asked to see you at eleven o'clock," she reported. "His secretary said it's important." Spencer grabbed the pink slips and ducked into his chambers. He was scheduled to render a decision on a variety of motions in a large civil suit in less than an hour and he wanted to review his notes. He found them tucked under the mail, which Miss Alice had left on his desk Friday. The already-opened Federal Express box from Las Vegas was on top of the heap. He'd forgotten all about Patrick McPherson and the rock. He reached inside the shipping box and pulled out the white stone that was still wrapped in plastic.

Why had McPherson sent it to him?

He unwrapped the bubble wrap and held the stone in his right hand, feeling its weight. Less than a pound, he guessed. It was smooth, as if it had been plucked from a creek bed where its sharp edges had been rounded by years of rushing water. He tossed it to his left hand, as if it were a baseball, and when he caught it, he felt a sudden sting. At first, he thought he'd pinched himself when the rock had struck his wedding band. But when he squeezed the stone, he felt another prick and recognized it. It was an electrical shock. He had not felt a jolt like that since his days as an undergraduate student when he and several of his friends had flown to Cancun, Mexico, for spring break.

His mind drifted back to that trip and the drunken, machismo game that they had played. They had been downing shots of tequila with beer in Señor Pepe's bar when an old Mexican carrying a small electrical generator approached their table and challenged them to test their manhood. He looked like an organ grinder—without a monkey—because he was holding the generator at waist level from a strap wrapped around his neck. There was a hand crank on the right side of the machine that he spun to create an electrical charge. The Mexican handed one of Spencer's buddies two copper pipes each about six inches long to grasp in each of his hands. Wires led from the pipes to the generator. The object was to see how long you could hold onto the copper pipes while the Mexican turned the crank sending an electrical charge through your body. Someone gave the Mexican a fifty peso note and he began spinning the generator's crank. An old gauge showed how strong the current was and when it reached the number two, the student holding the pipes yelled ouch and dropped the copper tubes. Everyone laughed. The Mexican had then handed the wires to another one of Spencer's friends. Once again, he began spinning the crank. When the gauge slipped by two, Spencer and his pals began to chant: "Go! Go! Go!" Their comrade bit down hard on his teeth as the gauge hit four, but when it reached five he screamed and the Mexican stopped. By this time, several women and other men from the bar had crowded around the table to watch as, one by one, Spencer's friends each took a turn. No one could hold on past nine.

Spencer, who was drunk, was the last to try and in his stupor, he was determined to reach ten. His hands were sweaty as he gripped the copper tubes and nodded to the Mexican.

"Go! Go! Go!" the crowd began to chant as the old man began turning the crank. Spencer could feel the electricity shoot up his arms. The dial hit one. He grinned and nodded confidently. The Mexican turned faster. The generator began emitting a high-pitched whirling sound as it spun and the crowd began cheering him on: "Go! Go! Go!"

Spencer closed his eyes and felt the current traveling from his right hand up along his arm, across his shoulders and down into his left hand. When he opened his eyes, the gauge was resting on five and he was panting, his forehead was drenched in sweat, and the pain was intense, but he nodded for more.

"Evan! Evan! Evan!" his friends yelled as the Mexican continued spinning the wheel, which now skipped to six. Spencer's hands and arms began quivering. Suddenly, he began to worry that the current could short-circuit his heart, but he was determined to continue.

He closed his eyes and tried to think of something other than the painful current racing through him. When he opened them, the gauge was on eight and Spencer felt as if he were pressing his hands against the red-hot burners on an electric stove. Still, he refused to surrender. Mind over pain. He smiled at his Mexican torturer who was now turning the generator's crank as fast as he possibly could.

The gauge popped to ten and the crowd burst into cheers. Spencer had done it! He immediately tried to release the copper tubes. But he couldn't drop them. The electricity was so strong that it was overriding his brain's commands to his hands. He panicked and screamed! The Mexican stopped cranking. Everyone was quiet. His guttural cry had surprised them. It was a scream that had come from a horrified man. Someone laughed and his friends doused him with beer.

The prick that Spencer had just felt from the rock would have been about a number two on the old Mexican's gauge, he imagined.

It's impossible! Rocks don't emit electricity.

He squeezed the stone with both hands as if he were Superman trying to crush it.

Without warning, he was hit with another jolt, this one so strong that it made him gasp for breath.

How can this be happening?

He tried to drop the stone but his hands wouldn't move. Suddenly, another jolt hit him, this one even stronger. Then another. Then a fourth, each becoming stronger than the last. His mind was spinning, searching for an explanation. But there was none. His hands and arms began to shake as the jolts became even stronger. Finally, his knees gave out and he fell forward, his body limp, as if his bones were a house of cards that was collapsing. As he fell, his chest struck the edge of his desk and he felt several ribs crack. He hit the floor with a thud, his head smacking the light blue carpet. He saw the ceiling above him and then blacked out.

It was cold and dark. Spencer was rocking back-and-forth to the motion of the sea onboard a small sailboat. He was freezing. But then, suddenly, it became hot. A cloudless sapphire sky appeared above him. The sun burned his face. He raised himself up on his elbows and reached over the boat's side to cool his face with water. But as soon as he broke the surface of the clear water, it turned murky green and he could see hideous creatures slithering underneath the boat. They were ghost white and when they spotted his hand on the surface, they raced up to him as if they wanted to snatch his arm, pull him overboard, and feast on his flesh. He jerked back his hand just in time and hid in the boat, afraid to move, thinking that after that it might capsize. After several moments, he raised up enough to peek over the side. Off in the distance, he saw a figure in white robes walking toward him on the surface of the water. The figure moved slowly, gracefully, with no fear of sinking, no fear of being devoured by the beasts from below. Spencer screamed: 'Save me! Please save me!'

When he opened his eyes, Spencer saw a pencil-thin green neon light on a monitor tracking his vital signs. There was an IV tube in his right arm. It was night and the room at Charlottesville General Hospital was dark except for streaks coming from the hallway through a six-inch opening because the door to his room had been left partly open. Spencer could see a nurse sitting behind a counter outside his door and he tried to call her, but his mouth was dry and there was no voice. He tried again but his words came out as a hoarse whisper. He decided to sit up, but the pain in his ribs when he moved stopped him. Instead, he probed with his hands along the sides of the bed until he found a remote control. He began pushing its buttons.

The nurse looked up, called to another nurse, and both hurried into his room. The sudden burst of fluorescent light forced him to shut his eyes.

"Judge Spencer, you're awake!"

"What's happened to me?"

"You scared us," one of the nurses replied. "We'll page your doctor. He'll answer your questions. The good news is that you're awake."

"How long have I been here?"

"Four days."

"Four days! It's Thursday?"

"Actually, it's Friday morning."

"Your clerk found you lying unconscious on the floor of your office and called an ambulance."

An hour later, Melissa arrived and a few minutes later his doctor joined them.

"Tell me what happened in your office," his doctor said.

"I was shocked," Spencer replied. "Electricity. I was holding this rock and I felt a jolt. It knocked me down."

"A rock?" Melissa asked.

"Yes."

The doctor asked: "Were you standing near a window?"

"There's one by my desk. But I was at least four feet from it."

"That doesn't matter. We think you might've been hit by lightning."

"Lightning?"

"It was raining Monday," Melissa added.

"You're lucky," the doctor said. "At least for a man who was hit by a lightning bolt. Do you have a headache?"

"No."

"Tinnitus—ringing in your ears?"

"No."

"How about dizziness, nausea, or vomiting, which frequently happens when someone is hit by lightning."

"No, I feel fine."

"Good."

The doctor looked at Melissa. "We'll do an EKG, CT scan, and MRI but I'm guessing they will be normal too because if he was hit by lightning, those types of anatomical tests aren't going to reveal any damage."

"Can you translate that into English?" Spencer said, annoyed that the doctor was talking to Melissa as if he weren't in the room.

"You got a computer, don't you, Judge?" the doctor said. "If an electrical shock was sent through your computer, the machine's metal case would still probably look okay—just like your body looks okay to us. The circuit board also would probably look okay and not be fused or melted. I'm guessing the same is true about your body—a CT and MRI will show that no parts of your brain have been fried. But when you boot up your computer—even though it looks fine—it could have difficulty accessing files, making calculations, sending messages to your printer. That's what could happen to you too. I'm going to order some neuropsychological tests to see how your brain is working. It's possible you may suffer from short-term memory loss or you may experience a change in your personality because of frontal lobe damage."

"What sort of personality change?" Melissa asked.

"Spencer might become irritable and get angry easily. Oftentimes, someone struck by lightning may not recognize that something is wrong with them, or they might deny it and claim everything is fine when it really isn't."

"I wasn't hit by lightning," Spencer interrupted. "I told you it was the rock. It shocked me." He suddenly realized just how incredibly stupid that sounded.

"See what I mean?" the doctor said, laughing. "Listen, I'll order the tests. We'll run the CT and schedule the MRI and neuropsychological testing. If everything goes on schedule, you should be out of here within a few days. The only pain will be from those broken ribs in your chest, and there's nothing we can do about those but wait for them to heal."

A few minutes after the doctor left them, Melissa said she had to leave. Her father was expecting her to help host a fund-raising dinner that night at the country club for Ducks Unlimited and she needed to prepare for it.

"It's not even nine A.M. yet," Spencer protested.

"I have a lot to do," she replied. "Don't be a baby about this."

Spencer was alone until seven o'clock that night when Taylor Cauldwell peeked in.

"Spencer, you old dog," he cracked as he entered the room. "You'll do about anything to get out of meeting with me, won't you?"

"When I know you're looking for a campaign contribution, I will," he replied.

"Damn, you've gotten your senses back. I was hoping you'd write me a check before you understood what was going on."

"It's not my money you're after. You know my wife is the one who's loaded."

They had been good friends since both of them were law students at the University. Even Melissa, who found both politics and law dull, had always been interested in Cauldwell's political career and had made certain that she and her father had contributed to each of his campaigns.

"Guess you heard about the murder?" Cauldwell said.

"Murder?"

"You really have been in a coma, haven't you? Frank and Maxine Arnold's daughter, Cassie, was kidnapped Sunday night. Her parents called the police Monday morning. Maxine told them that she'd just found a ransom note."

"Jesus Christ! That little girl was kidnapped?"

"The note demanded $118,000 in small bills and it was filled with a bunch of crap about how the girl had been snatched because her father was exploiting workers in Mexico where his razzle-dazzle computer switch is made. But that was all bullshit!"

Cauldwell pulled a stool over to Spencer's beside and continued: "On Monday afternoon, Frank Arnold and the cops go downstairs in the basement to look around and, bingo, Arnold finds his own daughter's body right there in the basement on the floor. The little girl had been bound, gagged, sexually tortured, and strangled—just like in the JonBenet Ramsey case. I mean, it's almost identical to that Boulder, Colorado, murder. Even the $118,000 ransom demand—it was exactly the same figure the killer in the Ramsey case wanted."

"A copycat?"

"It sure as hell looked that way. Within a few hours, we had CBS, NBC, CNN, ABC, and a whole bunch of foreign networks rushing into town. You picked a poor time to end up in the hospital."

Spencer had just taken some pain-killer medication and wasn't certain that he was hearing everything that Cauldwell was saying. It didn't seem to make sense. Why would someone kill Cookie?

"We got our killer though," Cauldwell continued. "The cops arrested that black punk, Lester Amil, who lives with the Arnolds. Found him at the bus station on Monday night trying to flee out of town."

"Why'd he do it?"

"Who knows? We're still investigating. But the forensic guys have found all sorts of newspaper clippings about the JonBenet Ramsey case in his room. The state crime lab came through with the clencher. It found the black kid's semen splattered all over that dead little girl's pajamas."

Spencer's thoughts flashed back to Sunday when he had seen the Arnolds floating peacefully above VanDenvender Hall in a hot air balloon. Now Cauldwell was informing him that eleven-year-old Cassie—who had waved down to him from the sky—had been kidnapped from her bed, sexually tortured, and murdered. It was hard to imagine.

Cauldwell leaned in close and spoke softly: "Spencer, you realize I was coming to see you on Monday to get a contribution, but now the game has changed. Listen closely. I'm going to need you to do me a big favor, a really huge one, probably the biggest favor you've ever done for me in your life."

Spencer didn't have a clue what Cauldwell wanted.

"We've been friends for a long, long time and you know I wouldn't ask you to do this unless it really was critical," he continued.

"Okay, okay, get on with it," Spencer replied. "What exactly do you want?"

"I'm going to intervene in this case," he whispered. "I'm going to step in and prosecute this Amil kid personally. And I'm going to seek the death penalty."

"You can't prosecute a murder case," Spencer said. "Unless the general assembly has rewritten Virginia's constitution while I was in my coma, attorney generals aren't allowed to prosecute cases in circuit courts."

"You're absolutely right. It's never been done before," Cauldwell replied. "But I've found a way. Virginia statute 2.2–551 specifically states that an attorney general shall have no authority to institute or conduct criminal prosecutions. But then it says 'except in certain cases.'"

"Yes, but those exceptions deal with things such as air pollution, illegal waste dumping—crimes that cross local boundaries and fall more into the commonwealth's bailiwick than into a local prosecutor's," Spencer recalled. "They don't include murder."

"Ah, but you're wrong. Read exception number six," Cauldwell replied. "It's the key. It says the attorney general can intervene if a case involves 'child pornography and sexually explicit visual material involving children.'"

"But this is a murder case, not kiddie porn."

"You're right, but guess what the cops found on Lester Amil's computer? Little girls tied up. S/M. Explicit stuff that he'd downloaded off the Internet. And that, my dear friend, is my portal into this case."

"Do you really think Governor Anderson is going to sit by and watch you intervene—knowing that you're going to run against him?"

"Hey, the governor has already set the precedent—the brain-dead newsman case. Besides, even if he has the cajones to complain to the Virginia Supreme Court, it's stacked with Democrats. There are only two people who can stop me from jumping into this murder investigation."

"Who?"

"The local commonwealth's attorney, Jacob Wheeler, could protest. But you and I both know Wheeler is shaking in his JCPenney loafers right now. He's scared he'll screw this up and he just might if he doesn't get any outside help. Trust me, Wheeler will be thrilled to let me prosecute this matter. Besides, Wheeler's got a legitimate reason to invite me into the courtroom to help him. He's never prosecuted a death penalty case."

"And the other person who can stop you—or do I even need to ask?"

"It's you! There's no way in hell I can intervene in a circuit court murder case unless the presiding judge lets me," Cauldwell explained.

As far as Spencer knew, no attorney general in Virginia

had ever prosecuted a capital murder case. If Spencer allowed it, he would be establishing a dangerous precedent. There'd always been an undisputed "No Trespassing" line drawn between the state's circuit courts and the AG's office. It was the attorney general's job to argue appeals before the Virginia Supreme Court, not prosecute local murder cases.

"There hasn't been a death penalty case in Charlottesville in at least twenty years," Spencer noted. "I'm not certain the town will stand for it."

Charlottesville was a conservative Southern city, but compared to its ultraconservative neighbors, it was a beacon of liberalism. The University was the reason.

"I genuinely believe the death penalty is justified in this case," Cauldwell said. "This punk kidnapped a child, sexually tortured her, and then strangled her in the basement of her own home while her parents were sleeping upstairs. That's every parent's nightmare."

Spencer looked directly at Cauldwell. "Taylor, I've known you a long time," Spencer said, "long enough to know that this is really about something else. I'm guessing it's publicity, getting your face on the front pages and television news shows just before the gubernatorial election."

Cauldwell feigned shock. "Publicity? Me? Never!" But then he added: "Of course that's part of it. This case could be my ticket into the governor's mansion. My pollsters tell me the governor is vulnerable in only one area when it comes to his precious northern Virginia voters. He's miscalculated their views about the death penalty. Remember the Wydell Mower case?"

Spencer did. Mower had been a mentally retarded black man convicted of murdering an eighty-six-year-old grandmother in Richmond. A week before his execution date, Governor Anderson had agreed to let Mower's attorneys get a DNA comparison done. Mower's DNA did not match the DNA on human tissue found under the murdered grandmother's fingernails. Anderson had granted Mower an immediate and absolute pardon. No one had ever walked away before from Virginia's death row, and the Mower case had received national attention in the media. At about this same time, Illinois Governor George Ryan, a fellow Republican and death penalty advocate, had put a hold on all executions in his state after thirteen death row inmates had their executions overturned, mostly because of DNA evidence.

Cauldwell said: "I'm not sure why Governor Anderson decided to do what he did next—maybe it was his conscience, maybe it was because he wanted to show the world that he is not such a right-wing extremist—hell, maybe he was just taking some stupid political advice from an aide. But for whatever reason, our governor told Katie Couric on the *Today Show* that he personally had developed strong misgivings about the death penalty and no longer believed that he could morally support it."

Cauldwell paused dramatically to emphasize the importance of what he had just said and was about to say. "Now Spencer, you and I both know that Virginia is no ordinary state when it comes to executing people. Hell, we introduced the death penalty into the New World by hanging some unlucky sap in the early 1600s. We've executed more women and the youngest children of any state in the nation. Back in 1951, we executed eight men in a seventy-two-hour period. After the Supreme Court ruled that the death penalty was too arbitrary and capricious, our state legislators worked overtime to draft new laws so we could get back into the business of killing people. Since 1982, we've put more prisoners to death than any other state except Texas, which has a far larger population."

Spencer was familiar with the execution numbers.

"Not only does Virginia enjoy executing our criminals," Cauldwell continued, "we have streamlined the process. Just look at our appeals process. After a judge signs a death order, a defendant has only twenty-one days to find new evidence. If he doesn't find it in twenty-one days, then he can't introduce it in an appellate court no matter what he discovers. It doesn't matter if he finds proof. If it wasn't introduced at the trial, then it can't be raised in the appeal."

It was a sore point with defense attorneys, Spencer knew. There were others.

"The same is true about a defense attorney's objections," Cauldwell said. "Under the Contemporaneous Objection

Rule, lawyers are barred from raising objections on appeal unless they were brought up previously during the original trial. If a prisoner gets an incompetent lawyer, he's shit out of luck. Our commonwealth has another cute way of speeding a defendant into the electric chair. You know the Preservation of Evidence Rule as well as I do. The circuit court is under no obligation to preserve evidence from trials once they have concluded. In most cases, the evidence is destroyed. Try going back ten years to look at DNA samples in most Virginia cases. You can't do it!"

Clearly on a rampage, Cauldwell asked: "You ever wonder why the good citizens of the Commonwealth of Virginia make it difficult for death row inmates to appeal? It's because voters are sick and tired of seeing the court system bogged down with frivolous suits. They're convinced that the only way for the death penalty to be effective is if it is done swiftly."

"I've checked," Cauldwell continued, now pausing only long enough to catch his breath. "Do you know that no elected official in Virginia who has flip-flopped on the death penalty and voted against it has ever been reelected. Not one. There are some sins that conservative voters in Virginia will forgive. You can get caught fucking your campaign manager, as long as she's a woman, and you can steal but you sure as hell better not go soft on crime. Polls I have taken privately show 85 percent of Virginians favor the death penalty. Hell, even if you soften the question by giving them an alternative—by saying that a criminal would be sentenced to a mandatory life sentence without any chance of parole—a whopping 65 percent of Virginians still want that son-of-a-bitch to fry in the electric chair. So you tell me now, what's our illustrious governor going to do when I get this black kid, Lester Amil, convicted and I get a jury to sentence him to death? I can see the media circus now: I'll be demanding justice for the victim—an innocent little white girl who was kidnapped, sexually tortured, and strangled by a child pornographer. And Governor Anderson will be stuck on the other side trying to defend this crooked-hat-wearing, hip-hop-singing angry black punk from getting what he deserves. Every white parent in northern Virginia is going to put themselves in Frank and Maxine Arnold's shoes and be on my side. And I'm going to ride this case right into the governor's office. It's that simple. Remember Willie Horton?"

Cauldwell reached over and gently placed his hand on Spencer's shoulder. "Remember how we used to talk in law school," Cauldwell said, "about how I was going to become governor and you would run the state supreme court. This is our big chance. My pollsters tell me I can knock off Anderson—this murder case is his Achilles' heel. I would make a great governor and you deserve to be on the state supreme court."

Spencer was starting to feel uncomfortable. They were straying close to unethical ground. Judges aren't supposed to discuss murder cases with potential prosecutors nor was it a wise idea for Cauldwell to be dangling a supreme court job in front of him. Technically, the justices on the Virginia Supreme Court were appointed by the general assembly, but if Cauldwell were elected he could use his clout to get Spencer onto the highest state court.

"Spencer," Cauldwell said, "this isn't just about politics and our ambitions. The kid sexually tortured and murdered a child. Neither of us want him to walk away free and kill again. All I'm asking is for you to not object when I reveal that I've decided to intervene."

"When were you planning to reveal that?"

"The kid's preliminary hearing is scheduled for later today. I'm sure Judge George Gatlin is going to find sufficient evidence to send the charges to a grand jury. That's when I'm going to step in and turn this into a capital murder case. We're going to make it look like this was Jacob Wheeler's idea—to invite me in to help him prosecute."

"You've got it all worked out, don't you?"

"Spencer, this is my future and it's your future too!" Cauldwell said. "Can I count on you to be my friend here?"

Spencer thought for a moment. He'd always admired Cauldwell's balls-to-the-wall ambition. Cauldwell was a risk-task. In law school, he had been infamous for challenging conventional thinking in legal cases. He was opinionated, determined, focused, and utterly ruthless when it came to getting what he wanted. After he had graduated, Cauldwell had settled in Richmond where he'd worked as a prosecutor. He'd taken the weakest cases and somehow won them, earning the nickname Take 'em Down Taylor. From there, he'd moved to the U.S. Attorney's office where he'd shown the ferociousness of a pit bull, going after a deadly Richmond-based outlaw motorcycle gang. After that, he'd been elected as a state delegate to the General Assembly where he'd quickly moved through the committee ranks. And then he had risked it all by running for attorney general against a better-financed opponent. The rest was history. He'd won an upset and now he was pushing the envelope again, trying to unseat a sitting governor who was among the most popular in Virginia's history.

"I won't object to you intervening," Spencer said softly. "You have my word on it."

Cauldwell broke into a huge grin. "I knew I could count on you. You've made the right decision." He glanced at his watch. "Oops, gotta go. Oh, there's something else I should tell you. I had an informal chat earlier this week with Judge Gatlin and he's going to appoint Patti Delaney to defend Lester Amil."

"You're getting Delaney appointed to defend a death case?"

"Well, she really doesn't know yet that it's going to become a death case, remember? That won't happen until I intervene. Right now, it's just a simple murder case."

"Is she qualified to defend a capital murder case?"

"Listen, she's more experienced than you might think. She handled a death case appeal in Baltimore."

"That's not Virginia. Is she on the state commission's list?" he asked, referring to a list the state keeps that identifies defense attorneys who are qualified under Virginia guidelines to represent clients on trial for their life.

"To be honest," Cauldwell answered, "no, Patti Delaney is not on the list of qualified death row attorneys. But that's not going to present us with a problem. I'm certain that she'll have someone from the public defender's office helping her. After all, the state requires two defense attorneys in death cases."

"She was horrible when she appeared in my court," Spencer said.

"Really?" Cauldwell replied with a smile. "What a poor shame for Lester Amil."

"What if someone objects to her defending a death case?"

"Who's going to object?" Cauldwell said. "And even if someone does, Virginia statutes give you the authority as the presiding circuit court judge to declare her competent. But let's get real here, no one else in this community is going to want to touch this case."

Spencer knew that was true. Death penalty cases were notoriously time consuming, costly, and could ruin a local attorney. No decent resident of Charlottesville was going to hire Patti Delaney to defend them or even prepare a property deed once they learned that she had represented a black sexual predator and murderer.

"Why'd you pick her, besides the fact that she's incompetent," Spencer asked.

"I've got my reasons."

Cauldwell grinned again and then said, loud enough for the nurses outside to hear him, "Now Judge Spencer, I want you to get back to work as soon as possible. The Commonwealth of Virginia can't afford to have someone as important as you lying in this hospital flirting with all these pretty nurses!" He waltzed outside and shook hands with both women.

It was only after Cauldwell was gone that Spencer began to realize the enormity of his promise. In his years on the bench, he had never heard a capital murder case. He'd never had to look a defendant in his eye and sentence him to death either by lethal injection or by electrocution. In agreeing to help his longtime buddy—and possibly secure a seat for himself on the Virginia Supreme Court—Spencer had placed himself in an uncomfortable position, both ethically and morally.

How could justice be blind if Cauldwell's fingers were tugging at the scales?

Lying in bed, thinking about what he had just done, Spencer felt a sudden pain in his left hand. It was as if someone was slicing his skin with a dull knife. He raised his hand and noticed that a tiny red line had begun to appear in the center of his palm.

"What the hell?" he said, touching it. It was tender and, as soon as he felt it, the red line began to throb.

5

AFTER LANDING AT LOGAN INTERNATIONAL AIRPORT, THE Rev. Dino Angelo Grasso and his traveling companion, Kyle Dunham, caught a cab to Beacon Hill, a posh section of Boston. Before Patrick McPherson had committed suicide inside the Luxor, he had lived here with his wife in a Greek Revival town house. Carol McPherson greeted Grasso and Dunham in a contemporary foyer, which had pale green walls and a zebra skin on its blond hardwood flooring. She led them into an adjoining living room where the walls were painted bright peach, the window coverings were bloodred, and there were two white overstuffed sofas facing a fireplace that had a plum-colored mantel. Grasso's deformed body was immediately swallowed up when he sat on the smaller of the sofas.

"Can I offer you anything? Tea, coffee, a soft drink?" she asked.

"No, no, I'm fine," Grasso replied, having been taught in his childhood at the monastery never to be an inconvenience to anyone.

"I'd love a beer if you've got one," Dunham said. He was a third-year student at Catholic University, a bright boy with an inquisitive mind whom Grasso had asked to accompany him to Boston since his physical handicaps and age made traveling alone difficult.

"Of course," Mrs. McPherson said.

Grasso examined her as she summoned her housekeeper. Although she was only in her early forties, she looked much older. She was slender and plain. Her black hair was pulled back tightly in a bun. No makeup. A simple black dress, no-nonsense black shoes, no jewelry except for her diamond and gold wedding bands. She had been reluctant to talk about her husband when Grasso first telephoned, and she'd tried to politely put him off, but he had been persistent. Now, as they waited for beverages, Grasso complimented her on her house's colorful decor, hoping to make her feel at ease.

"I did all of the decorating myself," she replied, "or, I should say, I hired the work crews and told them what to do. The entire interior of this house was gutted. I had a steel five-story circular stairway installed to save room and give the place a more modern feel. I know the colors are a bit, shall we say, exotic. I was inspired by a trip I made to Tuscany."

The difference between her own minimalist appearance and the brightly painted rooms seemed peculiar. She lit a cigarette as the maid entered carrying a silver tray with a mug of beer for Dunham, a silver pot of coffee, two cups, and a plate of finger sandwiches. Mrs. McPherson poured coffee for Grasso but he was sitting so low in the sofa, he couldn't reach the table with his good right arm. Dunham came to his rescue, handing him the saucer before turning his attention to the stack of finger sandwiches.

"My husband was showing signs of severe mental illness before his death," Mrs. McPherson began, "although I am not certain about the exact diagnosis. When he first began acting oddly, I suspected he was bipolar. I am a psychiatrist here in Boston but I don't see many patients. Research is my speciality. I have spent my career studying schizophrenia, extreme cases where people have escaped deep into a world of delusions and fantasies. Ironic, isn't it, a psychiatrist married to a lawyer who kills himself because he is delusional. . . ." Her voice trailed off.

"Dr. McPherson," Grasso said, "when did you begin noticing that your husband was acting strangely?"

"Are you familiar with bipolar disorder?" she asked.

Grasso had heard the term.

"It comes on unexpectedly, often when people are under great stress. I'm surprised you haven't encountered it because college students, especially ones about to graduate and be sent out into this big, frightening world of ours, are frequently struck by it, as are adults entering middle age and the much dreaded midlife crisis. My husband had no history of any mental disorder. As you can see, we lived very comfortable lives here and abroad. All of this and one day, I woke up with a Jackson Pollack in my bed."

"You said something usually sparks the disorder," Grasso said.

"Patrick was often at his best when he was under a tight deadline or when handling extremely complex legal matters. Stress didn't bother him. Or, at least, it never had. Whatever caused him to begin acting strangely is still a mystery to me. But I don't believe it was stress. The first sign something was wrong was when he became fixated on a rock, a white, round stone. He told me it had magical powers."

"A rock?"

"Yes, God knows where he got it. He claimed he could tell if people were lying to him because of this rock. It was crazy talk but really not that unusual for a bipolar patient. Most develop feelings of grandiosity and they often fixate on objects, such as a movie—you know, seeing themselves as the main character. My husband had a brilliant legal mind and incredible wit but when he talked about this rock, he sounded like an imbecile."

"Was your husband a deeply religious man?"

Mrs. McPherson smiled, revealing perfectly straight and brilliantly white teeth. "So you know about the strange mark on his left palm," she said. "The one that looked like a crucifix. Is that what this is all about?"

"The mark is quite unusual."

"Yes, at first he tried to hide it from me. He was afraid I would think he was making it himself, you know, cutting his own palm. And that is exactly what I'd suspected. But he insisted the rock created the mark and when I examined the cross closely, I could tell it was not self-inflicted. He claimed it was a sign from God."

"What sort of sign?"

"Father Grasso, I told you my husband was suffering from some sort of mental illness. He claimed he had been, for lack of a better word, cursed, and the only way for him to lift this curse was to seek forgiveness from people whom he had harmed in the past. Each time he got someone to forgive him, the mark on his palm would get bigger. One night, he woke me and told me he had found a way to free himself from the rock and its curse. He babbled on and on about discovering some secret code in the Bible. It was going to show him how to get rid of this rock. It was all crazy talk."

"A curse like in voodoo?" Dunham interjected, picking up a seventh finger sandwich.

Mrs. McPherson ignored him. "Reverend Grasso, are you familiar with Haldol?"

"No."

"It is a powerful antipsychotic drug. We give it to patients who are having psychotic episodes and no longer can tell the difference between fantasy and reality. I gave my husband three doses of five milligrams, a standard daily dose. It had absolutely no impact. So I slowly began upping the amount. I soon was giving him more than one hundred milligrams, along with a powerful cocktail of mood stabilizers, and they had absolutely no effect on his delusions. Nothing. None. It was unbelievable. It should have knocked him out. I've seen deeply disturbed patients snap out of their delusional state with much smaller doses of Haldol, but he was completely unaffected. I tried Depakote, Zyprexa, Lithium. Not one of these drugs made a difference. He still claimed he had been cursed, still claimed he had supernatural powers, still claimed it was the rock that was tormenting him. What was odd was how he was completely lucid when he talked about everything else going on in his life. He could discuss the weather, date, time, cases at work, current events. He was in total touch with reality, except when it came to this rock. He knew I was giving him drugs and he insisted there wasn't anything wrong with his brain, there was no chemical imbalance, it was his soul, he told me, that needed healing. Near the end, his ideas became too fast for him to even explain. He didn't need to sleep. I began giving him Ambien, a sleep aid, but there was no effect. He made long lists of people whom he said he had wronged. Silly stuff, really, like when he was five years old and stole some malted milk balls from a neighborhood candy store. He actually tracked down the store's owner and when he discovered he had died years ago, he found the owner's son. He mailed him a long apology and money for those malted milk balls."

"Why was he so worried about being forgiven?"

"It was that damn rock! During one of his worse days, I found him in our bedroom sobbing. He told me that . . ." Mrs.

McPherson paused. Grasso could see tears forming in her eyes. "He told me that he had had an extramarital affair. He said he had fallen in love with this young lawyer in his firm. It had been a long time ago—ten years—but he brought it up and asked me to forgive him. I was stunned, humiliated, and furious. I felt totally and utterly betrayed. I screamed at him. I refused to forgive him. How dare he! After all these years of keeping quiet, he suddenly develops a conscience and wants to feel better about himself, so he confesses. I told him to leave, to get out of our house."

"Is that when he flew to Las Vegas?"

"No. It wasn't my rejection that sent him there. It was your God." She smashed out her cigarette in a silver ashtray. "I'm sorry. I shouldn't have said that. This is not easy for me. Patrick moved back into our house two days after our fight. I forgave him. I thought now, maybe, this horrible nightmare was going to end. But he was as tormented as ever. He told me there was something even more horrible than adultery that he had committed. I said, 'What's more horrible than adultery?' He wouldn't say. Then he told me he had to go to Las Vegas to redeem himself. I said, 'Why Las Vegas?' He'd never been there in his life. He said, 'The Bible is ordering me there. It's hidden in the scriptures. I have to go.' I was afraid but I couldn't stop him. He called me from where he was staying out there, that pyramid-shaped hotel, whatever it's called. He told me he'd finally found a way to be forgiven for all of his sins." She began to cry.

"I'm sorry your husband was in so much pain, that you both were," Grasso said sympathetically. "Did your husband ever seek help from a priest?"

Mrs. McPherson reached for a tissue. "I don't mean to be rude," she said, "but my husband saw plenty of priests, Protestant ministers too. More than a dozen. That was early on, that was when he first began his search for answers. I told you he was obsessed. None of them had an answer that satisfied him, so he began diagraming verses in the Bible on his own, hundreds of them, looking for a secret code. I've never seen a mental illness like what he had. Not only didn't the drugs work, neither did logic. He told me he was trying to become like Jesus. He had to. The rock was forcing him to become perfect." She was having trouble speaking now because of her tears. "None of what he said made any sense."

"Perhaps," Grasso said gently, "if we examined his papers, we could find some clues to this puzzle."

"They're in his library," she said, standing. "If you follow me, I'll show you where."

Grasso tried but was not strong enough to free himself from the sofa. Dunham pulled him to his feet. McPherson's library was the only room that his wife had not decorated. It was all walnut bookshelves and leather chairs. Cartoons from *Punch* magazine about lawyers were framed on the walls. An autographed photograph of William Jennings Bryan fanning himself while seated at a table during the famous Scopes Monkey Trial was hanging on one wall.

"I suspect letting you look at all this can't do any harm," Mrs. McPherson said. She sat down in one of the library's chairs and took out another cigarette. "Being in this room reminds me of Patrick. He loved the law, the rightness of it." Grasso examined the books stacked on McPherson's desk. There were more than a dozen and each described a different technique for interpreting biblical scriptures.

"Dr. Grasso," Dunham said, "check this out." He handed Grasso a yellow legal pad that McPherson had written on. It contained a list of seventy-three different biblical verses. The first was from chapter sixteen, verse five, in Genesis: *"May the Lord judge between you and me!"* Grasso quickly scanned the others.

"Each of these scriptures contains the words judge, judgment, or justice," he noted. "It appears Mr. McPherson was compiling a list of every scripture in the Bible that dealt with judgment."

"Here's something else," Dunham said, handing Grasso another legal tablet. McPherson had written the words *Psalm 27, verse 1* at the top of the page:

> [A] The Lord is my light and my salvation:
> [B] Whom shall I fear?
> [A] The Lord is the stronghold of my life;
> [B] Of whom shall I be afraid?

Underneath the scripture, McPherson had scribbled "*A-B-A-B.*"

Grasso showed the pad to Mrs. McPherson. "It appears your husband was using his legal training and exactness to diagram these scriptures," Grasso said. "Many Old Testament books, such as Psalms, Proverbs, Lamentations, Micah, and Obadiah, are actually long Hebrew poems. However, the Hebrews didn't use the same rhyme or meter that English writers use in poetry. Some scholars call this Hebrew style 'parallelism' because many of the Hebrews' poems repeat the same thought in a slightly different way. Let me show you." Grasso took a blank sheet from the legal pad. "Look at what happens if we put the two lines that McPherson has marked with the letter *A* side-by-side." Grasso wrote:

> *[A] The Lord is my light and my salvation.*
> *[A] The Lord is the stronghold of my life.*

"These two sentences repeat the same message. See? Now, let's put the lines marked *B* together." Grasso wrote them out.

> *[B] Whom shall I fear?*
> *[B] Of whom shall I be afraid?*

"Once again, these lines say the same thing," Grasso explained. "They parallel each other."

"Congratulations," announced Mrs. McPherson. "Patrick showed me that same *A* and *B* trick one night. But he called it 'mirror imaging.' He told me the Bible contained hidden messages that could only be unscrambled if you knew a special code. That's what all of these diagrams are about. He spent hours dissecting biblical passages."

"Do you know if he found this code?" Grasso asked.

"Yes, at least, he thought he had. He showed it to me." She flipped through one of the yellow pads that her husband had used and stopped on a sheet that contained a scripture from Isaiah, chapter 6, verse 10:

> [A] Make the heart of this people fat,
> [B] and make their ears heavy,
> [C] and shut their eyes;
> [C] lest they see with their eyes,
> [B] and hear with their ears,
> [A] and understand with their hearts . . .

"See how this verse repeats the same pattern: the heart [A], the ears [B], and the eyes [C]?" she asked. Grasso and Dunham nodded. "Now look at this scripture on the next page." She showed it to them. It was from Isaiah, chapter 55, verses 8 and 9.

> [A] For my thoughts are not your thoughts,
> [B] neither are your ways my ways . . .
> [C] For as the heavens are higher than the earth
> [B] so are my ways higher than your ways,
> [A] and my thoughts higher than your thoughts.

"Obviously, *A* and *B* mirror each other—thoughts mirrors thoughts, ways mirrors ways," she explained, "but there is no sentence that mirrors *C*." McPherson had underlined *C* on the legal pad.

> *[C] For as the heavens are higher than the earth*

"This was my husband's great discovery: that there are lines in the poems that are not mirrored. They stand alone. These then are God's secret messages. In this case, the secret message is: *heaven is higher—or above—the earth.*"

"Wow, that's cool!" Dunham gushed.

"Don't be deceived here, my young friend," Grasso said. "While this may be a clever approach, I'm afraid, in the end, it doesn't make much sense."

"How come?" Dunham asked.

"To begin with, the Holy Scriptures were not written in English," Grasso explained. "The finest scholars in the Vatican can't agree on which verses in the Holy Bible are legitimate and if these verses were transcribed and interpreted accurately. There are words the Hebrews used which are completely unlike any words in English. Yet Mr. McPherson is using his legal training to literally look behind the verses and see a hidden message. That's the first problem."

"And the second?" asked Mrs. McPherson.

"Your husband believed God had hidden messages for him in the Bible. Why? There is no reason for God to hide messages. What God intends for us to know, He tells us. It's mankind who makes His message difficult to understand. The importance of these notes is not *what* your husband's amateur biblical scholarship produced," Grasso continued, "but rather *why* was a man who had no strong religious convictions suddenly so obsessed with religion that he was diagraming hundreds of verses? I think we should ask ourselves *why* he was writing these pages. What was his motivation? We need to ask what was driving him down this desperate path—rather than trying to follow in his footsteps and search for a secret message from God hidden in the Holy Bible."

Grasso and Dunham continued inspecting McPherson's papers while Mrs. McPherson smoked and watched them. After a half hour, she let out a loud sigh. "Dr. Grasso, I'm going to the kitchen to have another cup of coffee. Is there anything I can bring you two?"

"No thank you," Grasso said, this time answering for both of them.

"There is a copying machine in the corner that you can use," she said. "I will be back in a few minutes." She left.

Something was troubling Grasso. "On the first pad that we examined," he told Dunham, "McPherson listed every verse in the Bible that mentioned judgment. Yet, there are no diagrams of these 'judgment' verses on the legal pads that we've found. If McPherson was fixated on judgment and seeking forgiveness for his own sins, then where are those verses and what secrets did he discern when he diagramed them?"

"Maybe he took those legal pads to Vegas with him," Dunham suggested.

"Perhaps, but let's check the trash in case he destroyed them so his wife would not realize that he was going to Las Vegas to commit suicide."

Underneath a paper shredder in the corner, they found a bag filled with yellow and white strips that had come from a mixture of shredded legal pads, letters, and envelopes. Dunham took out a handful of the strips and spread them on McPherson's desk. While reconnecting them was impossible, they found two strands that hadn't been completely separated. The words on them read: *"strikes a man so that he dies . . ."*

"Do you recognize this verse, Dr. Grasso?" Dunham asked.

"Yes I do, it's from the Old Testament. It's one of the early laws set down by the Hebrews." Grasso picked up a worn copy of the Holy Bible from McPherson's desk and opened it to Exodus. He found what he was searching for in chapter 21, verse 12. *"Whoever strikes a man so that he dies shall be put to death . . ."*

Something in McPherson's Bible caught his eye. He turned back a few pages to Exodus, chapter 19, which describes Moses's encounter with God on the mountaintop at Sinai. McPherson had covered the margins in these pages with notes.

"This is interesting," Grasso said. "McPherson has written initials or specific names next to each line of the Ten Commandments. Next to 'Thou Shall Not Steal,' McPherson had jotted down 'McMillian's Corner Candy Shop'. Alongside verse thirteen, 'Thou Shalt Not Kill,' McPherson had written the initials 'B.D.' The next verse, fourteen, had the name 'S. Dickens' penned next to it.

"I want you to make a copy of this page—the Ten Commandments and his scribbled notes next to each verse," Grasso said, handing the Bible to Dunham. While he was doing that, Grasso looked in the bookshelves and found a directory of Boston lawyers. He looked up the name "S. Dickens." There was only one listed. When he dialed the number, a woman answered.

"Miss Dickens," Grasso said. "I apologize for bothering you at home, but I need to speak to you about a matter of importance. My name is Father Dino Angelo Grasso. I'm a professor at Catholic University and I'm in Boston investigating a delicate matter. I think you might be able to help me."

"What are you investigating?"

"Patrick McPherson's death."

Dickens didn't respond.

"I think you know the reason why I'm curious about it."

Again, only silence.

"Please, I don't wish to embarrass you in any way with my questions," Grasso continued. "Whatever you say will be kept completely confidential. I give you my promise as a priest. Please also know that this is very, very important. Can we meet in person?"

Again, there was no reaction.

"Miss Dickens, are you there?"

"I'm married now," she said. "Dickens is my maiden name but I still use it because of my legal practice. How much do you know about Patrick and me?"

"Only the basics, but I believe you may be the only person who can tell me the real reason why he killed himself."

For several more moments, she didn't speak and then she relented. "Okay, I'll meet you, although I really don't know why I should. But not here at my house. Meet me at an Irish pub called O'Leary's on Beacon Street in forty-five minutes."

As soon as Grasso put down the phone, Dunham asked: "Who's she?"

"Commandment seven," he answered.

"Huh?"

"No time for questions now," Grasso replied. "We've got to get to a pub."

Before they left, they said good-bye to Mrs. McPherson. "My husband was a good man," she said softly, as she escorted them to the front door. "If you discover what caused his illness, please let me know. We were happy, so happy, before he got fixated on that damn rock."

"I will," Grasso promised. "By the way, do you know what happened to the rock?"

"No," she said. "He must have taken it with him because it's not in his office. I looked."

O'Leary's was the epitome of Bostonized Irish pubs. Its decor was a mixture of American and Irish kitsch. Grasso always stuck out in crowds because of his deformities, but he looked even more out-of-place than usual standing inside the jammed pub, amid a sea of the city's young and upwardly mobile professionals. Dickens recognized Grasso from his cleric's collar and suggested the two of them walk down the street to a less-crowded cafe. They left Dunham behind nursing a beer. Once they had settled into a booth and ordered coffee, Dickens asked: "How'd you find me?"

"Ironically," Grasso replied, "it was Patrick McPherson who told me your name. His wife said that he had once had a sexual affair with someone in his law firm, but she didn't mention anyone by name." Grasso removed a slip of paper from his pocket, unfolded it, and slid it across the Formica tabletop to her. It was the copy of the Ten Commandments that Dunham had made with McPherson's handwritten notes in the margin.

Susan Dickens, a slender African-American woman in her thirties, glanced down at the words "S. Dickens" penned next to verse fourteen, the Seventh Commandment: *Thou shalt not commit adultery.* She slowly folded the paper.

"I was born in Monroeville, Alabama, raised primitive Baptist, and, quite frankly, my people have little respect for the Roman Catholic Church," she said, "so I don't have some great need to confess my sins to you."

"I'm not here to hear your confession or criticize you," Grasso replied. "I just want to learn about Patrick McPherson."

"I hated him," she said coldly. "I also loved him." She paused, trying to decide if she really wanted to tell him her story, and then she continued. "It happened ten years ago. I was fresh from law school, trying to prove myself. You have no idea how difficult it is for a young lawyer in one of these big Boston firms. You get every horrible assignment. They work you eighty hours a week, pay you next to nothing, treat you as if you are stupid and worthless. It's part of an initiation. Back in those days, there was a lot of sexual harassment and the fact that I was a young black woman trying to make it in a white, male-dominated world in one of the most racist cities in America made it even more difficult. There were plenty of senior partners who didn't want me to succeed. Patrick's law firm had been forced under threat of a lawsuit to hire minorities, but they made it clear, I wasn't really welcome."

"And McPherson, how did he treat you?"

"He didn't think like those other old bastards. He took time to help me, give me advice and encouragement. There was one partner, a racist old fart who really was making my life a living hell. He was trying to make me quit, wanting to prove blacks couldn't cut it as lawyers. I hated him so much I came up with a plan to get revenge. It sounds silly now, but I decided I would seduce one of the partners and then sue the firm. I wanted to embarrass those rich self-righteous bigots. I looked around and Patrick stood out. He was my only shot. I knew he had a wife and appeared happily married but I didn't care. I worked late whenever he was in the office, made sure I was there to help him with cases. I flirted with him, teased him. It was different from what I had imagined it would be, but he ended up falling hard for me."

She cleared her throat, took a sip of her coffee. "Of course, I ended up falling in love with him too. Right out of a Hollywood B-movie script, huh? The tangled webs we weave. We kept our love affair a secret. We were together for more than three years. That's not a short time, especially when you're in your twenties. Then one Christmas, I woke up alone in my bed and I was angry. I wanted to be married, not some white man's black whore. I told him, 'Enough! Either you leave your wife and we start a new life together or I'm out of here.' I thought he would leave her but he just couldn't do it. I tried to reason with him, tried to sell myself, made promises of how great it would be. I felt like a fool but I couldn't walk away either. And then I thought of a way to force him to choose me. It was my lowest moment."

The waitress appeared with coffee, momentarily interrupting her story.

"You know," Susan said, seconds later, "I'm a well-educated woman. I've overcome tremendous odds to obtain the success I've achieved. But in total desperation, I did what those dumb-ass, ignorant black teenagers who live on the outskirts of Monroeville do when they want to trap a man. I got pregnant. You know, he and his wife couldn't have children, something wrong with her, and he'd always wanted to be a father. Now he had a child on the way, a half-black child. That was going to shake that rich, white family tree of his down to its roots. I thought it would be enough to win him over, make him choose me. I thought he wouldn't have any other choice. But he came to me and said he'd figured out a way to arrange it so he and his wife could adopt our baby. No one would ever know I was the mother and his wife would never know he was the father. I was outraged. I went off on him. He wanted me to give up our child! He wanted me to provide a baby to him and his sterile wife! He had no intention of leaving her for me. When I realized that, I told him I was going to abort the baby. I'd rather kill it than have him and his wife raise it. He was horrified."

She looked at Grasso, searching for a reaction, a sign of horror. But he remained stone-faced.

"I had a law professor tell me once that in every trial there is a deciding moment when the balance tips. A great attorney knows when that moment has arrived and knows how to tip the balance in his client's favor. We'd reached that point in our relationship. I had to take my best shot, go for broke. I told Patrick that I wanted him to drive me to the abortion clinic. I was forcing him into a corner, making him take responsibility for what I was going to do. He either had to divorce his wife and marry me, or see our baby aborted. It was all very dramatic. The truth is I wanted him to be in as much pain as possible. I didn't think he would drive me to that clinic. I didn't think he could be that cruel. But he did it. He took me there, came inside with me, paid the bill, and was there when I came out. I had never done anything so terrible in my life. I hated that I had aborted our child and I hated him for letting me do it. How had I sunk to such a low level? I resigned from the law firm and told him that I never wanted to see or hear from him again. It took me years, and I mean years, to get over him. All of that time, he never tried to contact me and that made me despise him even more. He'd simply gone on with his perfect life. He'd rejected not only me but our baby. Eventually, I met my current husband and fell in love. That was what finally made it possible for me to get on with my life and stop thinking about him and hating him. Then one day a few months ago, Patrick shows up at my law firm. No warning call, no note, no e-mail. I didn't know how to react. He tells me he has come to apologize. He's sorry for hurting me, for causing me so much pain. He asks me to forgive him. I mean he literally gets down on his knees in my office with tears rolling down his face and he tells me he's sorry."

"And you forgave him?"

"Hell no, not at first! I didn't want to. I still hated him, but seeing him so upset and so distraught, it was unbelievable to me. I told him that he had ruined my life. But then I started crying too and suddenly I blurted out the truth: how I had intentionally seduced him and how I had gotten pregnant on purpose. I told him that I was the one who needed to be forgiven. He disagreed. He said he was older, should have known better, was married. I said, 'Let's just forget the past, forget any of this happened.' But he couldn't, not even after I had forgiven him and he'd forgiven me. It was the abortion that was eating away at him. He referred to our dead child as Baby Doe."

"What did he say about Baby Doe?"

"He said there was only one way that he could make things right. That scared me. A few days later, one of my law partners came running into my office and blurted out: 'Patrick McPherson killed himself in Las Vegas!' The newspaper speculated he had done it because of gambling debts. But I knew better."

She held her coffee cup with both hands, taking in the warmth. "You want to know why he killed himself?" she asked. "It was because of the abortion."

Grasso was trying to think of something comforting to say, but he had never developed a good bedside manner. He was an academic, not a parish priest. "The Lord works in mysterious ways," he finally said. "Perhaps, this is part of some mysterious, master plan. Perhaps some good will come from it."

"Spare me your bullshit clichés, father," Dickens replied bitterly. "I grew up being told that rubbish about how God has some grand plan, about how He is weaving a tapestry and we are each a piece of thread and can't see the total design. I don't believe a word of it. You want to lecture me about the struggles of Job? See, I know my Bible. But I don't buy it! God created Job and it was God who created our pain and our suffering." She leaned forward and spoke quietly but bluntly to him. "If all of this is part of God's master plan, then the next time you pray to Him, give Him a message for me. Tell Him: His plan sucks." With that, she stood up and walked swiftly from the restaurant.

Grasso was exhausted by the time he hobbled back to O'Leary's tavern. He found his young protégé asleep with his head on a table. They hurried to the airport and caught the last shuttle to Washington, D.C. En route, Grasso said a prayer for Susan Dickens.

The next afternoon, Kyle Dunham reported to Grasso's office as ordered.

"What did we learn in Boston?" Grasso asked, falling easily into his role as a teacher.

"Patrick McPherson felt he had to be forgiven for every sin he'd committed," Dunham replied.

"Correct," Grasso said, "and based on what Ms. Dickens told me, we know he was haunted by the abortion of their child." Grasso unfolded the copy of the Ten Commandments. "McPherson wrote *B.D.* next to *Thou Shalt Not Kill.*" Grasso said. "I think it's safe for us to assume *B.D.* stands for *Baby Doe.*"

"He believed he'd committed murder by aborting Baby Doe?"

"Yes," Grasso said.

"What does McPherson's secret code have to do with any of this?"

"I'm afraid we will never know for certain," said Grasso. "But I suspect the answer is in a thousand strips of shredded paper in McPherson's trash can. At some point, he must have diagrammed a verse, probably in the Old Testament, that told him that the only way he could redeem himself was by ending his own life. There are plenty such verses in the Old Testament. Exodus twenty-one, verse twelve says: *'Whoever strikes a man so that he dies shall be put to death.'*"

"He killed himself so he could be forgiven for aborting Baby Doe?" Dunham asked.

"Some refer to it as blood atonement."

"Then he was really nuts."

"Was he?" Grasso replied. "Then how do you explain the mark on his hand?"

"Psychosomatic."

"What if the mark on his hand was some sort of mystical stigmata and the stone that he touched was, in fact, a holy relic?" Grasso asked.

"That's a bit far-fetched, isn't it?"

"Why, the church has thousands of relics on display across the world and most are believed to possess mystical powers."

"Are you saying God wanted McPherson to kill himself?"

"Of course not. That was McPherson's misguided decision based on this silly secret code that he'd come to believe in," Grasso replied. "But let's examine the facts. Fact one: McPherson is not a religious or superstitious man. Fact two: He tells his wife that he's found a magical stone and it's making him feel guilty about sins that he has committed. Fact three: An outline of a cross appears on the palm of his left hand. There's no medical explanation for what is causing it. Fact four: He begins searching for ways to rid himself of this mark. Fact five: He seeks forgiveness for all of his sins. Now, are those actions really so odd? If we believe, just for a minute, that this magical stone actually exists and it makes you feel guilty, then McPherson's actions are not crazy at all. What was the first thing McPherson did after he touched the stone? He reached out to the experts by contacting priests and ministers. When they couldn't explain what was happening to him, he began reading textbooks about biblical interpretation. He was trying to find his own solution, and when he couldn't do that, he began searching for some secret code to end this 'curse' that was disrupting his life. I would argue that a man who has just been diagnosed with cancer would react the exact same way: he would consult doctors, read all that he could, and if the traditional methods didn't cure him, he would try to find some new cure. Would you declare him crazy?"

"No, but do you really believe McPherson found a magic stone?"

"I believe we can't assume that he didn't," Grasso replied. "Not yet. Think rationally. If there is a magic stone, then there should be a record of it. Chances are, Patrick McPherson wouldn't have been the first to touch it."

"Okay," Dunham said sarcastically, "That simplifies things.

All we have to do now is find someone who keeps records about magic stones! Duh!"

Grasso smiled. "My young friend, you have much to learn. Inside the Court of the Belvedere next to the Vatican Library in Rome, there is a room where records about unexplained happenings are kept. They're part of the Vatican's Secret Archives and they date back to the beginnings of Christianity. If a magic stone exists, there will be a record of it there."

"We're going to Rome?"

"No, *I'm* going to Rome," Grasso replied. "You'll stay here and find a solution to the next problem that we will encounter if, in fact, the records inside the Secret Archives substantiate what I suspect."

"What problem is that?"

"Finding the stone."

6

CHARLOTTESVILLE, VIRGINIA

THE ALBEMARLE COUNTY SHERIFF'S DEPUTY STATIONED BE-hind the two-inch-thick protective glass inside the county jail's control center asked Patti Delaney for her Virginia Bar Association identification card after she explained that she was representing Lester Amil. She slipped the card through a slot to him and he turned it over several times. Then he re-membered. "Hey, you're the woman lawyer who had that kid wear stolen clothes to court, right?"

Delaney tried not to blush. "Yes, I'm new here. That's why you don't recognize me."

"Your client was pretty funny," he said. "We all got a good laugh when we heard about it." He smiled, revealing a row of crooked yellow teeth stained from cigarettes. "I'll have your client taken to the attorney-client interview room. How you want him?"

She didn't understand.

"How you want him?" he repeated. "With or without bracelets?"

"Huh?"

"Handcuffs," he snapped. "You want him with or without them?"

Delaney didn't know much about her new client except what she had read in the warrant that had been issued against him. Amil was accused of kidnapping, statutory rape, and murder. Still, she didn't want him to think that she was afraid to be alone with him. "Leave them off," she said, and then she hesitated. "I mean, isn't that how most other attorneys see their clients?"

As soon as she asked, she wished she hadn't. The deputy was clearly enjoying making her feel stupid. He shrugged and pushed a red button that opened an electronically controlled door a few steps away. She made her way through a series of steel gates until she reached a windowless room that contained three chairs and a table. Ten minutes later, two deputies brought in Lester Amil. One deputy was carrying a long black club, the other had his hand clasped around a pair of handcuffs, which held Amil's wrists tightly behind his back. The deputy removed the restraints.

"Thank you, guards," Delaney said.

"Correctional officers," one of the deputies grunted. "We ain't guards."

She'd only said three words and yet her inexperience was screaming out. "Guards is an insult to them," Amil explained as soon as they were alone in the room. "We call them BOSS only BOSS doesn't mean respect. Prisoners think of the letters in reverse: they stand for Sorry Sons of Bitches—BOSS! Get it?"

He chuckled. "Things like that help us pass time and passively fight back against our oppressors."

Delaney mustered an uncomfortable smile. "I've been appointed to represent you today at an evidentiary hearing," she explained. "Because you have been accused of three felonies, including murder, the judge has appointed two attorneys to represent you. Unfortunately, the other attorney is currently detained at the courthouse representing another client. He'll join us at the hearing."

"I want you to know that I didn't kill Cassie. She was like a kid sister to me!"

"Let's focus on what's going to happen today," Delaney replied, "because we don't have much time. You'll be taken before a judge in what's called a general district court. The commonwealth's attorney will call witnesses who will tell the judge why the police have arrested you."

"That's easy," he said, interrupting. "I'm black!"

"While I suspect racism might be playing a role in all this, the commonwealth's attorney wouldn't have filed a murder charge against you unless he had some evidence linking you to the crime. Do you know what it might be?"

"I didn't do anything wrong. When will I get to talk to a judge?"

"Virginia has an unusual court system. The first step is having the police or a magistrate issue a warrant for your arrest. Then you are taken before a general district court judge. That's what's scheduled today. He will decide if there's probable cause to believe you murdered Cassie. If there is, he'll 'certify' or send the charges against you to a higher court. It's called the circuit court. Once that happens, the process starts all over. The commonwealth's attorney will prepare what's called a 'bill of indictment' against you. He'll take that indictment before a grand jury, that's usually a panel made up of six people all from Albemarle County."

"Any of them black?"

"I don't know. It's a secret proceeding."

"Just like the Ku Klux Klan."

"The grand jury will decide if you should be indicted. If you are, and I'm guessing you will be, then you will finally go before a circuit court judge and be put on trial."

"I'm being framed because I'm black."

She ignored his remark. "This hearing today is very important."

"Why? You just said I'm not going to be put on trial until we get to a higher level court."

"Because the hearing today is going to be one of the few opportunities we'll have to discover what the prosecution has as evidence against you. In other states, prosecutors are required to tell us what sort of evidence they intend to present at a trial, including a list of their witnesses. But in Virginia, all they are required to give us is a copy of any statement that you made to the police and any exculpatory evidence that they uncovered that would help prove that you're innocent. Today's hearing is like a game of poker. We'll be trying to discover as much as we can about their cards, and they'll be trying to keep those cards hidden."

"Who's paying you? I don't have any money."

"You've been declared indigent and that means the commonwealth has to pay me. You don't have to worry about paying any of my bills."

"I wasn't going to," he replied. "What you're telling me is that the same folks who want to lynch a nigger are paying you."

"Listen," she said, irritated by his implication, "if you'd rather be represented by someone else, you can request a different lawyer at the hearing today."

"Really?" he replied. "Then get me the Rev. Jesse Jackson, and if he's tied up, then get me Al Sharpton."

She couldn't tell if he was serious or just being flippant. "Mr. Amil, the Reverend Jackson and the Reverend Sharpton are not lawyers. It looks like you are going to have to trust me today."

"Trust you?" Amil repeated. "I don't know you. Do you trust me?"

A deputy interrupted them. It was time for court.

General District Judge George Gatlin was a no-nonsense, short-tempered, impatient judge. He'd been diagnosed with lung cancer but continued to stay on the bench and smoke. Sometimes he would sneak a cigarette during a long trial by ducking his face down close to the top of his desk; the attorneys appearing before him could only see the top of his bald head and clouds of cigarette smoke rising up. Because there are no jury trials in Virginia's general courts, Gatlin knew the murder case against Lester Amil was going to be automatically sent up to Judge Evan Spencer's circuit court. He didn't see much point in belaboring the process. "Let's get this over as quickly as possible," he grumbled.

"Before we call witnesses, the Commonwealth would like to amend its criminal complaint against the defendant," Jacob Wheeler announced. "The state medical examiner's office informed us this morning that there was no vaginal penetration of the young victim. Therefore, we are reducing the statutory rape charge to sexual assault."

Gatlin looked to see if Delaney had any questions or objections. She didn't. It suddenly dawned on him that she was the only defense attorney standing next to Amil. "Didn't I appoint two defense attorneys to represent this client?" he asked. "Where's your cocounsel?"

"You appointed Christian Hicks from the public defender's office but he is busy representing another client in a different courtroom," Delaney said. "I'm sure he will be here in a half hour if we can wait."

"I don't wait, especially for defense attorneys," Gatlin declared. "Mr. Christian knew what time this hearing started, so we'll go on without him."

"But your honor," Delaney said. "I'd prefer he was here."

"And so would I, but he isn't," Gatlin snapped. "And that's his choice. So let's go."

Wheeler's first witness was Detective Dale Stuart of the Albemarle County Sheriff's Office, a slightly balding, portly man of about thirty with a handlebar moustache.

"A woman who identified herself as Maxine Arnold telephoned the sheriff's department on Monday and said her daughter had been kidnapped," Stuart said. "I went immediately to the Arnolds' house." Stuart was speaking in a monotone voice. His words sounded memorized and probably had been. "Frank and Maxine Arnold told me that Lester Amil, the defendant, lived in their basement. He was not there. During a search of the house, the body of Cassie Arnold was found. She'd been strangled and sexually assaulted. Her clothing was sent to the state crime lab for analysis."

"I have no more questions," Wheeler announced.

Judge Gatlin motioned to Delaney. "Your turn."

"Detective Stuart, what time did you arrive at the Arnolds' house on Monday?"

"Approximately nine A.M."

"Was there anyone else in the house when you got there?"

Wheeler rose from his chair. "I object, your honor. This line of questioning goes well beyond the scope of direct."

"Sustained," Gatlin declared. "Move on, Ms. Delaney."

"Your Honor, are you saying that I can't even ask who else was in the house?"

"This isn't a trial, young lady. All the state has to do is prove a crime was committed and your man is a likely suspect. Now, let's keep this hearing moving."

For the next several minutes, Delaney tried to pry more information from Stuart, but Wheeler objected to every question and Gatlin ruled in his favor. When she paused for a moment out of sheer frustration, the judge asked: "You done? Good." She sat down.

Wheeler's second witness was Dr. Yuki Nyguen Nang, a pathologist with the state medical examiner's office. Like Detective Stuart, she seemed to have been coached. Her testimony came in simple, bland, declarative sentences. "We examined the victim's clothing. There was male semen on the victim's pajamas. The DNA in the semen matched the defendant's DNA."

"I have no more questions," said Wheeler. "The commonwealth rests."

As soon as Delaney began her cross-examination, Judge Gatlin started tapping his pen nervously on his desk. After she had asked a total of three questions, he interrupted her.

"Can we hurry this along?"

"Judge, this may be my only opportunity for discovery before a murder trial," she replied. "I'm entitled to thoroughly cross-examine this witness."

Gatlin looked angry and was about to speak when Wheeler butted in: "Judge, I would be happy to open all of my files to Ms. Delaney. We've got nothing to hide. She can come into my office next week and look through my records at her leisure."

Wheeler's offer sounded too generous to be true to Delaney, but Judge Gatlin accepted it without question. "There you go, Ms. Delaney," he declared. "The Commonwealth is giving you open access, so there shouldn't be any trouble with discovery in this case. Now, let's wrap this up, shall we?"

Delaney sat down.

Gatlin quickly dispensed with several legal formalities and ruled that there was sufficient cause to send the charges against Amil to the circuit court for trial. The hearing had taken less than twenty minutes.

Delaney stopped Wheeler as he was leaving the courtroom. "I'd like to see your files as soon as possible," she said.

"No problem. How about the middle of next week? That will give me time to make sure all of the police and forensic reports have been processed."

Public Defender Christian Hicks was pacing inside the attorney-client conference room at the county jail when Amil and Delaney returned from the courthouse. A slender, tall, elegantly dressed black man, Hicks was in his sixties and had represented dozens of defendants accused of murder during his thirty-two-year career. Nearly all had been young black men. The first words from his mouth were aimed at Lester Amil.

"I don't want you to tell us anything about this crime, not a single word, you understand?"

Amil nodded. Hicks then turned to Delaney and asked: "How'd it go?"

"We're headed to circuit court," she replied.

"No surprise there. What's the state got as evidence?"

"DNA. His semen was found on the victim's pajamas."

Hicks began firing questions at Delaney, asking her what she had learned about the Commonwealth's case. She couldn't answer any of them.

"Didn't you cross-examine their witnesses?" he asked.

"The judge wouldn't let me!" she replied. "But Wheeler promised in court that we could look through his files. He said we could see them next week."

"And you believed him?" Hicks stammered, making it sound as if she was a complete sucker. "Don't you know there's only going to be a single sheet of paper in his files and all it's going to say is: 'Your client is guilty!' You didn't get us a goddamn thing today!"

"I guess you should've been at the hearing," she bristled.

"Yes," he said. "I clearly made a critical error, but then, I assumed you were competent enough to handle it without me."

Delaney thought about slapping him but didn't.

"Give me a moment to think," Hicks said. It was quiet in the room for several minutes and then Hicks spoke directly to Amil. "I have represented sixty-five clients accused of murder in Virginia. I'm not going to bullshit you. Most of them ended up with life sentences. Our best chance would have been to cut a plea bargain, but this is such a high profile case that just might not be possible. Even so, I'll talk to Wheeler and see if I can get you fifteen years."

"Fifteen years! But I didn't kill that girl!" Amil blurted out.

"I didn't ask if you did," Hicks snapped, "and, quite frankly, it really doesn't matter. What you need to understand, young man, is that in a courtroom, there is no such thing as the truth. The only thing that matters is what the jury believes. As far as I know, an alien spaceship could have come down, landed next to the Arnolds' house and a team of little green men could have sexually assaulted and killed that little girl. But I'm telling you right now, no jury would believe that story even if it were true."

"But I'm innocent! That's got to matter! Doesn't it?"

"It doesn't, not really," Hicks replied sternly. "You aren't listening to what I'm saying. Let's say there are twelve white crackers on a jury and every one of them thinks black men are stupid and lazy. Now, if I stand up in court and tell them that you're an energetic black man with an IQ that surpasses Albert Einstein, do you think they'll believe me? Hell no, they won't. Even if I bring in witness after witness and each one claims you're brilliant. They'll assume I'm lying because everyone assumes defense lawyers will say anything to get their clients off, and they'll assume the witnesses are getting paid or are all your friends. But if a prosecutor stands up and says you're stupid and lazy, then those white crackers are going to believe it. Why? Because that's how they perceive the truth. That's what they already believe. It's 'their' truth. You getting this?"

"I think so," said Amil.

"Good, now what we have to do is find a way to persuade

twelve jurors that 'their' truth and 'our' truth are the same," said Hicks.

Amil still seemed confused but Hicks didn't seem to care.

"Our biggest problem is going to be coming up with a reasonable explanation for how your semen got on that little girl's pj's," Hicks said. "Okay, let's try this. Now this is just off the top of my head, but it may give us something to work with. Cassie Arnold was eleven years old. Many young girls that age are beginning to menstruate, they're becoming curious about their bodies and sex. You and the victim slept under the same roof. You were friends. She developed a crush on you. No, it was more than that. She became infatuated. On the night of the murder, she comes to see you. The two of you began joking around. Maybe you even have a pillow fight in your bedroom. Innocent horseplay. You start tickling each other and all of a sudden, things turn sexual."

Delaney couldn't believe what she was hearing.

"One thing led to another," Hicks continued, "and suddenly Cassie Arnold was touching your private parts. You know she's young but it feels good so you don't stop her and she ends up masturbating you. It's embarrassing, especially now that she's dead, but it's what happened and you're just being honest about it. There was nothing sinister—just two young people fooling around. That's how your semen got splashed all over her pajamas and why there were no signs of any vaginal penetration. It was her masturbating you. She was fine when she left your room. Someone else must have kidnapped her later that night."

Hicks was clearly pleased with himself. "Think about what I just said," he told Amil. "I think that is an explanation that we could sell to a jury."

"You can't do this!" Delaney protested. "You're creating an alibi for him!"

"No, Ms. Delaney," Hicks said. "I'm simply doing what skilled and experienced defense attorneys do. As officers of the court, you and I are bound by ethical guidelines. If our client tells us what happened on the night of the murder, then we would be obligated to stick to *his* version of the facts. However, if we study the evidence and use our experience to determine on our own what happened, then we have not violated any ethical guidelines. Do you understand what I am saying? We can deliver a very plausible explanation to the jury with a completely clear conscience."

"This is how you practice law?" she said. "You tell your clients what *you think* happened so they can regurgitate it back to you?"

Hicks was getting angry. He didn't like her attitude. "I'm sure Mr. Amil can tell us how his semen got splattered all over that dead girl," he said. "But I hope he's smart enough to say, 'Mr. Hicks, you're a genius. You figured it out! Cassie gave me a hand job that night.' Because that is an explanation that a jury could believe."

"Maybe he should just try telling us the truth," Delaney replied.

"Goddamn it," Hicks said. "Haven't you been listening to me? I don't have time for your naivete. If you want the truth, join a local Baptist church. But if you want to help get our client the best deal possible, you need to get real! This man's future is at stake and he needs to understand that there is no second-place trophy in a courtroom. You either win or you go to prison forever."

Hicks stared at Amil. "It's obvious Ms. Delaney is on a different page than I am when it comes to defending you," he said. "You're the client so you need to make the decision here: Who goes, who stays? The state prefers that you have two attorneys in murder cases, but you can get by with one—especially if they disagree about how you should be defended."

Amil exchanged glances with Delaney and then with Hicks. "I want to talk to each of you alone," he said. "First her, then you."

Hicks started to leave but paused when he reached the door. "Just remember, Ms. Delaney, that anything he says to you is protected by lawyer-client privilege—even after he fires you."

As soon as they were alone, Amil asked Delaney: "Do you think I'm guilty?"

"Mr. Amil," she replied, "my opinion doesn't matter. It's my job to defend you regardless of—."

"Bullshit!" he shouted, slapping the table with his open palms. "I need to know: if I say I'm innocent, will you believe me?"

"What I was trying to explain is that my opinion doesn't count," she said, struggling to keep her voice calm. "We are trained in law school to . . ."

He slapped the table once again. "Damn it! You walked in here this morning and said to me: 'Trust me. Do what I tell you.' You expected me to automatically trust you and you got angry when I asked who was paying you. Why? Because you consider yourself to be an honest person. The fact that I was suspicious was offensive. But you will not extend that same courtesy to me."

"I'm afraid you still don't understand how our legal system works," she replied. "I don't have to believe you are innocent in order to represent you. My job is to pick apart the Commonwealth's case. I'm the devil's advocate. I'm here to make certain the state has done its job. If it can't prove beyond a reasonable doubt that you are guilty, then we win."

"No, Ms. Delaney, I'm afraid you're the one who doesn't understand," Amil replied. "What you're telling me is law school bullshit that you hide behind so you can sleep at night. It makes it possible for you to avoid taking personal responsibility. It makes it possible for you to represent the most reprehensible people on the face of this planet, and if you get a rapist off, then you can soothe your soul by saying it was the prosecution's fault, not yours. They didn't have enough evidence. But the truth is that it was your fault. You got him off. It's called rationalization."

She was about to argue but he stopped her by holding up his hand. "Please let me finish," he said. "I know what you thought when you first saw me. You thought: 'This nigger raped that little white girl. The DNA proves it.'"

"Wait a minute," she said. "I'm not a racist. The fact that you're black doesn't have anything to do with this."

"The hell it doesn't," he shot back. "Race has everything to do with everything a black man does, and if you ain't hip to that, then you really are naive."

"But I'm not a racist just because I'm white," she stammered.

"Oh yes you are! All whites are. Only people in control can be racists and you whites have been in control for hundreds of years in this country. But that's not my point. My point is that you automatically assumed I was guilty. Don't be ashamed of it. Hell, Mr. Hicks is a brother and he thinks I'm guilty too. That's why he's cooking up this bullshit hand-job theory of his. He assumes he can concoct a better alibi than I can. That's why I want you to answer my question: if I tell you I'm innocent, will you believe me—because if my two attorneys, one white and one black, who are supposed to be on my side—if they automatically assume I'm guilty, then what chance do I got with a jury?"

Delaney wasn't certain how to respond. "Regardless of what I or Mr. Hicks might think," she said carefully, "you still need an attorney. I believe both of us are professional enough to keep our own personal feelings out of this case."

Amil let out a loud sigh and folded his arms across his chest. "Ms. Delaney, I don't want an attorney who is going to keep his personal feelings out of this case. I want an attorney who believes I'm innocent. No, let me rephrase that. I want someone who *knows* I'm innocent. A jury is going to do exactly what you did this morning. Jurors are going to walk into that courtroom, see my black face, hear about the DNA, and sentence me to life in prison. I don't have any credibility. The cops say I did it and everyone is going to believe them. I know it sounds cliché but it's also true. That's why I need someone who is like the jurors—is one of them—to stand next to me. I need someone who can point a finger directly at my face and say, 'This man is not guilty! The cops got the wrong guy! I know he was framed!'"

"Why are you asking me to do that rather than Mr. Hicks?"

"A jury is going to see him for what he is: A black public defender who represents all the poor black mutherfuckers who no one gives a shit about. But jurors will look at you and think, 'Damn, this woman lives in Charlottesville. She's white. She's someone's daughter, just like Cassie was. Maybe she's got a little girl of her own.' Then they will say to themselves: 'She believes this man is innocent. She's putting her ass on the line.' That's my edge, my only hope. You've got to believe in me if you want to defend me!"

He paused to gather his thoughts. "Ms. Delaney, I'm why you became a defense lawyer. I'm an innocent man. I did not kill Cassie Arnold." He stuck out his right hand and said: "I'm going to ask you one last time: Do you believe I'm innocent?" It was Delaney's turn to answer. She looked at his eyes and then at the slender fingers of his black hand. She reached over and shook it.

"I will trust you, Lester, until you give me reason not to," she said.

"And I will do the same with you," he replied. "Now, let's fire Mr. Hicks and I will tell you what I know about Cassie's murder."

7

CASSIE ARNOLD'S BODY WAS FOUND ON A MONDAY. LESTER Amil was arrested later that day. His evidentiary hearing before Judge Gatlin was held on Friday that same week. Commonwealth attorney Jacob Wheeler presented his case against Amil to a grand jury on the next Monday, exactly one week after the murder. Miss Alice telephoned Patti Delaney that afternoon and announced that Judge Spencer had scheduled a hearing for Tuesday morning to review the grand jury's indictment and to select a trial date.

Lester Amil was clearly on a judicial fast track.

Evan Spencer peeked through a crack in a side doorway of the Albemarle County Courthouse as the crowd jammed into his courtroom for Tuesday morning's hearing. The first person he spotted was Walter Corn, a pudgy reporter for the *Charlottesville Courant,* sitting in the front row. Spencer had overheard Corn asking Miss Alice about seating assignments the day before.

"I'm holding a lottery," she'd explained. "Except for the victim's family, everyone else will be given a number. I'll pick numbers from a hat until all of the seats are filled."

"But you can't do that!" Corn had protested. "I'm the local reporter. Our community is counting on me to be their eyes and ears!"

"Mr. Corn," Miss Alice had replied, clearly enjoying her authority. "I know how important you are. Why just the other day, some of us were talking at the Albemarle County Historical Society about how wonderful it would be if you began covering our meetings so you could write stories about our club's activities."

Corn caught on quickly.

"I can assure you," he'd replied, "I'll be at your next meeting."

With his promise secured, Miss Alice had slipped Corn into the courtroom before the lottery.

Spencer didn't like Corn. He was a tired-looking man with a perpetually nervous stomach. He always seemed to be chewing antacid tablets and usually had a toothpick sticking from his mouth. Young, ambitious reporters eager to move to a big city newspaper might be guilty of exaggeration and hyperbole in the hope that their sensationalism might get them noticed. But a middle-aged reporter such as Corn understood that his glory days had passed him by, and if he sensationalized a story, it was not because he was seeking a career boost—it was because he had an ax to grind. In Spencer's eyes, Corn was much more dangerous than the bevy of national reporters who'd been lucky enough to win seats.

The rectangular Albemarle circuit courtroom was divided in half by a waist-high railing. On one side were wooden pews for spectators. There were thirteen benches divided by a center aisle. Much like a wedding, where the relatives of the groom sat on one side of the church, and the bride's sat on the other, it was usual for a defendant's supporters to congregate to the left of the courtroom while the prosecutor's chose the right.

On the opposite side of the railing is where Judge Spencer, Miss Alice, the court reporter, the jurors, the attorneys, and the defendant sat. Spencer noticed that Delaney was dressed in a tight black skirt and a bright blue, short sleeve blouse with a fluffy white collar made of what looked like bird feathers. It wasn't professional garb, but no one in the courtroom seemed to be paying much attention to her eccentric wardrobe. All eyes were on Frank and Maxine Arnold, who had been escorted inside by deputies just a few moments before the hearing was scheduled to begin. They sat on the prosecution's side. Frank Arnold was staring straight ahead, focusing on nothing in particular. He was wearing a gray Italian silk suit, crisp white shirt, silver tie. Maxine was seated on his right in a simple black dress. She had twisted her long blond hair tightly in a bun. Her eyes were puffy and red.

Taylor Cauldwell had not yet arrived, but Jacob Wheeler was nervously rocking in his swivel chair at the prosecution's table. He was sitting directly in front of the Arnolds. Fifteen empty juror chairs, enough for twelve jurors and three alternates, lined the wall to Wheeler's right. The witness box was also on the right side of the courtroom next to the judge's bench so the jurors could see it clearly. There was a wooden podium located between the defense and prosecutor's tables. It's where the attorneys were supposed to stand when they questioned a witness or spoke to the judge and jurors.

Wheeler kept glancing back over his shoulder at the courtroom entrance. He was wearing a bright gold tie that had what looked like a gravy stain on it. A few moments before the hearing was about to start, Taylor Cauldwell made his grand entrance. He hustled up the room's center aisle and slipped into the chair next to Wheeler.

Delaney was puzzled. *Why was Virginia's Attorney General sitting at the prosecution's table?*

With the stage now set, Miss Alice entered and proudly declared that the Albemarle Circuit Court in the sixteenth Judicial Circuit of Virginia was in session with the Honorable Judge Evan LeRue Spencer presiding. Everyone rose as Spencer entered. Miss Alice took care of several procedural matters and then two deputies led Lester Amil inside. He was dressed in an orange jumpsuit with the words "AC JAIL" stenciled in black on the back. It was shorthand for Albemarle County Jail. Spencer was struck by how different Amil looked from when he had sung his defiant hip-hop song at the Arnolds' outdoor party. Back then, he had been the poster child for what many in white America feared: a self-proclaimed "nigger with attitude." Now, he simply looked young and scared. His hands were restrained with handcuffs and his legs with a chain. As soon as Amil spotted Frank and Maxine Arnold, he mouthed the words: "I didn't do it!" But Maxine immediately turned away while Arnold simply glared at him.

Spencer asked if both attorneys were ready and Delaney rose from her seat and stepped to the podium. "Your Honor, I'd like to request that from now on when my client is brought into the courtroom that he not be restrained, and I'd also like to ask that he be provided with a suit to wear so a jury will not be prejudiced by his appearance here."

"The Commonwealth has no objection to the defendant being given a decent set of clothing," Taylor Cauldwell announced as he too stepped to one side of the podium. "In fact, we appreciate Ms. Delaney's continued interest in making certain that all of her clients are well dressed."

There were a few snickers among spectators who understood Cauldwell's reference to Delaney's former burglary client and the stolen clothes that he had worn into court. "But," Cauldwell continued, "we oppose the removal of the defendant's restraints because we feel they are necessary to protect the public."

"Excuse me!" Delaney said, "But I'm not certain why the attorney general is even here this morning. This is a circuit court murder case. It has nothing to do with him!"

The moment that Cauldwell had masterminded had arrived. He announced, in a voice loud enough for every reporter in the courtroom to hear, that he was intervening in the Amil case under the authority of Virginia statute 2.2–511.

"I don't believe that statute gives you the authority to prosecute a circuit court murder case," Delaney replied.

Cauldwell reached over to the prosecution's table and picked up a black volume of the Virginia Code, which he dramatically flipped open. "I'd like to cite exception six of statute two-two-five-eleven," Cauldwell said. "It authorizes the attorney general to prosecute, and I quote: 'criminal laws involving child pornography and sexually explicit visual material involving children.'" He slapped shut the book. "In addition to felony kidnapping and sexual assault charges," he explained, "the Commonwealth is now charging this defendant in an indictment issued by the grand jury with violations of Virginia's child pornography laws. This new charge is being filed because of graphic and obscene materials found by detectives on the defendant's personal computer. The requirements of exception six are clearly met by the filing of this new charge."

Delaney was caught completely off-guard. "Your Honor," she stammered, not certain what to say next, "I deeply resent the fact that no one from either Mr. Wheeler's office or the attorney general's office gave my client any warning about this new charge."

"Excuse me," Cauldwell interrupted, "but the Commonwealth doesn't usually tell criminals in advance that they are about to be arrested and charged."

Several members of the audience snickered.

"Ms. Delaney," Spencer said. "I've read the statute and I believe the attorney general is fully within his rights to intervene in this matter. Because of that, I'm ruling that he can continue as the lead attorney in this case."

"Thank you, Your Honor," Cauldwell said, before Delaney could protest. "Now there is another matter I'd like to raise. The Commonwealth of Virginia—in today's indictment—also will be modifying the murder charge. Because of the vicious nature of this crime, the indictment will charge Lester Amil with capital murder. And I will be seeking the death penalty."

"What?" Delaney asked, clearly stunned.

Her question was drowned out by several spectators who had started to applaud. Spencer smacked down his gavel. "I'm not going to tolerate any outbursts," he warned. "This is going to be an emotional trial. I will clear the courtroom if there are any more disruptions."

"This is unbelievable!" Delaney muttered.

"I'd also like to state for the record," Cauldwell continued, "that I'm here at the invitation of commonwealth attorney Jacob Wheeler. He has specifically asked for my help in prosecuting this case because it involves the death penalty."

"That's right," Wheeler volunteered, springing from his chair.

Amil reached over and touched Delaney's arm. She bent down to listen to him. "They're seeking the death penalty? Is that what he just said?"

"Yes," she whispered. Turning back to Spencer, she said: "Your Honor, I do not believe that this case meets the statutory requirements to be a capital murder case."

Cauldwell interrupted her. "First of all, it's up to the Commonwealth to decide if it wants to seek the death penalty, not a defendant," he declared. "Second, the law says the death penalty is appropriate if the crime was 'outrageously or wantonly vile, horrible, or inhuman in that it involves torture, depravity of mind, or an aggravated battery to the victim.' I'd say that kidnapping an eleven-year-old girl, sexually torturing her, and then strangling her meets those criteria."

Maxine Arnold began to cry.

"Ms. Delaney," Spencer said, "you can file a motion challenging the Commonwealth's actions if you wish, but I can tell you right now that I will rule in favor of the attorney general." Looking down at the calendar in front of him, he said: "I'd like to begin this trial in nine weeks. Because this is now a capital case, the defendant must have two attorneys representing him. I thought Judge Gatlin had already assigned someone from the Public Defenders Office to help you, Ms. Delaney."

"We had a difference of opinion," she replied.

"That being the situation, I will review the list of local attorneys who are prequalified to represent defendants in capital murder cases and appoint one by five o'clock this afternoon to assist you."

Delaney was boiling but tried to keep her tongue in check. "Your Honor, nine weeks is not sufficient time for me to prepare an adequate defense."

"It will have to be," Spencer replied. "I'd suggest that you contact several Virginia law schools and ask for their help. I understand, in some cases, entire classes of promising young law students can be put at a defense attorney's disposal in capital murder cases."

"What about discovery?" she asked. "Mr. Wheeler promised in general court that he would open his files to me."

"Your Honor," Cauldwell said. "The defense will get exactly

what they are entitled to under the law: their client's statements
to the police and any exculpatory evidence that we find. But
I'm not going to let Ms. Delaney rummage through our files.
This is now my case and our files will be closed to her."

"What about Mister Wheeler's earlier promise?" she demanded.

"I'm in charge now," Cauldwell repeated.

Delaney looked at Spencer, expecting help. But he didn't
say a word.

He had to have known about these last-minute changes, she
decided. *Cauldwell wouldn't have risked the public humilia-
tion of being tossed out of court if Spencer hadn't supported
him in advance. Her client was being railroaded.*

"If there is nothing further," Spencer said, "we'll adjourn."

"Your Honor," Delaney said. "You've not given me an answer. I asked that my client not be brought into court in
shackles."

Spencer glanced over at Cauldwell. "And what's your view
on this, Mr. Attorney General?"

"I've already said that the defendant is dangerous and could
pose a threat to people in this room," he replied. "He'll also be
an escape risk. The shackles should remain on."

"We have deputies here to protect Mr. Cauldwell if he is
frightened," Delaney countered.

Spencer said: "Let's not get cute, Counselor." Addressing
the deputies, he said: "From now on, I want the restraints removed from the defendant after he is seated at the defense
table, but I also want extra deputies posted in the courtroom."

A crumb, she thought.

"Your Honor, there's one more thing," Delaney said. "You
have referred to Mr. Cauldwell as the attorney general several
times. Mentioning his title during a trial will prejudice our
client's chance to an impartial trial."

"What would you prefer that I call him?"

"Oh, I can think of a number of fitting names," Delaney
quickly replied, "but most are not appropriate to be uttered in
a courtroom."

Several onlookers laughed.

"Ms. Delaney, this not a comedy club or a costume ball,"

Spencer said. "Please conduct yourself accordingly." He noticed her cheeks turning flush with anger. "However," he continued, "your point is well taken. I will refer to the attorney general by his name or as counselor from now on."

Asshole! she thought.

Spencer spent the next several minutes handling paperwork procedures. Then he had Amil taken out through a side door. As soon as Spencer left the courtroom, reporters engulfed Cauldwell and the Arnolds. Delaney, meanwhile, closed her briefcase and tried to weave her way through the mob. But the crowd wouldn't let her pass and she soon found herself being gently pushed toward Frank and Maxine Arnold. When she was about two feet from them, the room became eerily quiet.

"How can you defend that monster?" Maxine Arnold shrieked.

Delaney elbowed the reporters blocking her exit and pushed through them. Walter Corn caught up with her outside the building as she was walking briskly across the courthouse lawn.

"Pretty brutal, huh?" he asked. She ignored him. "Any comment?" he persisted. "Any comment at all? How do you feel about Cauldwell intervening—making this a capital case? How about the judge only giving you nine weeks?"

Delaney froze. "You want a quote?" She could feel her Irish temper flaring. "Here's one! I'm wondering if the trial date in this case was set early because the judge is interested in swift justice or if he simply wants this trial to be held at the same time his buddy, Taylor Cauldwell, is running for the governor's office!"

As she stomped away, she thought: *Oh shit! What have I done? I shouldn't have attacked the judge!*

Back in his chambers, Spencer suddenly thought about the stone that Patrick McPherson had mailed to him. The last time that he had seen it was when it had shocked him. He'd been discharged from the hospital during the weekend and had searched for the stone as soon as he had returned to his office on Monday morning. But the rock was nowhere to be found. He'd even gotten down on his knees and peered under the couch and chairs, thinking that it might have rolled under them after he had collapsed, but it wasn't there. He'd finally decided that one of the paramedics had picked it up and taken it.

Miss Alice rapped on the door to his chambers.

"There's an attorney out here named Charles MacDonald who'd like to see you," she announced. "Says he wants to volunteer to help defend Lester Amil."

Moments later, a white-haired man in his late sixties walked into Spencer's chambers and extended his hand. Spencer noticed that MacDonald was wearing a wristwatch on his right, rather than his left, hand. The watch was a white gold Rolex, Oyster model. Expensive.

"Thanks for seeing me," MacDonald began. "I settled in Charlottesville four years ago, came down from Fairfax County, just outside Washington, D.C., where I'd had my own legal practice. My wife and I met at the University in 1950 and we'd always wanted to retire here. But she died on me a year ago, and quite frankly, I've been lost and stir crazy ever since. I'd like to volunteer to be a cocounsel in the Amil capital murder case."

"What sort of experience do you have?" Spencer asked.

"Judge," MacDonald said. "I'm not a nut seeking publicity." He withdrew a folded typewritten sheet from the inside pocket of his sports jacket. "Here's my resume and a list of references, but let me give you the short version. I joined the District of Columbia Police Department fresh out of college. That was back in the days when few cops had college degrees. Most schools didn't even offer criminal justice courses. I worked up the ranks and eventually became a homicide detective. I spent ten years investigating homicides, in all, several hundred murders. At age fifty-five, I faced mandatory retirement because of the danger of the job. So I entered law school at Georgetown and because of my former occupation I chose to specialize in capital cases. It was 1982 and Virginia had just reinstituted the death penalty so I had plenty to choose from. What made my practice unique was that I only accepted cases where I personally believed the accused was innocent. I had a decent pension and my wife and I could afford to live without me working."

"Exactly how many capital cases have you been involved in?"

"Fifteen," MacDonald replied. "Five acquittals, reduced sentences in six more."

"The other four?"

"Two are still sitting on 'the row,' as it's called. Two others were executed. And, yes, before you ask, I was there when both of their sentences were carried out. They each chose lethal injection and, yes, again, I still am convinced that both were innocent. You'd think that before the Commonwealth carried out the ultimate sanction it would make damn sure the condemned was the right man, but there's a greater chance of an innocent man being found guilty in a capital case than in a simple robbery. Never made much sense to me but that's how it is."

"Why does the Amil case interest you? Think he's innocent?"

"Like everyone else, the JonBenet Ramsey angle caught my eye at first," MacDonald replied. "But as odd as this might sound, it was a photograph of that kid that really made me show up today for his hearing. Do you believe in the occult, sixth sense, premonitions, that sort of mumbo jumbo?"

"No," Spencer said firmly. "I don't believe in the supernatural."

"As a detective," MacDonald continued, "you learn to read people by watching them, by looking at how they move, how they carry themselves, by looking into their hearts through their eyes, as the poets say. Sometimes you risk believing in things you can't explain."

"And you looked into Lester Amil's eyes and saw an innocent man?"

"I don't think he's a killer, especially one who kidnaps, sexually assaults, and then murders an eleven-year-old child. I don't see it in his face. It takes a lot of anger to kill a child."

They chatted for another twenty minutes and Spencer found himself becoming fond of MacDonald. He was articulate, clever, and easygoing. "I'll need to review your credentials," Spencer said, "but based on your experience, you might just be the most qualified person in all of Albemarle County at this moment to defend a capital case. I'll let you know my decision later today."

* * *

From the courthouse, Charles MacDonald drove directly to Patti Delaney's office, which he found tucked into a tiny strip mall that contained a dry cleaners, Chinese carry-out restaurant, vitamin store, and bagel shop. He introduced himself and told Delaney that he had just volunteered to become her cocounsel.

"I want to help," he said, "so even if Judge Spencer doesn't appoint me, I'll lend you a hand as a criminal investigator. Like I told the judge, I have a hunch this kid is innocent."

MacDonald charmed Delaney, just as he had won over Spencer. She liked his soft-spoken, folksy style. He was confident. At one point, he asked: "You Irish?"

"The red hair gives it away, huh?" she replied. "How about you?"

"Everyone assumes I am because of the name, but my ancestors came from Scotland. Now my wife, she was a green-eyed beauty from the Emerald Isle. Had red hair too, just like yours. I asked her to marry me on our first date but she was playing hard to get and didn't say yes—until the second one!"

Delaney laughed.

"We had forty-four years together before she passed on and I couldn't have asked for a better partner, lover, and friend. There isn't a day that goes by that I don't think of her at least a thousand times."

"Any children?"

"One but she's gone now too. It happened years ago. An accident. Now it's just me sitting in a big empty house with a stray cat named Romeo that just showed up one day, and I never really have liked cats much. Good reason to get out more."

As they were talking, Miss Alice telephoned Delaney and announced that Judge Spencer had appointed MacDonald as her new cocounsel.

"We're now officially a team!" Delaney said as she put down the phone. She stuck out her hand and he shook it.

"Then let's get started," he said. "What do we know about the Commonwealth's case?"

"Not nearly enough. Our client gave the county sheriff's

department two statements, and in both he denied taking any part in the murder."

"That's good," said MacDonald. "How about this child pornography charge they sprang today: totally unexpected?"

"Totally, in fact, I'm wondering if it's a scam that Taylor Cauldwell conjured up so he could intervene. That's one of the things we need to ask our client."

They rode to the county jail in MacDonald's Acura SUV rather than her ancient Saab. En route, they discussed defense strategy.

"Based on my experience, there are actually only five possible defenses in a murder case," MacDonald said. "The first is to deny that a murder happened. You can claim the person killed himself. Obviously, that won't work here. Then there's the ever-popular self-defense alibi where you admit killing a person but insist that he made you do it. Again, that's not going to do us any good. The third defense has become more popular in recent days. I call it—'the victim needed killing and I was just the one to do it'—tactic. But that only works if your client has been a battered spouse or abused child. The fourth is the stall defense where you file so many motions and get so many continuances that the prosecution finally throws in the towel and negotiates a plea bargain. And then there is the fifth defense and the most widely used, which is: 'Hey, the police got the wrong guy.' I'm guessing our man is claiming the cops got the wrong guy—even though his semen was found on the dead girl's clothing. Now that's going to be tough to explain!"

When they reached the jail, Delaney said: "I'm really happy we're going to be working on this together, especially since you're a former homicide detective. I don't want to screw up and I was beginning to feel that I was in way over my head during that hearing."

He reached over and patted her hand. "You were bushwhacked, sweetie. The judge, Cauldwell, Wheeler, they set you up. Listen, all you need to remember is to follow your instincts. I'm a big believer in gut feelings."

Amil was skeptical of MacDonald.

"I'd rather have a black attorney," he said. "No offense, but that would give me one white, one black. If I'm getting two, I might as well cover all of my bases."

"That's understandable," MacDonald replied, "but there are a few reasons why you're better off having me. If a jury ends up convicting you, then the appeals process will kick in. It's going to be important for us to look for ways now to lay the groundwork for a successful appeal. That means we've got to cram as many motions and objections as we can into this case so a good appellate attorney will have lots of angles to work with. Not having a black attorney could be something you can raise later on. I'd keep the race card in your back pocket right now."

While Amil was mulling this over, MacDonald offered another nugget. "I've handled a slew of death penalty cases, but Ms. Delaney tells me that she's never been involved in a capital murder case in Virginia. I'd like to propose that she does all of the talking in court. I'll keep in the shadows. Again, if we lose this case, then you can claim Ms. Delaney was inexperienced and I was a retired old fart who didn't do anything." MacDonald glanced at Delaney. "Sorry," he said, "but in death penalty cases when a man's life is at stake, every appellate attorney claims the accused wasn't well represented anyway. It comes with the job."

"I understand," she said.

Amil began warming up to MacDonald.

"Tell me about what happened Sunday," MacDonald said.

"Mr. Arnold decided that morning that we'd all go on a hot air balloon ride. It took most of the day. After we got home, we ate pizza. I left around nine o'clock that night and drove to a party at a friend's house. There were maybe sixty of us there, just chilling, drinking beer, smoking some weed. This girl introduced me to this guy, everyone called him GAT, I didn't know his real name. He listened to some of my beats and rhymes and said he was interested in helping me cut a record. About two A.M., he left and I ain't gonna lie to you, I got wasted."

"How?"

"Beer, weed. I was feeling pumped about meeting him and I'd been stressing because of all this shit, ur, excuse me, stuff happening at the Arnold house. I got so drunk I ended up passing out and I never made it back to the Arnolds' house that night. The next day around noon, GAT calls this girl where the party was held at. He says he left his backpack there and he asks me to bring it and come up to D.C. that Monday night because he'd already arranged for us to get some time at his buddy's recording studio. He tells me I need to get my butt over to the bus station. The next thing I know, the cops snatched me up. Hell, I didn't even know Cassie had been murdered until they told me."

"Anyone see you at this party?" MacDonald asked.

"Yep and nope. Plenty of folks saw me get drunk and pass out, but I got up around three A.M. because this guy next to me threw up and the room stunk. I went out on this back porch on the house and curled up on a sofa there until about noon when the girl who gave the party came out and told me GAT was on the phone and he wanted me to come up to D.C."

"So no one can swear that you didn't leave that house during the night?"

"That's right. Besides, I don't know how many folks at this party are going to want to testify. There were a lot of drugs being passed around."

"One of the first things we need to do is find GAT," MacDonald said. "I can make some calls in D.C. Now, did you telephone the Arnolds on Monday to tell them you were riding the bus to D.C.?"

"No," Amil said, glancing nervously at Delaney.

"Go ahead," she urged him, "tell him why you were reluctant to return to their house that Monday."

"Maxie, I mean, Mrs. Arnold, we were, ur, ah, well, we sorta had a thing going on, if you know what I mean."

"You've got to be more specific," Delaney said. "Tell him everything. Start at the beginning. It's easier."

"Okay, one day I was just chilling at their swimming pool in California and she asked me to rub some lotion on her back, and then she undid her top and one thing led to another. It was stupid but that didn't stop me."

"You had sex?"

"Yes."

"Was this a one-time incident or more?"

"More. We was real discreet at first. She'd wait until Mr. Arnold was traveling and then come to my room late at night after Cassie was asleep. The truth is I fell in love with her and she said she loved me too. We even talked about her divorcing him. I said, 'Girl you're crazy because I don't have no money,' and she said in California, she'd get half his cash if they split up. She's a lot younger than him and she used to tell me that he couldn't, you know, keep her happy in the bedroom. She has a real strong sex drive, real strong. And he was lousy in bed and kinky too."

"What do you mean?" MacDonald asked.

Amil again looked at Delaney who nodded for him to continue. "She'd want it maybe four times a day. I've never known a woman who wanted that much sex."

"What about him being kinky?"

"She told me he liked to be spanked. I thought that was funny."

"Did she say anything that might make you think he was molesting his own daughter?"

"Hell no!"

Delaney interrupted: "Tell him why you didn't go back home on Monday, the day that Cassie's body was found."

"I was scared," Amil said. "Things had gotten freaky. I mean, Maxie and I had been having sex for a couple months but we'd all sit down at dinner like we was one big happy family, and here I'd been looking at her, knowing we'd had intimate relations a few hours earlier and him just sitting there, clueless, or at least I thought he was."

Amil was beginning to sweat. "Sorry, talking about this stuff makes me real nervous. I mean, she's white and married. I'm black and we're in Virginia. This ain't good."

"No, it isn't," said MacDonald.

"A couple weeks ago, I'd had enough. I told her to make her choice: either him or me. She and I got into a nasty, nasty argument. We didn't talk for a few days and Mr. Arnold knew something was up. Then it was time for the Arnolds' big house party. Maxie and me acted cool at that party, but I knew Frank was suspicious of us. I'd heard him and Maxie fighting earlier that day but I didn't know why, only that she was screaming at him and he was yelling at her. They held it together during the party, but then it got really weird."

"How so?" MacDonald asked.

"Cassie went to bed and the rest of us—me, Maxie, and Frank—were sitting in the living room. It was maybe four A.M. and all of us were shit-faced drunk. Maxie pulls out a joint and fires it up. I already knew she smoked weed but Mr. Arnold starts ragging on her about smoking dope in front of me, you know, how it's a bad influence and such. She gets really pissed and suddenly she hands me the joint. I looked at him and I could tell he was really, really angry, so I said 'No thanks, Maxie' and handed it back to her without taking a hit and then, suddenly, she's really pissed off at me. She starts calling me names and then calls him names."

"What sort of names?"

"She says we're both frauds. Liars. Both pretending to be something we aren't. Frank gets so angry he storms out of the room. I figured he was going up to bed."

"He left you two in the living room alone?" MacDonald asked.

"Yeah, so I decided I should go to bed too. But when I stand up, Maxie says to me: 'Forty-four,' which is my street nickname, 'Let's fuck. I'm really, really horny!' I said I didn't want to because I knew this was going to end up with me getting into more trouble. But she started getting pushy. It was the dope and booze. She grabbed me and pulled me back down on the sofa and then she stood up in front of me and began taking off her clothes, stripping real seductive right there in the living room. When she was naked, she said: 'C'mon, just this last time. Then it'll be over. Come and get some of mama's white pussy!'"

Amil paused to clear his throat.

"I knew it was really stupid but I began taking off my clothes and she started helping me, and the next thing, we're doing it on the sofa. That's when I looked up and saw Mr. Arnold standing near the doorway watching us. He wasn't saying anything and he wasn't moving toward us, he was just standing there, watching. It really freaked me out! But Maxie has her eyes closed. I didn't know what to do, so I whispered: 'Maxie, Frank's watching us!' But she didn't even open her eyes so I figured she didn't understand. I said. 'Frank's watching us for christsake!' She opens her eyes and turns her head to look, but he's gone. I asked her what we were going to do and she says. 'Nothing.' She tells me to just keep my mouth shut. She'll handle it, she says. The next day, Saturday, I didn't say a word to her and I avoided being anywhere near him because I thought he'd want to kill my ass. Then on Sunday, Maxie told me that we were going on this balloon ride together as a family."

"Wait, Frank Arnold still hadn't said a word to you about what he saw—how you were having sex with his wife?" MacDonald asked.

"That's right, not a word, nothing. So after the balloon ride, I asked Frank if we could talk in private and when we got back to the house, we went into his office and he says, real casual like, 'What's up?' and I said, 'It's about the other night. I think I need to move out of the house.' He says, 'Don't worry, I liked the song you sang at the party'—meaning the rhyme I did for his guests. Now I'm really confused. I'm not sure if he is playing me or if she is playing me or if they are both playing me. Or if I was so drunk I imagined him watching us or what? Then Frank puts his arm on my shoulder and says, 'Everything is cool. There's no bad blood between us, bro. You're still welcome in my crib.' He always tried to talk to me like he was from the street. Not long after that, I left for my Sunday night party."

"He never acknowledged that he'd seen you having sex?"

"No. But it didn't matter. I knew I had to get out of there before something bad happened."

"Can you prove you were having a sexual affair with Maxine Arnold?" MacDonald asked.

"Prove? How could I prove that?"

Abruptly switching subjects, MacDonald asked: "How'd your semen get on Cassie's pajamas?"

Amil didn't reply at first, instead, he stared down at the table. For the first time during their conversation, MacDonald sensed that Amil was embarrassed. Either that, or he was trying to hide something. "I used jackets, you know, condoms when Maxine and I had sex. She told me her husband had had a vasectomy and she wasn't gonna risk getting pregnant. She said she was allergic to latex so she could only use these expensive rubbers made from animal membranes. She always had one. Afterward, she'd wrap them in toilet paper and put them in the trash in her private bathroom when we was done. She didn't trust me to do it because she was afraid I'd just toss one into a trash can and the housekeeper or Mr. Arnold would see it."

"Did you use a condom that night when you had sex on the couch? When Frank Arnold saw you?"

"Yeah, she made me put one on."

"And then she took it with her after you were done?"

"Yeah. She went into the kitchen with it. I left before I saw what she done with it."

"Are you telling me that Maxine Arnold took your semen from a condom after you had sex and later smeared it on her own daughter's pajamas as part of a plan to frame you?"

"Well, someone must've because, as God is my witness, that's the only way my semen could have gotten all over Cassie's pajamas!"

Now it was MacDonald who sat quiet for several moments, thinking. "Getting a jury to believe this is going to be damnnear impossible," he finally said. He changed subjects again. "What's all this about you downloading kiddie porn off the Internet?"

Once again, Amil was sheepish.

"That was a really, really dumb mistake. Everyone my age looks at porn on the Internet and one night when I was surfing, I hit this Web site that had young girls on it. The next thing I knew, it had automatically sent me into another site, someplace in Thailand and it had a bunch of pictures of these young boys and girls tied up and shit like that. I'd never seen anything like that. I was curious. So I downloaded a few of them. I was going to show them to my friends because they were just really sick. But I wasn't into that. I swear!"

"Did you send them to anyone else?"

"I sent a couple to guys I know but just because it was wacko stuff."

During the next two hours, MacDonald continued to grill Amil but he never changed his stories. Nor did MacDonald catch him in any obvious lies. It was late by the time that Mac-Donald and Delaney left. He bought her dinner at the Chinese carry-out next door to her office.

"If we want a jury to believe Amil didn't murder Cassie," MacDonald said, "then we're going to have to provide jurors with a more likely suspect. I hate doing that because it's not up to us to catch the real killer. But the Commonwealth is going to show the jury photographs of Cassie Arnold, and those jurors aren't going to let our guy walk out of that courtroom as a free man unless they're convinced that some-one else is going to be punished for killing her. It's just hu-man nature."

"I think Cassie's mother, Maxine, did it," Delaney said. "She's our best suspect."

"Why?"

"Because I don't trust her. I believe she seduced Amil and I think she killed Cassie. I don't know why but my gut is telling me it's her."

"Then that's where I'll start digging," MacDonald replied. "First thing in the morning."

8

DELANEY HAD NEVER REALIZED HOW QUICKLY NINE WEEKS could slip by. She tried to interview Frank and Maxine Arnold but they refused to meet with her. The Arnolds' neighbors turned her away too. MacDonald stopped at the county sher-iff's office to speak with Detective Dale Stuart and other deputies who had helped investigate the murder, but none of them would cooperate. As promised, Taylor Cauldwell pro-vided Delaney and MacDonald with two statements that Lester Amil had made after he was arrested but neither con-tained any new information. Ironically, their best source for information turned out to be the *Charlottesville Courant*. The local newspaper printed stories by Walter Corn almost daily about the murder and upcoming trial, and every one of them was based on leaks by the prosecution.

By Walter Corn
Charlottesville Courant Staff Writer

The *Charlottesville Courant* has learned that detectives have recovered a key piece of evidence that further ties Lester Tidwell Amil to the brutal murder of Cassie Arnold, the eleven-year-old daughter of computer wunderkind Frank Arnold and his wife Maxine. . . .

According to well-placed sources, members of the Arnold household routinely wore small plastic badges, known as personal identifiers, whenever they were inside the house. These badges contained a chip that fed signals into the house's main computer so it could track the house's occupants at all times. The "personal identifier badge" assigned to Lester Amil was found near Cassie Arnold's body after she was murdered. Detectives believe it was torn from his shirt during a struggle.

Another Corn "exclusive":

By Walter Corn
Charlottesville Courant Staff Writer

Albemarle County sheriff's detectives found more than two hundred newspaper clippings that described the JonBenet Ramsey murder case when they searched the basement bedroom of accused murder suspect Lester Tidwell Amil, according to informed sources.

A highly placed official, who asked that his name not be used in this article, said Amil was "totally captivated" by the still-unsolved JonBenet Ramsey killing, so much so, that he filled twelve different spiral notebooks with poems and hip-hop lyrics about the horrific murder. "This kid probably knows more about the JonBenet murder than the Boulder Police Department, which investigated the case," one detective said.

Cassie Arnold was found strangled in the basement of her home. Detectives believe her murderer was trying to replicate the crime scene in the JonBenet case. "This was a copycat killing," said one source. "It was clearly done by someone who knew every detail of the Ramsey case."

The daily onslaught of newspaper stories caused Delaney to seek a change of venue, but Spencer refused to move the trial outside of Charlottesville. It was the first of seven defense motions that he'd rejected. Finally, on the day before jury selection was scheduled to begin, Delaney and MacDonald got a break. MacDonald learned that Maxine Arnold had a younger sister named Carol Webis and that the two women were estranged. Afraid that Webis would simply hang up if he telephoned her, MacDonald caught a flight to Spokane, Washington, where Webis lived with her husband and their four children. Delaney stayed behind to pick jurors.

Judge Spencer had set aside three days to impanel a jury and Miss Alice had arranged for sixty potential jurors, three times the normal number, to report to the courthouse. By the end of the first day, Delaney had used two of her five strikes. She'd removed a middle-aged homemaker, who was the mother of six girls, and a local businessman, whose brother was a federal prosecutor. Cauldwell had struck a black high school history teacher and a heavily tattooed bartender.

MacDonald telephoned Delaney from a Spokane motel later that night to ask her about her first day of *voir dire*.

"It was rough," she said. "They're going to decide Amil's fate and I'm having trouble finding a sympathetic face. Cauldwell got a fundamentalist preacher on the panel today. I'm planning on using a strike tomorrow to get rid of him." Their strategy was to avoid older jurors, especially parents, and to try to get as many minorities and college age candidates as possible on the jury.

She asked about Webis. MacDonald replied: "I went out there this afternoon but no one was around. I'm getting ready to try again. It's sad. They live in an old trailer home park. You know, rusty cars jacked up in the driveway and mailboxes decorated to look like fish or pigs or cows."

"Hey!" she exclaimed. "I've always wanted one of those tacky pink plastic flamingos. If you see one, get it for me."

He thought she was joking. She wasn't.

It was a thirty-minute drive from his motel to the Red Robin Mobile Park. The Webis's trailer was ancient. Despite the wheels attached to its undercarriage, the trailer was never meant to be moved. There were weeds peeking out from around its base. The trailer itself was a faded two-tone: aqua and white. An El Camino was parked under the metal carport next to it when MacDonald pulled up. Plastic toys were strewn across the patch of worn grass that served as a yard. Hopscotch squares were scribbled in bright yellow chalk on the concrete walkway that led to the front door. He knocked and a tired woman wearing a bandana in her hair slipped open the door and greeted him with a skeptical scowl. MacDonald introduced himself and asked if he could ask her a few questions about her sister.

She looked at him and then glanced out to see what model of car he was driving. It was a rented Lincoln. She asked: "What's in it for me?"

MacDonald tried to sway her on moral grounds. Maybe Webis could tell him something that might help him save an innocent man. She didn't bite. "You think I feel sorry for your client?" she said incredulously. "That son of a bitch was living high on the hog with them. They're treating him better than their own people." Once again, she studied MacDonald, and then said: "Five hundred. If you want to talk to me, that's what it'll cost. You're a lawyer. You can afford it."

MacDonald said no. "It's against the law for me to buy testimony," he added.

"I ain't planning on testifying, Mister," she replied. "I was just going to send you looking in the right places."

He fished a hundred-dollar bill out of his billfold. "One now, another when we're done. That's my final offer."

She spit out an expletive and then snatched the bill. "For a hundred bucks, you ain't getting much." She opened the door for him and he stepped into the trailer. He could hear a television blaring in a back bedroom and children arguing. There were plastic plates with uneaten food resting on the speckled Formica counter that separated the main room from the cramped kitchen and also served as a breakfast bar. One of the thinnest men MacDonald had ever seen was sitting in a wooden rocking chair smoking a cigarette in the main room. "That's my husband, Harold," Webis said. Harold didn't get up, even after MacDonald stepped toward him and shook his hand. MacDonald sat next to Webis on a couch that had small balls of white cat hair permanently ensnared in its checkered brown and yellow fabric.

"Our daddy's name was George Finley," she began. "He was a helicopter mechanic in the military, so we moved a lot. Me and Maxine was both born in Germany, all of us four kids were born overseas. Daddy didn't move back to the U.S. until Maxine was fifteen and I was ten. That's when he got himself stationed at Nellis Air Force Base outside Las Vegas. My daddy was all military. When he got home at night, we'd line up so he could ask us what we'd done that day. Then he and Mama would retreat into the parlor to have a few cocktails. Maxine was left in charge. She had to feed us, get us our baths, put us into bed, and she hated it and she hated us. She always said, 'I'm never going to have any rug rats of my own.'"

Webis plucked a menthol cigarette from a soft pack and lit it, blowing the smoke from her lips as if she had suddenly revisited her past and was now dismissing the memory with a puff.

"I guess she changed her mind because she had Cassie," MacDonald offered.

"You think?" she answered with a smirk. "Okay, Mr. Big Spender, let's get something straight between us. If I tell you something and you subpoena me, I will deny ever meeting you. You understand? My sister is a bitch and she has enough money to ruin anyone she wants by siccing lawyers after them. As long as you understand that me and you never talked, then I'll give you your two hundred worth."

MacDonald said, "Okay."

"Let's play a little word game here. I'm going to give you a clue. You can figure out the rest. Just don't let Maxine trace it back to me. If a teenage girl is miserable at home and can't afford college and can't find a job—or doesn't want to—what's the quickest way out?"

"Run away?"

"Naw," she replied. "Get some local chump to knock you up and marry you. Now for question two: What do you do after you've escaped from your family but you're still stuck, only now you also got yourself a new baby and a deadbeat husband, and you don't really love either of them?"

"What do you do?"

She held out her hand for the other one hundred dollars. He reluctantly handed it to her. She got up and opened the front door for him to leave.

"You'll find the answer in Las Vegas. Look in the public records there. Try death certificates," she said, enjoying herself.

Death certificates! As he stepped toward the door, Mac-Donald tried to think of a way to keep her talking. "Can I ask you just one more question?" he said.

"Sure you can, but I'm not answering unless you got another hundred."

Harold, who hadn't said a word, suddenly laughed.

"Why do you hate your sister?" MacDonald asked.

She glared at him and then said, "I'll tell you that for free. Look around at this dump. My husband's got a bum leg. Car accident. Four months ago, he got laid off. I clean houses with a bunch of Mexicans who can't even speak English. Maxine and Frank are rich. You figure it out."

He stayed put, as if he expected more. She said: "Maxine thinks she's better than us. Hell, you know how she met Frank? She was at that COMDEX convention in Las Vegas. Biggest computer show in the world. They hired her to hand out brochures. Ever been to COMDEX? It's a hell of a sight. Computer nerds with their taped-up eyeglasses and pocket protectors, and showgirls with silicon tits passing out information about computers that not a single one of them girls would even know how to turn on. Geek brains and giant boobs. Except for Maxine, of course. She's flatter than Harold. But she's clever. When she discovered how much Frank was worth, she went after him. She learned more about that invention of his than his own salespeople knew. He noticed her chatting up customers and introduced himself and that's when she reeled him in. Only took her two weeks before she had him walking down the aisle."

"What do your parents think of her?"

"They're dead. Maxine didn't even come to Mama's funeral but when it came time to read the will, this lawyer shows up and says Maxine is going to sue and keep my Mama's will tied up in probate unless we agreed to let her go through everything first and take what she wants. If she wants something or gets herself in a corner, she's capable of doing anything."

"Even murder?"

"You've had your freebie," she grunted. "I got no more to say."

Because of the time difference between Spokane and Charlottesville, it was too late for MacDonald to call Delaney and report. The next morning, he booked a flight to Las Vegas. Before it took off, he left a message on the answering machine in her office. "Know you're in court picking jurors. I'm off to Las Vegas. I'll call you later to explain why. I hate leaving messages on machines. If I'm not back before the trial begins, knock 'em dead with your opening statement. And remember, follow your gut. That's why I'm heading to Vegas."

Follow your gut. It was quickly becoming their motto.

9

SPENCER HAD JUST FINISHED EATING BREAKFAST ON THE VEranda of VanDenvender Hall when Melissa appeared wearing a knit shift designed by Gala Moseevsky, a Russian fashion designer from Moscow. She was one of Melissa's new discoveries. The shift was black around the bodice but faded to heather gray, and then finally a pale sky blue at the hem, which rested just above her knee. She was carrying a sky blue purse and wearing black heels.

"I think I'll stop by your courtroom today," she declared. "Is there some specific time that's best?"

She was completely overdressed for the Albemarle County Courthouse. "The murder trial begins at nine o'clock," he said, opening *The Washington Post*. "But there aren't going to be enough seats for all of the spectators and media, so Miss Alice is holding a lottery."

Melissa had never before shown any interest in his job. She leaned forward and kissed his cheek. "Surely you can reserve a seat for me," she replied. "I mean, you are the judge. Now, I'll probably be a bit late. I'm getting my nails done at nine. Close to the front would be nice." It was as if she were ordering tickets to a Broadway play.

She sat down in the white wicker chair next to his and noted that a light morning fog was lifting from the still damp meadow. He noted that she was not wearing a bra but kept that to himself.

Spencer had realized early in their marriage that Melissa was self-absorbed and intellectually lazy. What had surprised him was that he and everyone else let her get away with it. Her narcissism seemed perfectly normal because she was both rich and stunning. If Melissa broke a fingernail—an irritating but mundane event in most women's lives—she would react as if it were a major calamity. Incredibly, so would everyone else around her. It was as if the everyday events in a rich person's life were somehow more momentous simply because of their wealth.

What surprised Spencer was that Melissa remained generally unenthusiastic about her life despite the special treatment that she received. She automatically disliked nearly everyone whom she knew or met, and there wasn't much that seemed to genuinely excite her. She had no goals, no ambitions, no life plan, and few interests. She did love her horses and she worshiped her father, but she really didn't seem to care about anything or anyone else. And that included Spencer.

Her flaws hadn't mattered to him when they were first married. Women such as Melissa, Spencer had decided, served only one real purpose: to be envied. He had a wife whom other men lusted after and other women wished they could be. From the start, he had chosen to be blind to her faults, not out of love but because being married to her had made him feel superior. Melissa gave him an edge over other men. He had won her. That was his payoff. Why she had agreed to marry him had never been quite as clear.

"I was out riding Little Thunder yesterday," she said, interrupting his thoughts. "I was with DeDe Gilmore and she told me about this brash woman who has been appointed to defend that black murderer."

"Lester Amil hasn't been tried or convicted yet," Spencer replied, "and I'd hardly call his defense attorney brash." He pretended to be engrossed in a news story but was really eager to hear more of what their gossipy neighbor had said.

"DeDe told me that this woman," Melissa continued, "oh, what's her name?"

"Delaney, Patti Delaney."

"Yes, that this Patti Delaney woman had just horrid taste in clothes and that she had moved here after she caught her husband under the sheets with another man. She must be a lousy fuck."

Spencer folded his newspaper and looked at his wife. Although she rarely used profanity, she occasionally enjoyed its shock value. "What?" he asked.

"Oh Spencer, don't go prude on me," she replied. "What's the first thing every man thinks when he meets a lesbian? He says to himself, 'I could make her forget all about the joys of eating pussy if I got her between my sheets just for one night.' So why are you acting offended now when I suggest this woman must be lousy in bed if her husband was forced to get his sexual needs met by another man?"

"Melissa," Spencer said, "this is perhaps the most nonsensical breakfast conversation we've ever had. Do you really think Patti Delaney drove her husband into a homosexual frenzy because she sucked in bed?"

He cringed at his poor choice of words but she gratefully let it pass. "You're right," she said, "I mean, if every man around here whose wife was a lousy lay decided to become gay, then we'd suddenly be overridden with fags!" She laughed at her own joke. "Of course, that wouldn't be a problem in your case," she added, "now would it?"

He intentionally changed subjects. "Why are you coming to the Arnold case?"

"To support Frank and Maxine," she replied. "The Arnolds are going through a horrible, horrible ordeal and I think they will appreciate me stopping by the courtroom."

"Yes," he replied, "especially in your new dress."

Melissa lit a cigarette. "Spencer," she said, "sometimes you bore me."

When Spencer was a child, there were three places where the public could hear great orators. The first was at political rallies where impassioned, partisan speakers electrified crowds. The second was in church where preachers painted vivid images of lambs lying down next to lions, and devils prancing across burning embers. The third was in a courtroom. The birth of television and Marshall McLuhan's observation that "the medium is the message" ended the need for great oratory at political events. Politicians now spoke in sound bites. At least once a month, Spencer and Melissa attended Saint Luke's Episcopal Church, which the VanDenvenders had helped found, but the minister there was dull and timid, afraid to offend his privileged flock. This left the courtroom, and although most of the lawyers who appeared before Spencer were lackluster, Taylor Cauldwell was both a skilled debater and clever prosecutor. Spencer had always marveled at his friend's command of English but his effective use of language was only part of his oratorical skill. Cauldwell was charismatic and always had been whether he was in or out of the courtroom. Spencer had noticed years ago that Cauldwell lived his life as if he were constantly in front of an audience. Even when Spencer and Cauldwell had been students at UVA, there had never been a moment when Cauldwell had not been onstage. Meanwhile, his innermost thoughts remained private. Spencer had noticed another Cauldwell-ism. He was an excellent listener and he was especially adept at using the information that he gleaned to his advantage.

It had taken Delaney and Cauldwell only two days to impanel a jury so the trial began on a Wednesday, a day earlier than Spencer had initially planned. The twelve jurors were a varied lot: four blacks, five women. They included a fireman, retired plumber, grandmother, stay-at-home mom, executive secretary, telephone company manager, aerobics teacher, the owner of an apple orchard, an unemployed artist, a first-grade public school teacher, a city bus driver, and a college student. They ranged in age from twenty-six to sixty-nine.

In Virginia, the Commonwealth's attorney gives his opening statement first before the defense attorney, and at the end, he gives the final closing argument, ensuring that the first and last words that jurors hear are from the prosecution. Cauldwell began by removing his jacket and rolling up his sleeves, a rather hackneyed symbolic gesture that he was readying himself for an arduous chore.

"Of all the crimes we human beings commit, there is none worse than a murder," he announced. "Unlike disease or an accident, murder is intentional, a violent act against a fellow human being. The worst, the most heartbreaking, the most devastating, the most disgusting of all murders are the ones done by adults against children. A child, so young and so innocent, is cheated from the wonderful joys that make all of our lives worthwhile. And we are cheated because we never will know what this child might have become." Cauldwell's voice sounded sad. "This case is about a cruel murder. Cassie Arnold, called Cookie by her friends, was killed by the defendant." Cauldwell looked and pointed directly at Lester Amil. "He is the man sitting right there."

Continuing, he said, "I want you to etch her name into your memory. Cassie Arnold. Remember that she once was a breathing, intelligent, loving, laughing, and wonderful child." He turned to his right and gestured toward the front row of spectators. "Her parents, Frank and Maxine Arnold, are sitting over there. They loved her and she loved them."

For the next several minutes, Cauldwell described Cassie. He wanted the jurors to develop an emotional connection with her. He then described the murder as chillingly as he could.

"The killer came into Cassie's bedroom while she was sleeping. He jabbed a high-voltage stun gun against her tiny body to immobilize her and prevent her from screaming. He then carried her down into the basement where he had already prepared a spot on the cold concrete floor. He placed her down on newspapers and then used duct tape to bind her hands and cover her mouth. By this time, she had regained consciousness and was wide awake. He pulled down her pajama bottoms and pushed up her blouse, exposing her. Then, he fashioned a garrote around her neck. He used a broken piece of a paintbrush handle to tighten the rope slowly as he stood above her and pleasured himself by masturbating. He eventually ejaculated over her body, perhaps at the same moment as he twisted the garrote a final time, strangling her. We can't be certain if she died then or when he took a blunt object and slammed it into the side of her skull. But what we do know is that the final moments of little Cassie Arnold's life were horrific."

Cauldwell had used inflections in his voice to highlight key phrases that he wanted jurors to remember: "came into Cassie's bedroom while she was sleeping . . . jabbed a high-voltage stun gun against her . . . was wide awake . . . pulled down her pajama bottoms and pushed up her blouse . . . twisted the garrote a final time . . . pleasured himself by masturbating . . . eventually ejaculated over her body." In all of his years as a prosecutor, he proclaimed, he had never seen such a ruthless and perverted crime.

Cauldwell's speech was suddenly interrupted by a woman sobbing. It was Maxine Arnold. Frank helped her to her feet and led her out of the courtroom. After waiting several moments for the commotion to die down, which called even more attention to it, Cauldwell launched into the final part of his statement. He outlined the evidence that he said confidently would prove that Lester Amil was guilty. The strongest proof was Amil's DNA. It matched DNA found in the semen splattered on Cassie's pajamas.

Cauldwell then said: "A law professor once told me that I should never say a defendant's name in a murder trial. He taught us to always call a defendant the 'accused' to remind jurors that a crime had been committed and to dehumanize the defendant. But ladies and gentlemen, I'm not going to follow that learned professor's advice today. Because Lester Tidwell

Amil is a cold-blooded sexual predator—a child molester, a child killer—and I want you to remember his name and also remember exactly what he did."

As he was about to deliver his final lines, Cauldwell walked close to the defense table and pointed his finger directly at Amil. If you were going to accuse a man of murder, you had to show the jury that you weren't afraid to call him a killer to his face.

"This man," he said, "tortured and murdered an eleven-year-old girl. Don't you dare forget his name and what he did! And don't you dare forget the name Cassie Arnold and how that little girl suffered because of him!"

Several spectators were crying as Cauldwell returned to the prosecution table. Patti Delaney stood slowly and stepped up to the podium. By now, Spencer had become used to her un-professional choice of courtroom attire, but the tan vest that she was wearing today seemed even more inappropriate than usual. It was decorated with pieces of men's ties. Three nar-row ties—one a bright yellow, another with black-and-white polka dots, and the third with red-and-green stripes—were hanging on each side of her chest, as if they were military medals. Black bow ties, meanwhile, had been sewn on each shoulder. She looked like a walking tie rack. Just as she was about to begin, the door of the courtroom opened and Melissa VanDenvender waltzed inside. A deputy escorted her to a space on the front row where Miss Alice had taped a sheet of white paper with the word "Reserved" hand printed on it. Had it been anyone else, Spencer would have been furious. But he said nothing as everyone watched his wife's showy entrance.

Patti Delaney waited for Melissa to be seated and then looked directly at the jury. "That was an amazing opening statement that Mr. Cauldwell just gave. He is an extremely ca-pable prosecutor. For those of you who might not know it, he is also the attorney general of our state and if this trial goes well for him and if what the newspapers are reporting is cor-rect, Mr. Cauldwell may even be elected as our next gover-nor." She paused and looked over at Cauldwell. "I doubt there are many defense attorneys east of the Mississippi who can match wits with him in a courtroom," she said. "In fact, and I want you to remember this, Taylor Cauldwell is good enough to convict an innocent man." Without saying another word, she returned to her seat.

A visibly irked Cauldwell sprang from his seat. "Your Honor, I'd like to meet with you and the defense counsel in your chambers."

Spencer looked at his watch. It was nearly noon. "We'll adjourn for lunch," he said, "but before we leave, there is something I wish to say." He addressed the jurors. "The prosecutor and defense attorneys in this case have a legal right to say just about anything in a courtroom. What you need to remember is that nothing either of them just said is evidence and your job is to reach a verdict based only on the evidence that will be presented. You should ignore the innuendos and the lawyers' persuasive powers or lack thereof."

"I've never been so offended in my life," Cauldwell complained, as soon as he entered Spencer's private chambers. Tagging along behind him, Jacob Wheeler said nothing.

"Which part of my opening statement offended you?" Delaney asked. "The part where I said you were a capable attorney?"

Cauldwell glared at her. "Cute, very cute," he snapped. "I thought you didn't want the judge referring to me as the attorney general but that's the first thing you tell jurors. And I resent you implying that I am trying this case because I want to be elected governor. Politics has nothing to do with this crime!"

"It had nothing to do with the crime, but it has everything to do with how this crime is being prosecuted," she replied.

"Judge Spencer," he said, "this isn't the first time she has implied that politics is driving this case. I'm certain you saw her quote in the *Charlottesville Courant* where she accused you of picking a trial date with the gubernatorial election date in mind. She's not only impugned my character but the court's too!"

Delaney had hoped that Spencer hadn't seen her quote—though that was unlikely—or that during the last nine weeks he had forgotten about it—which was also unlikely.

"That's enough," Spencer said. "Mr. Cauldwell, the fact you're running for governor makes you an easy target. That shouldn't surprise you. If anything, I find it cliché and cheap." Addressing Delaney, he said, "If you have a problem with my decisions or you wish to question my motives, I'd suggest you do it with the appropriate state ethics committee and not a newspaper reporter."

"I apologize, Your Honor," she said. "I spoke out of frustration. May I offer a suggestion?"

"Go ahead."

"Mr. Cauldwell insists politics aren't at play here. If that's true, why don't you put a gag order on both of us?"

Cauldwell was shocked. "That's unnecessary," he stammered. "She wants a gag order because she doesn't have a credible defense!"

"I simply don't want you riding into the governor's mansion on Lester Amil's back. I also resent having my client lynched on the front page by leaks from 'anonymous sources.'"

Before Cauldwell could respond, Spencer said: "Actually, I think a gag order is a good idea. By its nature, this is going to be a highly charged case. It would be smart to keep the rhetoric to a minimum."

"What?" Cauldwell replied incredulously. "You're agreeing with her?"

"I've made my decision," he said. "Now, if there's nothing more, I will see you both after lunch."

Cauldwell spun around and stomped from the room with Wheeler dashing after him. Delaney and Spencer looked at each other for several moments. Neither spoke. And then she said, "Thank you, Your Honor."

"There's no need to thank me. Regardless of what you may think, my decisions are not based on politics."

"Yes, Your Honor." She turned to leave but before she reached the door, it flew open, causing her to jump back to keep from being struck.

"Where are you taking me for lunch today?" Melissa Van-Denvender asked as she strolled inside. Seeing Delaney, she said: "Oh, I didn't know you weren't alone."

Spencer introduced them.

"I've never seen so many men's ties on a woman's vest before," Melissa said.

"I bought it at a craft show," Delaney replied. "And your dress?"

"It's by a Russian designer," she replied, "but I doubt if you've heard of her. She's very expensive."

Melissa wasn't through. "Ms. Delaney, you're from Baltimore, isn't that correct? You and your husband?"

Delaney correctly assumed Melissa already knew that she was divorced and why. "Baltimore is where I used to live before my husband decided he liked men," she replied bluntly. She nodded to Spencer and left.

"DeDe was certainly correct about her," Melissa said. "And that vest she is wearing is atrocious."

Spencer ignored her comment. "I've already asked Miss Alice to get me a sandwich from across the street for lunch. With court reconvening in thirty minutes, I'm afraid I don't have time to take you anywhere." She could tell that he was still irritated by her earlier entrance in court.

He walked over to a brass hook on the wall, which is where he hung his judicial robe, and started to unbutton it. But Melissa intercepted him. "Poor, poor Spencer. I've embarrassed you," she said. "Coming into your courtroom like that, bursting into your chambers. I simply don't know what you are going to do—to discipline me!"

She glided past him and stepped to the front of his desk. She had her back to him now. She spread her legs, hiked her skirt above her waist, and leaned down, her elbows now resting on his desk. Before him were an exposed pair of perfectly tanned legs and a black satin thong.

"What's wrong, dear?" she said, mocking him. "Afraid Miss Alice might walk in?"

He hadn't been thinking about Miss Alice at all. Actually, he didn't know why he was hesitating. This was not the first time that Melissa had surprised him by demanding sex at an inopportune place and location. Spencer assumed that most women differentiated between lovemaking and fucking. Melissa didn't. Looking back on it, she never had. She didn't expect flowers, soft candles, cuddling. It was physical. Animalistic. Predatory. Looking at her now, his mind told him to say: "No. This isn't appropriate."

But he didn't. Instead, he stepped forward, grabbed her hips, and spun her around so that she was now facing him. He went to kiss her but she turned her face.

"No time for that," she said.

A surge of anger swept over him and he reached under her arms and lifted her where she stood, shoving her back onto his desk so that she was now perched before him with her skirt still hiked up. He reached down and was about to grab her thong when there was a quick rap on the door and Miss Alice came in.

"Oh, oh, excuse me!" she squealed, as soon as she saw them. She turned and raced out the door.

Spencer was horrified but Melissa burst out laughing.

"It's not funny," he said.

"Yes, it is," Melissa replied. "It's quite funny, actually."

She pushed him away and slipped off the desk, still laughing. "I'm going riding this afternoon with DeDe so Miss Alice can give my reserved seat to someone else—if she hasn't had a heart attack and dropped dead from shock outside your door."

She smoothed her dress. "After our ride, we'll probably stop off at the club for drinks and dinner. I'm planning on being late so don't bother waiting up." She leaned forward and kissed his cheek. "Now wasn't that fun?"

Spencer removed his judicial robe and slumped into his desk chair. For nearly ten minutes, he didn't move. He was thinking. There was another knock on the door.

"Come in," he hollered.

Miss Alice gingerly walked inside. She was carrying a paper bag that contained the sandwich that he had ordered earlier. There was also something else in her other hand. For a moment, Spencer thought about apologizing for the spectacle that she'd interrupted, but just as quickly he decided that the less said, the better.

As she approached his desk, Miss Alice said: "I picked this up off the floor after you collapsed and were taken to the hospital." She lifted up the white stone that Patrick McPherson had sent him. "I thought it might have some sentimental value since that man went to the trouble of mailing it to you from

Las Vegas. I was afraid the cleaning people would throw it away if they found it on the floor. I put it in my desk drawer and forgot about it until now."

She held it out for him, but he pointed to a stack of papers on his desk and asked her to put it there. He didn't want to touch it. She turned to leave.

"Miss Alice," he said.

"Yes?"

"I'm sorry."

She left.

He stared at the stone. Miss Alice had just carried it to him without being shocked with electricity.

It couldn't have knocked me out! I must've been hit by lightning.

He started to reach for it but pulled back his hand.

Miss Alice knocked again.

"Judge, there's someone here who's asked to see you."

Maxine Arnold breezed by her without waiting to be invited inside. She was dabbing her eyes with a tissue.

"Frank doesn't know I'm here," she blurted out. "He's out in our car trying to make some business calls. Those horrible media people are swarming around him like piranhas, and every time he gets out of the car they stick microphones under his face. It's just so horrible. I'm afraid to go outside so I've been hiding in the women's bathroom."

For a moment, the thought of him and Melissa having sex on his desk flashed through Spencer's mind. They would have been interrupted by Miss Alice and Maxine Arnold! He must have been insane to have responded to her seduction.

"I'll find an office here in the courthouse where you and your husband can go before and during the trial," he offered. "I'll post a deputy outside its door so the two of you won't be interrupted."

"Oh, thank you!" she said. "That would be wonderful!"

He was waiting for her to leave but she didn't. "Is there something else?" he asked.

She tried to smile, but instead broke down and began sobbing. "This is all so terrible," she sniffled.

Spencer kept a box of tissues in his private bathroom. He moved from behind his desk to fetch them but before he reached the bathroom door, she stepped forward and without warning hugged him.

"This . . . is . . . a . . . nightmare. . . ." she stammered, her sentence interrupted by gasps for air as she continued crying. He didn't know how to react. She stepped back.

"I'm sorry," she said. "I know that was totally inappropriate. I'm sorry."

She hurried from the room.

What had just happened?

Spencer wasn't sure. On the surface, it had appeared spontaneous. Maxine Arnold had been distraught. She was a grieving mother. Just the same, he wasn't certain it hadn't been calculated.

He sat back down behind his desk and glanced at his watch. Five minutes before court reconvened. He reached for the deli sandwich. Unwrapping it, he took a bite and found himself once again looking at the stone on his desk. He reached forward and snatched it up.

Nothing. No sudden jolt. No burst of power. He relaxed. It was nothing but a rock. A simple stone. His doctor had been right. *Stones don't emit electrical blasts. Stones don't knock a man unconscious!* He started to put it back down.

And that's when it happened. He felt a prick and then a quick jolt! He tried to drop it, but his fingers refused to obey his mind and another surge of electricity shot up his arm.

It's happening again!

Suddenly, the walls of his private chambers disappeared.

Spencer was flying. He was passing through the ceiling above him, the rafters, the roof, into the blue sky. He could see the court square and now, like a bird, he was shooting above the city, darting quickly over the rooftops underneath him, like his childhood hero, Superman, being whisked along in some unexplained out-of-body experience. VanDenvender Hall came into view and he whipped over its tile roof like a heat-seeking missile locked onto a still unseen target. He passed through the stone walls of the stables and found himself standing in front of a horse stall.

He could hear sounds: a woman moaning, a slapping noise, like two hands clapping together in an out-of-synch rhythm. He saw movement to his left and walked quietly across the stable's floor for a better look.

The back of a naked man appeared before him. The man was standing up. He was having sex with a woman who was bent over in front of him. He had entered her from behind, and he was using his left hand to pull her hips back-and-forth against him. He had grabbed the woman's hair with his right hand, and he was jerking her head back with each thrust.

He heard a voice. "Yes, yes, yes, harder, harder, harder." It sounded like dialogue from a sleazy pornography movie. The woman moaned and he suddenly recognized her voice. It was Melissa.

Spencer stepped closer. They didn't stop. Didn't see him. Couldn't. But he could see Melissa's face clearly now. The man was slamming himself into her faster and faster and Spencer knew that she was near orgasm. "Ohhhhhhhhhh!!!!" Her eyes were squeezed tight, she was totally focused on the moment, carefully synchronizing her movements with his. "Yes, faster, faster," she demanded. He knew her well enough to know that she was lost in her own sexual pleasure, not really caring if the man behind her was ready to explode.

Spencer tried to make out the man's face but he couldn't. His wife's lover had bent back his head so that all Spencer could see was the butt of his chin and neck. Spencer couldn't take his eyes off the man. As he watched, his wife's lover slowly lowered his chin. It was a college student whom Melissa had hired during the summer to work in the stables. A neighbor. Jason Crew. "Harder, harder, yes, yes, yes! Aghhhhhhh!"

Young. Strong. Tight. Melissa reached back and grabbed Crew's butt with both of her hands, pressing him tight against her. Her fingernails dug into his flesh. But her euphoria was short-lived, interrupted by the sound of a car approaching. Her eyes flashed open.

"My husband!"

The boy disengaged and frantically reached for his pants. His penis still erect. Melissa, completely naked, fell forward into the hay and spun around, reaching for her shorts and blouse. She didn't bother slipping on her panties. As she hurriedly dressed, she began grinning. Crew was still fumbling with the buttons of his shirt. Smoothing back her hair, she hurried to the doorway, composed, delighted. She looked outside. Spencer could see himself now. He was standing near the house about fifty feet away. Melissa yelled to him:

"Be up in a minute."

He waved back and walked into VanDenvender Hall. He was completely oblivious to what had been taking place. Melissa returned to where Crew was hiding and stooped to pick up her panties from the hay.

"A souvenir," she said, tossing them to him.

He stepped forward to kiss her but she turned her cheek.

"No time for that."

The stone fell from Spencer's hand and he was back in his private chambers. He was breathing fast and drenched with sweat.

What had just happened? Had he been hallucinating? It had been so real. Like a dream but not a dream. How? Why? As his thoughts slowly became clearer, he remembered an afternoon when he had come home early and Melissa had waved to him from the stables. It had only been a few weeks ago. Yes, now it was all coming back to him—all of it and even more.

He remembered that she had had pieces of hay in her hair when she had come into the house. He tried to recall more details. Think! Yes, now it was coming to him. She had said something about how it had been Jason Crew's last day at work before he'd returned to college. They'd gotten into a hay fight in the stables, she'd said. Kid stuff. Innocent! Melissa throwing hay at some kid, reliving her youth, harmless.

The thought that she had sexually betrayed him had never entered his mind. Never! Not until now. He tried to remember every detail that he could and more came to him, slowly, in pieces and flashes. When he had gone upstairs that day to change clothes, he had seen Melissa undressing to take a shower. Now he remembered. She hadn't been wearing panties. At the time, he had thought it odd because she had been outside working in her shorts, and he had thought it must have been uncomfortable not wearing underwear while riding horses and carting around bales of hay.

Miss Alice knocked on his door.

"It's time," she called out.

He felt fine physically but emotionally he was spent and confused. He rose and stepped over to the brass hook to retrieve his judicial robe. As he reached for it, a pain shot through his left hand. He opened his palm. The red mark in its center had doubled in size. He peered down at his desk and the stone.

What was happening to him? And why? Why this? Why now?

10

THE VATICAN, ITALY

THE REV. DR. GRASSO TWISTED UNCOMFORTABLY IN THE WIN-
dow seat of the crowded airplane en route to Leonardo da Vinci Airport in Rome. He was in a row with three seats. An obese woman, sitting in the center, was asleep, overflowing on both sides of her seat and snoring loudly, much to the irritation of a gaunt man sitting on the aisle. He was reading the latest Nelson DeMille novel under a tiny beam of light shooting down from the aircraft's overhead console. The flight had departed several hours behind schedule because of increased security precautions at Dulles International Airport outside Washington, D.C. The flight was about midway across the Atlantic. They wouldn't be arriving in Rome until midafternoon. Grasso was too restless to sleep. Besides, his misshaped body didn't fit well into seats designed for average-size passengers.

Because of his reputation as a biblical scholar and his connections at Catholic University, Grasso had bypassed the strict requirements that most researchers face when they ask for permission to inspect the Vatican's most private documents. Technically, the *L'Archivio Segreto Vaticano* is open to the general public and has been since 1888. But having once worked there, Grasso knew that actually getting inside the Secret Archives was a formidable challenge. Applicants first had to submit a letter, written by a bishop or a high-ranking diplomat. It went to the prefect of the Secret Archives—the priest responsible for protecting the church's records. No one entered the archives, except for the pope himself, without the prefect's permission. Researchers lucky enough to be granted an audience were asked by the prefect to explain in painstaking detail how they intended to use the information that they hoped to find. The prefect, who was appointed by the pope for life, not only decided if the applicant's projects were worthwhile but also passed judgment on the researcher's moral character. Those who were deemed acceptable filled out a form addressed to the pope as *Beatissimo Padre*. Then they waited, sometimes weeks, sometimes months, until a permit arrived. It was good for a specific number of days, and once it expired, the researcher was no longer permitted inside the archives regardless of whether or not he had finished his work.

Grasso knew that only about two hundred requests per year were approved. The Vatican had several explanations for why it limited access. Many documents in the Secret Archives were fragile. Several were priceless. The archives had a small staff that consisted of the prefect, a vice-prefect, three archivists, and four *scrittori,* or helpers, and they could only help a handful of researchers. But Grasso also knew there was another reason for limiting access. The archives contained so many documents that no one—not even the prefect—had read them all, and to this day, it is impossible to know exactly what secrets are still waiting to be discovered there. Best to be careful.

The archives had started out as a library for early Christians who wanted to keep a record of Jesus Christ and his teachings. It became the "Secret Archives" after it was forced underground by Roman emperors, especially the lunatic Nero, who began persecuting early Christians. One of Grasso's favorite stories was about Lawrence the Librarian. In 258, Roman soldiers were sent to loot the archives of gold and silver that the church had collected for the poor. But Lawrence hid the valuables. The soldiers slowly roasted him alive in an attempt to make him squeal but he refused. His mummified skull is still kept on display in Vatican City as an inspiration to the librarians and archivists who have followed him.

As Christianity grew, so had its paperwork. The church bureaucracy began collecting hundreds of thousands of documents: financial records, membership rolls, baptismal records, theological rulings. In 1612, the pope designated the Vatican the permanent site of the archives and ordered all monasteries and churches to surrender their individual holdings to it. Today, the archives contain so many pieces of paper that if they were stacked on top of each other, they would reach one hundred miles tall. Its holdings included thousands of pages of indulgences—the "all your sins are forgiven" passes that the church sold to enrich itself. There are seven thousand books on its shelves filled with individual requests for indulgences. Some are from kings. The handwritten notes taken by secretaries of the Sacred Rota, a Vatican religious court, fill another hundred volumes. These records contained intimate details about the lives of church members who requested annulments and other dispensations.

But the archives' largest single holding is the papal registers, which contain the official letters of the popes, along with correspondence that was sent to them. There are more than five thousand thick papal volumes in the archives, dating back to Pope Innocent III in 1198.

Because he was intimately familiar with the archives, Grasso understood the difficult task that he was now facing. Unlike a modern library, there was no index, no central card catalog, no computerized record system in the archives. He would not be able to type the words "stigmata—left hand—magic stone" into a computer and receive an answer within seconds. Despite years of labor by librarians, there were still thousands of boxes filled with books identified only as *miscellanea* because no one had ever sorted through them. Inside one of these long-forgotten boxes might be the record that would tell him about a mystical stone.

There was another reason, besides his reputation, that explained why Grasso had been able to avoid the archives' normal entrance requirements. The prefect was his longtime friend, Father Petrocelli Zerilli, the Italian priest who had accompanied him years ago to Sicily to investigate the case of the young village girl who had been blessed with the mystical stigmata. Although they had not kept in regular contact, their experience with the dying girl had formed a lasting bond between them, and much to his delight, Grasso was greeted at the airport by a chauffeur dispatched by his old compadre. Rather than taking him to a hotel, the driver zigzagged through Rome's congested traffic and deposited Grasso at the Alberto Ciarla restaurant in the Piazza San Cosimato. Zerilli was already waiting inside.

"I thought you'd be hungry and thirsty after flying for such a long time," the prefect announced as he greeted Grasso affectionately with a hug. Grasso wasn't surprised that Zerilli had chosen a restaurant for their reunion. Fine dining was one of the few extravagances that the church permitted, and Zerilli had a well-deserved reputation in Rome as a priest who loved to eat. He was not embarrassed to charge the cost of his feasts on his Vatican-issued American Express card, although few restaurant owners ever presented him with a bill out of their respect to the church.

Zerilli was an oddity for an archivist who, much like librarians, were stereotyped as being quiet, contemplative, even mousy, souls. Standing six-feet-six, he weighed 320 pounds and was gregarious and loud.

"You must try the sea bass!" Zerilli bellowed. "The chef here can prepare it in three different ways. In fact, I would be happy to order for the both of us."

Grasso, who was exhausted, eagerly agreed and Zerilli, delighted to demonstrate his skills, instructed the waiter to bring them an appetizer of soup made from pasta and beans with seafood, a house specialty. Lifting his wineglass, Zerilli proposed a toast.

"To all of our departed brothers and sisters who now are with God and know the glory of being with our Lord Jesus Christ and his blessed mother, the Virgin Mary," he said loud enough for other diners to hear. And then, he added in a whisper intended only for Grasso's ears, "including a few who would be roasting in hell if it were not for our good Lord's willingness to forgive their many, many sins!"

Grasso glanced outside and noticed that the late afternoon sky was beginning to turn a brilliant pink. Was there ever a city as beautiful as Rome at twilight? He didn't think so. "Ah," Grasso said reflectively. "Rome really is a heavenly city."

"Yes, my friend," Zerilli replied, "you have been away for too long." For the next hour, they discussed mutual acquaintances and church gossip. Finally, Zerilli asked Grasso why he was in such a hurry to dig into the archives.

"A suicide," Grasso said.

"This person was someone close to you?"

"Actually, we never met," Grasso replied. "But the circumstances that surround his death interest me, especially a peculiar mark on his left hand. I believe it's the stigmata, but not in the traditional sense—like the one we witnessed in the village girl."

Zerilli's fork stopped midway to his mouth, a rarity. "A stigmata—on someone who committed suicide—impossible! God's gift doesn't drive one to self-destruction."

"This mark only appeared on his left hand," Grasso explained. "It was shaped like a cross and was so well defined you could actually see Christ hanging on it. He even was wearing a crown of thorns."

"Listen to what you are saying, my friend. This can't be a stigmata! Perhaps it's a birthmark or some self-inflicted wound of some sort. A cruel joke, no doubt."

"No. A thorough medical examination revealed it was identical to a stigmata. The man's wife said it began to develop after he touched a stone."

"A stone, you mean a rock?"

"Yes."

"This is preposterous!" Zerilli declared. His reaction was so abrupt and sharp that it surprised Grasso. Zerilli quickly lowered his voice. "Forgive me, my friend," he said, "but what you are saying is both ridiculous and outrageous."

"Why?"

"Please, we are old men, not starry-eyed innocents. Have you not been listening to yourself speak? A stone that causes a stigmata! My friend, you've not changed since we were both young priests. You still want to be both a scientist and a priest. You cannot. You must choose. Our church says thousands of miracles have occurred. The scientific community says none has. Does it matter? The faithful still believe. Don't you understand that this dispute lies at the core of our faith: true faith begins only after logic and scientific reasoning end. Once you understand this, then you will see that there is no point to your search here."

"I've never believed that God expects us to turn a blind eye to scientific knowledge," Grasso replied. "He gave us an unrestricted intellect. It's our nature to demand evidence, to question. If there is a mystical stone, and I believe there is, where did it come from? I believe the archives might hold the key to unlocking this mystery."

"See, it's exactly as I said," Zerilli said, laughing. "You've not changed. I'm afraid you're wasting your time, but then it's your time to waste. Where do you plan to start this search of yours?"

"I remember years ago examining a book written by a Monsignor Pico Ferrara, a priest who lived in the late 1200s and spent much of his life investigating mystical happenings. If there is a record of a cross-shaped stigmata or a magical stone, I imagine there will be some reference to it in his book. Are you familiar with this volume?"

"No, I've never seen it but we'll find it for you. But for now, let's have another drink and then dessert."

It was well past midnight when they parted. Grasso had been up for more than twenty-four hours. Still, he found it difficult to sleep so he rose before dawn to pray and then left to find a taxi. Rome was shaking off its slumber. Women swept the sidewalks in front of their shops, calling out greetings to one another. Other store owners raised protective metal grills, sending a click-clack-clacking into the morning air. The traffic deadlock of Fiats, taxis, and motor scooters already had started, accompanied by honking horns and obscene gestures. A still-groggy taxi driver delivered Grasso to St. Peter's Square and within minutes, he was hobbling past the Leonine walls, a last defense by Rome against the Saracens, and through the Gate of Ste. Anne into Vatican City. A Swiss Guard stopped him when he reached the Court of the Velvedere, where the entrance to the Secret Archives is located. He was stopped twice more by guards before he arrived at the marble staircase that led to the archives. Grasso paused there to catch his breath and examine an old friend: a statue of Hippolytus, thought by many to be the most important third-century theologian of the Roman church. Grasso had always quietly considered Hippolytus one of his religious heroes even though the outspoken theologian had revolted against the church by publicly challenging the papal election of Callistus in 217 and declaring himself as the first "antipope." He had died in a forced labor camp.

Grasso's uneven legs felt as if they were on fire by the time he reached the top of the stairs. He showed an archive employee the pass that Zerilli had given him and moments later, the prefect himself swept into the lobby.

"Welcome, welcome!" Zerilli proclaimed. "As I promised, we are ready." He led Grasso into an adjoining office so small that a desk and chair filled nearly every inch of its space. "Father Paul Montini will assist you," Zerilli declared. "He will bring you any records you request. I've asked him to start by bringing you the *fondo* (register) of Monsignor Pico Ferrara, as you requested last night. Although I will be busy during the day, I would like to dine again with you later this evening. How about seven o'clock? I have a wonderful restaurant already selected."

Before Grasso could reply, Zerilli was gone.

The leather-bound volume that Father Montini bought him was thirty inches in length and twenty inches wide. Monsignor Pico Ferrara had written an introduction, noting that he had investigated three hundred reports of supernatural acts during his lifetime and was now consolidating his findings into a single volume. Ferrara's handwriting was ornate and he had illustrated each page with drawings, including sketches of Draculas, women with bestial anatomical features, and other nightmarish creatures. The pages were not numbered, but midway through the book, Grasso came upon several passages that dealt with the mystical stigmata. Ferrara, who considered himself both a priest and a historian, explained that the first suspected stigmatic was St. Paul who had written in his Epistle to the Galatians, chapter six, verse seventeen: "I bear in my body the marks of the Lord Jesus." In Greek, the word that Paul used for "marks" was "stigmata." But it was not clear whether he was speaking figuratively or was referring to actual wounds of punishment and suffering he had endured. There were no other cases of the stigmata reported, as far as Ferrara's research showed, until nearly twelve centuries later. In 1222, a man living in Oxford, England, claimed he was suffering from five wounds similar to those inflicted on Christ at his crucifixion. However, a monk named Thomas Wykes had unmasked the man as a fraud who was self-inflicting the wounds to draw attention to himself. The imposter was sentenced to prison for life on rations of only bread and water. A second report, in 1234, said a French nobleman named Robert Carr, who was the Marquis of Monteferrard, had showed signs of the stigmata. But an investigation by a priest revealed that Carr was piercing his own flesh every Friday with nails in order to share in the suffering of Christ; he had never claimed the wounds were a supernatural gift.

The first verified case, Ferrara wrote in his book, involved St. Francis of Assisi. Shortly after his death, a fellow priest known only as Brother Elisas reported the appearance of the stigmata on St. Francis to religious officials in France.

> I announce to you a new miracle. From the beginning of ages, there has not been heard so great a wonder, save only in the son of God, who is Christ our God. For, a long while before his death, our Father and Brother appeared crucified, bearing in his body the five wounds which are verily the stigmata of the Christ; for his hands and feet had as it were piercing made by nails fixed in from above and below, which laid open the scars and had the black appearance of nails; while his side appeared to have been lanced, and blood often trickled therefrom.

A second Franciscan brother, identified only as Leo, had also signed the affidavit, stating that he too had personally seen the wounds.

After St. Francis, the number of reported incidents of the stigmata jumped. In 1231, a monk named Brother Dodo was killed in an accident and when his body was being prepared for burial, the stigmata was discovered. However, because it was impossible to tell if the wounds had been self-inflicted, his status as a stigmatic remained in question. In 1237, the Blessed Helen, a Dominican sister at a convent in Veszprim in Hungary reportedly became the first female stigmatic.

For several hours, Grasso read Ferrara's notes but there was no mention of a cross-shaped stigmata appearing only in a left palm or of any mystical stone. He did discover, however, that Ferrara had become cynical near the end of his life. Most reported miracles were not miracles at all, he concluded. Nearly all could be explained by science or they were frauds. On the final page of his book, Ferrara wrote:

> In regard to the mystical stigmata, I have come to believe that many of the faithful are inducing these wounds themselves in protest against the excesses and corruption of the Church. They are trying to give new importance to the suffering of Christ and His disregard for creature comforts.

Disappointed, Grasso closed the thick volume and pushed it to the side of the desk. His eyes were tired. He removed his reading glasses and rubbed his eyes. When he opened them, he noticed a tiny gap in the edge of Ferrara's book. He slid a fingernail into the gap and opened the book again. Nothing seemed extraordinary on the pages. But when Grasso examined the binding closer, he discovered that at least three pages had been neatly cut from the volume.

Father Zerilli arrived. "My friend," he proclaimed, "it's time for us to depart for dinner!"

Zerilli had his Vatican-assigned chauffeur drive them to the Agata e Romeo restaurant, owned by a husband and wife. As before, Zerilli ordered for them, this time selecting a sweet-tasting swordfish sliced thin and surrounded by capers and olives.

"I found something odd today," Grasso said, as they were eating. "I think someone has removed three pages from Monsignor Ferrara's book."

"Ah, unfortunately, this is not as rare as it should be," Zerilli replied. "The pages were probably stolen or perhaps destroyed. Who knows why? Perhaps they contained a drawing that someone thought would be worth selling. Or it's possible that a devout priest removed them because he thought they were offensive. I'm sure you noticed that Monsignor Ferrara was fond of drawing sketches of strange creatures, often seminude women, on the borders of his text."

While convincing, Zerilli's explanation seemed odd to Grasso but he wasn't certain why. "Surely, you keep track of who has had access to your materials," Grasso responded.

"Yes we do, but let's not be naive," Zerilli said. "Monsignor Ferrarra's book was written in the late 1200s. Do you know how many hands have touched it since then? Who's to say the pages weren't stolen in the 1400s or removed in the 1500s?"

It suddenly dawned on Grasso why he thought Zerilli's comments were odd. The night before, Zerilli had said he was unfamiliar with Ferrara's book. Now he was describing the drawings on its borders. Still, Grasso said nothing. He had not slept well and knew he was irritable. Perhaps he had misunderstood his friend.

"I have another *fondo* for you to inspect tomorrow," Zerilli volunteered. "It contains papers from Ste. Catherine of Siena. Perhaps you will find something there."

Father Montini was waiting the next morning. "Our records about Ste. Catherine of Siena are quite extensive," he explained.

"How many cartons about her do you have?" Grasso asked.

"More than twenty-five boxes and they are just the ones from the church in Siena. Because you are specifically interested in the stigmata, I have brought records only from the year 1375, which is when the stigmata first began to appear on her."

"Father Montini, I have a request," said Grasso. "Would you be kind enough to check your records and tell me who was the last researcher to examine Monsignor Ferrara's volume about supernatural happenings?"

"There's no need for me to check," Montini replied. "I already know. When the prefect asked me to get it for you, I wrote your name in our log and I noticed that the last person to read it, was Father Garampi, in 1952, shortly before he died."

"I remember him," Grasso said, smiling, "from when I worked here. He was a delightful priest."

"Yes, Father Garampi was well liked in the archives. He dedicated his life to writing an index of our books. He began when he was nineteen and worked on his index all of his life. He was still writing it when he passed away at age seventy. During that time, he completed six volumes. They covered books in the archives for 1250 to 1255. Imagine, he spent his entire life working on an index that only encompassed five years!"

"Will you bring me the index that Father Garampi did of Monsignor Ferrara's book about supernatural happenings?" Grasso asked.

For the next several hours, Grasso read reports about Ste. Catherine of Siena, who first began having mystical experiences when she was only six. She claimed that she could see guardian angels as clearly as the people whom they were protecting. There was no mention in her files, however, of any cross-shaped stigmatic mark or mystical rock. Around noon, Father Montini appeared with the index that Grasso had requested. Incredibly, he found what he was searching for within a few minutes. Under the words: "Stigmata, unusual shapes," Father Garampi had written: "Christ on the cross, left hand. See also: *giudicare* rock." Under "*giudicare* rock," which translated from Italian means "to judge rock," Garampi had written: "Touching causes Christ to appear on cross, left hand." The index noted that additional information about both the stigmata and rock could be found in Monsignor Ferrara's book about supernatural happenings.

"Ah," said Grasso to himself. "Now I know what was on those three pages cut from the text." Once again, Grasso summoned Father Montini.

"How long has the archives kept reliable records of who checks out its books?" he asked.

"Since 1950, we have had a strict policy: no one gets a volume without his name and the number on his research pass being logged into our records."

"Any exceptions?"

"Only two: the pope and the prefect. They look at whatever they wish, whenever they wish, without signing the log."

"How often does the pope come here?"

"Never. If he wants something, the prefect gets it for him."

That night, Grasso dined alone at a café near the famed Trevi Fountain. After he finished, he sipped coffee and watched people strolling past the cafe. He noticed a young couple toss a coin into the legendary fountain and his mind suddenly flashed back to his youth when he had come to this very same fountain as a novice priest and seen a different couple toss in a coin and make a wish. He could remember that day clearly and still could see the woman's face, even though it had been more than a half century ago. She had been the most beautiful creature Grasso had ever seen. Still a young man, he had felt a rush of sexual desire rise up in him that day and had turned away from her. But within seconds, he had found himself returning to gaze at her face. She had noticed and had nudged her boyfriend. Together, they had approached him.

"Father," she had said, since he was wearing his cleric's collar, "will you say a prayer for us? We are about to be married and are very much in love."

Her voice had sounded pleasing and innocent, like that of a young child's. Grasso had awkwardly mumbled a blessing and the boyfriend had slipped a coin into Grasso's left hand. Because it was his useless hand, the coin had fallen onto the pavement. Grasso had never been more aware of his physical deformities as he had at that moment, yet the woman had not appeared horrified by his appearance. She had bent down, retrieved the coin, and gently put it in his good hand, saying, "This is for the church, Father. Thank you for your beautiful words." Later that night, he had thought of her and in a sinful moment had wondered if she and her boyfriend were being physically intimate. He had tried to force the image from his mind and ultimately had gotten out of bed and onto his knees to pray for strength. But as soon as he had returned to his bed, she reappeared in his thoughts. As a boy being trained for the priesthood, Grasso had been instructed by the older monks on various methods to prevent what they described as "impure thoughts." One monk had taken a piece of string and tied a hangman's loop at one end. He had then told Grasso to slip the loop over his penis before he went to bed and to tighten it. After he fell asleep, if the devil entered his mind and he began having sexual dreams that caused his blood to engorge his penis, the string would become painfully tight and awake him so he could regain proper control of his thoughts and pray for forgiveness. Grasso had rarely used the string. The love of Jesus Christ had been enough to keep him satisfied. But on that night years ago when he had spotted the woman at the fountain, he had awakened three times in pain because of the looped binding. Now, he was an old man and had no need for strings. But the memory of that woman still made him smile and caused him to wonder. *What had happened to her? Had she been as happy with her choices in life as he had been with his?*

The next morning, Father Montini brought more cartons to him about another stigmatic, Ste. Veronica Giuliani, who received the marks on her hands, side, and feet on April 5, 1697, but Grasso found nothing useful there. Besides, he was distracted. He was trying to find a polite way to confront the prefect. That night they met for dinner at a restaurant named Boccondivino, which translated means "divine mouthful." Zerilli had already ordered whipped codfish resting on spikes of polenta for himself and a subtle blend of roasted turbot stuffed with foie gras for Grasso. They ate quickly and while they were waiting for their fruit-filled ice cream desserts, Grasso leaned close to his friend and quietly asked: "Why did you cut three pages from Monsignor Ferrara's book before you had it delivered to me?"

"What are you accusing me of doing?" Zerilli said slowly.

"I examined an index written by Father Garampi," Grasso replied. "According to it, Monsignor Ferrara wrote about both a stigmata that appeared in the shape of Christ on the cross and a '*giudicare* rock' in his book about supernatural happenings. Since I could not find any mention of them there, I can only conclude that Garampi's index was referring to the three pages cut from the text."

"Yes," said Zerilli. "That is logical, but it hardly proves I removed the pages. As I said, this is a very, very old book."

"My friend, the three pages were there in 1952 because that is when Father Garampi read them and included them in his index. According to the archive logs, no one has checked out the book since then except for me. There are only two persons who could have removed the pages without writing down their names. The pope and you."

Grasso searched Zerilli's face for a reaction, but there was none, so he continued: "I believe you removed the pages on the night we had our first dinner together after I told you why I was here. I further suspect you have been trying to waste my time by providing me with boxes and boxes of documents about stigmatics, knowing there is nothing useful in them. My question is why?"

Zerilli wiped his front teeth several times with his tongue as if he were polishing them. "You're a clever detective," he said. "I forgot about the index. I thought removing the three pages from Montini's book would be enough. I underestimated you."

"Why did you remove them?"

Zerilli took his time in answering. He chose his words with care. "I have decided to help you, really help you, but this is too sensitive for us to discuss here. We must return to the archives tonight."

They finished their ice creams in silence, thanked the owner, and left the restaurant without ever being presented a bill. Neither spoke on the drive to Vatican City. The guards nodded as Zerilli stepped past them into the Court of the Velvedere. Rather than climbing the staircase to the archives, the prefect slipped behind it and motioned to Grasso to follow him. There was a large metal door there without a knob, only a keyhole. Zerilli unlocked it and pushed it open.

"Watch your step," he warned.

There were no windows and when the door was shut behind them, it was so dark that it was impossible to see. Zerilli flipped on a light and led the way. The corridor took them into a cavernous room filled with giant steel bookshelves imported from the U.S. The shelves were so tall they formed two levels. Curved stairways led from the ground to the second level, where there was a labyrinth of passages between the rows of books. Zerilli moved quickly into another dark passageway. The electric lights, which Zerilli switched on as they walked, shut off automatically within a few minutes, so that he and Grasso were traveling in a constant island of light, with darkness behind and in front of them. They passed a stack of documents that Grasso recognized. They were the writings of Vatican scholars who had been recruited by the pope to refute the rebellious religious leader Martin Luther. Beside that bookcase was a large safe where the church kept seventy-eight seals made of gold and silver. It was the world's foremost collection. Two of the seals bore the marks of the Spanish Kings Philip II and Philip III. Each of the two kings' seals weighed nearly two pounds and was made of solid gold. There was another steel door at the end of this corridor. Grasso recognized it too. It led to the most secure and private of all chambers inside the archives. There was only one key to its lock and it never left the possession of the prefect.

"No one must ever know I have allowed you in this chamber," Zerilli said, as he reached under his frock and produced a huge brass key. "Only popes and their prefects have ever stepped foot in here."

The deadbolt made a loud "thunk" as he turned the lock. Grasso felt a burst of cool air escape when the door opened. The air in the room was filtered and kept at a perfect temperature for preserving documents. A light came on automatically. Grasso surveyed the interior. The chamber had steel walls, turning the entire room into a giant vault. Zerilli locked the door behind them and walked briskly to a safe. He spun in the combination, opened the door, and removed a large metal box.

"As you know, there are thousands of religious relics in the world, as well as numerous reports of miracles," Zerilli explained. "You have asked to hear the truth, so I will tell it to you. Nearly all of these religious relics are frauds and the reported miracles are not miracles at all. Some are hoaxes or legends or fairy tales or odd occurrences easily explained by science. Yet the church has chosen to perpetuate these myths because those who believe in them seem to receive some joy or inspiration from them. I'm certain you have always suspected this. What you don't know is that in the last two thousand years, there have been seven actual events that cannot be scientifically explained and for which there appears to be only one possible logical explanation. These seven events are miracles. They are bona fide acts of God."

Zerilli paused to give Grasso time to understand the significance of what he had just been told. "You and I have been fortunate to have witnessed one of these events: the young stigmatic in Sicily." Zerilli motioned with his right arm toward a series of shelves stacked with cartons. "Those boxes contain everything known about the young stigmatic whom we watched die. After we made our initial report to the Vatican about her death, the church quietly launched an intense and thorough investigation. Investigators and private detectives took detailed statements and affidavits from every person over the age of ten who lived in the village. They collected autopsy records, put together a detailed family history, gathered DNA samples. They even investigated us to make certain we were reliable. Nothing was overlooked. They spent years studying that case and they were unable to find a logical explanation for the girl's death or the marks on her body. What I am telling you is this: there is no doubt that this girl had the stigmata, and while the church publicly accepts hundreds of reports about the stigmata as being true, the reality is that this young girl is the only verified, authenticated example of the stigmata that we know happened. She was an actual stigmatic."

"What of St. Francis—of Ste. Catherine?"

Zerilli repeated: "The girl in Sicily is the only case that we have authenticated."

Zerilli opened the box that he had removed from the safe. "What you have stumbled onto, my good friend, is another one of the seven bona fide miracles—the *giudicare* stone. The church has been collecting evidence about it for two thousand years. It surfaces each generation, it seems. We usually hear about it after someone dies and the mysterious mark on their left hand is noticed. The mark is always in the shape of Christ hanging on the cross. It is also highly unusual because when it bleeds, it bleeds actual blood. This specific stigmata is always linked to the *giudicare* stone. There is another aspect of this miracle that is most bizarre. The person who touches the stone finds himself empowered with supernatural abilities, but he also becomes doomed and will die a horrible death. For years, we searched for an explanation: Where did this stone come from, what is the source of its power?

"But none of our research made any sense until 1943 when a boy playing in a cave in Jordan not far from the Dead Sea found an ancient clay pot that contained a parchment. We were able to obtain the parchment and because it was during the war and the boy and his father did not really understand the significance of what they had discovered, the church was able to keep its discovery a secret. Based on carbon dating, we have been able to determine that this parchment was written around 70 A.D."

Grasso stepped closer to the steel box. "I'm going to show you a section of this parchment," Zerilli said. "After you read it, you will know the source of the *giudicare* stone's power and understand why it is a most magnificent gift from God and, yet, at the same time, a terrible curse for those who encounter it and attempt to use its unique powers."

PART TWO

FACE TO FACE

O

Unless I see in his hands the print of the nails, and place my finger in the mark of the nails, and place my hand in his side, I will not believe.

The Gospel of John, Chapter Twenty, Verse 25

11

THE VOICE OF BROADWAY ACTRESS CAROL CHANNING WARNED Charles MacDonald to stay to the right of the moving walkway at McCarran International Airport so passengers in a rush could slip by him. It was a recording being played through a loudspeaker. Seconds later, another celebrity, Tommy Tune, warned that the walkway was coming to an end and he needed to watch his step. This was definitely Las Vegas.

He hailed a cab and went directly to the Clark County Courthouse. Carol Webis had said he needed to examine the death records there if he wanted to learn more about Maxine Arnold's first marriage. But Webis had not told him the name of Maxine's first husband, the man whom she had reportedly tricked into wedding her so she could escape from her dreary life at home. He'd have to discover it first.

MacDonald began by searching through yearly indexes that listed all of the marriage licenses issued in Clark County. Because several hundred thousand couples get married each year in Las Vegas casinos and at quickie wedding chapels along the Strip, it took him several hours before he found the license he was searching for.

Maxine Gunter Finley, age sixteen, married to Justin Thackery Wright, age twenty-two, on June 6 in the Little Chapel on the Strip.

MacDonald jotted down that information and walked across the hall into another courthouse office where divorce records were kept. Now that he had their names and a wedding date, retrieving their divorce decree was easy. The couple had stayed together only six months. Although Webis had claimed that Maxine had been pregnant when she was married, MacDonald could not find any mention of a child or a custody agreement in the divorce decree. He wrote down the case number and asked the clerk to bring him the settlement agreement that the couple had signed.

"It's such an old case," the clerk said, "it will take several days for us to get it from our storage facility."

"I don't have that much time," MacDonald replied. He showed her the police badge that he had carried when he worked as a Washington, D.C., homicide detective. He didn't mention that he was retired. She suggested that he drive to the courthouse's storage facility personally and look at the file there. "Since you're a detective, they'll let you do that." A half-hour later and twenty-five dollars poorer because of a long cab ride to the edge of the city, MacDonald found himself rummaging through cardboard file boxes in a warehouse. The folder that held *Wright v. Wright* was thin. He read it quickly. Once again, there was no mention of a baby. MacDonald discovered, however, that Maxine had taken nearly all of the property in the settlement that had any value, including a five-year-old Chevrolet Impala and $2,514 in a savings account. Her husband had been stuck paying $4,200 in debts. A wad of overdue bills had been stapled onto the settlement papers. MacDonald thumbed through them. They seemed routine until he came to a yellow slip: $854 owed to Brown's Funeral Home for the "interment of Cynthia Gunter Wright."

A secret revealed. There was a baby after all and her name was Cynthia Gunter Wright. Maxine Arnold had given birth to a daughter before she was married to Frank Arnold.

MacDonald did the math in his head: Maxine gets pregnant

at age sixteen. Justin Wright marries her and she gives birth to Cynthia Wright a month after their shotgun wedding. According to the date on the funeral home's bill, the baby had been buried four months later. Maxine had filed for a divorce, one month after that. She'd gotten to keep their car and the cash. It wasn't much, but it had been enough to tide her over until she met and married Frank Arnold.

Now that he knew the baby's name, MacDonald caught another twenty-five-dollar cab ride back to the Clark County Courthouse, where he returned to the records office, this time to search through death certificates. When he found Cynthia Gunter Wright's, he discovered that the infant had been pronounced dead on arrival at the emergency room in St. Josephine Hospital. No cause of death was listed. MacDonald copied down the hospital's address and hailed yet another cab.

At the hospital, he flashed his detective's badge at the clerk in the medical records office, but she balked at handing over Cynthia Wright's medical records. Instead, she referred him to the hospital's in-house lawyer. MacDonald was afraid the attorney wouldn't be fooled by his badge so he tried the truth. He explained that he was representing a capital murder defendant and needed a copy of Cynthia Wright's records. While sympathetic, the lawyer refused to give them to him. Nevada privacy laws prohibited the release of medical records. He'd either need a court order or a notarized release signed by a parent. MacDonald pleaded and then argued but got nowhere. By now, it was getting late so he hailed a cab and had it take him to Boulder Station, where he checked into the combination hotel, casino, restaurant, and shopping complex a few miles from the Strip. He telephoned Delaney's office and home but she didn't answer. After a half hour of mind-numbing television in his room, he decided to get something to eat.

Las Vegas was a difficult city for MacDonald. It had been one of his wife's favorite vacation spots. He missed Jean terribly. Forty-four years had not been enough time for them. He'd always been surprised when he'd heard other men complain about their wives. He and Jean rarely disagreed and never exchanged angry words. Maybe it was because he saw so much violence and marital discord on his job. Jean had idolized him and he had felt the same about her. Her fascination with Las Vegas had always amused him because she was quiet at home and frugal. He knew a number of cops who had always vacationed in Las Vegas during the sixties and seventies and that had also struck him as odd. After all, that was before gaming corporations had taken control of the Strip. La Cosa Nostra had been in total control back then. Jean always played the nickel slots while he tried blackjack. At night, they went to shows. She had loved the follies, even though he had felt uncomfortable watching topless showgirls. When they were first married, he'd been convinced that he could never love anyone as much as his bride. And then their daughter had been born. Even though he'd been warned that fathers sometimes have a more difficult time than mothers bonding with newborns, MacDonald had been instantly smitten. Over the years, he and his daughter had become best friends. He never missed her birthday parties, not a single one, even when he was working different shifts. When she was little, she was always waiting at the door for him when he came home. He'd spoiled her from the start and did his best to turn her into a tomboy. He taught her how to play baseball and football, and after a neighborhood group of boys refused to let her play in one of their sandlot games, MacDonald showed her how to box. Much to his delight, she was a gifted athlete. Baseball, soccer, basketball, swimming, field hockey, she played them all well. He coached her teams whenever he could. Even after she had become a teenager and had begun arguing with her mother, the two of them had stayed pals. He had known her innermost secrets. After high school, she was accepted for entrance in a California college and they planned her trip there together. It was just the two of them, driving across the country in a U-Haul rental truck. They made an adventure of it, stopping at the Football Hall of Fame in Canton, Ohio, and even visiting the Las Vegas Strip. He was miserable during her first year away, and he had an even tougher time when she fell in love and announced that she and her boyfriend were planning on getting married as soon as they both completed school. MacDonald thought he would despise her boyfriend, but when they met, he realized that she had made a wise choice.

The proudest day in his life was when he had walked his daughter down the aisle at her wedding. A real Kodak moment. Their relationship was how a father and daughter's friendship was supposed to be. There had been no way for either of them to know on her wedding day the tragedy that was only hours away.

MacDonald found a steakhouse inside the Boulder Station casino complex and ordered a T-bone and shot of Johnny Walker whiskey. When the bill arrived, he opened his wallet. A photograph of the two women he had loved looked up at him from behind the yellowing plastic window where most men kept their driver's licenses. He was standing between them, his arms draped around their shoulders. Carefree. Happier times. He was old school, never cried. But he felt overcome by a sense of abiding sadness. Clinical depression is what the psychiatrist had called it immediately after his daughter's death. He'd spent a full year trying to shake it. Drugs didn't help. He'd become so debilitated that the shrink had recommended electric shock treatments. MacDonald had rejected them. He'd find his own way out of the abyss, he said. And he had. He'd cured himself, or so he'd told them.

Sitting in the steakhouse, waiting to sign his credit card receipt, MacDonald thought about Frank and Maxine Arnold. Did Maxine miss her first daughter, Cynthia, and now her second child, Cassie, as much as he missed his daughter and wife? Did Frank Arnold feel the same hollowness in his life? MacDonald signed the credit card receipt and walked out into the casino. He headed directly to a bar there and ordered another shot of whiskey. It was going to be another tough night.

The next morning, MacDonald showed a cabdriver a paper with the address of the Clark County Coroner's office scribbled on it. He was following one of his gut feelings. It had dawned on him that morning that if there had been anything suspicious about the death of Maxine Arnold's first child, the Las Vegas police would have requested an autopsy.

And those records generally were open to the public. Perhaps he could find out how little Cynthia Wright had died.

12

THE COMMONWEALTH'S FIRST WITNESS WHEN THE MURDER trial of Lester Amil reconvened after lunch Wednesday was Albemarle County Sheriff's Detective Dale Stuart. He played a tape recording of the 911 emergency call that Maxine Arnold had made after she discovered her daughter was missing.

"She's been kidnapped!" she shrieked.

"Calm down please. Tell me your address so I can send a patrol car," the dispatcher could be heard saying.

"They'll kill her. Don't send a police car!"

Detective Stuart testified that he and two other officers had arrived fifteen minutes later in a white van. They wore green overalls with the words "Water Dept." stenciled on them. Frank Arnold had met them at the door and demanded to see identification. There was a pistol in his waistband.

"Mrs. Arnold was totally distraught," Stuart recalled. "But her husband was calm."

Under questioning by Taylor Cauldwell, Stuart took the jurors through the events of that morning.

He said that Maxine Arnold had gotten out of bed at eight o'clock to take Cassie to the private elementary school that she attended. Normally, their housekeeper, Theresa Montoya, fixed breakfast for Cassie and drove her there, but Montoya's mother had died on Saturday night and she was away at the funeral. Maxine had gone downstairs into the kitchen, removed orange juice and milk from the refrigerator, and put them next to a bowl of cereal on the table. She then had gone back upstairs to rouse Cassie from her bedroom on the second floor. The Arnolds' master suite also was on the second floor but at the other end of the house. Cassie's bed was empty and she wasn't in the bathroom that adjoined her room. Thinking that her daughter might have somehow slipped past her, Maxine had started to return to the kitchen when she spotted three pieces of lined white legal paper laid side-by-side on the hallway floor. It was a ransom note. It instructed the Arnolds to withdraw $118,000 in hundred dollar bills from their bank. They would receive a telephone call at five P.M. with instructions about where to deliver the money.

Cauldwell introduced the ransom note as an exhibit and then had Stuart read a portion of it out loud for the jury:

"At this time, we have your daughter in our possession. She is safe and unharmed and if you want her to live, you must follow our instructions to the letter. Do NOT call the police or your daughter will be killed. We are watching your every move and will be all day long until we get the money. Be sure to take a briefcase to the First Virginia Bank big enough to hold the money."

Stuart testified that the note had been written with a black, felt-tip marking pen.

"The blocky handwriting appears to belong to someone who was either extremely nervous or consciously attempting to disguise his or her normal style, possibly by writing with their weaker hand," the detective said.

"I object," Patti Delaney interrupted, rising from her chair. "This witness is not a handwriting expert."

"Sustained," said Spencer. He told the jury to ignore Stuart's analysis of the handwriting.

Taylor Cauldwell asked Stuart what he had learned from examining the ransom note.

"It mentions the Arnolds' bank by name, so the kidnapper obviously either knew them or had watched the family for some time."

Stuart further testified that the note had been written on paper that appeared to have been torn from a legal pad in Frank Arnold's home office.

"That's odd because kidnappers usually don't use materials in a victim's house," he testified. "They bring a note with them, already prepared."

There were "no signs of forced entry" into the house or into Cassie's bedroom. A window in the basement was broken, but there were no fingerprints found on it or footprints outside that would have suggested an intruder had used it to enter and exit the house.

Judge Spencer allowed Stuart to refer to notes that he had made on the morning when he had first interviewed Frank and Maxine Arnold. He testified that Maxine had become so overwhelmed with emotion that Frank Arnold had telephoned their family physician and asked him to come over to the house. He'd also called his attorney.

"Why'd he call his lawyer?" Cauldwell asked.

"He said an executive in his position didn't like making decisions without having a lawyer present," Stuart testified. "I didn't see anything suspicious about it since he also wanted his attorney to go to the bank later and withdraw the money for the ransom."

Stuart said the Arnolds had both told him that Lester Amil had gone to a party on Sunday night. Cassie had gone to bed around ten P.M., and Frank and Maxine were in bed asleep by midnight. At around four-thirty A.M., Frank Arnold heard one of the automatic doors to the garage opening and he woke up. He'd assumed it was Amil coming home and had gotten up to check.

However, Frank Arnold had not gone downstairs. Instead, he had verified that Amil was in the house by checking the status of Amil's personal identification badge on the computer monitor in the master bedroom. The computer indicated that Amil was indeed in the basement.

Stuart testified that Frank Arnold's stirring had awakened his wife. She had a headache and had gone into their bathroom to take two aspirin and a sleeping pill. They both had gone back to bed then and had not realized anything was amiss until the next morning.

"After I wrote down their statements," Stuart testified, "I told Mr. Arnold that I wanted to see how his home's computerized tracking system worked." They'd gone together into Arnold's home office.

"When he checked the computer program, Frank Arnold said to me, 'Hey, this says Lester Amil is still in the house right now! He's in the basement!' Apparently, no one had bothered searching all of it. They'd looked in Amil's bedroom and not seen him, but no one had gone into any of the other basement rooms," Stuart testified.

"I'm confused," Cauldwell said. "If this computer kept track of everyone, then why didn't it tell you where Cassie Arnold's body was?"

"Cassie had taken off her personal identification badge before she had gone to bed on Sunday night," Stuart explained, "so her badge was still on the nightstand in her bedroom."

At about the same time that Detective Stuart and Frank Arnold were going to search the basement, the Arnolds' family doctor and lawyer arrived at the house. The doctor had gone into the living room to treat Maxine Arnold. But the attorney had joined Stuart, Frank Arnold, and another police officer. Together, they all headed downstairs to search for Amil.

"Frank Arnold thought Amil might have surprised the kidnapper during the night and might have been killed or wounded in a struggle," Stuart explained. "At that point, Amil was not a suspect. We all thought he might have been murdered and his body hidden in another room."

The computer tracking device showed that Amil was in an area of the basement that the Arnolds used for storage. It was locked from the inside.

"I knocked several times and called out Lester Amil's name but there was no reply," Stuart explained.

Arnold had given Stuart permission to kick open the door. The storeroom was actually a large, unfinished area that contained four individual rooms. Tools were kept in one room, another contained storage boxes mostly filled with clothing. There was a room where the gas heater for the house was located, and there was a room next to it where the Arnolds kept several wooden crates filled with wine bottles, Stuart recalled.

"The Arnolds said they were planning on converting the room with wooden crates in it into a wine cellar. We all split up with each of us choosing a room to search. I went into the tool room," Stuart said.

"What happened next?" asked Cauldwell.

"I heard Frank Arnold utter this gut-wrenching scream." Stuart turned in the witness chair so that he was now looking directly at the jurors. "I came running out of the tool room and saw Frank Arnold carrying Cassie's body. I immediately told him that he needed to put his daughter's body back exactly where he had found her because this was now a murder investigation and I wanted the crime scene protected."

"Did he do that?" Cauldwell asked.

"No, he was so distraught that he carried Cassie upstairs and put her down on a sofa. Then he began calling for the family doctor to come help Cassie. But she was clearly dead. I immediately told everyone to leave the house, except for my two fellow officers."

"So the crime scene was disturbed?" Cauldwell asked.

"Most definitely. You don't move a body like he did without contaminating the scene."

Stuart said he immediately called the FBI and the Virginia Medical Examiner's office and asked them to send forensic crime scene specialists to the Arnolds' house.

"I was doing damage control," he testified. "I didn't want anyone else tampering with the murder scene. I also was worried because we still didn't know what had happened to Lester Amil. I assumed that his body was still down in the basement storeroom. I figured the kidnappers had murdered him too."

Stuart went down alone to finish searching the basement.

"That's when I found Lester Amil's personal identification badge on the floor in the storeroom—the same room where Cassie's body had been found. The clip on the badge was broken, which made me think maybe it had fallen off during a scuffle. But Lester Amil was not in the basement."

Taylor Cauldwell showed jurors a clear plastic bag that contained a small badge inside it.

"Is this the personal identification badge that you found on the floor?" he asked.

"Yes," Stuart replied, "that's Lester Amil's."

"Did you find anything else in the room where Cassie's body was found?"

"Yes, there was a fifty thousand-volt stun gun on the floor there too."

Cauldwell lifted up another plastic bag. This one had a stun gun inside it. He had Stuart identify it as the stun gun that he had found at the murder scene.

"Were you able to trace the stun gun back to its owner?"

"It had a serial number on it. We traced it to a local gun dealership and sales records there showed that it had been bought by Lester Amil two days before Cassie's murder."

"Did you find fingerprints on the stun gun?"

"Yes, we found prints that matched Lester Amil's prints."

"When and where did you finally find Lester Amil?"

"He was spotted shortly after five o'clock at the Charlottesville bus station where he had purchased a round-trip ticket to Washington, D.C. I'd put out an APB on him. He was taken from there to the sheriff's office here in the courthouse basement for questioning."

"Did he have any luggage with him at the bus station?"

"He was carrying a backpack that he said belonged to someone else—a friend of his who he was supposed to meet in Washington," Stuart replied. "He said he didn't care if I looked in the bag so I had him sign a release and opened it up. Inside, I found a small plastic container that was filled with a white powder substance that appeared to be cocaine. It was nearly an ounce. He said he'd never seen it before."

"Did you question Lester Amil about the Cassie Arnold murder?"

"I waited about a half hour before I brought it up," Stuart told the jury. "Before that, I focused on the cocaine. I wanted to see if he would bring up the murder on his own, but he didn't and when I finally mentioned it, he acted as if he didn't even know it had happened."

"I object," Delaney said. "The witness doesn't know if my client was 'acting.'"

"Sustained," said Spencer.

Stuart testified that Amil had been taken before a magistrate at nine P.M. and formally charged.

For the next fifteen minutes, Cauldwell questioned Stuart about similarities that the sheriff's office had found between Cassie's murder and the JonBenet Ramsey case. Stuart quickly outlined them. The ransom notes had been written with materials found inside the victims' houses. The wording of the ransom notes was almost identical. The two notes also contained the exact same dollar amount as a ransom demand:

$118,000. Both young girls had been murdered in a nearly identical fashion.

"This struck me as a copycat crime," Stuart said. "The killer of Cassie Arnold was clearly mimicking the murder of JonBenet."

"Did you find anything in the Arnolds' house that described the JonBenet Ramsey murder?" Cauldwell asked.

"Yes," said Stuart. "We found several hundred newspaper clippings and articles about the JonBenet murder case inside Lester Amil's room. When we searched his computer's hard drive, we discovered that he had visited dozens of Web sites about the JonBenet case. We also found six photographs of nude children. All of those photos showed them gagged and bound. They had been downloaded from a pornographic Web site that operates overseas."

Delaney started to object but decided not to call extra attention to the nude pictures.

"Did you find anything else that linked the defendant with the JonBenet case?"

"Yes, we found a copy of a hip-hop song that Lester Amil had composed about the JonBenet murder. He'd posted it on the Internet for people to download."

Cauldwell showed Stuart a sheet of paper. "Is this a copy of that hip-hop song?"

"Yes."

"Please read the jurors the verses that are highlighted in yellow marker—verses that Lester Amil wrote in his computer and later posted."

Stuart read:

Six-year-old video queen/ tapping shoes/ famed for
Singing 'cowboy sweetheart'/ mom's delight/ strangled, molested/
now tabloid raped/ another to join you at them pearly gates

"Please read that last phrase again, detective," Cauldwell said.

"It says 'another to join you at them pearly gates.' "

"During your investigation, were you able to develop a theory about a possible motive in this case?"

"Yes, based on my experience, I believe the defendant murdered Cassie Arnold because he wanted to call attention to the hip-hop song that he had written about the JonBenet murder case."

"Are you saying his motive was to promote a rap song?"

"Yes, in part. His song has numerous other phrases in it about the JonBenet case that suggest her killer is still roaming the streets, still looking for victims. Cassie's murder played right into that theory," Stuart testified. "Of course, I also am convinced that Lester Amil is a pedophile."

"I object!" Delaney snapped, leaping from her feet. "Detective Stuart is not qualified to analyze my client psychologically. His comment is outrageous and prejudicial to the jury!"

Spencer sustained her objection without even waiting for Cauldwell to react. He then reprimanded Stuart. "You've testified in a good share of criminal trials and know better than to make a statement like that." He instructed the jurors to ignore Stuart's pedophile comment.

But Delaney knew that the damage already had been done.

Patti Delaney had three goals when she began cross-examining Stuart. She wanted jurors to understand that no one had seen Lester Amil return to the Arnolds' house on the night of the murder. She wanted to introduce the idea that someone besides Amil killed Cassie and she wanted to undercut Detective Stuart's credibility.

Getting Stuart to acknowledge her first point proved fairly simple. Under questioning, he admitted that neither Frank nor Maxine Arnold had actually seen Amil come home that night.

"You testified earlier that Lester Amil's personal identification badge was found in the storage room." Delaney said. "But it's entirely possible that someone else might have planted it there, isn't it?"

"Mr. Arnold was a stickler when it came to making everyone wear their badges," Stuart replied. "And the Arnolds certainly assumed that Lester Amil was wearing his, otherwise Frank

Arnold wouldn't have checked his computer during the night."

"You didn't really answer my question," Delaney said. "You don't know if Mr. Amil was wearing that badge or if he had removed it before leaving Sunday night to attend a party. He could have left it on the desk in his bedroom in the basement in plain sight, where anyone could have picked it up and then dropped it in the storage room to frame him."

Taylor Cauldwell interrupted her. "Judge, is she going to ask a question or is she testifying here?"

Judge Spencer said: "Ms. Delaney, if you have a question, ask it."

She decided to switch subjects.

"Since you're such an expert on the JonBenet Ramsey case," she said sarcastically, "please tell us who were the initial suspects?"

"No one has ever been charged or arrested in that case."

"I didn't ask that," she replied. "Please answer my question."

"The parents became suspects."

"Were Frank and Maxine Arnold ever suspects in this murder case?"

"Family members are always suspects in a crime such as this," he said, "but we removed them from the list as soon as the evidence began pointing to your client."

"Yes, let's discuss some of your evidence-gathering techniques," Delaney replied. "Did you take a saliva sample from my client?"

"Yes, we did."

"Was that before or after you told him that Cassie Arnold had been murdered?"

For the first time since he had been on the witness stand, Detective Stuart hesitated. He knew she was setting a trap. "I'm not certain," he said. "But I do know that he signed a consent form giving us permission to take a saliva sample."

"C'mon detective, let's be truthful here," Delaney said. "You told my client that if he gave you samples of his blood and saliva, then you'd be able to tell if he had been using cocaine and other illegal drugs. He gave you those samples because he thought you were going to charge him with possession of drugs, and he wanted to prove to you that there was no cocaine in his system. You never mentioned anything to him about using those saliva samples in the Cassie Arnold murder investigation. You never told him the truth about why you really wanted them. You wanted them to conduct a DNA test, didn't you?"

Stuart didn't flinch. "The exact wording on the release, which he voluntarily signed, says 'the samples you are voluntarily submitting to the Albemarle County Sheriff's Office will be used in an ongoing criminal investigation that could result in the filing of misdemeanor or felony charges against you.' I asked him if he had read that statement and had understood it and he said he did. So I really don't think the timing of when I took the sample is important."

"Oh, I'm certain you don't," Delaney replied, mocking him. "Because you knew you were tricking him, misleading him. Tell me detective, did you even bother to check for drugs in his bloodstream?"

"Yes," Stuart said. "Our tests showed the presence of alcohol and some marijuana but no signs of anything else."

"Tell me, detective," she continued. "Do you know of any tests for drugs that use saliva? Isn't it true that saliva tests are primarily used for DNA?"

"I'm not sure," he replied calmly. "I'm not a pharmacologist."

Delaney was angry and she wanted jurors to realize it. It was time for a bit of theatrics, she decided. She started toward her seat but just before she sat down, she announced that she had one more question for Stuart:

"Isn't it true my client burst into tears when you told him Cassie had been murdered?"

"Yes, he started to cry."

"I'd say that's a pretty good indication," she said triumphantly, "that he was both shocked and horrified by the news!"

"Or maybe," Stuart volunteered, "your client was just sorry that he'd been caught."

"Judge, I object and want that last comment stricken! I didn't ask him to give us his opinion," Delaney declared.

Spencer refused. "You opened the door, counselor, when you gave the jury your interpretation of why he was upset."

Frustrated, her face turning red, Delaney sat down.

Taylor Cauldwell said he had only a few follow-up questions. "The defense has pointed out that no one saw Lester Amil come into the house on the night of the murder. Tell me, if you can, detective," Cauldwell said, "where does male sperm come from?"

Several spectators chuckled. But Stuart looked puzzled. "Do you mean human sperm?" he asked.

"Detective, this is not a trick question. Do you know where human sperm comes from?"

"A man's reproductive organs."

"And, detective," Cauldwell continued, "during your years as an investigator, have you ever known of a case where a suspect has left his semen or sperm at a crime scene without having been there personally?"

"No," said Stuart. "If you find a man's sperm, you pretty much figure he had to have been there."

Again, a few spectators chuckled.

"Even if no one saw him?" Cauldwell asked.

"Yep," Stuart replied. "Even if no one saw him."

It was nearly seven P.M. by the time Detective Stuart finished testifying. Judge Spencer was exhausted. His supernatural vision at noon that day of Melissa having sex in the stable with her college hired hand had been haunting him all afternoon. He was ready to adjourn for the day. Before he did, he went through the routine paces that judges are required to do. He warned the jurors not to discuss the case among themselves, took care of a few other judicial niceties, and then rose from his seat to leave the courtroom. As he stood, he noticed an older man in the rear of the courtroom who looked familiar but whose face he couldn't immediately place.

A few minutes later, Miss Alice rapped on his chamber door and announced that a professor from the University of Illinois wished to see him. "He says you were one of his students."

The man's face finally gelled with a name: Dr. Walter Benedict. It had been nearly thirty years since Spencer had been in his English class. Spencer greeted him warmly. It looked to Spencer as if Benedict was wearing the same tweed jacket with leather elbow patches that he had worn to class nearly three decades earlier.

"You still teaching?" Spencer asked.

"Oh no, no, no, my boy," Benedict replied. "I'm retired, have been for quite some time. Out here on a little vacation. Visiting my daughter. She's a professor of English at the University here."

"A chip off the old block," Spencer said, not knowing what else to say.

"I'm afraid this isn't entirely a social call," Benedict said. "I read about this Arnold murder case in the *Charlottesville Courant,* and I decided I needed to tell you something. Unfortunately, this is not going to be very pleasant."

Spencer couldn't think of any possible connection between Benedict and the Arnolds, but whatever the professor had to say, it was clearly making him uncomfortable.

"If this is information or evidence about the murder," Spencer said, "then you need to talk to the Commonweath's attorney, not me."

"Oh no, I need to talk to you because this is about you." Benedict crossed and then uncrossed his legs and fumbled with his bow tie. "I suppose you don't remember much about my senior English class?" Benedict continued. "You made it quite clear when you were enrolled in it that you didn't think much of the course."

"I'm afraid," said Spencer, "that English composition was not one of my strong suits."

"You were failing my class. It's difficult for me to remember all of the excuses students gave me. However, you pleaded for a second chance. I agreed to pass you if you turned in an extra-credit report and you chose to write about censorship. Much to my surprise, your paper turned out to be quite brilliant. Do you remember?"

"Yes," Spencer said, "but I'm a bit foggy about the details."

"Details, yes," said Benedict, "the devil is in the details. I gave you an A on that paper and you were allowed to graduate and then you went on to law school."

"It was most generous of you to give me a second chance."

"My last year of teaching, I had a student turn in a paper about censorship and it was equally brilliant, in fact, it was so brilliant that I suspected this student had cheated. He wasn't as smart as you. I suspected he had found your paper and copied it almost word for word. Over the years, I've learned that essays that earn high marks have been known to resurface periodically, even decades later. I dug through my records and, by chance, found your original paper so I compared them and my worst fear came true. This young man had copied your work. There was one line in particular that stuck out. 'If men were never allowed to speak unless they spoke wisely, a great silence would brood upon the earth.' That is what you wrote in your paper. Do you remember that line?"

Spencer didn't. "I hope you weren't too harsh on the student. Kids make mistakes in college," Spencer said.

"Yes, they do," said Benedict. "And your attitude is certainly forgiving. But in my field, plagiarism is the ultimate sin. It is theft, stealing another's words. It can ruin an academic's career and a writer's career too."

"What happened to the student?"

"I confronted him. I put his paper side-by-side with your paper and when I did that, he confessed. He had committed plagiarism. But he swore he had not copied your paper. He had taken the lines in his paper from a book."

Benedict removed a brown book from his briefcase. He read its title out loud: "*Cobb of 'The World'* published in 1924. It's a collection of newspaper editorials written by Frank I. Cobb, an editor at the old *New York World* newspaper. I've marked page 350. It's a speech that Cobb gave to the New York Economic Club on April 6, 1920. In particular, I've underlined a sentence from that speech." He read it to Spencer: " 'If men were never allowed to speak unless they spoke wisely, a great silence would brood upon the earth.' "

Benedict closed the book. "When I read this speech," he said, "I realized that you had cheated to pass my class. You *stole* Frank Cobb's words."

Now Spencer remembered. He had fallen behind in his classes because his mother had become ill and he had been cutting class to help her. By the time graduation had rolled around, he was behind in nearly every subject. He'd been in the library doing research when he had stumbled upon Cobb's book. The newsman's old speech had seemed perfect, and

Spencer had thought no one would ever discover his source. And no one had, until now.

Benedict placed the book on Spencer's desk. "This is for you," he said. "I have known about your plagiarism for some time and I was willing to forget it and keep quiet, but this morning when I got up, I felt compelled to come and confront you. You are a judge, a man who is supposed to be honest, truthful. You, of all people, should know that you can never run away from one of your sins."

Benedict left the room without offering to shake Spencer's hand or listen to his explanation. Spencer was humiliated, he felt as if he were still in college. He began to rationalize. *He'd been young. He'd made a mistake. Had Professor Benedict never cut a corner in his life? What right did he have to tell Spencer that he had sinned?*

Spencer picked up the book and tossed it into a trash can.

This had been a lousy day.

13

WEDNESDAY NIGHT, JUDGE SPENCER WASN'T IN A HURRY TO go home so he kept himself busy in his courthouse chambers. Melissa had warned him earlier that she would be staying out late that night at the country club. He wasn't in a rush to see her, especially now that he suspected her infidelity in the stables.

Around ten P.M., he felt hungry and recalled there was a pub a few blocks from the University that served a great Reuben sandwich along with a steaming pile of french fries smothered in white cream gravy. As a poor law student, it had been one of his favorite hangouts until he started dating Melissa. She had despised the place. He went downstairs and stepped outside the courthouse. It was a clear night. The sky was awash with stars. When he pushed the red button on his key ring, his Jaguar made a *beep beep* chirp and the stems of its door locks popped up. He drove toward the University and thought of years gone by. A trip down memory lane.

But when Spencer reached the pub's address, there was nothing there. The building had been replaced by a parking lot now crowded with students' cars.

Spencer began driving aimlessly in search of a restaurant and was soon lost. For twenty minutes, he took one wrong turn after another until he spotted a red neon sign that said RITCHIES. He pulled into its near-empty lot and went inside. It was dark and smelled old. Most of the light came from candles on about a dozen tables that had red-and-white-checkered plastic cloths. One side of the room was lined with booths. An older waitress seated him and jabbed a menu in his face. Ritchies served strictly Italian fare. He ordered Pellegrino and a prosciutto Parmesan salad. There was a young couple sitting in a booth and two older men eating at another table but otherwise the eatery was empty. Spencer thought about his wife. He prided himself on being an analytical thinker so he flipped over the paper place mat in front of him and drew a straight line down its center. On the left side, he wrote: *Reasons to Stay*. On the right side, he put: *Reasons to Leave*. By the time the waitress brought his salad, he already had written down ten reasons why he should stay married despite Melissa's suspected infidelity. He noticed that every one of them involved either financial security or social status. On the right side, he had written only one line: *Don't love her anymore*.

"Judge Spencer? Is that you?"

He flipped over the place mat, embarrassed that someone might read it, and looked up. Patti Delaney was standing next to his table. He didn't know how long she had been there.

"I wasn't certain it was you because it's so dark," she said. "This isn't exactly your sort of hangout."

"Oh really," he replied. "Why not?"

She looked around. The place reeked of cooking grease. Several strips of wallpaper—that showed a Venice gondola scene—had been torn from the wall. There was tomato sauce splattered on the clear plastic–covered menu that the waitress hadn't bothered to collect after he'd ordered. The most expensive entree cost eleven dollars. "Well, judge, no one is going to confuse it with the Fox Run Country Club."

Her comment irritated him, but he was in no mood for a squabble. Instead, he tried to make a joke. "I guess I was curious about what the 'common folk do,'" he said, mangling a lyric from the musical, Camelot.

He could tell from the blank stare on her face that she hadn't caught his clumsy effort at humor. "I just wanted to be polite and say hello," she explained. "I didn't mean to interrupt. You looked deep in thought. But then, I guess that's how judges are supposed to look."

Before he realized what he was saying, he was inviting her to join him. "As long as we don't discuss the trial," he said. "It will be okay." He thought he sounded a bit desperate. And he was.

She hesitated but after he stood and pulled out a chair next to his, she slipped into it. She was wearing blue denim jeans, running shoes, no socks, and a baggy UVA blue and orange sweatshirt. It was the first normal outfit that he had ever seen her wear, and he was struck again by how attractive he found her. Her red hair was tucked under a blue baseball cap. A pony tail came out the hat's back opening.

The waitress poured Delaney a glass of the restaurant's house red wine without asking, and said, "Miss Patti, your dinner will be out in a few minutes." She then served Delaney a cannoli.

"Dessert first?" he asked.

"Absolutely."

"You must be a regular. She didn't even ask what you wanted."

"The owners are friends. Former clients, actually. I helped them out of a tax jam. They were afraid they were going to lose this place. I eat here two or three times a week."

"Taking advantage of their generosity?"

"No, they didn't have much money so I agreed to take part of my payment in meals. I'm a lousy cook so eating here has been great—except for my waistline." She glanced around the room. "Funny how one man's dive is another man's palace."

"An attorney who is a hero?" he said. He was feeling

melancholy. "I've not known many real-life Atticus Finches. If I recall, he took a bag of nuts as payment from a client."

"My dad was a lawyer and a hero," she replied. "He never made any money because he was always defending some noble cause. Tilting at windmills."

"More Don Quixote than Atticus Finch, huh?" He seemed to be stuck on literary analogies.

"My father is why I became a lawyer," she volunteered. "He used to tell me when I was little: 'Patti-cake'—that's what he called me—'there's only one thing that separates men from beasts and that's the law.' To him, the law was sacred. After I got divorced, I was going to move home and practice with him. But he died before I got all of the details settled with my ex-husband. So instead, I decided to teach for a while. That's what brought me to Virginia, and then after that I moved here."

"Why Charlottesville?"

"Why not? Small enough for justice to have a human face," she said. "Big enough, especially with the University, to have culture."

He liked her answer.

"Want to know the real reason why I moved here?" she said, whispering. The wine seemed to have caused her to relax. "I've always had a crush on Sam Shepard, the actor and playwright, and I heard he and Jessica Lange live here. I came to steal him from her." She laughed.

"I'm not sure they do live around here," he replied, "although Charlottesville does attract its share of celebrities. Sissy Spacek has a two-hundred-acre horse farm close by. And the author John Grisham has an estate here."

"Judge, I didn't know you were interested in movie stars."

"I'm not," he replied. "But my wife keeps track of people whom she considers socially important." He intentionally switched subjects. "Where did you spend your childhood?"

"In a tiny town in Colorado. Believe me, you've never heard of it. It's a wide spot in the blacktop in what's known as the Arkansas River Valley, southeast of Pueblo. Lots of watermelons and cantaloupes and, in those days, Mexican laborers. My father lived there all of his life. The only time he left was for World War Two. There's less than a thousand in town and that includes the dogs and cats. When I was little, Hispanics weren't allowed to live within the city despite federal integration laws. No one would sell them a house. They lived in a shanty town just outside the city limits that was called 'the patch.' My father took out a loan and bought the house next door to our house and then sold it to a young Mexican couple. People in his own church refused to talk to him. There was talk of violence. But when he died and I went back home for his funeral, the longest line of cars that anyone had ever seen followed his hearse to the cemetery. There were Mexicans and whites there. Like I said, he never got rich but he helped a lot of people."

He noticed there were tears forming in her eyes.

"And your mother?"

"Oh, she's a character! She's crazy, absolutely nuts, but in a funny way. She still lives there. My father met her in England during the war and she came back with him to Colorado and has hated it ever since. She was from London and never fit into rural life. Can't stand farmers. Says they are always claiming they're poor when they own hundreds of acres. But she adored my father and she still lives there. She loves hats and wears a different one every day. People weren't very nice to her at first. But she didn't care. She refused to go to church and smoked my father's cigars in public. Mom used to tell me, 'Patti, never settle.' I got my taste in clothes from her. It may be childish and romantic, but it's my way of being independent, just like her."

"You're dressed pretty ordinary now," he said. "Ur, I mean, you look very nice but you look like everyone else."

"I don't know if that's supposed to be a compliment. I was in a hurry and live just around the corner. This trial is keeping me up late. You too, I guess." There was an uncomfortable pause and then she asked: "What about you, Judge? Why'd you become a lawyer or did everyone just expect you to become one?"

"What do you mean?"

"I didn't mean to be rude. I just thought, you know, based on who you are and who your wife is and the social circles you travel in, that you grew up in a family of lawyers or diplomats. You know: Ivy League, country club, VanDenvender Hall, that whole crowd. Silver spoons."

He was beginning to regret that he'd invited her to join him. "Silver spoons, as in, born with them in your mouth?" he asked.

"I apologize," she replied, wrinkling her forehead. "Hey, I have a talent for sticking my foot in my mouth. I admit it. Maybe, I'm envious. I grew up wondering what it was like to be rich. To never want for anything. Oops, I think I'm digging myself in deeper here. Maybe I should leave."

"No," he said. "I'd rather you stay. I'll let you in on a little secret—my dad was in the military. After he died, my mother did other people's laundry in addition to her regular job to make ends meet. I earned my millions the old-fashioned way: I married it."

She didn't laugh.

"That last part was a joke," he said. "It's my wife who married beneath her social class. Just ask her." He'd not meant to add that last dig but it had come out just the same.

"From what I've seen, the reverse is true," she replied.

Her frankness shocked him. He didn't know if he should be offended because she had just insulted Melissa or if he should thank her.

"Money has never impressed me," she said. "People let it control their lives, tell them what they are worth, make them feel superior."

"So given a choice, you'd rather be poor and happy, rather than rich and sad?" he asked.

"Wouldn't you?"

"Ms. Delaney, I remember after my father died, there were times when my mother and I didn't have enough money to buy each other Christmas presents. I've always had a sneaky feeling that people who claimed you can be poor and happy have never really been poor."

The waitress arrived with Delaney's entree—a large plate of ravioli—and Spencer grinned. "My god, I haven't eaten ravioli since I was a kid. My mom used to buy it in cans. What was the name of that brand—it had a guy wearing a chef's hat—?"

"Chef Boyardee!"

"Yeah, my favorite was SpaghettiOs."

"Now you're talking gourmet! But I think they were made by a different company. See, I loved them too."

She said, "Judge, I'm sorry if I offended you a few minutes ago. It seems every time we talk, I say or do something stupid, like bash into your new Jaguar. I don't know why I feel uncomfortable around you. I guess it's because I admire you. But, being honest, you scare the hell out of me too, if that makes sense."

Again, her honesty surprised him. Melissa would have thought it naive. He didn't know what to say and when he didn't immediately reply, she changed the subject.

"Your mother sounds like a hardworking and wonderful person, is she still alive?" she asked.

"Yes, but I don't see her much."

"Too busy?"

"No, she and my wife don't care for one another."

"That's terrible," she replied. "I mean, I'm sorry to hear that. If you don't mind me saying it, I was surprised when I met your wife. The two of you don't look like you go together really. Oh my, I'm overstepping my boundaries here. I'm sorry. It's been a long day and I think this wine is making me a bit loose-lipped."

"My wife can be a snob," he admitted.

"Really?" she asked sarcastically.

He suddenly realized she was mocking him but rather than getting angry, he laughed.

"I think I'll have a glass of wine too," he said. The waitress brought him one and poured a second for her. It tasted cheap, acrid, and at that moment, perfect.

"I'm a real movie freak," Delaney volunteered, searching for some meaningless chitchat. "When I was a kid, I'd go to as many on a weekend as I could afford. It was my escape from small-town life. Who's your favorite actress?" Before he could answer, she said: "I see you as a Julia Roberts fan? Maybe Meg Ryan, but Julia seems more moody, more intellectual. Besides Sam Shepard, I'm a big Kevin Costner buff. Absolutely nuts about him. And George Clooney, my god what a voice! Although I think Kevin made a real mistake playing Jim Garrison in *JFK*. I mean, Jesus Christ, everyone knows Garrison was a nut and was on the mob's payroll. Hey, I'd be curious, what do you think? Was there more than one shooter in Dallas?"

Spencer tried to recall the last time that he had talked to any of Melissa and his friends about something as frivolous as a movie star or as tedious as assassination theories. He was having a ball.

When the check finally arrived, he was surprised to discover it was nearly two A.M. and that they had drunk nearly two carafes of wine. He offered to pay the entire bill but she refused and they each paid separate checks. Outside, she shook his hand.

"Can I offer you a lift," he said, nodding toward the Jaguar.

"Naw, my place is only a block away and I've got this," she replied, removing a tiny canister of pepper spray from her purse. "My dad always insisted I carry it."

"He was a very wise man."

"I think he would have liked you, Judge," she said.

"And I would have been honored!"

"I want to thank you, Judge," she said. "For arranging for me to defend that burglary suspect, even though I really blew it. I heard about how you got me assigned to that case. It was sweet."

He watched her as she walked away and suddenly realized he was sexually aroused just by the sight of her. With Melissa, it took much more than a handshake and talking about movie stars.

Melissa was asleep when Spencer returned to VanDenvender Hall, and he intentionally rose early on Thursday morning so he could leave without speaking to her. He still wasn't certain how he wanted to confront her about the supernatural vision that he'd seen after he'd touched the rock. He had plenty of reason to be angry, beyond the obvious. Sex between them had always been an issue.

Melissa had already had numerous sexual partners by the time they met in college, even though she was only in her late teens. It had been the late 1960s and early 1970s. Free Love. The pill. Burning bras. Spencer had had only one sexual partner and she had been his high school sweetheart. He'd been wildly in love and she'd broken his heart when she dumped him. Because of his lack of sexual experiences, Melissa had taken it upon herself to educate Spencer. She'd joked that she was going to "deflower" him and during the early years of their marriage, she'd done just that. She introduced him to hard-core pornography, X-rated videos, sexual toys, and a few flirtations with kinky sex. Sometime during his forced "sexual awakening," Spencer had realized that the traditional roles in their marriage always had been reversed. Melissa was the sexual predator, the aggressor, the partner who considered sex nothing more than a healthy and much needed physical release. There was no affection and very little romance.

He wanted candles, holding hands, soft lights, snuggling at night, a soul mate. Getting fucked was enough for her.

At one point, Spencer had wondered if Melissa had been molested as a child. He had gone so far as to confide in a therapist who was a longtime friend and had been a classmate of theirs in college. After listening to Spencer describe their cold sexual relationship, the therapist said he doubted Melissa had been sexually abused. It was more complicated.

"Melissa was probably attracted to you in college out of curiosity and because you filled gaps in her own personality: you're warm, compassionate, caring, personable. She also knew you'd be safe and easily dominated," the therapist had explained.

Spencer had grimaced at those words. He certainly didn't think of himself as being a wimp.

The therapist had suspected for years that Melissa suffered from a borderline personality disorder that had left her emotionally cold, as well as narcissistic.

"I'm certain Melissa is convinced that she is too good for you and that you are extremely lucky to have married her," the therapist had said. "Deep down, she thinks of you as being incapable of satisfying her regardless of what you do, in and out of the bedroom. The very personality traits that first drew her to you are now viewed by her as serious character defects and weakness. She probably finds you repugnant because you're not strong and overpowering like her father."

Whatever.

Spencer wasn't a great believer in Freudian psychobabble. But he suspected there was some truth to what the therapist had said. Spencer just had a simpler way of putting it: Melissa didn't need anyone else's love because she loved herself. That was enough for her.

As time passed in their marriage, Spencer had gone through a series of stages that evolved from disappointment, to frustration, to anger, to bitterness. He'd also learned a lesson: the opposite of love was not hate, because hate required emotion. The opposite of love was complete indifference.

While driving to the courthouse that Thursday morning, Spencer began preparing himself mentally for the scene that he knew was sure to come. At some point, he would confront Melissa and dutifully cast himself in the role of the cuckolded spouse. He wasn't certain what role she would choose. He could see her erupting in fury, openly acknowledging that she had betrayed their wedding vows and then blaming him for her betrayal. Or she might adopt the persona of a woman going through a midlife crisis. Maybe she would accuse him of neglecting her. Or, if she really chose to be painfully honest, she would just come out and say the obvious: she was bored with him and their marriage.

Only a few short months ago, Spencer had told himself that he had a perfect life. Now it all seemed a lie.

He arrived much too early at the courthouse and made his way past Miss Alice's empty desk. He slipped into the cocoon that was his private chambers surrounded by his law books, his college degrees, and the other worldly signs of his success that helped define him.

Somehow he knew that this new view of his own life had been brought about by his touching of the small, smooth stone. The blinders had been removed from his eyes and he did not like what he saw.

14

"YOU'RE HERE EARLY TODAY," MISS ALICE NOTED AFTER SHE arrived at work and discovered Spencer was already in his chambers.

"Catching up on paperwork," he replied. "I need to run a short errand. Would you please take the materials on my desk into the courtroom for me in case I get back late?"

He slipped out the side door of the courthouse and walked briskly by the statue of Stonewall Jackson to a nearby coffee shop where he bought the morning *Charlottesville Courant*. Walter Corn's story about Detective Stuart's previous day's testimony was printed with an artist's illustration that showed Stuart being grilled by Taylor Cauldwell while Lester Amil and Patti Delaney looked on helplessly.

By Walter Corn
Charlottesville Courant Staff Writer

Defense attorney Patti Delaney attempted yesterday to show that Lester Tidwell Amil was not inside the home of Frank and Maxine Arnold when their eleven-year-old daughter, Cassie, was sexually tortured and strangled to death.

Delaney insisted that prosecutors had failed to prove that Amil had returned Sunday night from a party because no one had actually seen him enter the house through a garage door during the early morning hours when Cassie was brutally attacked. But in a clever move, Virginia Attorney General Taylor Cauldwell easily rebuffed Delaney's claim by asking Charlottesville Detective Dale Stuart an unusual question.

"Tell me detective, if you can," Cauldwell said, "where does male sperm come from?"

Cauldwell's question was meant to remind jurors of the Commonwealth's key piece of evidence against Amil. In his opening statement, Cauldwell told jurors that DNA tests will show that Amil's semen was found on the pajamas that the murder victim was wearing. Prosecutors claim Amil stood above his helpless victim and masturbated before he murdered her.

Under prodding from Cauldwell, a slightly embarrassed Stuart testified that a man and his semen are generally linked together. "If you find a man's semen on a murder victim," Stuart told reporters outside the courthouse, "then I'd say it's pretty obvious that he was at the crime scene too." Amil's fingerprints were also found on a stun gun left near the victim's body, Stuart added.

Because Chief Circuit Judge Evan Spencer has issued a gag order that prevents attorneys from discussing the case, neither Cauldwell nor Delaney would comment about Wednesday's opening session. But experienced courtroom observers said Delaney is doing a lackluster job of defending her client. She is supposed to be being assisted by another, more experienced attorney, Charles MacDonald, but he has not yet appeared in the courtroom. Delaney told Judge Spencer yesterday that MacDonald is still investigating potential leads.

Before Delaney was appointed to represent Amil, she was the butt of numerous jokes at the courthouse. In her first appearance in circuit court, she told her client, who was accused of burglarizing Hallman's Clothing Store, to dress nicely when he appeared in court. He took her advice literally and wore clothes that he had stolen from the store.

Corn's story continued for another twenty inches, but Spencer had read enough. As he hurried back to the courthouse, he saw Delaney sitting behind the wheel of her ancient Saab reading Corn's story. A hundred feet away, a crowd had gathered at the courthouse's front steps for the daily lottery for seats. Television camera crews were filming the spectacle. No one else noticed Delaney, and she didn't look up as he quickly whisked by her car.

Dr. Yuki Nyguen Nang, the senior pathologist at the state medical examiner's office, explained the results of the autopsy that she had performed on Cassie Arnold to jurors in emotionless, clinical terms. The eighty-nine-pound victim was four-feet, eleven-inches tall, Nang said, and appeared to have been a healthy young girl. A ligature had been tied so tightly around her neck that it had dug a furrow into her skin. It was a garrote, knotted in the back and fastened to a broken four-inch stick that had been used to twist it. The stick was part of a paintbrush handle that forensic tests later showed had been taken from the tool room in the Arnolds' house. This was identical to the way that JonBenet Ramsey had been strangled, even to the point of breaking off a paintbrush handle four inches long, Nang said.

Nang also told jurors that she had found two tiny burn marks on Cassie's body. In her opinion, these had been caused by a fifty thousand-volt stun gun, indicating that Cassie had been struck twice with it. Nang had found additional bruises on Cassie's lower back and her buttocks that appeared to be older than the other bruises on her body. The hymen was not intact, but there were no abrasions along the vaginal wall. "There was no evidence this victim was raped during the attack," Dr. Nang announced.

Continuing with her testimony, Dr. Nang said that when Cassie's scalp had been pulled back during the autopsy, there was a five-by-two-inch area of hemorrhage on the right side of her skull. Underneath this was an even larger skull fracture, approximately eight and a half inches long. A thin film of sub-arachnoid hemorrhage—bleeding under the membrane covering the brain—overlay the entire right cerebral hemisphere. Underneath, the gray matter of the brain itself was bruised. This indicated that Cassie had been struck by a blunt object or possibly slammed head-first onto the concrete.

Dr. Nang said she had not found any foreign objects under Cassie's fingernails, explaining to jurors that often victims scratch their attackers. She then provided the court with several gruesome color photographs of Cassie's body, including close-ups of the garrote, the burn marks made by the stun gun, and the bruises on her lower back and buttocks. These photographs were passed to the jurors after Taylor Cauldwell had them admitted as evidence. He wanted to make certain they saw for themselves how much this little girl had suffered during the final minutes of her life.

"I appreciate your thoroughness, Doctor," Cauldwell said, "but I am not a pathologist and neither are these members of the jury, so can you please give us the bottom line here? How did Cassie Arnold die?"

"In extreme pain. She was strangled with a garrote-style ligature that was tightened slowly by her killer. She also suffered massive blunt-force trauma to the right side of her head."

"Let's talk about the strangulation first," said Cauldwell. "Why would a killer use a stick to tighten a garrote—based on your experience?"

"When the killer slowly tightens the garrote while masturbating or raping the victim, it is a form of sexual torture and increases the sexual pleasure of the killer," Nang replied.

Patti Delaney was about to object because Nang was not an expert in sexual deviancy but she decided the quicker this line of questioning ended, the better for her client.

"Now, let's talk about her head trauma," said Cauldwell. "What caused it?"

"It's impossible to tell," Nang replied. "But we know that she did suffer a trauma to the head."

"Did she die from being strangled or did she die from being hit in the head?"

"There is some question about which happened first, but either would have been sufficient to kill her," said Dr. Nang. "The petechial hemorrhages on the insides of the eyelids, coupled with the lack of substantial bleeding from the head wound, suggest that the strangulation was first, so that by the time of the head injury, her heart was no longer pumping or was pumping only weakly. For that reason, I listed the cause of death as asphyxia by strangulation associated with craniocerebral trauma."

Dr. Nang's testimony was suddenly interrupted by the sound of a woman retching. Maxine Arnold had vomited. Her husband helped her from her seat and together with a bodyguard, whom they had recently hired to keep reporters away, they left the courtroom.

"We will adjourn for thirty minutes," Spencer said. He asked Miss Alice to call the janitor. When court reconvened, Maxine Arnold had composed herself and was again sitting in the front row holding hands with her husband. Cauldwell showed Dr. Nang and the jury a plastic bag that contained a pair of cotton pajamas.

"Do you recognize these?" he asked.

"They were on the victim when her body was found. They're pajamas for a little girl."

"What did you find when you examined these pajamas?"

"We found male semen at three different locations. The largest concentration was deposited in the immediate groin area where the legs of the pants come together. There was also a small amount on the back of the pajama bottoms and on the blouse near the neck."

"Were you able to identify whose semen this was?"

"Yes, we tested the DNA in the semen and determined that it was a perfect match with a sample collected by Detective Stuart from the defendant. I can state unequivocally that the semen in the pajamas came from Lester Amil, the defendant in this case."

"Can you re-create for us, based on your forensic investigation, the final minutes of Cassie Arnold's life?"

"I believe the killer used a stun gun to immobilize the victim in her bedroom. He carried her into the basement where he laid her on newspapers and used the stun gun a second time to keep her still while he attached the garrote around her neck, pulled down her pajama bottoms, and pushed up her blouse. She was not wearing underpants. He masturbated while tightening the garrote and then, after he ejaculated, he hit the victim with a blunt object."

As he listened, Spencer noticed that he could still smell the odor of vomit lingering in the courtroom. It seemed somehow appropriate.

Strangely, Delaney began her cross-examination by complimenting Dr. Nang on her choice of a profession. "I find forensic science fascinating," she said. "I've been told that by simply examining a few bones, you can determine a person's race. Is that true?"

"What you're describing is forensic anthropology," Dr. Nang replied. "Forensic anthropologists apply standard scientific techniques developed in physical anthropology to identify human remains. And, yes, by examining skeletal remains, even those that are badly decomposed, a skilled forensic anthropologist can often determine the race, age, sex, stature, and other unique features of a deceased."

"Wow!" said Delaney. She seemed genuinely impressed.

"Actually," Dr. Nang continued, "while these determinations may surprise nonscientists, most of these techniques are not new and are quite easy to perform. Some require only a quick examination. For example, you can often tell a victim's race by the alignment of his teeth. Caucasians often have bites that are in line while a Hispanic victim will have an overbite or an underbite."

"Really?" Delaney said. "I didn't know that. If I understand you correctly, a forensic anthropologist could look at bones from a skeleton and determine from those bones a person's sex and their age too—as well as their race?"

"That's correct. There are only sixty trained forensic anthropologists in the nation and I am proud to be one of them."

Delaney slipped a bag out of her briefcase. "I have two bones here that I borrowed from the science department at the University this morning. Could you give us a demonstration of your skill? Can you tell us, say, the sex and appropriate age of the victim based on these two small bones?"

Sensing a trap, Cauldwell objected. "Dr. Nang is one of the Commonwealth's most skilled forensic scientists," he said. "She has been recognized as an expert witness throughout the state in countless trials, and she has a long list of academic credentials and accreditations. I fail to see much point to this."

"Judge Spencer," Delaney countered, "Dr. Nang has just explained to the jury how she believes this murder happened based on her review of the forensic evidence. I don't think asking her to look at a couple of bones to determine a person's sex and age is going to present her with much of a challenge."

"I'm going to allow it," Spencer said.

Delaney handed Dr. Nang the bag and she took both of the badly yellowed bones from it. Each was less than two inches long. "Because I don't have my equipment, I will not be able to tell the exact age of this person. But you have given me bones from what appears to be a human foot and based on what is admittedly a quick and cursory examination of them, I can tell you that they came from a man."

"That's incredible," Delaney said. "Now could you, if you had the time and use of your instruments in a lab, be able to calculate how tall this man was based on these bones from his foot?"

"Yes. We'd also be able to examine the bones for possible diseases that he suffered. The body leaves many clues behind."

"Amazing, just amazing!" Delaney gushed. "Just by looking at those tiny foot bones, you could tell us how tall this man had been."

"That's correct," Dr. Nang said, clearly enjoying herself. "I can't be sure, but I'd guess the man whose bones are in this bag was about six feet."

"Would you be comfortable enough, say, to testify in a court that he was six feet tall?"

"Oh heaven's no!" Dr. Nang said. "I'd have to verify that in our lab."

"But you would be comfortable saying the bones were from a man's foot?"

"Yes, I would be comfortable testifying to that."

"Dr. Nang, I picked up these two bones this morning from a veterinarian lab at UVA. They're from a pig. They aren't even human bones."

Several spectators laughed.

"I see," Dr. Nang said, without any sign of embarrassment. "Well, I would like to point out that some pig bones and human bones are very similar."

Delaney had accomplished what she wanted: to show jurors that Dr. Nang, despite her impressive degrees and seemingly expert testimony, was capable of making mistakes.

"Dr. Nang, are you familiar with what happened in Oklahoma City not long ago?" Delaney asked.

"I assume you are talking about the police chemist situation?" Nang replied.

"That's correct, would you please tell the jurors about that?"

"A police chemist was accused of exaggerating her scientific findings in court. Unfortunately, these things happen."

"Isn't it true that this chemist helped convict a man who

had been wrongly accused of rape, and aren't authorities there reviewing another three thousand cases that she might have made errors in?"

"I object," Taylor Cauldwell said. "The fact that this chemist in Oklahoma City might have exaggerated doesn't have anything to do with this case."

"I'm simply trying to show that scientific testimony, while seemingly impressive, sometimes can be interpreted incorrectly," Delaney said. "In Oklahoma, that apparently happened three thousand times!"

"You've made your point," said Spencer. "Let's move on."

Delaney asked: "Would you please tell us again where semen was found on Cassie Arnold's pajamas?"

Dr. Nang repeated her earlier testimony—that semen had been found near the crotch of the pajama bottoms, on the seat of the pajama bottoms, and near the neck of the pajama blouse.

"You believe the killer masturbated while he was standing directly over the victim, who was bound and gagged on the floor underneath him—is that correct?" Delaney asked.

"Yes," Nang answered.

"Did you find any semen on Cassie Arnold's skin?"

"No."

"None?"

"That's right."

"If her pajama bottoms were pulled down around her feet, as you testified, and the killer was standing above her, wouldn't there have been semen on the victim's body, the floor, the newspapers, as well as on her pajama shirt?"

"I can't answer your question," Nang said. "I've never performed or seen any tests that would account for the trajectory of ejaculated semen."

Someone in the audience laughed and Spencer banged his gavel. "This is not humorous," he declared.

Delaney continued: "You found three samples on the pajamas. In other words, there was a glob in each spot. But you found none on her skin, the basement floor, the newspapers, or anywhere else. One of the locations where you found a sample was the rear panel—or the seat—of her pajama bottoms—isn't that correct?"

"Yes, we found some there."

"If the victim was lying on her back, as you believe she was, then how did it get on the seat of her pajama bottom?"

"I don't know," Nang said. "Perhaps she was struggling and lifted her legs."

"Your Honor," Taylor Cauldwell said, interrupting Delaney's cross-examination. "Dr. Nang has testified that the semen on the pajamas belonged to Lester Amil, and the defense, so far, has not challenged that. Who cares if it was on the front or the seat of the pajamas? It doesn't change the fact that he was there."

"What are you trying to demonstrate here?" Spencer asked Delaney.

"Judge, yesterday during Detective Stuart's testimony, the Commonwealth asked where male semen came from. Detective Stuart testified that if semen was found at a crime scene, then the person who had ejaculated, must have been there too. But that is wrong. In fact, we intend to prove that isn't what happened in this murder."

Cauldwell looked confused.

"The defense is not challenging the DNA tests that Dr. Nang performed," Delaney continued. "We're not denying that it was Lester Amil's or that it was found on the victim's pajamas. But by itself that doesn't prove anything because someone else put it there."

"What are you suggesting?" Spencer asked.

"We will prove that the real murderer collected Mr. Amil's semen from a condom. This condom had been worn by Mr. Amil when he had sex with a member of the Arnold household. The murderer then took the defendant's semen from the condom and wiped it on Cassie's pajamas in an attempt to frame Mr. Amil."

"I can't believe you're suggesting such a cockamamie story!" Cauldwell exclaimed.

"This explains why the location of the samples on the pajamas is so crucial," Delaney said, ignoring Cauldwell. "What Dr. Nang is describing is inconsistent with a man ejaculating over a body, especially a young man standing several feet directly over the victim. You have to ask yourself why did the semen fall only on the pajamas. Why wasn't it found elsewhere? And why did it fall in only three specific spots?"

"This is the most ludicrous defense I've ever heard!" Cauldwell replied.

Delaney turned on him. "If the prosecution would have done its job, it would have uncovered this!"

"Your Honor!" said Cauldwell. "Can we approach the bench for a sidebar before Ms. Delaney blurts out some far-fetched accusation and ruins someone's reputation?"

Spencer waved Cauldwell and Delaney toward him and reached under the bench to a shelf where Miss Alice had tucked several trial files. He was groping for a fresh legal pad from the stack that he kept stored there. As he reached for it, he noticed that Miss Alice had brought the stone, which had been sitting on his desk, along with his papers into the courtroom. She had placed it on top of the pads as a paperweight. Without thinking, he removed the stone with his left hand and grabbed a pad from the stack with his right hand. But before he could replace the stone, he felt a now familiar prick.

Before he could react, a bolt of electricity surged through him. It hit with such a force that it knocked him off his chair.

Spencer was inside Frank and Maxine Arnold's house. He could see himself walking upstairs. He was now entering Cassie Arnold's bedroom. It was dark and the little girl was in her bed sleeping. Suddenly, she opened her eyes and began crying. She kicked her comforter onto the floor. Her sheets were soaking wet and Spencer could smell urine. "Mama!" Cassie screamed. "Mama!"

Maxine Arnold came bursting into Cassie's bedroom.

"Goddamn it!" she cursed.

She grabbed her daughter's arm and jerked her roughly from the bed.

"How many times have I told you to wake yourself up and use the bathroom when you need to pee?"

Cassie began crying louder. "I tried!" she sobbed.

Maxine tugged at the bed's prefitted sheets, stripping them away from the soiled mattress while Cassie squatted nearby on the floor nearly hysterical.

"Get your clothes off," Maxine ordered.

Cassie had worn her street clothes to bed. She'd been too

tired to get into her pajamas after the hot air balloon ride and late dinner. When she was naked, her mother grabbed her and shoved her into the bathroom.

"Get in the shower and wash off!"

Cassie stepped into a shower stall while Maxine bent down and picked up a pair of pajamas that had been left on the bathroom floor earlier that morning.

"You can wear the same pajamas that you wore last night," she yelled. "The ones that you left on the floor this morning without putting them away. And stop your blubbering!"

Maxine left the room, carrying the soiled sheets and Cassie's wet clothing in her hands. She was furious and when she returned, she had become even angrier.

"Goddamn it, Cassie!" she cursed. "You peed so much I'll have to flip the mattress over!"

Maxine reached under the mattress, lifted it onto its side and then let it fall into place. She put new sheets on the bed. By this time, Cassie had gotten into the pajamas and rejoined her mother in the bedroom. She was still crying.

"Shut up!" Maxine screeched, but Cassie had worked herself into such a state of distress that she couldn't control herself. Maxine grabbed her and shook her violently. "I said shut up! Stop crying or I'll give you something to really cry about!"

Cassie tried to stop but couldn't.

Maxine slapped Cassie's face. Hard. The little girl fell to the floor and began wailing even louder. Maxine attacked, swinging both hands at the child. Cassie covered her head with her arms. Clearly out of control, Maxine lowered her aim and began hitting her daughter's back and buttocks.

Spencer had never seen such a violent attack.

"Shut up! Shut up! Shut up!" Maxine screamed. Finally, she pulled her daughter's hair, forcing Cassie to stand. As soon as she was upright, Maxine punched her hard across the face with a fist, knocking her down again.

It took Spencer several moments to understand the voices. He opened his eyes. He could see Cauldwell and Delaney standing over him. Now Miss Alice had joined them along with several strangers. It was the paramedics.

"Jesus, Spencer!" Cauldwell said. "You blacked out! You fell off your chair!"

Spencer's hands and legs felt numb.

"How long have I been out?"

"At least fifteen minutes," Cauldwell replied.

Spencer tried to sit up but the paramedics wouldn't let him. They were taking an EKG and demanded that he remain still. While lying on his back, he ordered Miss Alice to dismiss the jury and clear the courtroom. The paramedics carried him out of the courthouse on a stretcher. Doctors at Charlottesville General Hospital were waiting in the emergency room, but by the time he arrived there, he felt fine. Just the same, a series of tests were run that afternoon. None of them found a reason for his blackout.

This time around, Spencer didn't mention the white stone. He simply let his doctors stew over him.

Spencer did not believe in witchcraft, voodoo, or the occult. He did not believe in ghosts, goblins, or angels. If pushed, he would admit that he wasn't even certain that God existed. Mainly, he believed only in what his five senses told him. If he couldn't see it, smell it, taste it, hear it, or feel it, he was suspicious of it. And because of this, what he had experienced made him wonder if he were having a mental breakdown.

Logically, Spencer knew an ordinary stone could not possibly do what this stone had just done to him. Not once, but three times now. It didn't make sense. As he lay in the hospital, he thought about his most recent vision.

Was what I saw real? Did Maxine Arnold storm into Cassie's bedroom and beat her because she had wet her bed?

There had not been any mention in any investigative report by the police that said Cassie had wet her bed. Nor had anyone suggested that Maxine Arnold had struck her daughter.

But that's what I saw!

He replayed the scene in his mind. Over and over again. He remembered what it felt like to stand in Cassie's room. What it looked like. Although he had never physically set foot in the Arnold house, he felt confident that he could describe it accurately if asked. He had watched Maxine explode into a rage.

He'd seen her uncontrolled anger. He had heard Cassie's screams.

But was it real?

The more he pondered, the more convinced he became: *It happened. I'm sure of it.*

Somehow, in some supernatural way—the white rock had transported him into Cassie's bedroom and had let him see what had occurred.

I need to tell someone. Who?

Detective Stuart would demand to know how Spencer had discovered that Cassie had wet her bed.

How can I explain that a rock let me see Maxine beat her daughter? Everyone will think I was hallucinating.

Around eight o'clock, Spencer was discharged, but rather than going back to VanDenvender Hall, he took a taxi to the now-deserted courthouse. Slipping inside, he went upstairs and turned on the computer inside his chambers. Although Spencer was by no means computer savvy, he understood several fundamentals. One was that all e-mail correspondence could be traced, making it impossible to send an electronic message anonymously. But he also realized there were ways for hackers to circumvent this process and conceal their tracks. One morning, he had logged onto the *Charlottesville Courant*'s Web page to read a story from its archives. It had taken him several minutes to find the article and when it had finally appeared on his screen, he had noticed there was a line of blue type at the top of the page that said: "Click here to e-mail this story to a friend." Spencer had clicked on the tiny blue type and a small box had appeared: "Want to send a personal message with this story?"

He had typed "Hello Spencer!" and then had sent the story to himself so that he could read it later that night at home. Sure enough, when he had opened his e-mail that evening, the newspaper story had been waiting for him and when it popped onto his computer screen, the greeting: "Hello Spencer!" had appeared.

It was at that moment that he'd realized that the sender of the newspaper article was identified only as the *Charlottesville Courant*. There was no other return address that re-

vealed who had actually mailed it to him. Completely by accident, Spencer had discovered a way to send an e-mail message without revealing his own identity. All he had to do was
attach it to a newspaper story.

Spencer typed the Web address for the *Charlottesville
Courant* into his computer and called up Walter Corn's story
about yesterday's testimony in the Arnold trial. As soon as it
appeared, he clicked the blue type that said: "Click here to
e-mail this story to a friend" and entered Patti Delaney's e-mail
address. He'd found it in Miss Alice's directory of attorneys.

When the "send a message" box appeared, Spencer typed
five short sentences and then hit the computer's send button.

Patti Delaney was working at her computer in her office when
she heard the familiar voice from America Online announce:
"You've got mail!" But when she saw from the title that someone was forwarding Walter Corn's newspaper story to her, she
considered hitting the delete key without even bothering to
open it. Corn had made her seem like an idiot and she didn't
need someone sending her a copy as a reminder. Still, curiosity got the best of her and she finally opened it. A personal
note appeared at the top of the story:

> Cassie Arnold wet her bed on the night she was murdered.
> Maxine Arnold changed the bedsheets and flipped over the
> mattress. She lost control. She beat her daughter. That's how
> Cassie's lower back and buttocks got bruised.

Delaney immediately checked to see who had sent her the
message, but the *Charlottesville Courant* was the only name
listed on the return address. Her first reaction was that the note
was a prank. After all, she knew that after JonBenet Ramsey's
body had been found, the tabloid press had speculated that
JonBenet had wet her bed on the night that she had been murdered and that her mother had flown into a rage. There had
been absolutely no evidence to support that theory, but it had
made the rounds just the same.

Delaney printed out a copy of the note for her files, but
didn't pay much attention to it. She went back to what she was

doing. An hour later, Charles MacDonald telephoned Delaney from a pay phone at McCarren International Airport in Las Vegas.

"I've got it!" he exclaimed. "I've got the records this morning that describe how Maxine Arnold's first baby died."

Before Delaney could respond, MacDonald began describing how he had flashed his detective's badge at the Clark County Coroner's Office and persuaded a clerk there to let him read about the death of four-month-old Cynthia Gunter Wright.

"Maxine Arnold's first daughter died of SIDS—Sudden Infant Death Syndrome—and the coroner's office got involved because the Las Vegas police were suspicious," MacDonald blurted out. "They thought maybe the baby had been suffocated by one of her parents, but there wasn't enough evidence to prosecute."

"Maxine Arnold was a murder suspect?" Delaney asked.

"The autopsy didn't say anything about that," MacDonald replied, "but a clerk in the coroner's office remembered the case and told me that the cops thought Maxine might have suffocated her own baby by holding a pillow over her head. There was never any proof."

"My god!" Delaney exclaimed, "I got an e-mail tonight that said Maxine had beaten Cassie on the night of the murder because she had wet her bed."

"Who sent it to you?"

"I don't know. I assumed it was a prank."

Delaney's mind was racing. "Let's talk this through," she said. "Maxine is angry because Cassie wet her bed. She begins hitting her. At some point, Cassie falls and busts her head on a shelf or something—maybe a bedroom dresser. Cassie is dead. Maxine is horrified. But she doesn't panic. She knows she can't call the cops because they will check into her past and discover that her first baby died suspiciously. So Maxine decides to cover up the murder by blaming Lester Amil. She knows he is fascinated by the JonBenet case. She remembers the two of them had just had sex. The maid is gone to a funeral for the weekend, so no one has emptied the trash in her bathroom. She goes back to her bedroom where Frank is asleep. She fishes the condom out of the trash. Then she carries Cassie down into the basement and smears the semen from the inside of the condom onto Cassie's pajamas. Amil isn't home so it's easy to slip into his bedroom. She spots his personal identification badge on his desk and the stun gun that he has bought. She takes them both and then re-creates the murder scene to cover up what really happened. She makes it look exactly like the JonBenet case. Before she returns to her bedroom, she goes up to her husband's office and writes a fake ransom note."

"That's awfully cold-blooded," MacDonald said. He was trying to picture the scenario in his mind, trying to see if it made sense.

"How about Frank Arnold?" he asked. "Was he involved too?"

"I'm not sure."

After Spencer sent his anonymous e-mail to Delaney, he sat at his desk and simply stared at the stone. Miss Alice had collected it along with his legal papers from the courtroom and returned them to his chambers. He had now touched the rock three times and each time it had caused him to have a vision. The first now seemed unimportant. He had been floating in a sailboat. It made no sense. Seeing Melissa having sex in the stables—his second vision—had been more disturbing. And now he had seen Maxine Arnold beating Cassie.

Why is this happening to me? What's it all mean?

He decided there was a test that he could give himself to determine if the stone really did have some sort of magical power or if he were simply going nuts. He needed to touch it again. But he was afraid.

What if it knocked him unconscious again? Even more frightening: If the stone were mystical, what would it show him next? He leaned forward and started to reach for it, then stopped himself. *This is madness!* He grabbed it.

Nothing. No electrical burst. No vision. He held the rock for several minutes. Disgusted, he jerked open the bottom left drawer of his desk and dropped the rock into it. He slammed it shut and locked it. Now he was bewildered.

He felt exhausted but he didn't want to go home to VanDenvender Hall and face Melissa. His left hand hurt. He opened it. A second red slash had surfaced on his palm. *Where'd it come from?* The mark intersected with the slash that already was there. *It's a cross. There's a cross on my palm!*

He unlocked his desk drawer, opened it, and reached in for the stone. It was as if it were calling to him. As soon as it touched the cross in his palm, he felt a surge of power. That was the key. Left hand. Cross. Stone. Electricity. Vision.

He was standing outside the ranch-style house where he had lived when he was a child. Now he was walking inside. His mother was in the bedroom lying on the bed in her bright blue terry-cloth bathrobe. She was reading The Wizard of Oz *to a small boy cuddled next to her. Spencer recognized the boy. It was him when he was nine years old. He was wearing his pajamas, listening to his mother. He felt safe and warm. His father entered the room carrying a box wrapped as a birthday present. "This is for you." He watched the boy scramble to the foot of the bed and rip open the box. Boxing gloves. "C'mon champ, it's time you learned how to defend yourself." His father led him into the garage where they both put on gloves. "In a fight, you have to protect your head. You need to hold these gloves up in front of your face. But you have to be able to see. Hold your gloves like this." His father demonstrated the proper position. Evan tried to copy him. "No, you're holding them too close together. They're blocking your eyesight." His father gently shoved Evan's gloves apart. But Evan was afraid of getting hit in the face and immediately pushed the gloves back together to form a shield. Frustrated, his father smacked the gloves, causing them to snap back and hit Evan's nose. "Ouch!"*

His father laughed. "I told you to hold your gloves apart, like this." Evan tried to mimic him but as soon as his father lifted his own gloves, he instinctively pushed his pair together to shield his face. His father slapped his son's gloves harder, knocking them back into the boy's nose.

"That hurts!"

"Don't you dare cry! Part of boxing is getting hit, and the sooner you learn how to take a blow and not be afraid, the better off you will be." His father raised his own gloves into the

proper position and Evan once again hid behind his pair. Now angry, his father hit his son's gloves a third time—so hard they smashed into Evan's nose, causing it to bleed. Evan lunged at his father. His fists flew in all directions. Amused, his father placed his hand on his son's head, holding him at arm's length as Evan continued swinging his gloves wildly in the air. Finally, he fell forward onto his knees. His face a brilliant red.

"I hate you!" He tried to remove the boxing gloves, but couldn't because his father refused to untie them, so he ran into the house to his mother. "I hate him. I hate him." He reached out to her, but she shoved him away.

"He's your father! He loves you! You should honor your mother and your father. Now you go out there and apologize. Don't you know it's a sin to disrespect your father?"

"I hate him and wish he was dead! I don't care if it's a sin!"

It had been nearly forty years since Spencer and his father had boxed in the garage, but he had just lived through it once again. His father had been killed in an accident shortly after their confrontation.

"I'm sorry, Dad," Spencer said aloud.

He dropped the stone back into the desk drawer and locked it. He walked over to the leather couch in his chambers and lay down. *Am I crazy?* He suddenly thought about Patrick McPherson, the attorney who had mailed him the stone. He had killed himself.

Spencer spent the night on the couch trying to make sense of the events unfolding in his life, events that made no sense at all.

15

CHANCE AND COINCIDENCE ARE THE LIFEBLOOD OF LAS VEGAS. As soon as Charles MacDonald finished telephoning Patti Delaney on Thursday night from a pay phone at McCarran International Airport, he raced toward a gate where a flight from Washington Dulles Airport was unloading its passengers and about to board new ones for a return trip. As he dashed around a corner, he collided head-on with Kyle Dunham, the student who accompanied the Reverend Dr. Dino Grasso on his out-of-town travels. They had just arrived on the Dulles flight. MacDonald helped the dazed student to his feet, apologized, and then hurried to the gate. Neither he, Dunham, nor Grasso realized during the chance collision how fate would soon bring them together again.

The Most Reverend John Mackie of Saint Timothy's Parish was waiting outside the airport's baggage claim area to welcome Grasso and Dunham. But before they reached him, the two travelers had to make their way through a maze of slot machines and interior billboards. Dunham, who had spent most of the airplane ride reading about gambling, was mesmerized by the clanging sounds of quarters tumbling into stainless-steel trays and the eight-foot-tall showgirls dancing on monstrous plasma screens hanging above them.

"Welcome to the Devil's playpen!" Mackie quipped when they finally appeared. He led them out into the warm night air. Dunham's eyes were immediately drawn to the miles of neon lights on the Strip, which cast a yellow glow across the desert valley. The airport was more than a mile away, but the billion-dollar casinos were clearly visible.

"That green-colored one is the MGM Grand," Dunham said, eager to show off his new knowledge. "It's the biggest hotel in the United States, and see that tower at the opposite end of Las Vegas Boulevard that looks like the Space Needle?

It's the Stratosphere. It has a roller coaster that shoots around its top!"

While other cities displayed the local time and current temperature on billboards that welcomed travelers, the electronic digits outside McCarran Airport kept a running total of the progressive multimillion-dollar jackpot being offered by MegaBucks slots.

"Have you ever had a gambler leave casino chips in an offering plate?" Dunham asked.

"A few times," Mackie replied, "but like most stories told about this city, reports of gamblers giving their winnings to God are greatly exaggerated."

Mackie considered Dunham's enthusiasm for the city amusing, having lost his own fascination with gambling and glitz years ago. "My young friend," he lectured, "coming here should provide you with an interesting lesson. Evil rarely appears to us in the form of a frightening devil with a tail, horns, and a pitchfork. Rather, evil disguises itself in the most delicious temptations possible. The evil one seduces us with what we covet the most—fame, fortune, sex!"

Grasso listened to Mackie's minisermon in silence. He had decided long ago that Dunham was doomed to learn life's lessons, not by academic study or by heeding advice, but by blundering blindly ahead on his own.

It was a short ride from the airport into the sprawling subdivision that was home to Mackie's rectory. "Las Vegas has been America's fastest-growing city for nearly a decade now," Mackie explained. "Each time one of these new megacasinos opens, the size of our congregation swells. Gambling and God booming together!"

Saint Timothy's was a wood-and-brick contemporary building that could have easily passed for a community center except for the octagonally shaped bell tower that arose from its copper-covered roof. It was surrounded by cookie-cutter two-story stucco houses with red clay tile roofs and gray fieldstone patios, oval-shaped backyard swimming pools, and swatches of green turf enclosed behind six-foot-tall privacy walls made of brown adobe. Once, only scorpions and lizards dared to live in the scorching desert. Now it was home to four-wheel-drive SUVs, automatic lawn-sprinkling systems, and imported palm trees.

"I'm afraid our accommodations will not be on the same par as the Bellagio or the Venetian," Mackie warned, as they pulled into the church's parking lot. "But, you should find them adequate." He escorted them into a one-story brick dormitory behind the church. The guest room inside had brown linoleum floors and concrete block walls painted off-white. Crucifixes were hanging above each of the two single beds. A reproduction of the Madonna and child by the artist Raphael was the only decoration. There were two gray metal desks, two metal chairs, two sets of white towels. There was no television, no radio, not even a clock, but there were two copies of the Holy Bible. "This will do fine," Grasso said, ignoring the disappointed look on Dunham's face.

"Morning prayers are at five, breakfast at six," Mackie explained. "What time is your appointment at the casino?"

"Nine," Grasso replied.

"At seven, we have a Bible study group for men . . . several of them work at the casinos . . . perhaps you and Mr. Dunham would like to join us."

"I would enjoy that," said Grasso, "but I doubt my young friend will be awake that early."

The next morning, Grasso left a snoring Dunham and joined the other priests in the rectory's usual routine. He enjoyed himself and honestly could not imagine why anyone would prefer a high roller's suite at Caesars Palace over the simplicity and comradeship of the rectory. Dunham was still sleeping when Grasso returned at eight. Fifty minutes later, the car and driver that Mackie was providing them drove underneath the belly of the giant sphinx standing guard at the Luxor's entrance. The flesh-colored beast, with the face of a pharaoh, served as a grandiose portico to the black pyramid. Grasso walked slowly down the slight incline that led into the resort's entrance.

"Whoa!" Dunham exclaimed as soon as they stepped inside. He and Grasso were facing a life-size re-creation of the exterior of the Temple of Ramses II. The facade was more than forty feet tall and was decorated with stone columns, gilding, and hieroglyphic writing. In its center was an archway that led into the casino. Gargantuan twin statues of seated pharaohs were posted on each side of the arch. Blue-tinted pools of water flowed from the pharaohs' feet toward Dunham and Grasso like beckoning fingers. More stone columns and carvings of Egyptian princesses lined the pools, creating a semicircle that subtly funneled guests from the glass entrance doors toward the slot machines and gaming tables. The sound of craps dealers calling the dice, the clanging of electronic bells and shrieking whistles, and the cheers and curses of gamblers drifted seductively through the archway. Grasso sensed that Dunham was eager to try his luck. "Go ahead," he said. "I can make it from here." Dunham hurried into the casino.

Grasso hobbled into the Luxor's ornate lobby to his right and pushed open a glass door with the words "VIP Lounge: Invited Guests Only" etched in gold on it. An attractive young woman wearing a black business suit and white silk blouse stood immediately from behind her desk.

"How may I be of service to you?"

Grasso told her that the Luxor's general manager had agreed to let him interview the casino's chief of security. The woman telephoned the general manager's secretary and five minutes later a husky man with a crew cut arrived.

"I'm Gaetano Luzi," he said. "Chief of Security. Let's go to my office." He led Grasso out across the lobby to a private elevator that took them to the resort's basement.

"First visit to Las Vegas, Padre?"

"Yes," Grasso replied. "It's quite a spectacular sight."

They walked down a bustling hallway into a rectangular room that had a huge blackboard posted just inside its doorway with the names and assignments of all the security officers currently on duty scrawled on it in yellow chalk. There were at least a dozen gray file cabinets in the room and a sixty-cup coffee urn was sitting on a metal cart in a corner surrounded by stacks of Styrofoam cups, napkins, and pink packets of sweeteners. Two secretaries greeted them as they continued through this outer room into Luzi's private office. The security chief motioned Grasso toward an office chair covered with faded blue fabric sitting next to a four-foot-tall dead corn plant. Luzi's office was decorated with several framed educational certificates, a large plaster of paris FBI insignia, and nearly a hundred shoulder patches from different police departments that had been given to him by law enforcement officers who had stopped by to introduce themselves during their vacations. Many had also been looking for jobs.

Luzi removed a thin manilla file from a cabinet drawer marked "Suicides."

"Our policy is to NOT show outsiders our security reports," he explained. "When I came here ten years ago from the local FBI office, I implemented the same procedures that we had in the bureau. I even began using the same government 302 Report forms. Professionalism has been and still is my top priority."

"You worked at the FBI?"

Luzi smiled. "Italian name, casino security chief—let me guess—the FBI was not the first organization that came to mind when we met."

"I meant no offense."

"Don't worry, Father, I'm used to it. Most of the casinos here have former special agents or police chiefs running their security operations. The mob days are long gone, but if you're Italian and live in Las Vegas, everyone assumes you're connected. I think the tourists really enjoy believing we're all cousins of Tony Soprano. Actually, I was a special agent for fifteen years until the bureau wanted me to transfer back to Washington headquarters. My son was just entering high school and my wife and I really liked the area, so I quit and became a casino cop. Now Padre, let me ask you a few questions: Why are you interested in Patrick McPherson? Was he a close friend?"

"No, we never met. I simply want to learn why he killed himself."

"Padre," Luzi said, with a tone of skepticism, "we've had lots of suicides but you're the first priest who's ever showed up to investigate one. There's got to be more behind your visit than simple curiosity. Was he an important person in the church?"

"No. I'm afraid I'm not really able to tell you why I am interested because it concerns a religious matter, but let me assure you that I'm not here to investigate your handling of his suicide, nor am I searching for anything that might reflect poorly on the Luxor."

"Sorry to be so suspicious, but you wouldn't believe the nuisance lawsuits we get filed against us," Luzi said. "Everyone thinks a casino owes them something, especially if they've lost at the tables. We've had a couple sue us because the housekeeping staff forgot to empty a trash can and there was a used condom in it. They claimed they had been exposed to the AIDS virus. I just wanted to make certain you weren't working for a lawyer, posing as a priest."

Luzi handed him a three-page, typewritten report. "I've been instructed to allow you to read this. I was proud of my officers. Besides immediately securing the accident scene, they interviewed twelve casino patrons who either saw Mr. McPherson jump or who had spoken to him earlier in the casino. In addition, I have an itemized list of McPherson's personal property, which was returned to his widow."

Grasso read the suicide report slowly.

At approximately 21:30 hours, a hotel guest, later identified as Patrick McPherson, a white male in his late forties from Boston, Massachusetts, committed suicide by jumping from the twenty-eighth floor of the hotel into the atrium. His body landed in the McDonald's fast food restaurant, exploding, with his head parts hitting several guests.

The report went on to note that the Clark County Sheriff's Office had been notified at 21:40. At the bottom of the report, a small box next to the words "videotape" had been checked.

Grasso asked what that meant.

"We got video of him jumping," Luzi explained. "You see, Padre, everything, and I do mean everything, that takes place in the public areas of the Luxor is watched by the 'eyes in the sky' . . . our security cameras. We've got cameras that can zoom in on every gambling table in the casino, plus we've got cameras watching every inch of the lobby, the hotel corridors, the resort's perimeter, the casino cage—that's where we keep the chips and money—the count rooms—where we count the money, hell we got cameras everywhere, more than two thousand of them."

"You have a videotape of McPherson committing suicide?"

"Yep, we've got tapes of him gambling in the casino too. Listen, this might be easier to understand if I showed you our main security room."

Luzi led Grasso out of the office and down a long passageway. All of the glamour of the Luxor, with its marble floors and ornate Egyptian decorations, was missing here. The concrete floors were painted institutional gray, the walls were undecorated sheets of white wallboard. "This resort is like a small city," Luzi explained, "and this basement is our city hall. The resort's general manager is our mayor. I'm the equivalent of a city police chief, the director of retail sales is our chamber of commerce guy—there's about thirteen various directors in all and all of us have offices down here." Luzi stopped outside an unmarked door with a peephole at eye level. He knocked and then spoke into an intercom next to the doorway. "It's me and one guest."

It took a moment for Grasso's eyes to adjust after they entered the dark room. One wall was filled with flickering television screens: ten in a row, six rows high. Three men were sitting in front of the screens behind a panel of switches and dials.

"My officers here control the 'eyes in the sky.' They're the very best on the entire Strip at catching cheats. You know how I know they're the best? Because two of them are former cheats and the third is the guy who caught them. Between them there isn't a casino con that's been invented that one of them doesn't already know."

Grasso scanned the screens, trying to make sense of the pictures that changed every few seconds. Kyle Dunham's image suddenly appeared on a monitor. He was gambling at a blackjack table.

"That young man came into the casino with you," one of Luzi's officers said. "We watched you go into the VIP lounge and watched him enter the casino."

"Zero in on him," Luzi ordered. One of the men flipped a

switch and the video camera above the blackjack table focused on an unsuspecting Dunham and his cards. He had been dealt two queens.

"Your buddy doesn't know much about twenty-one, does he?" Luzi asked.

"Has he done something wrong?"

"The dealer has an eight showing," Luzi explained. "Your buddy has two face cards, which means he's got a lock on twenty, which should be a winning hand. But he just signaled that he is splitting his queens. That means he is separating the queens into two different hands. Watch what happens now."

The dealer dealt Dunham a seven to go along with one queen and a six to go with the other.

"Now he has a seventeen and a sixteen."

As Grasso watched, the dealer flipped over his card, revealing a ten, which gave him eighteen. The dealer won.

Luzi said: "Your buddy took a winning hand and turned it into two losing hands, probably because he got greedy."

Grasso watched the dealer on the TV screen collect Dunham's twenty-dollar bet.

"Father, be sure to thank him for the donation," one of the other men quipped.

Luzi instructed his officers to put on "the jumper tape," and the image of a man standing precariously on the ledge of the twenty-eighth floor flashed onto a monitor. "That's Patrick McPherson," Luzi said. As they all watched, McPherson released his grip and fell forward. Grasso noticed that McPherson seemed relaxed, almost serene.

"He's doing a swan dive," Luzi said. "Unbelievable, huh?"

"Yeah, a perfect ten," one of his men joked.

Luzi wasn't amused. "Sorry, Padre," he said. "You've got to understand that humor is one way we deal with things like this."

Grasso was preoccupied studying the tape. A crowd had gathered around what was left of McPherson's body. Grasso was searching for the *giudicare* stone. Unfortunately, he wasn't certain what it looked like. He scanned the video but didn't see it.

"We have video of him gambling too," Luzi volunteered.

Once again, McPherson's image appeared on a monitor, this time at a blackjack table.

"All of us remember this guy, but not just because he killed himself," Luzi said. "He was an incredibly lucky card player."

"He was the luckiest son of a bitch we'd ever seen," one of the men added.

"When we first spotted him," Luzi explained, "we thought he was cheating. We assumed he was a member of a card-counting team. You know about card counting, Padre?"

Grasso said no.

"At any time during blackjack, the deck is either going to favor the house or the players. A skilled gambler tries to figure out when the odds are most in his favor. He does it by counting cards. He doesn't really memorize the cards that have been dealt. Rather, he keeps a running count in his head of pluses and minuses. It's a complicated procedure. A mathematician invented it. But the point is that we get a lot of card counters in here and the really smart ones work as a team. One guy will count the deck and when it gets 'juicy'—in the player's favor—he signals his partner, who then runs over and puts down a large bet. It ain't illegal, but if we catch someone doing it, then we ban them from playing in the casino."

One of Luzi's men in the room picked up the story. "We thought McPherson was a card counter because he played the game perfectly. He knew when to bet big and when to lay low. I swear he knew what cards were being dealt before they came out of the shoe. He was either counting cards or somehow cheating us because no one is that lucky."

"We couldn't figure out how he was doing it," Luzi said. "We changed dealers on him to make certain he and the dealer weren't working together. We changed decks every few minutes to make certain he wasn't marking them somehow. We watched his every move and we still couldn't figure out how he was winning. What he was doing was mathematically impossible."

"What really blew our minds," one of Luzi's men added, "was when he finished playing, he always gave away his winnings. Of course, we didn't know he was going to kill himself. At one point, we sent one of our undercover security officers to play next to him. See that blond woman on the monitor up there—she's sitting next to him at the table—the one with the big tits?"

Luzi quickly apologized for his man's description, but Grasso didn't seem offended.

"Anyhow," the officer continued, "she's one of the slickest card players in town and she couldn't figure out how he was beating us. She got him talking and he told her that he'd never really played blackjack that much before. And she didn't think he was lying! He gave her all of his winnings just before he made his jump."

"We only noticed one thing odd about him," Luzi recalled. "The first time he came into the casino, he was carrying this rock. We get lots of customers with lucky charms—rabbits' feet, four-leaf clovers—for a while, our Asian players had a thing for fake eyeballs. They'd put them right on the table next to them. Now your friend McPherson pulled out this rock and said it was his lucky charm."

"Did the dealer touch it?" Grasso asked.

"No, McPherson just held it in his lap. He only brought it with him into the casino one time. After that, he didn't seem to need it."

"Do you have videotape of him with the rock?"

"Of course," one of the men replied. He flipped several dials and a new image appeared of McPherson sitting at a blackjack table with a smooth stone resting on his right thigh.

There it is! The stone!

"So tell me, Padre," said Luzi. "Was there something in the rock—you know—a computer chip or something?"

"No, as far as I know it was just a rock."

They watched the videotapes of McPherson for several more minutes and then returned to Luzi's office. "You mentioned you had a list of everything McPherson left behind at the hotel after he killed himself," Grasso said. "May I see it?" Luzi fished an inventory from the file folder and handed it to him.

"If you're trying to find that lucky rock of his," Luzi asked, "I already checked. It isn't listed there."

"Do you know what became of it?"

"I don't have a clue. My officers swear he didn't leave it behind in his hotel room, and it wasn't found on his body, or what was left of his body. I think if any of them were lying to me and stole it, I'd know by now."

"How?"

"I faxed a warning to the other casinos on the Strip when I first noticed how lucky McPherson was at the tables. We share information all of the time about big winners. After McPherson killed himself, I wrote a short note about him and mentioned his lucky rock. The other security chiefs gave me a hard time about it, kidding me, you know. But if someone had shown up with a rock as a good luck charm and had started winning big, believe me, they would've called here, especially if it was one of my own employees."

"Do you have a copy of McPherson's final hotel bill?" Grasso asked. Luzi pulled a receipt from the file and handed it to him. One of the charges listed there was for services provided by the Luxor Business Center. "What's that?" Grasso asked.

"It's an office away from home for hotel guests. There's a computer, fax machines, you can write e-mail, pick up packages, that sort of thing."

"There's a charge on McPherson's bill for forty-five dollars from the center," Grasso noted. "Can you find out what that charge was for?"

Luzi called the business center and asked its manager to check McPherson's original invoice. A few minutes later, the clerk called back with the information. "It seems Patrick McPherson sent a package by Federal Express," Luzi explained after he had hung up the telephone. "The clerk remembers McPherson because he was extremely nervous when he brought the package in to be mailed. The clerk was worried he might be sending something illegal, such as drugs, or maybe a large amount of cash because McPherson kept asking questions about what would happen if the package got lost or was ripped open by accident. Finally, the clerk asked him what he was mailing and McPherson told her it was his lucky rock. So I guess, Padre, you've solved the mystery of what happened to his magic rock. For a priest, you're a good detective."

"Did your clerk tell you just now where McPherson sent his lucky rock?"

"It was mailed to a Judge Evan Spencer at the courthouse in Charlottesville, Virginia."

Luzi escorted Grasso upstairs into the Luxor's lobby. "Padre, I don't know what's in that rock," Luzi said, "or why you're so interested in finding it. But if McPherson somehow found a way to use a stone to cheat us, I'd appreciate a call." Luzi paused and then added, "I also should warn you that I will be faxing a brief note to other casino security chiefs later today about our visit. No offense, but if you show up in Las Vegas in a few days with a lucky rock and begin winning, I'll be paying you a visit."

"I guess in your line of work, you can't afford to trust anyone, can you?"

Luzi pointed a finger at a black bubble in the lobby's ceiling. It was an 'eye in the sky' watching them. "Around here," Luzi said, "everyone watches everyone else and the cameras watch us all."

Grasso found Dunham feeding nickels into a slot machine. "I lost two hundred dollars playing blackjack," he confessed. "I read two books about gambling before we got here and it sounded easy."

"What do you expect," Grasso asked, "when you split two queens?"

A stunned Dunham glanced up from his seat at Grasso. "How did you know I did that?"

Grasso didn't explain. Instead, he led his young protégé outside to their waiting car. "Where we going now?" Dunham asked.

"Charlottesville, Virginia. There is a judge there we need to visit."

16

CHARLES MACDONALD CAUGHT A QUICK NAP ON THE RETURN flight from Las Vegas to Dulles Airport and then drove straight to Charlottesville early Friday morning so he could brief Patti Delaney before the third day of the murder trial began. Maxine Arnold was scheduled to take the stand as the day's star prosecution witness.

"We've got to get her to admit she had sex with Lester Amil twenty-four hours before Cassie was murdered, otherwise we'll never be able to prove how our client's semen ended up on Cassie's pajamas," MacDonald warned.

"She has to know we're onto her," Delaney replied, "because I've already said in court that someone doctored the pj's. She'll have her guard up."

They quickly decided the best way to entrap Maxine was by confronting her about Cassie's bed-wetting.

"She won't expect us to know about it," MacDonald said. "Then we can go for her jugular by asking her point blank if she beat Cassie to death that night and then framed our client."

Delaney hesitated. "We don't want jurors to think we're attacking a despondent mother. We've got to set the stage first by proving she's a liar and discrediting her, otherwise we'll just look like cold-hearted defense attorneys who will say anything to defend their client."

"Look, Maxine Arnold beat her daughter to death," MacDonald said. "She's a bitch. Push her and that's sure to come out."

"I don't think Maxine intended to kill Cassie. I think she lost her temper, you know, probably went nuts for a few minutes. I'm sure it was an accident."

"Hey," MacDonald said, his face suddenly filled with anger, "that woman murdered a child. She needs to pay for what she did."

The intensity of MacDonald's reaction surprised her. She'd

never seen him so passionate about wanting someone punished. She said: "I'm a little nervous about questioning her. We've got a lot riding on this theory and we're basing our entire strategy on an e-mail from a source who's afraid to even tell us his name."

With much empathy, Attorney General Taylor Cauldwell led Maxine Arnold gingerly through the events of the morning when she first discovered her only daughter was missing.

"I fell completely apart when my husband found Cassie's body," Maxine testified, her voice quivering. She looked past Cauldwell, her eyes settling on Lester Amil. "We trusted you," she said coldly. "And you murdered her! You bastard!"

"Objection!" Delaney exclaimed.

"The jury will disregard the witness's last statement," Spencer said. Turning to face Maxine, he said: "Mrs. Arnold, all of us are aware of how distraught you are because of your daughter's death, but you need to control yourself. I'm not going to have an appellate court sending this case back for a new trial because you failed to keep your emotions in check."

She nodded pitifully. "I'm sorry, Your Honor." Her eyes were wet with tears. "I apologize to you and to the jury. It's just so difficult. I want him to pay for what he did to my baby."

Delaney started to object but Spencer waved her down.

"Let's get on with this," he said.

Cauldwell asked his next question. "Mrs. Arnold, how did you come to know the defendant?"

"My husband is a genius. He's made plenty of money. More than we can ever spend. We already have several houses and too many cars. So we try to find ways to help others who are less fortunate. We were watching the television news in our Los Angeles home one night and there was a report on it about a black teenager living in one of the city's worst neighborhoods. The news reporter said Lester had five brothers and two sisters and all of them—except for him—had ruined their lives by getting involved in drugs and street gangs. Three of his brothers were in prison, two were dead, and both of his sisters were prostitutes—it's how they supported their crack habits. Then there was Lester. He'd never missed a day of school, had never joined a gang. He helped his mother around the house, sang in church on Sundays, earned good grades. His dream was to attend college but he couldn't afford it. At least that's what the reporter said."

"You were deeply touched by this news report?"

"Absolutely. The day after we saw it, my husband had his company's public relations manager call the TV station and arrange for us to meet Lester. We were going to pay for his college education. The news reporter set up a meeting but the day before it, a gang firebombed Lester's house. They were furious about the news story, I guess."

"His house was firebombed?"

"Yes, Lester's mother and one of his brothers, who had just gotten out of prison, were burned to death. Lester wasn't at home. He didn't have anywhere to live, so we invited him to move in with us."

"That was very generous of you."

Maxine Arnold lowered her eyes modestly. "It's what anyone in our position would have done."

Cauldwell asked if Amil had fit easily into the family

"Cassie idolized him. I think she even had a schoolgirl's crush on him."

"Sounds idyllic!" Cauldwell said. "A Cinderella fairy tale come true."

"It was wonderful at first. But then Lester changed, or maybe he just wasn't really the person who that TV news reporter said he was. When it came time for him to fill out college applications, he began making excuses. I thought he was embarrassed because the school in his neighborhood had been atrocious. I think he knew he'd flunk out if he went to a really good university, so we suggested that he wait a year to apply. We hired a tutor to help him."

"So you were still doing your best to save him from the ghetto?"

"Yes, we were. But Lester lost all interest in college. All he talked about was becoming a hip-hop star and writing rhymes—that awful gangster rap. Because Lester wasn't interested in college anymore, Frank gave him a job, public relations, basically a meet-and-greet position, working with other

African Americans. But Lester didn't want to do anything but focus on his music. He developed a real nasty attitude."

"What do you mean?"

Maxine turned in her chair so she could talk directly to the jurors. "Frank and I decided to host a party in Charlottesville to introduce ourselves to the community. Frank really liked a song that Lester had written about a determined, young black man who pulls himself out of the inner city. It's called: 'Gotta Believe!' Frank asked Lester to sing it at our party. Now this was our first party here, so we wanted to make a good impression. Well, you can imagine our shock when Lester betrayed us and sang a completely different song. Even worse, this song blamed all of the black man's problems on white America. It was insulting to our guests."

Delaney thought Maxine's testimony sounded rehearsed. Lester Amil leaned close to her at the defense table. "She's lying!" he said. "I sang the song they asked me to sing."

Maxine Arnold continued: "Frank felt betrayed. That night, he gave Lester one week to pack up his stuff and move out. The next morning was a Saturday and none of us talked much. On Sunday, I suggested we go on a hot air balloon ride. I thought it was funny, you know, since there had been a lot of 'hot air' being let off by all of us."

She forced a smile and then dabbed her eyes with a tissue.

"Do you need a break?" Cauldwell asked.

"No," she said, "I want to keep going." She dabbed her eyes again. "After that ride, Lester asked to speak to us in private Sunday night, and I assumed he was going to apologize for his belligerent attitude and rude behavior. But instead, he accused us of using him as a 'token house nigger'—those were his exact words."

" 'A token house nigger?' "

"Yes, and then he tried to blackmail us."

"Blackmail you?"

"Yes, he said if we didn't give him a hundred thousand dollars so he could make a record album, he'd hold a press conference and accuse us of making all sorts of terrible racist remarks in the privacy of our home. He said people would believe him and Frank's reputation would be destroyed, and then he made an even more horrible threat."

She was starting to cry and needed a moment to catch her breath.

"What did he say?"

"He said he'd tell everyone that I'd seduced him! It was a horrible lie. But he said he'd go straight to the *National Enquirer* and they'd print it!"

Spencer had to bang his gavel to quiet the whispers in the courtroom gallery. Delaney shot a disgusted glance at Mac-Donald. Maxine Arnold had clearly guessed where they were headed with their defense. She was launching her own pre-emptive attack by accusing Amil of lying about their relationship before he could reveal that they'd had an affair.

"Mrs. Arnold," Cauldwell said, "when Lester Amil tried to blackmail you, did you consider him dangerous?"

"Yes, I did!" She turned and stared straight at Amil. "But Frank thought he could handle him. He told him to go straight to hell and that he had twenty-four hours to get out of the house. But neither of us ever dreamed he'd hurt our little Cassie!"

Maxine began to sob. Miss Alice handed her a fresh box of tissues and after a few moments, it appeared as if she had regained her composure. But as soon as she caught her breath, she began sobbing again. "I'm sorry," she blubbered. "I'm not sure I can continue!"

Delaney surveyed the jurors. Three of them were about to cry too.

"Let's adjourn for lunch," Spencer said.

Following MacDonald's advice, Delaney didn't waste time with niceties when it was her turn to question Maxine.

"You testified this morning that you and your husband have more money than you'll ever need. That's why you decided to help people less fortunate. People like my client. Is that right?" she asked sharply.

"Yes."

"Then tell us about Carol Webis. Who is she?"

The question surprised her. "Why, she's my younger sister."

"So is she rich too?"

"No."

"In fact, your sister and her husband and their four children are on welfare, receiving food stamps—isn't that correct? Your brother-in-law lost his job several months ago, and when your sister called you and begged you for help, you and your husband turned up your noses. You called them losers, didn't you?"

Cauldwell objected. "This has no relevance, judge," he said. "She's badgering the witness."

"Ms. Delaney," Spencer said, "I'm having a difficult time myself seeing a connection here. What's your point?"

"It goes to the witness's credibility. She has testified that she and her husband are generous. But they haven't helped her own flesh and blood. I'm trying to establish that the Arnolds had other motives besides altruism when they reached out to Lester Amil."

"May I say something?" Maxine asked. Without waiting for Spencer to answer, she said: "My husband and I have been paying the rent on my sister and her husband's mobile home for more than a year now. We've established college trust funds for all of their children. I don't wish to badmouth my sister, but she and her husband are poor because they have made poor choices. We're doing what we can to help them, but we don't want to cripple them by simply giving them cash whenever they get into a jam."

Delaney glanced at MacDonald who was sitting on the other side of Amil at the defense table. Carol Webis had never mentioned the rent payments and college trust funds. And in his eagerness to believe the worst about the Arnolds, Mac-Donald hadn't asked about such things.

So far, Delaney's frontal attack was scoring points but for the wrong side.

Delaney decided to switch subjects. "Why'd you go directly downstairs after you woke up on the morning of the murder? Why'd you get the orange juice and milk out of the refrigerator in the kitchen before you went upstairs into Cassie's room to wake her? Did you already know she was missing?"

"Judge," Cauldwell said, once again rising to his feet. "She's not letting the witness answer. She's bombarding her with questions."

"Let's ask one question at a time, Ms. Delaney," Spencer said.

"Yes, Your Honor. Why did you go downstairs first before going into your daughter's room?"

"I wanted to let Cassie sleep a few minutes longer. We were all recuperating from the Friday night party and an exhausting weekend."

"I think most mothers would've made sure their daughter was awake before fixing them breakfast," Delaney said.

"Judge," Cauldwell interrupted, "who's testifying here?"

"Ms. Delaney," Spencer said, "please ask a question, let the witness answer, and then ask another question."

Delancy realized that she was looking amateurish to the jury. But she didn't mind. It was part of her strategy. She walked from the podium over to the defense table where she picked up a file folder. She took a moment to read something in it. When she returned to the lectern, she was still holding the file. "Mrs. Arnold, did you leave your bedroom on the night of the murder?"

"No," she answered, without any hesitation. "Frank woke me. He said he heard a noise. I had a terrible headache so I got up, went into our bathroom, took some painkillers and a sleeping pill, and then went back to bed. The last thing I remember is Frank saying that Lester had come home for the night."

"So you didn't leave your bedroom and go into Cassie's room on the night that she was killed?"

"No." Her voice had an edge to it. "I just explained that I never left our bedroom."

"You didn't go down to check on Cassie that night?"

"No," she replied. "I've already answered your question twice. My husband heard a noise. He woke me up. I went into the bathroom, took the pills, and then went back to bed. I did not leave the bedroom that night!"

"And you are absolutely certain of that, I mean, your testimony is that you never left your bedroom on the night of the murder?"

"Your Honor," Cauldwell said, again rising to his feet.

"Mrs. Arnold has said three times that she went back to bed without leaving the bedroom. Once again, the defense is badgering this witness."

In a stern voice, Spencer said: "Let's move on here."

Delaney looked at the file again that she was holding in her hand.

"Mrs. Arnold, why didn't you tell anyone that Cassie wet her bed?"

The question caught her completely off guard. "I'm not sure I know what you're talking about."

Delaney removed a sheet of paper from the file folder. "The forensic team that investigated your daughter's murder prepared an inventory of every item that was found in your daughter's room and in her bathroom. According to the report that I am now holding, there were several boxes of disposable diapers found in the cupboard in Cassie's bathroom. You kept those diapers there because your daughter had a bed-wetting problem—didn't she?"

"Ur, ah, well, she did wet her bed sometimes, but all children have accidents now and then."

"Your daughter was almost twelve, wasn't she?" Delaney replied. "That's a bit old for bed-wetting. You got angry when your daughter wet her bed, didn't you?"

"Not really angry, disappointed perhaps. I mean, I didn't like it. What mother would? But accidents like that happen."

"How did you react when Cassie wet her bed on the night of the murder?"

"I object," Cauldwell said. "The witness hasn't testified that Cassie wet her bed that night. She's simply acknowledged that Cassie wet her bed occasionally."

Delaney glanced down at the forensic report that she was still holding in her hand. She took a moment and silently read a portion of it. "Your Honor, I'll rephrase my question. Mrs. Arnold, according to this forensic report, ur, wait, let me rephrase my question again: Mrs. Arnold, if Cassie didn't wet her bed on the night of the murder, why were soiled sheets from her bed found the next day in the upstairs laundry room? You put them there, didn't you? You removed them from Cassie's bed and put them there."

For the first time since she had taken the witness chair, Maxine Arnold looked confused. She glanced at her husband who was seated in the front row. Then she looked at Cauldwell. She apparently was expecting the prosecutor to come to her aid by objecting, but he was busy rummaging through his files.

"Please answer the question," Spencer said.

"This has been a traumatic experience," Maxine replied. "I mean, you've got to understand the impact that losing Cassie has had on me, on us. I guess, I, ur, ah, I guess I must have blocked out some of the events that happened that night. Yes, you're right. Now that you have reminded me, Cassie did wet her bed on that night. She had fallen asleep in her clothes and I made her get into her pajamas while I changed the sheets. I'm really embarrassed. I'm sorry. I simply forgot."

"Your Honor," Cauldwell said, "I'm having difficulty finding any mention in the forensic reports about soiled sheets being found in the upstairs laundry. The report does say there were disposable diapers found in the bathroom, but there's nothing in my copies about wet sheets in the upstairs laundry room. May I ask what report Ms. Delaney is reading from?"

"I never said the forensic team found soiled sheets," Delaney said gloatingly. "If you will recall, I rephrased my question and simply stated that there were wet sheets found there."

Maxine suddenly realized that she had been tricked. Like Cauldwell, she had assumed that Delaney had read about the wet sheets in the typewritten report—when, in fact, the report had never mentioned them.

"Your Honor," Cauldwell said. "I'd like to know how Ms. Delaney knew Cassie had wet her bed that night and had wet bedsheets? Where's this information coming from—thin air?"

She knew because I sent her an e-mail and told her about them. I saw Maxine Arnold strip the bed and take the sheets out of the room, thought Spencer.

"The witness has confirmed that her daughter wet the bed," Spencer said. "She's also testified that she removed the soiled sheets from Cassie's room. Exactly how Ms. Delaney discovered this information is immaterial. Let's move on."

Delaney, however, wasn't quite ready to move on. She

wanted to make certain that the jurors understood what had just happened. She also wanted to reemphasize that the witness had lied to them.

"When I asked you earlier if you had left your room on the night of the murder, you said no," Delaney said. "In fact, Mrs. Arnold, you told me three times that you had never left your room that night. You were emphatic about it. You said you had never gone into Cassie's room. But now you're admitting that you did leave your room and that you did go into Cassie's room because she'd wet her bed and called you. Is that right? You went into her room, helped her into her pajamas and you changed the sheets on her bed. Is that your testimony now?"

"Yes," Maxine replied coldly. "I'd forgotten that I had gone into her room."

During the next several minutes, Maxine Arnold revealed a side of her personality that jurors had not seen earlier. The tears were gone, replaced by antagonism. Delaney pelted her with questions, irking her even more.

Was your daughter crying when you went to check on her?

Did you swear at her?

Were you angry?

Did you drag Cassie into the bathroom and tell her to take a shower?

Had you been drinking earlier?

What kind of pain medicine did you take?

Do you normally mix alcohol and pain medicine?

Maxine Arnold bitterly spat out her answers.

Finally, after pushing Maxine to the point where her voice was laced with acid, Delaney asked: "Did you fly into a rage and strike your daughter that night because she'd wet her bed?"

"How dare you!" Maxine screeched. Once again, she looked to Cauldwell for support, but the prosecutor didn't move from his chair.

"Your Honor, would you please instruct the witness to answer my question?" Delaney asked.

Maxine tried to calm herself. "Like all good and loving parents," she said slowly, "there were times, not many, but a few, when I physically disciplined my daughter. On those few occasions, I gave her a light pat on her bottom or a slap on her hand—just to get her attention and mostly when she was much younger."

"Dr. Nang testified that Cassie had bruises on her lower back and buttocks," Delaney replied. "Some of these bruises appeared to be older than others. Now, Mrs. Arnold, I'm going to remind you that you are under oath to tell the truth. Once again, I'm going to ask you: Did you strike Cassie when you went into her bedroom and discovered she had wet her bed?"

"I had a horrible headache that night when my husband woke me up. I was totally exhausted and I had just been awakened from a deep sleep. I don't remember my every move, but I can tell you this: I loved my daughter and I never would have harmed her."

"You haven't answered my question. Did you strike, hit, kick, or physically discipline your daughter in any way that night?"

Maxine replied slowly: "I may have given her a swat on her bottom. But I never beat her!"

"One swat does not leave bruises like those that Dr. Nang found," Delaney countered. "I'm asking you once again: Did you fly into a rage when you discovered your daughter had wet her bed?"

Maxine paused and took a few seconds to collect herself. Then she turned and faced the jury. In a controlled voice, she said: "I now remember what happened very clearly, and I can tell you that I did not strike, hit, or touch my daughter. I changed her sheets, tucked her in, kissed her good night, told her that I loved her. Then I returned to my bedroom and went to bed."

Spencer looked at the witness. *You're lying! I saw you beat her!*

Delaney didn't believe her either. "You didn't drag your daughter into the bathroom that night?" she asked, her voice rising.

"No!"

"You didn't smack her so hard that she fell and hit her head?"

"Absolutely not!"

"You didn't accidentally kill your own daughter?"

"I object," Cauldwell shouted, leaping to his feet.

"I'll withdraw my last question," Delaney replied. But she was not about to let up now. Instead, she changed subjects again. "Mrs. Arnold, who was Cynthia Gunter Wright?"

Maxine, who was still reeling from the earlier questions, replied: "Cynthia was my first daughter. I was married when I was a teenager for a short period of time. Cynthia only lived for five months." Then she added, "But I'm sure you already know that, don't you, Ms. Delaney?"

"How did Cynthia—your first child—die?"

"SIDS. She died in her crib from Sudden Infant Death Syndrome."

"Just to be sure, I want to make certain I understand your testimony," Delaney said, even though it was clear that she knew exactly what had been said. "You have given birth to two daughters: one was brutally murdered, and the first died under extremely suspicious circumstances?"

"Wait a minute," Cauldwell protested. "There's been no evidence presented that would suggest Mrs. Arnold's first child died mysteriously. The defense is slurring this poor woman's reputation here and misleading the jury."

"What kind of a lawyer are you?" Maxine Arnold unexpectedly declared. She glared at Delaney. "My daughter has been murdered and you have the gall to attack me!"

Spencer banged his gavel. "That's enough from everyone. I want both attorneys to approach the bench."

Cauldwell and Delaney dutifully stepped toward him with the Commonwealth's attorney, Jacob Wheeler, and Charles MacDonald in tow. Spencer leaned close and whispered so that Maxine, who was still in the witness chair, couldn't hear him.

"Ms. Delaney," he said, "do you have evidence that shows this witness was implicated in the death of her first daughter?"

"The Las Vegas police thought there might be foul play," she replied.

"I asked if you had any evidence," he said. "Was she charged with a crime?"

"No, but a high percentage of SIDS deaths are homicides."

Cauldwell had heard enough. "This is simply outrageous behavior by the defense," he complained. "She's implied that Mrs. Arnold had something to do with her first daughter's death. She's implied that the child was murdered."

"There will be no more questions asked about Mrs. Arnold's first daughter," Spencer said firmly. "It's not relevant. Is that clear, Ms. Delaney?"

"Yes, Your Honor."

After all four attorneys had returned to their respective seats, Spencer addressed the jury. "At times during a trial, especially an emotional one such as this, there will arise a need for the judge and the attorneys to talk privately. You should not draw any conclusions from these sidebar sessions nor should you let them influence your decision about the defendant's innocence or guilt. You have just heard Ms. Delancy ask the witness about the death of her first-born daughter from an earlier marriage. This infant died. That is a fact. The witness was never accused of harming this child, and no criminal charges were ever filed that would suggest that this baby died from anything other than a tragic medically recognized syndrome. Further, the defense has not produced any credible evidence that links the first child's unfortunate death to the murder of the second child. While I can instruct you to disregard testimony, I cannot erase words after they are uttered in this courtroom no matter how badly I might wish to do so. I will remind you once again, what the attorneys say is not always a fact. And your job is to listen only to the facts. You are to ignore the rest." He nodded to Delaney. "The defense may now continue."

Moving back to the podium, Delaney stared directly at Maxine and asked in a calm voice: "When did you begin having sex with Lester Amil?"

"Your Honor!" Cauldwell said. "I object!"

"Overruled," said Spencer, without waiting to hear his reasoning.

"I've never had sex with him," Maxine replied. "I said earlier that he had threatened to falsely accuse me of that. He was trying to extort us."

"So you never had sex with him?"

Judge Spencer interrupted. "You heard her reply the first

time. Now I have given you great leeway in your questioning of this witness. She said she hasn't had sex with your client. Move on."

"On the night of the murder, did you take Lester Amil's semen from a condom after the two of you had sex in the living room and smear it on Cassie's pajamas after she was killed?"

"Your Honor!" Cauldwell shouted, jumping to his feet. Spencer once again was forced to bang his gavel to silence the murmurs in the room. "Judge, the defense is abusing this witness," Cauldwell complained. "I don't care if the defense wants to come up with some outlandish explanation in her closing arguments, but she shouldn't be allowed to give testimony through asking questions! The witness said she never had sex with Lester Amil. Asked and answered."

"In the interest of justice, judges do not like to limit the questioning of witnesses by defense attorneys," Spencer said, aiming his comments to the jury. "Because of this, I am going to allow the question and will order the witness to answer it." He looked at Delaney and added: "However, I am warning you, Ms. Delaney, you are skating on extremely thin ice here."

"If you have forgotten," Delaney said without any sign of regret, "my question was: Did you take my client's semen out of a condom after having sex with him and smear it on your daughter's pajamas?"

Maxine Arnold was so livid she could barely speak. "No!" she testified. "I never had sex with your client! So it would have been physically impossible for me to smear his semen anywhere!"

"Just like you never left your room on the night of the murder, never went into Cassie's room, never became so furious that you struck your daughter, never had anything to do with the death of your first child!" Delaney shot back.

Spencer slammed his gavel. "I am instructing the jury to ignore the defense attorney's last declaration," he said.

"I'm sorry, Your Honor," Delaney said. "I have no more questions."

As soon as Maxine Arnold stepped down, Spencer adjourned court for the weekend and retreated to his chambers. He was irritated. He'd always prided himself on being cool in emotional situations, of being impartial, fair, honest—the sort of judge whom attorneys admired and respected for his insights and decorum. He had let the courtroom get out of control today. He'd given Delaney far more leeway than he usually gave defense attorneys.

He slipped behind his desk and rubbed his forehead.

It was because of the stone. It was against judicial ethics for him to be interacting with the defense by sending them e-mails. But he couldn't simply keep quiet about the bizarre sights that the stone was showing him. The stone. He unlocked the desk drawer. There it was. A simple rock. Or so it appeared. Where did its power come from?

He reached down and picked it up with his right hand. Then, he slowly transferred it to his left so it would touch the red slashed cross in his palm. He wasn't certain why he was doing this. No, that wasn't true. He did know. He wanted to experience another vision. He needed to see what the stone could show him. This time, he was not afraid. He closed his eyes, waiting for its power to surge through him

Spencer was inside the Arnold house. He could see Frank reading the newspaper at the kitchen table. Maxine was making coffee. Lester Amil was buttering a piece of toast. "Where's Cassie?" Frank asked. "She just got out of bed a few minutes ago," Maxine replied. Frank glanced at a wall clock. "We're going to be late for the hot air balloon ride. You need to light a fire under her little butt." Maxine started to pour herself a cup of coffee, but the kettle's handle was hot and it burned her hand. She dropped it. "Shit!" she exclaimed. "Damn it, why did Theresa have to go to that damn funeral."

Without bothering to glance up from his newspaper, Frank Arnold said: "Use the microwave. That way, you won't burn yourself."

Lester Amil stood up. "I'll go tell Cassie that she needs to get ready."

Spencer followed Amil as he walked upstairs. He watched as he knocked on Cassie's door but there wasn't an answer. Amil gently pushed it open, peeked inside, and then walked in.

"Cassie?"

The bathroom door was ajar. Spencer could hear a stereo blasting loudly from inside the steam-filled room. He could hear the sound of water splashing in a shower. Amil moved forward to the bathroom door and quietly pushed it farther open. As Spencer watched, Lester Amil peeked into the bathroom and then reached down inside the baggy sweat pants that he was wearing. In one quick move, he removed his erect penis. Spencer tried to turn away but couldn't stop watching. Amil came quickly, his semen spurting out in front of him, onto Cassie's pajamas, which she had dropped on the bathroom floor.

Spencer opened his eyes and put the stone back into his desk drawer. That was how Lester Amil's semen had gotten on the pajamas. He hadn't towered over her in the basement—as the prosecution claimed. Maxine Arnold hadn't removed his semen from a used condom and doctored her daughter's pajamas—as the defense claimed. Lester Amil had pleasured himself while peeking into Cassie's bathroom while she was taking a shower. Completely by chance, he had ejaculated over pajamas that she had left on the floor. Completely by chance, Maxine Arnold had spotted those same pajamas later that night and had ordered her daughter to put them on after she had wet the bed.

Spencer's next thoughts were about Delaney. He needed to tell her the truth. He began typing another anonymous e-mail.

It was nearly midnight when Spencer decided to go home. As he walked down the courthouse's stairway, he heard the sounds of two men laughing. He peeked around the corner. Cauldwell was standing outside of the Commonwealth's attorney's office talking to Walter Corn. Spencer quietly retreated back upstairs where he waited another half hour before leaving. He didn't want to run into Cauldwell and the *Courant*'s courthouse reporter.

17

PATTI DELANEY AND CHARLES MACDONALD DROVE DIRECTLY to the county jail late Friday night as soon as they read the new anonymous e-mail about Lester Amil. Both were steaming by the time their client was brought by deputies into the attorney-client interview room.

"You lied to us!" Delaney charged.

"I should've known that condom story was crap!" MacDonald exclaimed.

"What are you talking about?" Amil asked. He seemed genuinely confused.

MacDonald wanted to reach across the table separating them and grab him by his throat. But he didn't.

"You told us someone had taken your semen from a condom and planted it on Cassie's pajamas—that's how your DNA got there and that's what we've told the jury," Delaney said. "We bought it—hook, line, and sinker!"

"But that is what happened!" Amil replied.

"Like hell it is!" MacDonald snapped. "Sunday morning, you masturbated in Cassie's bedroom while she was taking a shower."

"What? How'd you find that out!"

"So it is true!" Delaney exclaimed. "I can't believe I fell for your lies."

"No, wait, let me explain."

"What, more lies?" MacDonald interrupted. "Save your breath."

"I never saw Cassie taking a shower. I'm not a pervert! I'll admit that I, ur, pleasured myself in her room. But I wasn't watching her. It was Ester Vargas."

"Who?" Delaney asked.

"Theresa Montoya's sister. Theresa is the Arnold's housekeeper and cook—it was her sister in the shower that morning, not Cassie. Ester is twenty years old."

"What are you talking about?" MacDonald said.

"Ester is from El Paso and she was visiting her sister. They got word on Saturday that their mother had died in Arizona. Theresa left that night to make funeral arrangements, but Ester's flight home to Texas didn't leave until Sunday. The Arnolds didn't want her to spend Saturday night alone in her sister's apartment, so they invited her to stay at the house with us."

"That doesn't explain why you were watching her," Delaney declared.

"I'd gone upstairs to get Cassie. Mr. Arnold was getting nervous about being late for the hot air balloon ride. When I checked her room, she wasn't there, but I heard the shower running. The door wasn't fully closed and when I looked in, I saw Ester. The guest room shares the same bathroom as Cassie's room. I know what I did was creepy, but when I saw her, well, I got turned on and didn't think anyone would ever find out."

"She didn't see you watching her?"

"No, she was washing her hair and had her eyes closed because of the shampoo."

"Where was Cassie?"

"She'd already gotten dressed. She was in her parents' bedroom watching cartoons. I didn't tell you about it because it didn't have anything to do with Cassie's murder."

"It didn't?" Delaney replied. "Cassie's pajamas were lying on the bathroom floor when you decided to please yourself over them. That's how your DNA got splattered on the pajamas!"

Amil appeared stunned.

"C'mon," MacDonald said, "are you telling us that you didn't see her pajamas that morning on the floor?"

"No, I was watching Ester. I thought Maxine or Frank were trying to frame me. I thought they'd taken my semen out of a condom. It was the only explanation I could think of."

Delaney and MacDonald were still fuming when they left the jail later that night. As they were walking across the parking lot, MacDonald said: "I don't remember any mention of any Ester Vargas in the police reports. I'm going to call the Arnolds' housekeeper and verify that her sister was actually visiting that weekend."

"Maybe it's better if you don't ask," Delaney said sadly. "What if he's lying? At this point in the trial, I'd still like to believe our client is innocent!"

"He is innocent," MacDonald replied confidently. "He's not the killer. His semen just happened to be in the wrong place at the wrong time."

"That's a novel way to say it," Delaney replied. "What do we tell the jury now?"

"Nothing. We just keep focusing on the real killers: the Arnolds. I don't know yet why they murdered their daughter, but they did it."

"How can you be so sure?"

MacDonald stopped walking and turned so he was facing her. "I feel it in my gut," he said, smiling slyly. "Besides, it's a bit late for us to be changing horses, isn't it?"

Spencer rose early Saturday morning, leaving Melissa asleep in their bed. He still had not confronted her about her infidelity. And now that three days had passed, he was no longer in a hurry to demand an explanation. Although the hurt and anger that he felt had not subsided, in a strange twist, he now found himself savoring his secret. She had cheated on him and that gave him a moral advantage. He wanted to think about how he could best use it.

Spencer planned to spend the day at the University of Virginia doing research. There were fourteen different libraries on campus, including ones that specialized in astronomy, biology-psychology, chemistry, education, fine arts, health sciences, law, mathematics, music, physics, and science-engineering. Surely, he thought, he could find a book somewhere in those stacks that would explain the stone and the red slash marks still spreading across his left hand. He would begin in the school's main reference center, the Alderman Library, located just northwest of the center of campus. He parked his Jaguar in a visitor's lot off Emmet Street, near the school bookstore, and then walked along Newcomb Road until he reached the massive rectangular library. A student at the information desk directed him to a section of books about the occult and religion.

Spencer wandered through the shelves, scanning the different titles. Unknowingly, he was following the same course that the stone's previous owner had taken. Patrick McPherson had studied interpreter Bibles, looking for clues.

Spencer found twenty-nine different biblical verses in the Abingdon Bible Commentary that mentioned "stones." The most common reference was to "stoning," when an angry mob threw stones at a person to kill him after he had broken a religious law. But there was nothing in the Bible about a magical stone that allowed its owner to have visions. By noon, Spencer was both hungry and discouraged. He strolled over to the student center, bought a sandwich, and ate alone while sitting outside on a bench. Several students were playing touch football, and as he watched the young men and women jostling one another, he felt very old.

Returning to the library, he began examining texts that described religious beliefs outside mainline Christianity. A book called *The Holy Scriptures* caught his eye. It looked exactly like a Bible but contained chapters that he didn't recognize. He discovered it had been published by the Church of Jesus Christ of Latter-day Saints. It was the Mormon's version of the Holy Bible. According to its foreword, it had been transcribed during a three-year period by the church's founder, Joseph Smith, Jr., who said that God had ordered him to rewrite the Bible because it contained several mistakes. He'd also translated the Book of Mormon, which was the cornerstone of his church's faith.

Spencer knew a little about Mormonism because two of his friends in college had been Latter-day Saints. They'd told him that an angel named Moroni had appeared to Smith in the 1820s and shown him several solid gold tablets that had been hidden in a box conveniently located close to the Smith family farm outside Palmyra, New York. These plates contained the history of a band of ancient Hebrews who had been led by God to the American continent several centuries before the birth of Christ.

Spencer began flipping through an illustrated book about Mormonism and paused when he reached a page with a drawing of two smooth stones called the "Urim and Thummim."

The caption called them "seer stones." The book said Moroni had given the Urim and Thummin to Smith so that he could see into the past and future and also translate the golden plates.

Maybe this is it!

Hurrying to a study cubicle, Spencer began reading. He discovered that the Book of Mormon—unlike the Bible—contained more than four hundred different verses that described various stones with magical powers.

It's got to be one of them!

It was nearly seven o'clock by the time Spencer had reviewed every stone-related verse. Not one of them described his stone. He had wasted his time.

Disgusted, he decided to try a different approach. Rather than searching for a historical reference to the mysterious stone, he decided to see if he could identify it by examining the visions it had caused. Maybe he'd find a pattern to them.

On his notepad, he wrote:

1st vision: Sailboat, terrified, call for help from figure walking on water.
2nd vision: Melissa in stables having sex.
3rd vision: Cassie Arnold wets bed. Maxine beats her and later lies in court.
4th vision: Boxing with father.
5th vision: Lester Amil masturbates while peeking in bathroom.

He also jotted down:

6th: Visit from former professor, caught me plagiarizing.
7th: Patrick McPherson sends me stone then kills self.
8th: Bloody cross appears on hand.

He studied the list, looking for dots to connect. What did the visions and the three events have in common? Nothing jumped out. After several minutes of going down the list, he reversed himself. He started at the list's bottom and read up it.

8th: Bloody cross appears on hand.

Wait! What does a cross represent? Christ crucified. Why was he crucified? To take away the sins of the world. Sins. Could that be it?

7th: Suicide.

It's a sin!

6th: Plagiarism. Theft.

Another sin!

5th vision: Lust, impure thoughts.
4th vision: He didn't honor his father.
3rd vision: Maxine beats child, curses God's name, perjures herself in court.
2nd vision: Melissa commits adultery.

The formula fit. Everything on the list, except his first vision, involved sins.

Once again, Spencer had independently and unknowingly reached the same conclusion about the stone as Patrick McPherson. Sin was the connecting point. As he stared at the list, he noticed another pattern. The stone was not only revealing sins that others had committed—Melissa, Maxine Arnold, and Lester Amil—it was showing him sins that he had done too.

Spencer returned the library books to the shelves and left the building. A thought occurred to him. If he had figured out the pattern, then he would soon be confronted by a sin from his past. It was his turn. The question was: *What else have I done?*

Patti Delaney rarely slept late, but on Sunday, she kept hitting the snooze button on her alarm. By the time she finally crawled from under the covers, it was nearly eleven. She made coffee and went to get her newspaper. Ever since she had become Lester Amil's attorney, she dreaded opening the *Charlottesville Courant,* but she felt obligated to read Walter Corn's daily dribble. Today's was spread across the front page and was even worse than what she could have imagined. Someone had tipped off Corn to a scandal and it was from her past.

DEFENSE LAWYER IN ARNOLD KILLING FREED RAPIST WHO MURDERED AGAIN

By Walter Corn
Charlottesville Courant Staff Writer

Patti Delaney, who is defending accused child slayer Lester Amil, is no stranger to gruesome murders or controversial defendants. Her actions in a horrific rape and serial killer case in 1986 outraged the Baltimore area, where she previously practiced law.

In 1983, Baltimore was being terrorized by a rapist who preyed on young female real estate agents. He'd lure them to houses that were for sale by posing as a potential buyer. After twelve agents were brutally raped, the Baltimore Police Department created a task force to capture the "realtor rapist." They even had undercover officers pose as sales agents.

There were no new attacks for several months and then police found a real estate agent stabbed to death inside a model home. She'd also been raped. During the weeks that followed, two more women were raped and murdered. The task force then arrested Alfred Lloyd, a thirty-two-year-old insurance claims adjuster, who was married and the father of three young children.

The case against Lloyd was based entirely on testimony from a convicted burglar, who claimed that he had served as a lookout for Lloyd during several of the killings. A jury found Lloyd guilty and sentenced him to death. But in 1986, Lloyd hired Delaney to appeal his conviction and she uncovered what she claimed was damning evidence of police misconduct.

Detectives had testified that their star witness had always told the same story about the killings and was not paid any reward in return for his testimony against Lloyd. But Delaney claimed the witness had told the police several conflicting stories. It was only after several hours of coaching that his story became believable. He'd also collected $25,000 in rewards.

An appellate court overturned Lloyd's conviction, setting

the stage for a new trial. Delaney, meanwhile, was able to get her client released. One month later, a twenty-eight-year-old real estate agent was found raped and stabbed to death. Lloyd's fingerprints were found on her body. When they went to arrest him, they found Lloyd's wife, his elderly parents, and his own three children shot to death. He'd arranged their bodies in a row in the family's living room based on their age. Lloyd's body was upstairs. He'd shot himself after writing a suicide note. In it, he personally thanked Delaney for getting him released. He explained that he had needed to kill a total of ten persons before he could kill himself. His note didn't explain why.

In the story's next several paragraphs, Corn had recapped Delaney's "haphazard" handling of the Lester Amil defense. He'd saved his most vicious attack for the final paragraph. It was a quote from "a source familiar with the prosecution's case who asked not to be named."

You've got to wonder if Patti Delaney has been hoodwinked again—just as she was in the Lloyd case. I mean, this woman is responsible for freeing a serial killer. He went home and slaughtered his entire family. Now she's trying to get an accused child killer turned loose. How does she sleep at night?

Delaney crushed the newspaper into a wad and tossed it into her kitchen trash can. She assumed Corn's "source intimately familiar with the prosecution's case" was Taylor Cauldwell, but there was no way for her to prove it.

Her phone rang. It was MacDonald.

"Read the paper?" he asked.

"Yep," she replied, trying to mask her emotions.

"From what I read, you didn't do anything wrong," MacDonald said. "The Baltimore police screwed up."

"I've been over this a million times since it happened," she said. "It doesn't matter. Seven people, including three children, are dead because I got Lloyd out of prison. He's why I stopped practicing for a while."

For several moments, neither of them spoke and then Delaney said, "Maybe I should resign from the Amil case. We both know jurors aren't supposed to read the newspaper, but there's no way they aren't going to find out about Lloyd and I don't want my past to hurt our client."

"Stop being stupid. And stop feeling sorry for yourself."

His brusqueness shocked her. "That's easy for you to say," she replied, "because you're not the one with blood on your hands."

"When I was a D.C. cop," he replied, "I shot a murder suspect fleeing from a crime scene."

"You killed him?" It was difficult for her to imagine because MacDonald seemed grandfatherly.

"The shot blew off half his skull. But I never lost a second of sleep over it. Because I was doing my job."

"But I should have known that Lloyd was going to kill someone!"

"How? Why? Do you think killers look different from the rest of us? Some of the most vicious murderers I've seen wouldn't have stood out in a crowd. It's that old 'banality of evil' theory. You couldn't have known what Lloyd was going to do. Just look at the Arnolds, the uppity Frank and Maxine, with all of their wealth and their power and their prestige. They may think they're above the law and untouchable. But you know what? This time, they aren't. This time, they're going to pay."

She didn't respond.

"So? Are we still a team?" he asked. "Are we still meeting later today to go over tomorrow's testimony?"

"Yes," she replied. "I'm not running away from my past again."

"Hey," he said. "Everyone's got skeletons in the closet."

18

"DO YOU HAVE ANY IDEA WHO'S SENDING YOU THESE e-mails?" MacDonald asked.

"No," Delaney replied. "The author attaches them to news stories from the *Charlottesville Courant,* so there's no return address for him."

"How does he know what happened in Cassie's bedroom?" MacDonald was studying a printout of the most recent e-mail. "Hey," he said, "our e-mailer made a mistake in this message. He says Amil was watching Cassie in the shower, but our client claims he was watching someone else."

"It's a mistake only if Lester Amil is telling us the truth."

"But suppose he is. That means our e-mailer could see Lester Amil in Cassie's bedroom but he couldn't see the person in the shower."

"Okay, but why's that significant?"

"Frank Arnold loves high-tech electronic gadgets, right? He's got his new house filled with computerized tracking gizmos. I'll bet he's got a camera hidden in Cassie's bedroom! That's how our e-mailer knew Cassie had wet her bed, gotten a whipping, and that our client had frolicked with himself on Sunday morning."

"If there's a hidden camera in there, why didn't Frank and Maxine tell the police about it?"

"Maxine may not know and Frank probably doesn't want the cops to see whatever else is on his videotapes. Hell, he might have cameras hidden all over the house!"

Delaney considered what MacDonald was suggesting. "It sounds logical, but why would Frank Arnold send us e-mails? Why would he want to help us?"

"Maybe he's not helping," MacDonald replied. "Maybe he's trying to use us, trying to manipulate the case. Who knows? But there is one thing I do know: I'm going to find out if there is a camera in Cassie's bedroom."

"And I'm going to contact the *Charlottesville Courant* after court on Monday to see if I can trace these e-mails," Delaney declared.

Frank Arnold was scheduled to be the first witness on Monday, but when court convened that morning, Taylor Cauldwell announced that he was calling a new witness: Truman Moody. Simultaneously, Delaney and MacDonald asked Amil: "Who's he?" Their client shrugged his shoulders.

Two sheriff's deputies escorted a short, muscular black man in his early twenties into the courtroom. He was restrained with handcuffs and wearing a county jail jumpsuit. Moody slouched so low in the witness chair that spectators could only see his shaved head.

"Please tell the court where you currently reside," Cauldwell asked.

"The Los Angeles jail."

"Why are you in jail?"

"They say I sold drugs."

"Anything else?"

"They say I'm in a street gang."

"Anything else?"

"They say I was part of a murder."

"Are you a member of a Los Angeles street gang?"

"Sorry, Chief, but I gotta plead the fifth on that one."

Spencer interrupted. "I don't know what sort of behavior is tolerated in California courtrooms, but in Virginia, we do not address attorneys as 'Chief,' nor do we chew gum while testifying, nor do we slouch in our chairs. Now get rid of the gum and sit up straight, or you'll be spending more time in our county jail than you might wish!"

Moody shot up in the witness chair. Miss Alice handed him a tissue for his gum.

Cauldwell continued: "Do you know Lester Tidwell Amil?"

"No, can't say I ever met the dude."

"Your Honor," Delaney said. "If this witness doesn't know Mister Amil, then what's the point of having him testify?"

"My next question will answer that," Cauldwell replied. Pointing directly at Amil, the prosecutor asked: "Do you know this man, the defendant in this case?"

"Sure do," Moody smirked. He nodded at Amil and said: "Hey, dog!"

"Please tell the court who this man is," Cauldwell continued.

"His name be Delbert, Delbert Amil."

Spencer rapped his gavel to quiet the courtroom while Delaney and MacDonald, once again, simultaneously turned in their seats to question their client. But this time, Amil had bowed his head and was avoiding eye contact by staring at the top of the defense table.

"Just so I'm clear on this," Cauldwell said, emphasizing his point, "is it your testimony that the man sitting here—the defendant in his case—is not Lester Amil, but is, in fact, Delbert Amil, his brother?"

"I don't know nothing about any Lester Amil. I don't know if Delbert even gots a brother. All I'm telling you is that man sitting there is Delbert."

"How can you be so sure?"

"Because we done time together in prison."

Delaney immediately objected and a visibly upset Spencer stopped Cauldwell. "I want both counselors in my chambers—now!"

As soon as the attorneys—Cauldwell, Jacob Wheeler, Delaney, and MacDonald—entered Spencer's chambers, he shouted: "What the hell is going on?"

"We learned this weekend that the defendant is not Lester Amil," Cauldwell explained. "He's Delbert Amil, one of a set of triplets. His mother, Danyella Amil, gave birth to Lester, Delbert, and a third son named Jackoby. We didn't know he was an imposter until Truman Moody telephoned my office from the Los Angeles jail late Friday. He'd seen the defendant on the television news and recognized him."

"Didn't anyone check Amil's fingerprints when he was arrested?" Spencer asked.

"It appears a number of mistakes have been made."

"I'm listening," Spencer snapped.

"The sheriff's deputy who took the defendant's fingerprints in jail accidentally smudged them. The jail's computer was down so he took them the old way by using ink rather than having him press his hand onto a computer screen. Apparently, when the FBI's lab in Washington got them, the technician wasn't able to find any matches because of the smudge. So he sent back a report that said there was no record of Lester Amil ever having been arrested. After Moody called us, the sheriff had the defendant fingerprinted again, this time with the computer screen, and the FBI informed us Sunday that the defendant is actually Delbert Amil."

Cauldwell removed several sheets of paper from a file folder with the FBI lab's logo on them and handed them to Spencer and Delaney.

"Judge, it's pretty much like what Maxine Arnold testified on Friday," Cauldwell continued. "Lester Amil was the subject of a very complimentary television news report. By coincidence, that news program aired on the exact same day that Lester's brother, Delbert, was paroled. The next night, the Amil family's home was firebombed and two persons were burned to death. One was Danyella Amil, the mother. Everyone thought the other burn victim was Delbert."

"Who firebombed their house?"

"A neighborhood gang. Everyone assumed the gang was angry about the television broadcast and the TV station really pushed that theory—that the gang was trying to drive Lester out of the neighborhood because he was such a good kid and instead ended up killing his mom and brother. The station's ratings went through the roof."

"What really happened?"

"The Los Angeles Police Department's gang unit says Delbert was a member of the Black P Stones gang. It operates in the West Adams area of the city and has been fighting a war with a rival gang, known as the Eighteenth Street Gang, for years. The Black P Stones are African Americans. The other gang is Hispanic."

"Cut to the chase, Counselor," Spencer ordered.

"Delbert was arrested six years ago and was sent to the Fred C. Nelles Youth Correctional Facility in Whittier. That's where he became pals with our witness, Truman Moody. At some point, the L.A. police department offered Delbert an early release date in return for providing information about an Eighteenth Street Gang murder."

"I said, cut to the chase."

"Gangs don't like snitches. As soon as Delbert was freed, he became a target. His mother and brother just happened to get in the way."

"Lester Amil—the good kid—is dead, right?" Spencer asked. "And Delbert—the gang member turned snitch—is sitting in my courtroom pretending to be his brother."

"That's it in a nutshell," Cauldwell answered. "Apparently, Delbert went out to buy cigarettes a few minutes before the Molotov cocktails came bursting through the windows. By the time the cops got there, the fire was out and Delbert knew his mom and brother were dead. When the cops questioned him, he identified himself as Lester."

"No one bothered to check?" Delaney asked.

"There were no autopsies or a dental record check of the bodies," Cauldwell said, "because the cops considered it just another gang incident and Delbert—posing as his brother— had already identified both bodies."

"And none of their neighbors said anything?"

"He was a triplet," Cauldwell replied, "and this isn't a neighborhood where people stick their noses in someone else's business. Besides, Delbert was a good enough imposter to fool the television station reporter."

"How about Frank and Maxine Arnold?"

"They didn't have a clue about the switch. They thought they were inviting a good kid into their home."

"This is turning into a soap opera," Spencer complained. "Do either of you have any other surprises you need to tell me? What about the third triplet? Should I expect him to turn up in the courtroom—as a juror?"

Jacob Wheeler laughed but stopped when everyone else scowled at him.

"The other Amil triplet was killed a few years ago," Cauldwell replied. "At least, that's what the L.A. cops told me."

"Judge," Delaney said, "how can we know for certain that any of this is true?"

Cauldwell handed her another sheet of paper. "Here's a copy of the fax that we received from the L.A. gang unit, along with your client's rap sheet."

"If Delbert had everyone fooled," Delaney asked, "then how'd your witness see through the ruse?

"Moody is a prison tattoo artist. He put a tattoo on Delbert's neck while they were incarcerated together. It's a knife with a teardrop falling from its blade. Moody thought Delbert had burned to death until he spotted that tattoo on a Court TV broadcast about the murder."

Delaney suddenly realized that she'd been set up. "Judge, the Commonwealth knew all of this before court convened this morning but instead of telling the court and us, Mr. Cauldwell intentionally put Truman Moody on the witness stand. Why? Because he wanted the jury to know that our client had done time in prison with a gang member and murder suspect." Her voice raising in anger, she said: "You knew the law wouldn't let you introduce Delbert Amil's criminal past into the trial record so you snuck it through the back door!"

"Check the court transcript," Cauldwell cockily replied, "and you'll see that I didn't ask the witness a single question about the defendant's past!"

"That's because you let your witness do it for you," she complained. "Judge Spencer, I want a mistrial!"

"Whoa, first things first," Spencer said. "I want to review the FBI fingerprint records and research the law."

"How can our client get a fair trial now, especially since the jury knows he has been posing as his brother and also has been in prison?" Delaney asked. "You've got to declare a mistrial!"

"I don't *have* to do anything. Do you actually think your client is going to do any better with twelve new jurors? With all of the national media sitting in the courtroom, everyone in the nation is going to hear about this fiasco, and I'm not willing to stop this trial and go through all of the time, expense, money, and inconvenience of starting again. He's still your client, whether his name is Lester or Delbert. He's still the man who was living at the Arnolds. And he's still the man accused of murdering their daughter. Even if you got a new trial, the Arnolds would still be called to testify and their testimony would still reveal that your client had posed as his dead brother. There's no way I can shield jurors from that."

"But, Judge, this isn't . . ."

Spencer cut her off. "Your client dug himself into this hole and my suggestion to you, Ms. Delaney and Mr. MacDonald, is that you use the next few hours to take your client out behind the woodshed and get some truth out of him."

As soon as Amil was escorted into the attorney-client room at the jail, Delaney exploded: "Just who in the hell are you?"

"I'm Delbert," he meekly answered. "Lester was my brother."

"Jesus Christ!" MacDonald exclaimed. "We're screwed! No juror is going to believe anything we say now!"

"If I hadn't pretended to be my brother, I'd be dead. When I was watching my momma's house burn, I knew my momma and brother were dead and it was my fault. I was just going to disappear. But when that television reporter called, well, people treated me different when they thought I was my brother. Everyone respected him. They was proud of him. I decided acting like him was a way to honor him by carrying on his name."

"Oh brother!" MacDonald grimaced. "Now that's rationalization!"

"Becoming my brother was my ticket out of that neighborhood," he continued. "Then I blew it by having sex with Maxie. All that other stuff I told you, I swear it's true!"

"It doesn't matter now. No one is going to believe you now," Delaney said.

"Especially when it comes to a pissing match between you and Maxine Arnold about sex," MacDonald added.

"But I can prove she and me were having sex. She told me a bunch of personal stuff about her husband—like he can't get a hard-on unless he takes Viagra."

"That's hardly convincing evidence," MacDonald said.

"But I didn't kill Cassie! You got to believe me!"

Delaney slid a copy of his rap sheet across the table.

"You've got a long history of burglaries, petty thefts, even an armed robbery," she said. "That's not a big help."

Spencer was determined to continue the trial. He spent nearly an hour writing an explanation to read to jurors. He wasn't certain an appellate court would agree with his decision, especially if Amil were found guilty and sentenced to death. All death sentences are automatically appealed in Virginia, and appellate defense attorneys are always looking for loopholes. But he was not going to end this trial now. Before he had Miss Alice bring the jurors into the courtroom, Spencer warned Cauldwell that the Commonwealth was not going to be allowed to delve into Amil's criminal record. The fact that Delbert Amil had posed as his brother did not give the Commonwealth carte blanche to parade his previous crimes in front of jurors.

It took fifteen minutes for Spencer to read his explanation. He told the jury that the name, Delbert Amil, had been added to the criminal complaint, as if it were an alias. When Spencer finished, Truman Moody was called back to the witness chair. Cauldwell questioned him for another five minutes, mostly about the tattoo on Amil's neck, that he'd used to identify him. Then Cauldwell sat down feeling quite happy with himself.

Delaney understood the significance of the damage that Moody had done. She had decided not to ask him a single question in order to minimize his courtroom appearance. But as she was rising from her chair to tell Spencer that the defense didn't have any questions, she changed her mind. She wanted to get Moody to explain how an L.A. street gang had been trying to murder Amil. She thought it might help jurors understand why he'd been eager to switch identities with his dead brother.

"Are gangs in L.A. dangerous?"

"The police seem to think so."

"Would you be afraid if a Los Angeles gang wanted to kill you?"

"Yes," he replied, looking at her as if she were a moron. "I do believe I would be."

"Would you try to conceal your identity by posing as someone else?"

"Sure. If I could."

It was her next set of questions that Delaney would later deeply regret.

"Isn't it true that a gang in L.A. wanted to kill my client? Didn't they want him dead because he had told the police about a murder? Wasn't he doing what any honest, law-abiding citizen would do in giving the police information?"

"Oh, them dogs wanted him dead, all right," Moody replied. "When you're in a gang, you don't ever snitch, especially to cops."

Delaney felt as if someone had sucker-punched her abdomen. She sat down and naively hoped the jurors hadn't realized what Moody had just told them.

But Cauldwell was already on his feet: "Did you just say that the defendant was a member of an L.A. street gang?"

"I object," Delaney said, "this has nothing to do with this case."

"Judge," Cauldwell protested, "she opened the door!"

"And I'm shutting it," Spencer replied. "The objection is sustained. Ask your next question or sit down!"

Cauldwell sat down.

Moody's testimony had been a disaster for the defense.

Patti Delaney watched jurors as Spencer announced that it was time for a lunch break. She felt certain that every one of them had already made up their mind about Amil. They knew that her client was an imposter, a former prison inmate, and now a gang member.

As she searched their faces for clues, she quickly drew another conclusion. From their return glances, none of them seemed to think much of her either!

19

SPENCER HAD BEEN EXPECTING A SIN FROM HIS PAST TO SUR-face and after court adjourned Monday afternoon, it arrived in the form of a Washington, D.C., lawyer.

Miss Alice announced that Kevin Michaels had been waiting for several hours to see him. Michaels, a distinguished-looking man in his early sixties, entered Spencer's chambers dressed in a wool suit made by Henry Poole of Savile Row and carrying an unlit Cuban cigar in one hand and a battered leather brief-case in his other. After dropping his briefcase on the floor, he presented Spencer with an embossed business card.

KEVIN MICHAELS
Senior Partner, Member of Board of Directors
Boyd, Stackhouse, and Brown,
Attorneys at Law
2143 Connecticut Avenue, N.W.
Washington, D.C.

Spencer recognized the firm. It was one of the most presti-gious in the nation's capital. Spencer guessed Michaels billed his clients at least six hundred dollars per hour. What was so important that he had made the two-hour drive to Char-lottesville, and then spent his afternoon waiting for Spencer?

Michaels got right to the point. "Our firm represents the heirs of Ambrose and Ethel Worthington. As you probably know, Ambrose was a close friend of your father-in-law, Au-gustus VanDenvender VI. In fact, when Ambrose died some twenty years ago, the law firm of VanDenvender and Wythe handled the probate of his estate."

"I remember," Spencer replied, "although I'd just joined my father-in-law's firm."

"That's correct. If I'm not mistaken, you'd been out of law school less than a year. Yet, our records show that you handled the Worthington probate. That was quite an undertaking con-sidering the complexity of the estate."

"Actually, I'd only been on board a month. My father-in-law thought the Worthington probate would be a good way to break me in. Baptism by fire, so to speak. Although, after all of these years, I don't recall many specifics. Is there a problem?"

Michaels opened his briefcase and removed a thick stack of documents, which he rested on his lap. "Unfortunately, there is," he said. "You might recall that Ambrose left his entire for-tune to his wife, Ethel, but to avoid excessive taxes, nearly all of his money was shielded in various trusts. Because of that, his estate was tied up in probate for nearly two years."

"Yes, I recall it took some time."

"His wife proved to be a healthy old bird. She died two months ago at the age of one hundred and three. She spent her final years in a private, Washington, D.C., extended-care facility, which is why, I suppose, her children came to our firm to settle her estate since we are based in the capital." He glanced around the room. "Do you have an ashtray? I've gotten myself addicted to these damn, hand-rolled Cuban cigars. I've got extra if you'd like to join me."

"This is a public building. Smoking is prohibited. Besides, I don't smoke cigars."

Michaels frowned. "The size of Ethel's estate is more than a half-billion dollars. Ambrose proved to be a shrewd investor."

"I'm sorry," Spencer said, interrupting, "but since the Worthingtons are no longer clients, I'm not sure I should be hearing any of this."

"Judge Spencer," Michaels said firmly, "trust me, you're going to find what I have to say to be very interesting. You see, the heirs decided to liquidate most of their mother's stock holdings so our firm has been conducting an audit. It turns out that Ambrose bought a large number of shares in a company called Circus Circus Enterprises when it first started. Are you familiar with the company?"

He wasn't.

"It began in the 1960s as a tiny casino in Las Vegas," Michaels explained. "They called it Circus Circus because it was actually inside a circus tent—a large pink and white big top. The fellow who started it was the same entrepreneur who had built Caesars Palace and initially he was going to give it a Roman orgy theme too. He was going to call it 'Roman Circus Maximus.' But he ended up just calling it, Circus Circus. It had live circus acts performing there while people gambled. They even had an elephant walk around pulling the handles on slot machines but they had to get rid of the pachyderm because it pooped all over the floor. Imagine stepping in elephant crap while you're gambling!"

Spencer began drumming his fingers on his desk, but his impatience didn't speed up Michaels, who was clearly savoring the moment.

"Two colorful characters bought Circus Circus just before

it was about to go bankrupt, and during the coming decades, they miraculously turned the company around. In fact, these two men were ultimately responsible for sparking a revolution in the gaming industry in Las Vegas. They helped transform the city from a mob town into a destination resort city."

"I'm sorry, Mr. Michaels," Spencer said, "but this has been a very long day and I still don't understand what any of this has to do with me."

Michaels pitched the thick folder from his lap onto Spencer's desk. "Circus Circus is now part of a huge conglomerate," he said bluntly. "It owns sixteen megaresorts and has more hotel guest rooms on the Las Vegas Strip than any other casino operation in the world. Last year, it collected two billion dollars in revenues. Ambrose Worthington bought a million shares of Circus Circus when it was worth nearly nothing. That stock is now worth more than a hundred million dollars. The reason I'm here is because our audit turned up an irregularity. It's all documented in those papers I just gave you."

"And you think I might know something about it?"

Michaels's jovial manner suddenly disappeared. "You'd better," he said coldly. "During the two years it took you to get Ambrose Worthington's estate through probate, the Circus Circus company announced that it was splitting its stock. Mr. Worthington's holdings were supposed to go from one million shares to a million-and-a-half shares. But somehow that split was overlooked and the estate never was credited with the additional half-million shares. They vanished! Ethel Worthington knew her husband owned a million shares, but she wasn't that savvy about investments and didn't know about the stock split. When her husband's estate was finally released from probate, she checked, saw that the million shares were still there, and never realized that she'd been cheated out of an extra half-million shares."

"Cheated?" Spencer replied incredulously.

"Out of respect for you and VanDenvender and Wythe," Michaels continued, "our firm sent me to personally bring this oversight to your attention. We'd like to know what happened to those extra half-million shares?"

Spencer didn't have a clue. "I'll have to examine our firm's records," he said. "But I'm certain this was an innocent mistake—if what you say, of course, is true."

"Oh, it's true, all right," Michaels abruptly replied. "And just for the record, that missing stock is now worth fifty million dollars. Plus, my firm is tacking on a twenty-percent collection fee. That comes to sixty million dollars." Michaels took out a match and defiantly lit his Cuban cigar.

Spencer glanced up from the papers. "I told you this is a no-smoking building."

Michaels took a long puff. He was looking much more like a thug sent by a bill collector than a refined Washington attorney.

"Put it out!"

Michaels tapped his cigar on his shoe, knocking the ashes onto Spencer's floor. He gently pushed the cigar's tip against the shoe's sole, extinguishing it, but not damaging the cigar. "Judge, you've got a much bigger problem to worry about than my smoking. We want our money within a week, and if we don't get it, then the heirs are going to file a civil suit against you personally and your father-in-law's firm. We'll also contact various federal and state regulatory offices and provide them with our audit. This smells like several felonies to me."

He snapped shut his briefcase and stood. "I understand you may be in line for appointment to the Virginia Supreme Court, assuming Taylor Cauldwell is elected Virginia's next governor," he said. "Obviously, this little oversight is something best handled discreetly. Good day, Judge." He left without either of them offering to shake the other's hand.

As soon as Michaels was gone, Spencer rushed three blocks from the courthouse to the law offices of VanDenvender and Wythe at the corner of Seventh and East Market Streets. Although as a judge, Spencer had severed nearly all of his ties with the law firm, his former secretary still worked there and was responsible for keeping track of his old cases. Traci Sugarman was about to leave for the night when he burst onto the building's second floor where the firm's senior partners had their offices. She was the only employee still at work.

"It's been a long time, Judge!" she said warmly. "Good to see you!"

"I need everything in our files about the Ambrose Worthington probate," he said, slightly out of breath. "And I need it right now!"

He waited nervously inside the firm's conference room, which was decorated with paintings of hounds chasing foxes. About fifteen minutes later, Sugarman wheeled a metal cart with ten cartons of files into the room.

"I'm sorry for being so abrupt," he said. "I didn't mean to bark out those orders."

"It's okay, Judge," she replied. "All of us have our bad days now and then."

Two hours later, Sugarman knocked timidly on the door. "Judge, it's almost eight o'clock and my kids have been waiting for dinner since six. I thought maybe you have forgotten— I'm a single mom."

"I'm sorry," he replied. "I lost track of time. Please, please go home!"

Spencer continued reading until well after ten o'clock and what he discovered outraged him. He left the cart next to Sugarman's desk and returned to the courthouse, this time walking very slowly. In his chambers, he carefully read through the audit papers that Kevin Michaels had left him. By the time he had driven home to VanDenvender Hall, he knew exactly what had happened.

He discovered Melissa perched in front of a fire in the library reading a book about a racehorse named Seabiscuit and sipping Merlot.

"Your father just fucked me!" he declared as he walked into the library.

Melissa slowly closed her book, slowly removed her reading glasses, and slowly looked up at his angry face. "What in the world are you saying?"

"Your father used me as a patsy when I first joined his firm. He called me into his office, told me he was going to do me a big favor, and showed me a huge stack of legal documents. It was his buddy Ambrose Wellington's estate and it was going into probate. He wanted me to be the attorney of record. He acted like he was giving me a present of sorts. It would look good to the firm's other partners if his new son-in-law took fiduciary responsibility of a multimillion-dollar estate during his first month on the job. Only your dear, old daddy wasn't really doing me any favors. He was setting me up so he could steal a half-million shares of Wellington's stock!"

Her face did not betray a single emotion. She placed her book on a table next to her chair and rose gracefully. "How dare you burst in here," she said in a controlled, low voice, "and call my father a thief. I have no interest in speaking to you about this subject until you can control your emotions." She started toward the doorway but he slipped in front of her, preventing her exit.

"Your father did all of the probate work. He handled the account personally. All I did was sign the papers that he handed me. I was a fool. He offered me the credit and I took it. I never even bothered to read the probate papers. I trusted him and I wanted everyone to think I was clever enough to handle that estate!"

"Spencer," she said dryly, "this matter is between you and my father, and quite frankly, I don't see why you are making such a big deal about a few shares of stock."

"The big deal," he shouted, "is that those few shares are worth fifty million dollars! The big deal is that my name is the only one on all of the probate documents! The big deal is that it looks like I stole the money!"

Without warning, she slapped him hard across his right cheek. During their entire twenty-three-year marriage, she had never struck him. For a moment, he considered smashing a fist into her ivory cheek. Instead, he grabbed her wrists to prevent her from slapping him again and squeezed them hard. "Your father stole fifty million dollars and now the Worthington heirs want it back, plus ten million dollars more," he continued. "And if I don't come up with the money in a week, they're going to ruin me!"

"Let me go!" she demanded, her voice still controlled. "I resent how you are blaming my father. He's a hundred times the lawyer you are and a thousand times the man!"

Spencer lost it. All of the years of anger, frustration, resentment, and bitterness that he had held back during their marriage suddenly came gushing out. "You're defending him?

You're my goddamn wife and you're taking his side! Didn't you hear me? Your father set me up! He stole fifty million dollars and left me holding the bag! And you're slapping me and choosing him over me?"

"Let me go. Now!"

"I know you fucked that neighborhood kid in the stables!" he blurted out. "I saw you doing it!"

Melissa tried to pull away but he continued to hold on to her wrists. She no longer was dispassionate. She became furious. "You're hurting me!" she screamed. "Let me go now! You bastard!"

Instead, he squeezed even tighter. "I saw you in the hay! I saw you give him your goddamn panties as a souvenir."

Melissa stopped struggling and then in one quick move jerked her arms downward. He released her.

"You handed him your panties and laughed. It was all a goddamn joke to you!"

"This entire marriage," she said coldly, "has been one big goddamn joke!" She stepped by him and walked from the room.

"That's it," he shouted. "Pretend nothing is wrong! Just like you've done all of your life. Are you denying what I saw in the stables? Are you saying your father didn't set me up?" Suddenly, he turned sarcastic. "This actually is quite funny. You've cheated on me with some college kid. And your father screwed me too. You VanDenvenders are a real tag team!"

She had been walking toward the stairs, but now stopped and turned around. Like him, her anger came gushing out. "You disgust me! You're a sniveling, dull, contemptuous little man who has convinced himself that you matter when, in fact, you're insignificant. If you weren't married to me, no one would pay any attention to you! You have no friends, no life, nothing! My father and I gave you a future and now you're whining about some trivial misunderstanding over some stupid shares of stock."

"What about you? The queen of the manor, the ice princess, the daughter of the great VanDenvender dynasty. I saw you being bent over by some acne-faced college kid in the stables. You were banging away like a cheap middle-aged slut! How many other times have you cheated on me? How many other men have screwed you?"

"Get out!" she screamed. "Get out of my house!"

Spencer went upstairs to their bedroom to collect some clothes. When he returned, she was standing in front of the library's fireplace with a poker, jabbing the burning logs. She glared at him but didn't say a word.

Neither did he. He stormed out the front door and climbed into his Jaguar. He floored the pedal, sending gravel spitting up from behind. When he reached the main road, he called information on his cellular phone and asked to be connected to the Clifton Hideaway, a bed-and-breakfast resort just outside Charlottesville. It was a favorite of the monied crowd.

"Is the Randolph suite available?" he asked the Hideaway's receptionist. The 1799 house had been built by Thomas Jefferson's son-in-law, Thomas Mann Randolph. The suite had once served as Randolph's law office and was Spencer's favorite.

"I'm sorry, sir," she said. "The only opening we have is the Honeymoon Cottage."

The idiocy of the moment made him chuckle. "Why not?" he said. "I'll take it. This is Judge Evan Spencer. I'll be arriving in a few minutes."

"Will Mrs. VanDenvender be arriving with you?"

"No," he said icily. "Does that really matter?"

"I'm, uh, sorry," she said. "I only asked because we know she likes fresh-cut roses in her room. How long will you be staying?"

"Indefinitely," he replied, hanging up.

By the time he reached the Hideaway, he had replayed his confrontation with Melissa a hundred times and had thought of dozens of clever lines that he now wished he had yelled at her. He checked in and made his way to the Honeymoon Cottage, a square white brick building behind the main house. Its front door opened into one large room with a queen-size sleigh bed resting on pine planks. There was an antique armoire and fireplace. A bathroom was hidden behind double French doors. He tossed his bag in the direction of the armoire and laid down on the bed's thick white comforter. All he could think about was how stupid he had been to have trusted Augustus VanDenvender

VI. They had never liked one another. Augustus had always felt his daughter had married beneath her.

As Spencer lay there, his left hand began to bleed. He hurried into the bathroom and thrust his palm under running water. He dabbed it with a towel, but it continued to ooze blood. He pressed harder with the towel, applying direct pressure, but the blood refused to coagulate and quickly saturated the terry cloth. Now he began to feel a sense of panic.

He grabbed another hand towel but that too failed to slow the bleeding. Spencer felt nauseous. He lifted the toilet seat and vomited. Seconds later, he retched again. His face was now covered with sweat. Exhausted, he collapsed on the white tiled floor next to the porcelain toilet bowl. He checked his palm.

The flow of blood had slowed enough so that he could see the outline of the cross. It looked as if a figure were hanging from it.

He was hit with another round of nausea and stuck his head over the bowl.

What is happening? What have I done to deserve this? What sin have I committed this time? Once again, he leaned over the bowl and vomited. *This isn't fair! Why am I being punished? I didn't steal the Circus Circus shares!*

20

AN E-MAIL MESSAGE WAS WAITING WHEN PATTI ARRIVED AT her office early Tuesday morning.

Frank Arnold killed his daughter. His motive was money. Your client is being set up as a patsy.

She had just finished reading it when Charles MacDonald stepped up behind her, startling her. "Ah!" she shrieked. "I didn't hear you come in!"

"Sorry. Didn't mean to scare you. I got here early and was down the hall in the little boys' room. Did you get another message?"

"Yes, but there's something odd about this one."

He read it. "Why? I've always suspected it was Frank Arnold."

"In the other e-mails, our source gave us clues: the bed-wetting, the stuff about Lester pleasuring himself. All this e-mail says is Frank did it. His motive was money. Where's the evidence?"

She read it again. "Besides, I thought we'd decided Frank was the guy sending us these e-mails. Why would he implicate himself?" Remembering their last conversation about the e-mails, she asked: "Did you find out if there was a video camera hidden in Cassie's room?"

"The cops said there wasn't one."

"Then who's sending these e-mails?"

"Does it really matter anymore? The point is that we now know that Frank is the killer."

She read the message one more time. "I just don't get it. How is money the motive? Frank Arnold's already rich."

"Maybe killing Cassie didn't make Frank richer," MacDonald volunteered. "Maybe the murder kept him from getting poorer."

"You've lost me."

"Let's assume," MacDonald began, "that Frank Arnold sees his wife having sex with our client. He's furious and wants to divorce Maxine, but under California divorce statutes, she'll get half of his money, maybe more, and that's $225 million! Frank is not the sort of man who happily gives up half of his fortune, especially to a cheating wife. He begins looking for a cheaper way out. Cassie wets her bed. Frank hears Cassie screaming and knows Maxine is beating her. He sees an opportunity. After Maxine comes back to their bedroom, she swallows a couple of sleeping pills and knocks herself out. Frank gets out of bed, kills Cassie, and makes it look like it's a copycat crime of the JonBenet killing."

"How does that help him get rid of his wife?"

"Remember, Frank Arnold got rich by thinking two steps ahead of everybody else. He makes the murder look like a copycat killing because he wants the cops to arrest Amil. Why? Because he knows that Amil is eventually going to squeal about his sexual affair with Maxine. Frank knows about his wife's past and how her first baby died from SIDS. He knows she has a violent temper and he knows she beat Cassie on the night of the murder. He figures that either the cops or a good defense attorney are going to find out all of these things. Bingo! Maxine is implicated. If Frank is really lucky, both of them will go down—Amil and Maxine."

"But why go through all that?" Delaney asked. "Why not just hire a hit man to kill them both?"

"Too risky. An outsider might try to blackmail you later. Besides, Frank Arnold has a huge ego and he's a macho guy. He's going to want to handle this personally."

"Yeah, but killing your own daughter?"

"Under California law, if Maxine gets sent to prison, he can divorce her without paying her a cent. Besides, Cassie ain't really his kid."

"What?" she stammered.

"One reason the cops were so concerned about the SIDS death of Maxine's first baby is because she'd already gotten herself pregnant again. The cops were afraid she might harm her second baby after it was born. Maxine was about four-months pregnant when she and her first husband divorced. The COMDEX convention was held six months later. That's when she met Frank Arnold. The way I figure it, she gave birth to Cassie about a month before she met Frank. He legally adopted Cassie on their wedding day, but he wasn't her real father or whatever the politically correct term is now."

"Her birth father," Delancy said. "Did you just say that Maxine met Frank a month after giving birth?"

"Yeah, why? Is that significant?"

"Ur, no, it's just impressive."

"Huh?"

"Most women I know take more than four weeks to get back in shape after they've pushed out a baby!"

"C'mon, Delaney," MacDonald said. "You're missing my

point. Frank Arnold wasn't really murdering his own flesh and blood."

Delaney was still skeptical. "I think we're better off arguing that Maxine did it, you know, lost control during a moment of rage. But if I were on that jury, I've got to tell you, I'd find our client guilty."

"I know you would," MacDonald replied. "And that's exactly what Frank Arnold wants. The guy is pulling everyone's strings and we're all dancing. The only ones who seem to see it are your anonymous source and me. Has your source ever been wrong? Sure he made a mistake about who was in the shower, but he's never been wrong. He says Frank's the killer and so do I."

"What happened to your hand?" Miss Alice asked when Spencer arrived at the courthouse Tuesday morning. It was bandaged.

"I cut it but it's not as bad as it looks."

He hid in his chambers until it was time for the murder trial to start.

Taylor Cauldwell called Frank Arnold and for more than an hour the prosecutor tossed him cream puff questions. Arnold's testimony dovetailed perfectly with his wife's.

Spencer was listening but having trouble concentrating. His left hand was throbbing. He began sweating. Delaney noticed.

"Your Honor," she said, interrupting Cauldwell's questioning, "are you feeling okay?"

Everyone stared at him.

"No," he grunted. "I need a short recess." He rose and several spectators gasped. The bandage on his left hand was soaked with blood. Spencer hurried into his chambers and its private bathroom, locking the doors behind him.

"Do I need to call a doctor?" Miss Alice called through the outer door.

"No," he hollered. "Just give me a few minutes."

He wrapped paper towels around his palm and then stumbled out of the bathroom to his desk chair. He seemed to know instinctively what he had to do. With his right hand, he unlocked the bottom drawer. With his left hand, he grabbed the stone. As soon as it touched his palm, there was a searing sound and the smell of burning flesh.

Spencer is in the Arnold's master bedroom. Frank and Maxine are asleep. The digital clock reads three A.M. Cassie screams. As Spencer watches, Frank Arnold nudges Maxine. "It's Cassie. Sounds like she's wet the bed again."

"Shit!" she groans as she pulls herself from the bed, still half-asleep. Meanwhile, Frank rolls over. Moments later, Spencer hears Maxine cursing and Cassie begins screaming. Frank hears it too. He sits up and begins to climb out of bed but then stops, even though Cassie is screaming louder. He rolls back in bed.

Maxine returns but she doesn't say anything to Frank. Instead, she walks into the bathroom. Spencer follows. She opens a bottle of sleeping pills, gulps several down, and crawls back in bed next to her husband.

Whoosh! Spencer is now in the basement. Cassie is lying on newspapers on the basement floor. Her legs, wrists, and mouth are taped. Someone has fashioned a garrote around her neck and turned it so tight that it's cutting into her skin. There's a man standing over her. Spencer steps from the shadows so he can see the man's face. It's Frank Arnold. He's crying. "I'm sorry, Cassie! Please, please, forgive me! Forgive us!" The little girl doesn't move. Arnold leaves the storeroom. Spencer follows. Arnold goes upstairs and into his office where he opens a drawer, removes a blue and silver pen, and begins writing on a legal pad.

Spencer moves in closer. Arnold is writing a ransom note with his left hand. When he finishes, he walks down the hallway and carefully lays the pages on the floor. He realizes he is still holding the ink pen and opens a nearby closet. He tucks the pen into the inside pocket of a man's black leather jacket.

The pain in Spencer's left hand stopped as quickly as it had begun.

Frank Arnold is the killer! Delbert Amil is innocent! Cassie's own father murdered her!

Spencer put the stone back into his desk drawer and locked

it. He walked back into his chamber's bathroom and washed his face.

I've got to tell Delaney!

Returning to his desk, he logged onto the Internet and called up the *Charlottesville Courant* Web page. He began typing:

> Frank Arnold killed Cassie. He used his left hand to write the ransom note. He used a blue and silver ink pen. He hid it in a black leather jacket in the hall closet near where the ransom note was found. He forgot to wipe off his prints. Find the pen.

"Judge Spencer?" It was Miss Alice calling to him through his locked door. "Is everything okay in there? Should I let the jurors and people leave?"

Spencer hit the SEND button on his computer. "Everything is fine now," he hollered. "I'll be right out. Have everyone stay put!"

When he returned to the courtroom, he said: "I'd like to apologize. I cut my hand last night and I've been battling a cold. I'm sorry if I alarmed everyone. Since it's almost noon, I've decided that we should adjourn for lunch. We will reconvene here at one o'clock."

Spencer slipped out of his judicial robe and hurried downstairs. He saw Patti Delaney walking toward a deli.

"Ms. Delaney."

She stopped. "Are you feeling better, Your Honor?"

"Yes, are you going to your office now?"

"No, I was going to grab a bite to eat. I skipped breakfast this morning."

"You might want to skip lunch too and get back to your office," he blurted out. "I mean, you'll be cross-examining Frank Arnold this afternoon and he's obviously very important. I think you'll need to be better prepared than you have been!" He turned and stepped away.

Delaney was stunned. What right did he have telling her that she needed to spend her lunch break studying in her office? She continued toward the deli, but by the time that she reached it, she'd reconsidered. Maybe he was right. She turned and headed toward her office.

* * *

Patti Delaney rarely turned off her computer and she usually left it connected to the Internet even when she wasn't in her office. When she sat down at her desk, she noticed that she had mail. It was the e-mail that Spencer had just sent her. As soon as she read it, she grabbed the phone and called the Albermarle County Sheriff's Department.

"I need to speak to Detective Dale Stuart. It's an emergency." A few moments later, Stuart answered. Delaney asked: "Did you ever find the ink pen that the killer used to write the ransom note?"

"No. Why?"

"It's a blue and silver pen and it's in the inside pocket of a man's black jacket hanging in the hallway closet at the Arnold's house!"

"Did your client tell you this?"

"No!" she replied. "Frank Arnold killed Cassie! He put the pen there."

"Frank Arnold's handwriting didn't match the writing on the note, we already checked."

"Of course it didn't," she replied, becoming irritated. "That's because he used his left hand and he's right-handed."

"Ms. Delancy, is this some sort of trick? I mean, the timing of this all seems a bit convenient. You're telephoning me during a noon break in the trial to tell me that Frank Arnold killed his daughter, and somehow you know where he hid the ink pen he used to write the ransom note? How do I know your client didn't hide it there?"

"Delbert Amil doesn't know anything about the ink pen. He didn't tell me about it!"

"Then who did? Who would know where it is hidden except the killer or someone who was planting evidence?"

"Look, just go to the Arnold house and get that pen! All I'm trying to do is help you catch the real killer!"

"We already have," he said. "He's your client." He hung up.

Delaney dialed another number.

"This is the *Charlottesville Courant*," a voice answered.

"I need to speak to the person who maintains your Web page on the Internet," Delaney said. "It's important."

The receptionist connected her to the newspaper's librarian, who gave her the number and address for an outside company called S&K Designs. Delaney dialed the number but the line was busy. She tried again a few seconds later, and then again, but it was still busy. She was out of time. She hurried back to the courthouse just as the afternoon session was about to begin.

"You found your daughter's body in the storeroom, isn't that right?" Taylor Cauldwell asked.

"Yes," Frank Arnold replied, his eyes wet with tears.

"I know this is difficult for you, but can you tell the jury what you saw when you first walked into that storeroom?"

"Cassie was lying on newspapers. Her pajama bottoms had been pulled down and her arms and legs were wrapped with duct tape and I—" Arnold stopped midsentence. He was becoming too emotional to continue. "I'm sorry, Judge," Arnold said. "I just need a moment."

Delaney scanned the jurors. Arnold had them eating out of his hand. About a half hour later, Cauldwell finished his questioning.

"You testified earlier that you never left your bedroom on the night that Cassie was murdered," Delaney said, adding: "Is that still your testimony?"

"Yes. It's the truth, I've got no reason to change it."

"You don't, huh?" she replied. "You didn't get up to check on Cassie after you heard your wife beating her?"

"I object!" Cauldwell protested. "There's been no evidence produced that suggests Maxine Arnold ever beat her child!"

"I'll rephrase my question," Delaney volunteered. "Did you go into the basement that night?"

"I already said that I didn't."

"You really aren't Cassie's father, are you?" she suddenly asked.

Arnold looked angry. "If you mean: Was she adopted? The answer is yes. I adopted her when she was less than a year old."

"But you never told the police that, did you?"

"It's nobody's business, but you have obviously been digging into our past, looking for garbage. Is that the best you found?"

Delaney knew her questions were alienating the jury. She was coming across as cruel. But she pushed on.

"Were you angry when you discovered your wife and my client were having a sexual affair?"

"I object!" Cauldwell shouted.

"Judge," Frank Arnold said, interrupting Cauldwell, "if you don't mind, I'd really appreciate the chance to answer that."

"Go ahead," Spencer replied.

Arnold turned so that he was now facing the jurors. "Ms. Delaney keeps implying that my wife was sexually involved with the defendant. At one point, I did walk into a room and surprise her with the defendant. But they weren't having sex. She was giving him a motherly hug. She'd been trying to help him prepare for entrance exams for college and he was upset and depressed. Of course, now we understand why—he really wasn't Lester Amil, he was an imposter."

"Mr. Arnold," Delaney complained, "a simple yes or no will do here. Were you angry because of their sexual affair?"

"My wife never had sex with him!" Arnold declared. "He threatened to accuse her of that as part of a plot to extort us. But I trust my wife completely. If I didn't have Maxine to lean on, I wouldn't want to go on. She owns my heart!"

"What a wonderful endorsement," Delaney replied sarcastically. "Did it take your public relations firm long to write it?"

"Your Honor!" Cauldwell said.

"I withdraw the question." Instead, she asked: "Mr. Arnold, do you use Viagra?"

One of the jurors groaned.

"Your Honor!" Cauldwell complained. "What could this possibly have to do with anything?"

"The defense has a right to ask about this witness's sex life," Delaney replied, "especially since one of our contentions is that Maxine Arnold was having a sexual affair with the defendant and he knew about it!"

"I'm going to allow you to continue but not for very long in this area," Spencer ruled.

"Do you use Viagra?"

"Yes. I'm a busy man, under tremendous stress, and sometimes I have trouble focusing. But that doesn't mean my wife and I don't have a great sex life."

Delaney wanted to ask him about the ransom note, but she was afraid to call attention to the blue and silver ink pen. If Detective Stuart was ignoring her tip, then Frank Arnold could return home and destroy it. She paused and looked toward the back door of the courtroom.

"Are you expecting someone?" Spencer asked.

"No, Your Honor." But she was. She was praying that Stuart would come bursting into the courtroom, carrying the ink pen with him, just like in a good Perry Mason episode. That apparently only happens in television shows.

"Ask your next question or sit down," Spencer said.

"Mr. Arnold, are you left- or right-handed?"

"Right."

"Can you write with your left hand?"

"I've not tried since I was a kid. I'm sure it wouldn't be legible."

Delaney heard a noise behind her. Detective Stuart came walking down the aisle. He handed Taylor Cauldwell a note.

"I'd like to ask for a short recess so the attorneys for the prosecution and defense can meet with you in your chambers," Cauldwell said. "I've just received information that should not be discussed in front of the jury but which may be important."

"What's happening?" Charles MacDonald asked Delaney, as they both headed toward the judge's chambers. She hadn't had time to tell him about the new e-mail and the ink pen.

"I'm about to get my Perry Mason ending!" she gushed.

"About an hour ago," Cauldwell explained in Spencer's chambers, "Detective Stuart recovered a blue and silver ink pen from the pocket of a man's leather coat at the Arnold's residence. He believes the killer used this specific pen to write the ransom note."

"How do you know this is the right pen?" Spencer asked.

"It's made by a company called David Oscarson. Our forensic specialists had already identified the ink found on the ransom note as being a special blend that only David Oscarson uses in his pens."

"So you're a hundred percent certain?"

"No, Judge, we need to take an actual sample of ink from the pen and compare it to the ink on the ransom note. But I'd say we are ninety percent convinced."

"How did Detective Stuart know where to look?"

"He received a tip from Ms. Delaney telling him."

"And were there any fingerprints on this pen?"

"Yes. Mr. Arnold's prints are all over it."

Delaney was beaming inside.

"Mr. Cauldwell, are you now telling me that Frank Arnold killed his daughter?" Spencer asked.

"No, Judge, we still believe Delbert Amil is the murderer."

"What!" a dumbstruck Delaney exclaimed. "You just said Frank Arnold's prints are all over that pen!"

"That's true, but how did you know where the pen was hidden?" Cauldwell replied.

"What exactly are you suggesting?" Spencer asked.

"Ms. Delaney has been pulling cheap theatrics from the start of this trial. First, she accused Maxine Arnold of beating her daughter to death. Now, she's claiming Frank Arnold is the killer. I want to know how she knew where that pen was hidden!"

"Why should that matter?" Delaney asked.

"It matters because we think your client planted it there."

"That's ridiculous!" Delaney shrieked.

"Judge," Cauldwell said, "Delbert Amil could have used that pen to write the ransom note and then hidden it so he could use it later to throw us all off his track and frame Frank Arnold."

"But his fingerprints aren't on the pen! Arnold's are!" Delaney protested.

"That's because your client used gloves. He could've held that pen at its very tip between his thumb and forefinger and written with it."

"This is insane!" Delaney exploded. "What do we have to do to prove our client is innocent?"

"Just tell us how'd you know where the pen was hidden," Cauldwell replied. "If your client didn't tell you, who did?"

Delaney glanced at Spencer.

"I'm afraid I can't tell you!" she said softly. "It's a confidential source."

"Ms. Delaney isn't a priest or a psychiatrist," Cauldwell complained. "She's never been granted any special confidentiality privilege."

Spencer and Delaney's eyes met. *Does she know I sent her the e-mail? Is she trying to protect me?* He couldn't be sure. He had another thought. *What if she mentions the e-mails and they're traced back to me? How am I going to explain them?*

Spencer asked Cauldwell: "How long will it take for you to do forensic tests on that ink to make certain it's the correct pen?"

"By late tomorrow afternoon we can be sure," Cauldwell answered.

"I'm going to adjourn court for today," said Spencer, "and we aren't going to meet tomorrow either. On Thursday, you will provide the defense and the court with the test results. We will reconvene on Friday morning. Between now and Friday, I would strongly suggest that Detective Stuart should do his job and find out what Mr. Arnold has to say about this ink pen."

"No," Cauldwell snapped. "I want you to ask her right now how she knew where that pen was!"

"Mr. Cauldwell, do I need to remind you that you're not the judge here?"

"But Your Honor, we have a right to know!"

"You may become the next governor," Spencer replied, "but I'm still the chief judge, and I just told you how we're going to handle this! If this is a defense ploy, I'll deal with that accordingly on Friday."

"Yes," Cauldwell answered bitterly.

"There's one more thing," Spencer continued. "I'd like to remind both of you but you in particular, Mr. Cauldwell, that my gag order about this murder case is still in effect. I don't want to read about the discovery of this ink pen in tomorrow's *Charlottesville Courant*. I think Walter Corn has had enough scoops lately. Don't you, Ms. Delaney?"

Once again Spencer and Delaney locked eyes.

"Yes, Judge," she said. "I've read enough trash in that paper lately."

* * *

Detective Stuart brought a video camera and tripod with him when he knocked on the front door of the Arnolds' house. He always felt strange returning to an old crime scene. Regardless of what changes had been made, he still would see everything in his mind exactly as it had been just after the crime occurred. The housekeeper led Stuart and another officer into a living room where Frank and Maxine were waiting.

"What's this all about?" Arnold asked. "More questions?"

"Yes, you might want to call your attorney before we get started."

Maxine erupted: "Goddamn it, Frank, this has to do with that goddamn defense attorney. Why can't that bitch leave us alone?"

Stuart introduced his partner and once again suggested that Arnold call his lawyer. While Arnold was in his office making that call, Maxine offered to make everyone a cocktail.

"No, thank you," Stuart said, "and I'd rather that you and your husband didn't drink while we're here."

Some twenty minutes later, the Arnolds' personal attorney arrived and huddled briefly with his clients. "I've advised Frank and Maxine not to answer any of your questions," the attorney said. "But Frank has decided to ignore my advice."

Stuart began the interview by stating the time, date, and name of everyone in the room. He then asked Maxine Arnold to leave, explaining that they might need to question her separately later.

"This is bullshit!" she screeched. "Our daughter's dead and you're treating us like criminals!" She stormed out.

"Mr. Arnold," Stuart said, "we believe the killer used a David Oscarson ink pen when he wrote the ransom note. Do you own such an ink pen?"

"Yes, as a matter of fact, I do. My wife gave me a blue and silver one last year for my birthday. It's magnificent! Now that you mention it, Delbert Amil had seen me use it and had asked me about it. He knew where I kept it in my desk drawer."

"Is that pen missing?"

Arnold paused, clearly trying to decide what he was going to say next. "I hadn't thought about it until just now, but because you've jarred my memory, I do believe that pen is miss-ing. In fact, I haven't seen it since my daughter was murdered. I bet Amil stole it! It's a Henrik Wigstrom limited edition worth about $4,300."

"Just so we are clear on this," Stuart said, "you're now telling me that you haven't seen that pen or used it since the murder—is that correct?"

"Well, if I haven't seen it, I couldn't have very well used it, could I?"

"That would mean that the last person to use that pen was the killer."

"Yes, I guess I'd agree with that," Arnold replied. "But what's your point?"

"The point is that we've found the pen and your fingerprints are the only ones on it."

Arnold's attorney whispered in his ear, pleading with him to stop talking, but Arnold refused to listen.

"You've found my pen," Arnold repeated, "and because my fingerprints are on it, you're suspicious of me?" He shook his head in disgust. "Didn't it ever occur to you geniuses that the killer might have worn gloves? Of course, my prints are on the pen! Why wouldn't they be? It's my pen!"

Stuart was struck by how calm Arnold appeared to be. He was too calm. The fact that he had ignored his attorney's warning about answering questions seemed foolhardy. But it appeared as if Arnold was actually enjoying himself. When Stuart had met him for the first time on the day of the murder, he'd been surprised by how detached Arnold had seemed for a father whose only daughter had just been reported missing. In contrast, Maxine had been an emotional wreck. Nor had Arnold shown much shock later that afternoon when Cassie's body had been found. At the time, Stuart had assumed Arnold had been suppressing his feelings so that he could deal effec-tively with the calamity swirling around him. Now, as he watched Arnold, the detective wondered if Arnold had been calm because he had already known that Cassie was dead. He had another thought. On the morning when Cassie was found, Stuart had not seen anything sinister about Arnold being the first to find her body. Now he wondered if Arnold had hurried into the storeroom because he had wanted to contaminate the crime scene. Scooping up Cassie's body and carrying it upstairs had made it impossible for detectives to examine the storeroom exactly as the murderer had left it. His actions had also given him the perfect excuse if detectives later found his fingerprints or other evidence linking him to the murder.

"We found your pen in a very odd place," Stuart continued. He was watching Arnold's eyes. He'd always thought the best chance at catching someone in a lie was by watching their pupils change size. He decided to trick Arnold by lying to him. "We found your pen under the bed in your bedroom, between the headboard and the wall, on the side you sleep on. How do you explain that?"

"I don't have to," Arnold said coldly, "because you're lying."

Stuart didn't say anything for a moment and then he said: "You're right. I was lying. We actually found your ink pen in one of your pockets in a black jacket in the hall closet. Now, doesn't it seem strange that the killer would put an expensive ink pen inside your coat in a closet after he was done using it?"

"I don't know. Why don't you ask Delbert Amil?"

"Putting that pen there—that sounds more like what a man would do if he had a sentimental attachment to a pen because his wife had given it to him as a birthday present."

Arnold glared at Stuart.

"Why don't you admit it?" Stuart asked. "You instinctively picked up that pen that night from your desk to write the ransom note. Then you realized your mistake. But you couldn't part with that pen. So you hid it in your own jacket, thinking no one would ever look there. And if they did, so what? You just figured you'd bluff your way out. Isn't that what really happened? Isn't that what's happening now?"

Arnold's entire demeanor changed. He began sweating profusely. His eyes darted between his attorney and Stuart. His attorney whispered to him but Arnold wanted to say something. It was as if he felt a need to explain.

"You think you're smart, don't you, Detective?" Arnold said. "But the truth is, you don't have a clue as to what really happened that night. So I'm going to do you a favor, I'll tell you the truth."

"I'm listening."

"On the night of the murder, I woke up because Cassie was crying. She'd wet her bed. Maxine went down to Cassie's bedroom. I heard Cassie screaming and knew Maxine was going off on her. She loses her temper easily. When she came back to our bedroom, she took some sleeping pills and got back into bed. I dozed off, but I was worried about Cassie, so about an hour later, I went to check on her."

"That would make it a little after four A.M." Stuart said.

"Yes. Only when I got there, Cassie wasn't in her bedroom. I couldn't find her so I went downstairs and looked in the kitchen. But I couldn't find her there either, so I continued down into the basement. There was no one in Amil's room. He hadn't gotten home yet—or so I thought. Then I heard a noise. I began checking the other rooms and when I got to the storeroom, I saw Cassie lying on these old newspapers. I rushed over to her and felt for her pulse but she didn't have one. She was dead."

"She'd already been murdered?"

"That's right!" Arnold exclaimed. "I was in shock. I kept telling myself, 'You've got to think this through! Cassie is dead! There's nothing you can do about that now!' My next thought was: 'Maxine killed Cassie!' I assumed it was an accident. She'd probably hit Cassie too hard or knocked her head against something."

Arnold paused, tears began to flow down his cheeks. "Detective, I love my wife. I'd already lost my daughter and I didn't want to lose Maxine. So I decided that I'd stage the murder. I'd make it look like the JonBenet killing."

"Why?"

"I know this all sounds insane now, but it all seemed to make perfect sense when I was doing it. A few days before, I'd caught Maxine and Amil having sex in the living room. She does that—cheats on me—it's how she relates to men, how she controls them. I've always forgiven her but I hate it. I decided to frame Amil! It seemed perfect. I'd rescue Maxine from going to prison and get rid of him at the same time. Plus, I knew she would be obligated to me forever because I'd be the only one who knew the truth—that she had killed our daughter. If she ever tried to divorce me, I'd threaten to expose her." Stuart glanced at the video camera to make certain it was recording Arnold's confession. It was.

"I took a magazine article from Amil's room that described the Ramsey crime scene and I began replicating it. I was the one who planted Amil's stun gun and his personal identification badge on the floor."

"Did you also duct tape your daughter's hands?"

"Yes," he said. "It was horrible but I did it. Like I explained, I was in shock." He covered his face with his hands and for a moment sobbed. "The next morning, Maxine got up first and I heard her go downstairs. Then she comes running back into our room with my ransom note and says, 'Cassie's been kidnapped! I just called the police!' She was really scared. It struck me that she really didn't know that Cassie was already dead. I thought: *If Maxine didn't kill her, then Amil must have!* Later that night, you told me that Amil had been arrested and his semen had been found on Cassie's pajamas. I knew I had tampered with the crime scene, but it really hadn't mattered because I had helped frame the actual killer."

"Does your wife know that you suspected her and made the crime look like the JonBenet murder?"

"No. How could I admit that to her?" He looked pleadingly at Stuart. "I want to be perfectly clear here: I did not kill Cassie. I admit that I made it look like the JonBenet case, but I didn't kill my daughter! Delbert Amil killed her!"

PART THREE
RESURRECTION

O

For now we see through a glass, darkly: but then face to face; now I know in part; but then shall I know . . .

First Corinthians, Chapter Thirteen, Verse 12

21

PATTI DELANEY HAD TO DISCOVER WHO WAS SENDING HER anonymous e-mails. As soon as Spencer adjourned court on Tuesday, she drove to S & K Designs. The Web page firm was housed on the second floor of a dilapidated building in a poorer section of Charlottesville. A coin-operated laundry took up the ground floor. No one answered when Delaney pushed a buzzer next to a battered wooden door that had a cheap plastic sign nailed onto it that simply said WEB DE-SIGNS. Delaney could see lights burning upstairs, so she scooted through a narrow passageway between the building and its equally antiquated neighbor and entered an alley. A rusty metal fire escape ladder led to a second-floor window.

It was the only way up.

She began climbing, and when she reached the window, she peeked inside. A cute, twenty-something woman wearing baggy blue overalls, a clinging yellow tank top, and a New York Yankees baseball cap backward on her head was perched barefoot in a chair in front of a computer screen. Delaney tapped on the windowpane and the girl jumped.

"Hello!" Delaney mouthed through the closed window.

The girl came over. "Whatdayawant?" she asked, her words coming out as one.

"Are you with S & K Web Designs? It's important."

The girl unlocked the window, opened it, and helped Delaney step inside. The room was a catastrophe. It was cluttered with junk: boxes of computer parts, empty soda cans, discarded pizza boxes, and stacks and stacks of computer paper.

Delaney explained that she was a defense attorney working on a death row murder case.

"I've read about you in the newspaper, like, you're the attorney representing that black kid who's accused of killing that girl whose dad is Frank Arnold who invented the Arnold FNZ3600 Intelligent Optical Switch," the girl replied. She spoke in one run-on sentence, although she occasionally used the word "like" instead of a period when she changed subjects. "My name is Kathy but everyone just calls me Kat because it's, like, a nickname my brother Steve gave me years ago when we were little, like, he didn't like cats, you know, or me, but now, like, since we opened this place, we run it together and, like, we've become best friends and it's kind of funny, you know?" She took a breath. "I only work here part-time since I'm still a student and, like, since I'm studying criminology, I've been following your murder case real close and it's, like, just amazing to me to meet you, like, why are you here?"

"I need your help," Delaney said. She explained how she had been getting anonymous messages tagged onto news stories from the *Charlottesville Courant*'s library.

Kat said: "Wow, that's pretty clever, like, me and my brother never thought about that problem when we set up the page, you know, so how many messages have you gotten from this person and, what does he say when he sends them to you or can you tell me or is it, like, you know, secret trial stuff?"

Delaney took out a copy of the most recent e-mail message. "Before I show you this," she said, "you've got to promise you'll not tell anyone. You've got to swear that this will be our little secret."

"Wow, this is just like on television, oh man, hey, no problem, you can trust me because me and my best friend, her name is Cathy too, except she spells her name with a 'C,' we share all sorts of secrets and I've never told anyone anything unless it's my brother Steve but he doesn't really count because, like, he doesn't talk to anyone anyway, because he is always on his computer surfing the net, trying to break into other people's systems, but don't worry because I won't even tell him unless you say it's okay because, like, he's really smart and maybe he can really help you solve this thing because when he was little, they had a brain teaser at his elementary school each week and the kid who solved it won a prize, and he won it every week for the entire school year, so they, like, told him he couldn't do it anymore and we all thought that was really unfair."

Listening to Kat was wearing her out. "Here's a copy of the e-mail," Delaney said, "can you tell me who sent it?"

Kat read it and began typing on her keyboard. "Do you think I'll be called as a witness or something because I've never really been in a courtroom before and, like, I wouldn't mind it especially if it's like that television show about lawyers on Sunday nights cause, like, it's one of my absolute favorites except for the guy who plays the lead attorney, like, I mean my friend, Cathy, she says he's really hot, you know, what's his name, but I think he's really too hypocritical and intense, you know?"

Delaney interrupted: "Kat, I really need you to focus on finding who is sending me these messages. It's important and I'm sorry, but I'm in a hurry!"

"Sorry, my friend Cathy says I get carried away sometimes talking you know, it's just a bad habit, but I've always liked to talk or at least that's what Steve tells me." She was still typing. "Do you want me to tell you what I'm doing because it really isn't that difficult, first I gotta get into the newspaper's mainframe and then I gotta get into its library and then I gotta find the newspaper clipping that this guy sent you with his message attached to it to hide his identity." She took a breath. "There's a fairly good firewall around the newspaper's archives but since me and my brother put it there we can slip right through it because we left a trap door so we could do that and it, like, shouldn't be that difficult, in fact, I'm in the library right now and here's the story that your source tagged onto and when I push this little button right here we'll be able to see the history of everyone who's ever called up this story and then we can see who forwarded the story to someone else and then we can find the one that was sent to you and see who sent it, like, does that make sense to you?"

"Yes," said Delaney, although it really didn't. She simply didn't want Kat to repeat it all again.

Kat clicked the key and a series of Web addresses flashed on the screen. To Delaney, they looked like gobbledy-gook, but Kat jumped up from her chair, raised her right hand in the air and screamed, "You go, girl, like, give me five!" Delaney slapped Kat's open palm. "Now, let's see which one of these addresses sent you this newspaper story, okay, like I got it." She struck a few more keys as she talked. "Here it is."

Delaney looked at the letters on the screen:

CJES@CO.ALBEMARLE.VA.US./Circuit Court.

"I'm guessing these are probably someone's initials and he gets his mail at the courthouse, which is really wild because that means someone in the building is your anonymous source, like, this reminds me, did you see the episode on television when these lawyers were getting e-mails from this guy who actually is the real killer and he's tormenting them, you know, telling them stuff that . . ."

"Are you certain it's CJES?" Delaney asked, interrupting.

"Yep, that's who it is, like I said, me and my brother designed this entire tracking system, only now, it's like kids' stuff, because we've been setting up far better systems than this, like, wow, I can hardly wait to tell Steve about you."

"Wait a second!" Delaney said. "Remember, this is our secret. Mum's the word! That's what we agreed on, remember?"

"Oh yeah," said Kat, "but I need to tell my brother, okay, but, like, I'll swear him to secrecy, but he'll be good about it, cause he really doesn't have anyone to talk to anyway, remember?"

"I want to pay you," said Delaney. She wrote her name, address, and telephone numbers on a piece of paper. "You can just send me a bill. I really appreciate what you've told me. Now remember, this is a secret." She looked around the room. "Can I leave through the front door?"

"Naw, the lock is all busted and Steve says he's going to fix it but he never does and really I don't care because, like, you probably noticed, this isn't the best neighborhood and some creeps tried to break in here once so me and my brother just use the window and I just keep a can of Mace by the window, and since we don't ever get anyone coming here very often except for the pizza delivery guy, who is sort of hot and doesn't mind climbing up the fire escape, just like you did, well, I figure the window works just fine."

Delaney climbed out the window while Kat continued jabbering. "When this case is solved, do you think you could, like, send a letter to the producers of that television show on Sunday night because I think it would make a good plot for a story on television, especially the part about me finding out who was sending you those messages, like, you know, cause hacking has been on television a lot but this would be, like, something that was true."

"I'll call you later," Delaney yelled when she reached the alleyway. She drove back to her office. She wanted to make certain that her hunch about the identity of *"CJES"* was accurate. She took out a directory entitled *Albemarle County Public Officials* and looked under the letter "S." There was a Clifford Sanford listed there but he was an engineer at the city zoning board. She continued down the list until she got to Evan Spencer: *CJES*. She easily deciphered it: *Chief Judge Evan Spencer*.

She had suspected him since their encounter earlier that day. The tip-off had been when he had abruptly told her that she needed to return to her office rather than eating at the deli. The e-mail about Frank Arnold had been waiting there for her.

The fact that she now knew that he was the source still didn't answer the bigger questions: How had Judge Spencer known where Frank Arnold's ink pen was hidden? How had he known that Maxine Arnold beat her daughter after Cassie had wet her bed? How had he known about Delbert Amil masturbating? She tried to imagine a possible explanation. There was none. Then she wondered: Why is he helping me?

She looked in the telephone book for Judge Spencer's home number. She found it listed under his wife's name. Delaney called VanDenvender Hall.

"Hello," a woman answered.

"This is Patti Delaney. I'm an attorney in the—"

"I know who you are. This is Melissa VanDenvender," she replied sharply. "What do you want?"

"I'm sorry to disturb you at home, but I need to speak to the judge. It's urgent! Can you get him for me, please?"

"No!" She hung up.

Delaney hadn't expected to be treated so impolitely. She dialed the number again but after the third ring, Melissa picked up the receiver and put it back down.

What a bitch! Delaney thought. She found Miss Alice's home number in the directory and dialed it. After she apologized for bothering her at home, Delaney asked: "Does the judge have a beeper or a cell phone, or is there another number I can call at VanDenvender Hall to reach him? His wife keeps hanging up on me!"

"Call the Clifton Hideaway," Miss Alice said. "Ask for the Honeymoon Cottage. He's staying there."

"The Hideaway?"

"Don't tell him I told you how to find him," she added. "Let's just say that he and Melissa VanDenvender are having a bit of a spat."

"Excuse me, but did you say the Honeymoon Cottage?"

Miss Alice laughed. She was clearly enjoying this. "That's right!"

Delaney called but the Hideaway receptionist refused to put her call through. "The judge said he did not want to be disturbed for any reason."

Delaney went outside, got into her Saab, and headed toward the resort.

Sorry Judge, she thought, *but you have some explaining to do.*

Melissa VanDenvender had just served coffee to her two guests when Patti Delaney's calls rang at VanDenvender Hall. She had not appreciated the interruption. The Rev. Dr. Dino Grasso and his young traveling companion, Kyle Dunham, however, had not seemed offended.

"As I was saying," Melissa said, after ridding herself of Delaney, "my husband is adjudicating a rather ghastly murder trial in the city. Perhaps you've read about it or seen news reports on television?"

"The Arnold girl murder case?" Grasso asked.

"Yes," she replied. "Often when my husband becomes involved in cases such as this one, he works late. Out of courtesy to me, he stays in Charlottesville. I have a busy schedule and require a good night's sleep."

Dunham was fidgeting in his chair because he was hungry. They had flown from Las Vegas to Dulles Airport and had driven to Charlottesville without eating. Dunham had tried to convince Grasso to stop at several fast food restaurants, but the priest had been intent on getting to town as quickly as possible. He didn't want the trail of the *giudicare* stone to go cold. Dunham had gobbled down three candy bars from a vending machine at a gas station where they had gotten directions to VanDenvender Hall, but he was starving. Melissa had offered them coffee, but nothing else, although there were some mints in a jar on a table next to Dunham's chair. He began popping them, one after another, into his mouth.

Melissa was meeting with them in the library. It had high ceilings with exposed wooden beams. The floor was wide planks made of a dark hardwood. The walls were painted off-white and decorated with oil portraits. Melissa noticed Dunham staring at them.

"These are my ancestors," she said. "The VanDenvender family can trace its roots back to when this country was still called the New World."

"Ah yes," said Grasso. "Several years ago, I read the autobiography that Augustus VanDenvender had written about his role in the Revolutionary War. It was most interesting."

"His portrait is hanging over the mantel," she said, motioning with her right hand to a large canvas. The portrait showed an aristocrat in a white wig dressed in the militia uniform of the 22nd Regiment of Virginia, which featured a blue coat with scarlet facing. "He served in the same unit as George Washington and that portrait was painted by Charles Wilson Peale. He later painted a nearly identical portrait of the president, which today hangs at Washington and Lee University in Lexington, Virginia. According to family history, Augustus became furious when he learned that Peale had used his portrait as a test, of sorts, for the one that he later did of President Washington.

Augustus threatened to burn his portrait but instead demanded that Peale refund the fee that he'd charged for painting it."

"Did he get his money back?" Dunham asked.

"Yes," she said. "Not only did he get a full refund but he secretly loved the painting and how it was done before George Washington's."

"This portrait is of you, isn't it?" Grasso asked, nodding toward a painting of a woman seated in a chair with a distinguished man standing behind her. Unlike the others, which were traditional realistic paintings, it was done in a modern, softer, impressionistic style.

"Yes, it was painted five years ago by a Russian who is well known in Europe but not here. I have a special fondness for Russians. Tell me, Father Grasso, what is your view on reincarnation?"

"I don't believe in it."

"That's a shame! I asked because I happen to share the same day and month of birth as Alexandra Fyodorovna, the wife of Russian Emperor Nicholas II. I have read quite a bit about her and believe we share numerous personality characteristics. I've always been curious about whether or not I may have lived before. When I arranged for the Russian artist to come here for two months so he could paint my portrait, he and I had several interesting conversations about the similarities."

"That painting must have cost you a fortune," Dunham said. "Is that your husband in it with you?"

"You must forgive my young friend for being rude," Grasso said. "I assume the man standing behind you is your father."

"You're correct," she replied. "My father doesn't like to have his photograph taken or to pose for paintings. Having him pose with me was a way to force him into it."

"You're beautiful," Dunham said, clumsily hoping to make amends for his social blunder.

"Can you tell us where we can find your husband?" Grasso asked.

Melissa wrote a telephone number and directions on a card and handed it to him. "I don't think you have told me why you wish to see him? I assume it's a legal matter?"

"No," Grasso replied, "it has to do with religion."

"Religion?" she replied. "Spencer has never shown much interest in the Bible."

"May I ask you, have any strange marks appeared on his hands?"

She thought for a moment. "My husband has a red mark on his left hand. He tried to hide it from me but I noticed it one day. He's also been having fainting spells. At one point, we think he was struck by lightning. But what does that mark have to do with religion?"

"We're trying to find a stone," Dunham volunteered, but before he could say another word, Grasso interrupted.

"We're not entirely certain what we're searching for," he said, "but after I speak to your husband, I should know more and perhaps then I can explain it to you."

Grasso thanked her and said good-bye. Outside in their rental car, he gently chided Dunham for mentioning the stone.

"I'm sorry," Dunham said. "I was just trying to help. They're married so I didn't think mentioning it was any big deal."

"How many rooms do you think are in VanDenvender Hall?" Grasso asked.

"Twenty, thirty, maybe even fifty?"

"Then tell me this: Why would a judge, who lives alone with his wife in a thirty-room mansion only a short drive from his office, have to stay in a hotel if he wanted privacy?"

The gravel road leading to the Clifton Hideaway was only a few turns off a main thoroughfare just outside of Charlottesville, but because the manor house sat deep in the woods, it seemed remote. It was a clear night and there was a full moon, bright enough that at ten o'clock Delaney could have turned off her car's headlights and still seen clearly. She parked her Saab at the front entrance of the traditional two-story colonial manor house. A receptionist welcomed her as soon as she stepped into the foyer.

"I wondered if I could get a brochure that would tell me more about your wonderful bed and breakfast?" Delaney asked. The woman took one from an antique secretary.

"My husband and I are thinking about celebrating a second honeymoon," Delaney continued. "You do have a honeymoon suite, don't you?"

"Yes, it's set apart from the main house for privacy."

Delaney stepped outside under the front porch lights. There was a tiny map inside the brochure. According to it, the Honeymoon Cottage was at the end of a white stone path that also led to a croquet court and rose garden. Delaney had just started down the path when her cell phone rang. She grabbed it quickly. She didn't want to attract attention and have someone ask her why she was walking through the resort's grounds.

"Is this Ms. Delaney, the attorney in the Arnold murder trial?" a voice asked. Delaney recognized the caller. It was Kat from S & K Web Designs.

"Hi Kat. This isn't a good time for me."

"Oh, sure, sorry, okay, but like, there is something you've really gotta know and I thought you would want to know it as soon as possible so, like, that's why I am calling you on your cell phone."

"What is it?"

"You told me, like, how you had gotten several e-mails from this anonymous source and you know, you remember how me and you checked that one and I told you some guy named CJES had sent it to you from the courthouse?"

"Yes," Delaney replied impatiently.

"Well, okay, like after you left, I decided to look back and pull up every e-mail this CJES guy sent you and I hope you don't mind, but I was curious and I wanted to see what else he had to say to you, sorry, but, like, so I went back in the computer's history and found all of the other e-mails that had been forwarded to you and sure enough every one of them was from this CJES guy except for one that wasn't."

"What?" Delaney asked. She stopped walking. Until now, she hadn't been paying close attention. "Kat, I need you to stop talking and listen closely now to what I'm going to ask you," Delaney said.

"Cool, this is kinda like you questioning me, like, if I were on the witness stand right? I mean . . ."

"Kat, are you saying that one of the e-mails sent to me anonymously didn't come from CJES? Just answer yes or no and nothing else because that is how we'd do it if we were in court."

"Wow, cool, ur, I mean, yes, that's what I am saying, Ms. Defense Attorney."

"Good," Delaney said. "Now, Kat, I want you to tell me which message did not come from CJES? Remember, you must answer yes or no. Was it the first message about Cassie wetting her bed and her mother beating her?"

"No!"

"Was it the second message about Amil masturbating?"

"Yuck, no. That one came from CJES too!"

"Was it the third message that said Frank Arnold was the killer?"

"Yes, that came from someone else. I got the message right here. The message says: 'Frank Arnold killed his daughter. His motive was money. Your client is being set up as a patsy.' Your CJES guy didn't send that message."

"Then who sent it to me?"

"Okay, well, like that's the really crazy part of this whole thing because, like, it's so weird because when I traced that message back, it turned out that you had, like, sent it to yourself."

"What?"

"Wow, you're surprised then too, right, because I thought, like, how could she have sent this to herself and not know it, so I checked it again and, yep, you e-mailed it to yourself or at least someone used your computer to send the e-mail to you."

"How?"

"You ever leave your computer turned on and connected to the Internet because I do that all of the time and my brother Steve is always coming in and then writing me some stupid e-mail and sending it to me so it looks like I got mail from myself and when I open it, it says something like 'Hey stupid you left your computer hooked up to the Internet again.' "

Delaney was trying to think of who, besides Charles MacDonald, had been in her office alone.

"Oh," Kat said. "I spoke to my brother and, like, he says we should charge you twice our normal fee because you're a lawyer and lawyers make a lot of money so he is putting together a bill right now and I don't think that's right and I told

him I was going to tell you that I didn't think it was right because it will be, maybe, like two hundred bucks, but he wants
to do it anyway and I wanted to warn you because you seem
really nice."

"It's okay, Kat," Delaney said. "Trust me, you've earned it."

"Wow," Kat said. She began rambling about how she was going to use her share of the money to buy a pair of shoes but Delaney had heard enough. "Sorry," Delaney said. "I need to run."

When she reached the Honeymoon Cottage, she climbed
the three wooden steps that led to its door and knocked gently.

Judge Spencer opened it. "Ms. Delaney," he said, "you're
my second surprise of the evening!" He swung the door completely open so that she could see inside. There were two men
in the room. One was young, the other was an odd-looking
Roman Catholic priest.

"Please join us," Spencer said.

22

PATTI DELANEY SPOKE SOFTLY BECAUSE SHE DIDN'T WANT
Spencer's two guests to hear. "Judge," she said, "I've come to
talk to you about several anonymous e-mails I've received
concerning the murder."

"Do you know who has been sending them to you?"

"Yes," she replied. "You!"

Spencer felt a sense of relief. "I think you need to come
inside."

After she stepped in, he closed the door and introduced her
to Father Grasso and Kyle Dunham. They were sitting on the
only two chairs in the suite so he directed her toward the bed.
She sat next to him on its edge facing the two men.

"Ms. Delaney is a defense attorney in the Arnold murder
case," Spencer said. "I'd like you to explain to her what
you've just been telling me."

Grasso seemed reluctant. But Spencer said: "Father, trust

me, she needs to hear this, otherwise, she'll never believe me or understand what I've been doing these past several weeks."

Grasso asked Delaney: "Are you a religious person, Ms. Delaney?"

"I was reared in the United Methodist Church," she replied. "I don't go to church every Sunday, but I believe in God and I have a fairly good understanding of the Bible."

"Do you believe in miracles?"

"I believe things happen which we cannot explain," she replied. "Whether or not they are caused by God or are events that we aren't intelligent enough to comprehend is open to debate."

"Spoken like a true attorney," Spencer quipped. He began unwrapping the bandage on his hand. When it was completely off, he turned over his palm so she could see the red slashes on it.

"Oh my God!" she exclaimed. "It's a crucifix!"

"Patti," Spencer said quietly, "what Father Grasso is about to tell you is going to sound, well, pretty unbelievable. I had a hard time understanding it when he told me, and it's happening to me. All I ask is that you keep an open mind and keep it secret."

"My first obligation is to my client," she said. "But if it doesn't interfere with my ability to defend him, then I'm willing to keep it confidential."

Grasso addressed Dunham. "Kyle, please read us verse twenty in chapter nine of the New Testament book of the Gospel of Matthew." Dunham opened a Bible and began:

"And behold, a woman who had suffered from a hemorrhage for twelve years came up behind him and touched the fringe of his garment; for she said to herself, 'If I only touch his garment, I shall be made well.' Jesus turned, and seeing her, he said, 'Take heart, daughter; your faith has made you well.'"

"What do we learn from this passage?" Grasso asked rhetorically. "We learn that this woman was healed simply because she touched the garment that Jesus was wearing!"

He instructed Dunham to read another verse, this time from chapter fourteen of Matthew, verse thirty-five:

"And when the men of that place recognized him, they sent to him all that were sick and besought him that they might only touch the fringe of his garment; and as many as touched it were made well."

"Once again, the scriptural message is clear: Jesus was so pure, so divine, that people were healed just by touching the fringe of his garments," Grasso continued. "This is what I want you to remember: that by simply touching an article that Jesus had touched, a miracle occurred."

Grasso asked Dunham to read from chapter eight in the Book of John, but before he began, Grasso said: "Even though this may be a familiar story to you, Ms. Delaney, still listen to it very closely, please."

"The scribes and the Pharisees brought a woman who had been caught in adultery, and placing her in the midst they said to him, 'Teacher, this woman has been caught in the act of adultery. Now in the law, Moses commanded us to stone such. What do you say about her?' This, they said to test him, that they might have some charge to bring against him. Jesus bent down and wrote with his finger on the ground. And as they continued to ask him, he stood up and said to them, 'Let him who is without sin among you be the first to throw a stone at her.' And once more he bent down and wrote with his finger on the ground. But when they heard it, they went away, one by one, beginning with the eldest, and Jesus was left alone with the woman standing before him. Jesus looked up and said to her, 'Woman, where are they? Has no one condemned you?' She said, 'No one, Lord.' And Jesus said, 'Neither do I condemn you; Go, and do not sin again.' "

"Yes, I'm familiar with that story," Delaney said. "As a child in Sunday school, we used to talk about how horrible it would've been to have people throw stones at you until you were dead. I also remember that saying—'Let him who has never sinned throw the first stone!' "

"Excellent," Grasso said. "Now, I'm going to share a secret with you, something that I do not believe the church will ever publicly acknowledge, but which is, nevertheless, true. I have just returned from the Vatican and while I was there, I was taken into a vault hidden deep inside the Secret Archives and I was shown a section of an ancient scroll that is kept there hidden from the public. This scroll was found in a cave in Jordan not far from the Dead Sea during World War Two. The writing on this scroll is Greek. There were other scrolls found in other clay pots in this same cave but they were not in Greek. This has led to speculation that someone was translating an original Greek document into Syrian."

"That means the Greek one is the oldest document," Dunham gushed.

"Thank you," Grasso said patiently. "Ms. Delaney, I don't know if you are aware of it, but the validity of the story about the stoning of the adulteress has been hotly debated by biblical scholars for centuries. Mainly because there is no mention of this story in the church's earliest known manuscripts. Absolutely none. It can't be found in the Syrian translation of Cureton, in the Sinaiticus, the Gothic translation, or in the Coptic and Armenian translations, or in the oldest manuscript of the Itala."

Grasso could tell by the blank looks on Delaney and Spencer's faces that neither had ever heard of any of those early manuscripts. "Forgive me," he apologized. "I'm beginning to sound like the boring old professor that I am. I'm referring to ancient writings that have survived over the centuries and are accepted as the most accurate accounts we have about the life and teachings of Jesus Christ. They were written long before the Holy Bible was organized, assembled, and approved by the church."

"Exactly what are you saying?" Delaney asked, "that this passage about the stoning of the adulteress in the Book of John may have never happened?"

"No," Grasso replied firmly. "All I am saying is that there is no mention of it in any of the earliest texts about Jesus. But please understand that this does not mean it didn't occur. You see, many biblical scholars believe the earliest writers intentionally omitted the story because they found it offensive since it dealt with adultery. This has led them to believe that the story was added later by writers who felt it was important to make a complete record of Christ's actions."

"What does the scroll that was found in the cave say?" Delaney asked.

"Ah, you have a quick mind," Grasso replied. "You know where I'm going with this. Before I answer your question, I must give you a bit more history. Using carbon-dating techniques, the church was able to establish that the scroll in the Jordan cave was written earlier than nearly all other known accounts about Jesus Christ. Do you understand what this means? This means this scroll is a truly remarkable discovery. Just imagine, it's the oldest record, the one written closest to Christ's actual life! Of course, we have no clue who the author might have been. That remains a matter of speculation. But this scroll tells many of the same stories that are told later in other scriptures. It verifies them. What makes this scroll so compelling is that it contains details about the adulteress story that were omitted later when the story was finally added to the gospel." He paused a moment so that she could realize the significance of what he had just told her.

"What sort of details?" she asked.

"The scroll says Jesus bent down and picked up a stone from the ground. He then showed this stone to the mob gathered around the woman. Then Jesus wrote in the ground just as the Book of John later reports."

"That's all?" Delaney asked. "He picked up a stone! That was the only real difference between the scroll and the story that's in the Gospel of John?"

"It seems like such a minor detail, doesn't it," Grasso said. "Insignificant, really, or so it would seem. You can understand why—by the time that the Gospel of John was written long after Jesus died—this minor detail may have been easily overlooked or forgotten. Yet the discovery that Jesus picked up a stone is actually quite astonishing."

"Why?" Delaney asked. "Jesus picked up a stone—so what? I don't mean to be disrespectful, Father, but what's the big deal! And, quite frankly, I'm having trouble seeing how any of this relates to the Arnold murder case."

"Patti," Spencer said, "I have the stone."

"What?"

"I have the stone that Jesus touched."

She looked at him and then at Grasso and then back at Spencer. "You're joking, right? You're telling me that you have a stone that Jesus Christ actually touched more than two thousand years ago?"

"I have it locked in a drawer in my desk at the courthouse," Spencer explained. "It was sent to me, a few days before Cassie Arnold was murdered, by a Boston attorney. Within a few hours after he mailed it, he killed himself."

"Some Boston attorney sent you this stone and then killed himself?" she repeated, still bewildered by what she was hearing.

"Just before you arrived," Spencer said, "Father Grasso was telling me that in the Vatican, it's known as the *giudicare* stone—the 'judgment stone.' I knew there was something special about it, but until tonight, I didn't know what. The first time I touched it, I was knocked unconscious by a bolt of electricity. I woke up in the hospital. This stone is, for lack of a better word, supernatural. It's what has been showing me the visions that I've had about Cassie's murder. That's how I knew the information that I sent you in those e-mails."

He could tell by the expression on her face that she still didn't understand.

"Patti," he said, "think about it. How would I have known that Cassie Arnold wet her bed on the night when she was killed? How would I have known that Maxine Arnold went into her daughter's room and beat her? How would I have known that your client masturbated over Cassie's pajamas? How would I have known that Frank Arnold hid his ink pen in his coat jacket?"

"I thought there were cameras hidden in the house," she replied. "I thought maybe there were videotapes that showed those events and the police were hiding them from us! I never thought you'd tell me that you'd had visions caused by a stone!"

"I know it's difficult to believe, but I did have them. And I had those visions after I touched the stone—the same stone that Jesus picked up off the ground when that angry mob was about to stone that woman to death! It's the stone that has allowed me to see the truth, to know what was going on when Cassie was killed."

For a few moments, he let her quietly mull over what he had said. Then Spencer continued: "The stone transported me into the Arnolds' house. I saw Frank Arnold standing over Cassie's body. I saw him write that ransom note and hide his ink pen. I saw Delbert Amil masturbating over Cassie's pajamas! And I was there when Cassie Arnold woke up because she had wet her bed and called for her mother! I saw Maxine Arnold come into that bedroom that night! I saw her hit her daughter! I know it sounds impossible! It should be impossible! But I was there!"

Delaney asked: "I still don't get it! How can touching a stone give you visions?"

"Ms. Delaney," Grasso said, "do you remember the first two verses that we read? In both, people were healed just by touching the hem of Jesus Christ's garment. If you accept those scriptures as being true, is it so far-fetched to believe that a stone, which Jesus held in his hand, also has powers?"

"Father," Delaney said, "the scriptures said those people were healed. It didn't say they had visions. This is a bit daunting. I'm sorry, but I've never been a believer in relics— you know, nails that people claimed were from the cross, sacred water, statues crying blood, all that sort of mumbo jumbo."

"Neither have I," Grasso replied with a smile. "But I assure you, this stone is genuine. The Book of John says that Jesus wrote twice in the sand when he was speaking to the crowd that had gathered to stone the adulteress—do you remember that line of scripture?"

"Yes," she said. "But the Bible didn't reveal what he wrote. Does your ancient scroll tell?"

"It does," Grasso replied, "but we've only been able, so far, to transcribe one of the messages that he wrote in the ground. According to the scroll, Jesus wrote two."

"What does the message say—the one that you transcribed?"

"It says: *'By the stone, ye shall judge and ye shall be judged.'* Let me re-create the scene for you. A woman is dragged out into the street and thrown before Jesus. The crowd demands that Jesus judge her. He bends down and writes in the dirt: 'By the stone, ye shall judge and ye shall be judged.' Then he picks up a stone and shows it to the mob. He tells the mob that the person who has never sinned should throw the first stone. He then offers the stone to the crowd—the first stone—to anyone willing to take it. No one does. At that point, the mob disperses and Jesus tells the woman to go and sin no more."

"Did the scroll explain what happened to the stone?" Delaney asked.

"No, we don't know what he did with it," Grasso replied. "But we know that ever since that incident, periodic reports about a *giudicare* stone have surfaced. The first was received by the church in 220 A.D. and since then there has been one incident reported about every two hundred years or so. The stone surfaces and then it seems to disappear."

"If this is such a miracle stone, then why haven't I heard about it before? Why has the Vatican tried to keep it secret? Why hasn't someone who touched it gone public?"

"I'm not certain if I can answer your questions," Grasso said. "The church has been desperately trying to locate the stone for centuries, but until now it has always learned about the stone's whereabouts after it had already been passed on to someone new. This is because nearly everything we know about the stone has been learned after the person who touched it was found dead."

"Dead?" she said. "If they're dead, then how'd you know they touched the stone?"

"Because in every case, a stigmata of a crucifix has been found on their left palm," Grasso explained. "The stigmata is identical to what Judge Spencer just showed you on his palm."

"So the stone leaves a crucifix on the people who touch it?" she asked.

"Oh, it does much more than that," Grasso said. "The *giudicare* stone appears to be both a wonderful blessing and a deadly curse. It gives its owner the ability to tell if someone is lying—to discern the truth. The stone apparently can also transport its owner to an actual event so they can see it happen. I believe this is why the church has tried to keep the stone a secret and has been trying to recover it quietly. It doesn't want the stone to be used inappropriately."

Grasso suddenly began coughing and couldn't stop. Dunham got him a glass of water. After he had taken a sip, he apologized. His voice was hoarse and his eyes wet with tears from the coughing. He continued: "I'm afraid there is a tragic side to this stone. To understand this, you must remember what Jesus wrote on the ground: *'By the stone, ye shall judge and ye shall be judged.'* You see, Jesus was saying there are two parts to judgment: 'By the stone, ye shall judge'—that's part one. The owner of the stone has the power to judge! But then he added, 'and ye shall be judged'—that's part two. Jesus seems to be saying, 'If you judge someone, then God is going to judge you too!'"

"Isn't there a scripture in the Bible that says, 'Judge not, lest ye shall be judged?'" Delaney asked.

"Yes," Grasso replied. "That verse continues by asking: 'Why do you see the speck in your brother's eye, but not notice the log that is in your own? First take the log out of your own eye, and then you shall see clearly to take the speck out of your brother's eye.' The concept is exactly the same: no one should judge another person until they have dealt with their own sins. And this is the curse that the stone brings: it forces its owner to confront his own sins and then be judged accordingly."

Delaney looked at Spencer. "Are you telling me that Judge Spencer is somehow being judged by this stone?"

"No, he's not being judged by the stone," Grasso said. He paused for a moment. "I think we should take a step back here. The stone was sent to Judge Spencer by an attorney named Patrick McPherson. When Kyle and I went to Boston and met with his widow, she told us that her husband had become obsessed with seeking forgiveness. He had contacted dozens of people, some from his early childhood, and asked each of them to forgive him. The stone was showing him sins from his past and his guilt was forcing him to seek forgiveness."

Grasso asked Spencer: "Is this same phenomenon happening to you? Has the stone made you confront your own sins?"

Spencer glanced down at the crucifix in his palm. "Yes, it has been doing exactly that." He told them how he had been caught plagiarizing a college term paper. "The professor discovered it years ago but hadn't felt compelled to confront me until after I touched the stone. When he finally did come to see me, he specifically said that it was a sin for me to steal someone else's work. Not long after that, I had a vision. I was a small boy and I told my father that I hated him. In that case too my mother specifically told me that it was a sin not to honor my parents."

"You appear to be on the same path as Patrick McPherson," Grasso said somberly. "Although I must say that neither of those two sins appears to be very significant. Have there been others?"

Spencer didn't want to tell them about the missing half million shares of Circus Circus stock so he said: "No. Not yet!"

As soon as he lied, a pain shot through his left palm and the crucifix started bleeding. Spencer hurried into the bathroom to bandage it, leaving them alone.

"What's happening to his hand?" Delaney asked.

"I believe the judge has been marked by Christ," Grasso answered. "Once a person touches the stone, it causes him to receive a stigmata. I'm not certain why. However, in our studies of stigmatics, we've found they end up suffering, much as Christ did, for sinful acts. They literally take on the sins of others, just as Christ took on the sins of the world."

"Are you saying that Judge Spencer is being punished for other persons' sins?"

"I don't think punished is the correct word," Grasso replied. "Again, I'm not certain how the *giudicare* stone works. But I believe that each time Judge Spencer has a vision or is confronted by one of his own sins, the stigmata on his hand grows and becomes more painful. I must warn you that I believe the judge will eventually be overcome by it and he will suffer the same fate and pain that Christ himself suffered when the sins of the world were cast onto him. If these sins proved too much for Christ, then how can a mere man survive?"

"The stone is going to kill him—is that what you're telling me?"

Grasso paused because Spencer had just reentered the room. But the judge had heard enough to understand what they were discussing.

"What's the answer?" he asked. "Is this stone out to kill me?"

"We don't know enough about it to be certain."

Spencer knew Grasso was sugarcoating his answer.

"Father, give it to me straight: Is the stone going to kill me?"

"The answer, I fear, is yes. The stone is either going to drive you insane or it will ultimately kill you. We know of no one who has survived."

"How long do I have?"

"Judging from the mark on your palm, not long. It is almost as complete as the mark that was found on MacPherson's palm. All that is missing is the Christ figure."

"Can I get rid of the stone, somehow? Just throw it away or send it to someone else?"

"I'm going to contact a colleague of mine at the Vatican and learn if there is some sort of exorcism or ritual we can perform," Grasso said. "Meanwhile, you must stop touching the stone. Each time that you touch it, you will be moving one step closer to death. And, please, don't try to dispose of the stone. If we do discover a cleansing ritual, we'll need it. Oh, and finally, you must also make certain that you do not commit any new sins!"

"Damn!" Spencer said aloud. "There go the whiskey and orgies!"

No one laughed.

"It's a joke," Spencer added. Then he asked: "Father Grasso, do you think I could see Cassie Arnold actually being murdered if I touched the stone one final time?"

"Wait a second," Delaney interrupted. "I thought you told me that Frank Arnold murdered his daughter?"

"I received a telephone call earlier tonight from Taylor Cauldwell and Detective Stuart," Spencer said. "Obviously, they haven't notified you yet. Frank Arnold has admitted writing the ransom note as part of a ploy. He wanted the murder to look like a copycat crime. But he insists that Cassie was already dead when he found her in the basement."

"And you believe him?" she asked.

"Patti, I don't know who actually killed Cassie: it could have been your client, Maxine, or Frank Arnold."

He repeated his question to Grasso: "Could I see the killer's face if I touch the stone?"

"I think so, especially if the murderer is testifying or is even in the same room as you. However, you'd be risking your life."

For the next hour, Grasso discussed the stone with Spencer and Delaney until he was so exhausted that his eyes began drooping. Spencer and Dunham escorted him to the Hideaway's gravel parking lot and helped him into the car.

"I will try to find a way to free you from this stone," he promised Spencer. "I will pray about it."

Delaney was waiting in the Honeymoon Cottage when Spencer returned. "I'm sorry, Judge," she said.

"About what?"

"That you're going through all this, and that I didn't trust you when this trial began. I assumed you were helping Taylor Cauldwell."

"I was," he said bluntly. "I'm sure that's one of my sins. Cauldwell came to see me before the trial. He never said anything directly but he implied that I'd get a seat on the state supreme court if I'd let him prosecute your client in my court. That's the *quid pro quo:* me letting him into my courtroom in return for some behind-the-scenes string-pulling if he gets elected governor. I'm paying for that now, I guess."

He looked down at his palm, which was no longer bleeding.

"If you were on Cauldwell's side," she asked, "why did you send me those e-mails?"

"I've never really been on his side. I agreed to let him into my courtroom to prosecute the case. But that's all I've done to help him. And I felt guilty about that. That's why I issued the gag order—to soothe my own conscience."

"And the e-mails? Why risk your career by sending them to me?"

"You might not believe this, but I've spent my career on the bench trying to be a fair judge. Finding the truth in cases is much more difficult than anyone knows—except for another judge. Every day you make decisions that will alter someone's life. I've never knowingly let an innocent man be punished or allowed a murderer to walk away free. Nothing in politics is worth that."

"I believe you."

Changing the subject, he asked: "How did you discover that I was sending you the e-mails?"

"I got the people who run the newspaper's Web page to trace your notes. By the way, how many messages did you send me?"

"Three. Why?"

"Because I got four e-mails."

"How's that possible?"

"I'm not positive but I've got a hunch." She glanced at her watch. It was nearly five A.M. "I need to go while it's still dark outside. It probably would be best if I weren't seen coming out of the Honeymoon Cottage at daybreak!"

"Yes," he said, smiling for the first time that night. "That would give Miss Alice a real mouthful of gossip."

"Not to mention how angry it would make your wife!"

He suddenly looked sad again, so sad that he reminded Delaney of a hurt little boy. Without thinking, she reached out and touched his cheek. He closed his eyes. "Thank you," he whispered, "for understanding and for coming by here tonight. I didn't want you to think I was a dishonest judge. I didn't want you to despise me."

"I'm going to help Father Grasso find a way to help you rid yourself of this stone," she said. "I promise."

She stood, walked to the doorway, and slipped out into the morning darkness.

23

THE RINGING TELEPHONE JARRED SPENCER AWAKE. HE'D been asleep only two hours. It was Melissa calling.

"My father and I want you to meet us at eleven this morning on the verandah at VanDenvender Hall," she said. She hung up before he could reply.

Melissa and Augustus VanDenvender VI were the last two people in the world whom he wanted to see. But he crawled out of bed and drove to VanDenvender Hall as ordered. The front door was locked, and when he tried his key, he discovered it didn't work. Melissa had changed the locks. He walked around the side of the house and as he rounded its back corner, he spotted Melissa and her father sitting at a table on the verandah eating brunch. VanDenvender had just started to spread orange marmalade on a triangle of toast when Spencer reached their table. He noticed that no one had set out a plate for him, but he didn't care. He didn't bother to sit down and neither of them bothered to suggest it.

Van Denvender got right to the point: "How much is it going to cost me to get you to fall on your sword?" he said.

"Is that why you summoned me here? You want to know if I'm going to fight the prenuptial agreement that I signed two decades ago?"

VanDenvender glanced up from his plate. "What in the hell are you talking about?"

Spencer looked at Melissa who was taking a sip of coffee. When she had finished, she said: "Daddy, Spencer moved out of Van Denvender Hall. We're going to get a divorce."

Van Denvender slowly removed the white linen from his lap and used it to wipe toast crumbs from the edges of his mouth. After he finished, Spencer noticed there was a huge smile on his father-in-law's face.

"This is the best news I've received in years," he declared. "A divorce! Thank God! Good for you, dear!" Spencer knew Van Denvender had never liked him, but still the lightheartedness of his father-in-law's reaction surprised him. He was about to utter a retort but Van Denvender didn't give him the chance.

"The divorce is Melissa's problem," he said. "She can take care of herself. You're here because we need to talk about that lawyer from Boyd, Stackhouse, and Brown—the one who's investigating the missing Circus Circus stock."

Spencer studied his father-in-law's face. At age seventy-two, Augustus VanDenvender VI had snow-white hair and a white moustache that he kept carefully trimmed. His face was ruddy, a reflection of his lifelong love of the outdoors. His eyes were sky blue and piercing. He was tall, lean, and mean—a man who had been reared privileged and had never

doubted for an instant that he deserved all of the good fortune
that had befallen him. He did not believe in luck. As only an
arrogant child born-to-privilege could, Augustus VanDenvender VI viewed himself as a man of greatness, destined to stand
above other men simply because of his family's pedigree.
Spencer truly loathed him.

"So that's what this is all about," Spencer said. "Melissa's
told you that I know you stole that stock and tried to frame
me?" He paused for a second and then sarcastically added:
"Dear old Dad."

"As a man whose entire life is about to come crashing down
on him," VanDenvender replied, "you'd better wise up. Let me
keep this real simple for you. I didn't 'try' to frame you. I have
framed you. You're going to take the blame for those missing
half-million shares no matter what you do or say. It's your
name—not mine—on all of those probate documents. Luck-
ily for you, I'm willing to help you find a way out of this
mess."

"Help me like you did before—by setting me up?"

VanDenvender took another bite of his toast. "You can
blame me, but you're the one who wanted to be a big shot and
prove you could handle a complicated, multimillion-dollar estate even though you were fresh out of law school. All I did
was hold out the bait. You're the sucker who swallowed it
whole."

Spencer struggled to keep his temper in check. "The mistake I made was trusting you," he replied.

"Well, you've finally said something I agree with. You're
right!" VanDenvender admitted, without any hint of remorse.
"In business, you should always be suspicious of your own
relatives because they'll be the ones who will be the first to
fuck you."

Spencer glanced at Melissa. She was calmly cutting through
the poached eggs and Hollandaise sauce on her eggs Benedict,
seemingly oblivious to the two men's conversation.

"You said there was a way out of this mess—what is it?"
Spencer asked.

"I pay you five million dollars. Free and clear."

"A bribe?"

"Call it whatever you want. It's still more money than you will ever earn on your own."

"And what do I have to do in return?"

"Leave. Run away. Get out of the country. But before you do, you'll sign a full confession, acknowledging that you stole the shares of stock and no one else was involved."

"And what happens if I refuse and tell the media what really happened?"

VanDenvender put down his toast and looked at Spencer. "Then you're even stupider than I imagined. What proof do you have that I stole those shares? Absolutely none. There are only three people who know the truth: you, me, and Melissa. And just in case you haven't figured this out yet, Melissa and I are both going to swear that you stole 'em."

"If I'm going to take the blame anyway, why shouldn't I take you down with me, or at least try?"

"Because not only would you be losing five million dollars, you'd be making me an enemy. I'll do everything in my power to destroy you."

"I'm not scared of you."

"Really?" he replied. "You should be. But let's talk about the positives here first before we discuss the negatives. If you play ball and do as you're told, you'll not only pocket five million dollars, I'll pull strings for you."

"What strings?"

"I'll use my political connections to keep the Commonwealth's prosecutors and Taylor Cauldwell off your back. I'll see to it that no one files criminal theft charges against you for those missing shares. You won't be a felon. Hell, legally, you won't even be a thief. At most, all you'll face is a civil suit filed by Boyd, Stackhouse, and Brown. And even a second-rate attorney such as you has to know there is no extradition in civil suits. As long as you stay overseas, Boyd, Stackhouse, and Brown can't touch you."

"What do you mean? You'll keep Cauldwell off my back?"

"That's none of your concern. I'll handle him. But if you decide to fight me on this, then I'll see to it that you are indicted on a huge slew of felony theft charges. I can guarantee you that you will be convicted and you will end up receiving a very long prison term. Don't forget, I know a few judges in this state, and I'm certain they'd be outraged that one of their own stole money from a little old widow. In fact, I'm guessing that you'd be thrown in a Virginia prison cell for the rest of your life. And if that's not bad enough, don't forget that I know a lot of wardens too."

Van Denvender was really savoring this. "I'd be willing to wager that you'd end up in a cell with a big black son of bitch who'd have a real nasty hard-on for white boys." He smiled again. "Then you'll be calling him Daddy!"

Melissa grinned.

"So the choice is yours," VanDenvender concluded. "You can sign a confession, pocket five million, and live in comfort overseas, or you can stay here and end up being sent to prison where you'll spend the rest of your life being lathered up in the shower and passed around for a game of hide the hot dog."

"Do you really think you can buy everyone—that everyone has a price tag?" Spencer asked.

"I not only think that," Van Denvender declared, "I do it every day."

Spencer thought for a moment about Van Denvender's cash offer. Then he said: "You wouldn't be offering me five million dollars unless you were worried about something. I know you're not afraid of going to prison. You've got too many connections for that to happen. Besides, all you'd have to do is simply pay back the money. There's got to be another reason why you're offering to pay me off."

Suddenly, it hit him.

"This has to do with insurance, doesn't it?" Spencer said. "If I take the blame, then Boyd, Stackhouse, and Brown really can't do much to you personally or to your law firm. Sure, they can file a civil suit against VanDenvender and Wythe, but your insurance carrier will be obligated to step in and pay the cost of settling it because I was a dishonest employee. It's perfect. Boyd, Stackhouse, and Brown believes I stole the money so it spends its time and resources searching for me. Your insurance company is stuck paying for any damages that your law firm might face. And you get to sit back and keep all the stolen stock plus your reputation. But if I implicate you personally, then the insurance carrier is off the hook. That leaves VanDenvender and Wythe exposed. All of your trust-sucking relatives aren't going to like that—are they? The truth is that none of this is really about giving me a way out, it's about protecting you. You pay me five million to take the fall and run. That leaves you still holding the stolen shares and no potential liability."

"Congratulations, you actually figured it out," VanDenvender said, clapping his hands together twice in mock applause. "So what? Nothing you just said changes anything. You'll still go to prison unless you accept my offer. And by the way, we're not talking about stock anymore. That stock disappeared more than twenty years ago. Did you think it was hidden under someone's mattress?"

"So how much is the money that you stole worth now? Fifty million, a hundred million, or even more than that?"

"Let's just say it's been well invested."

As much as Spencer hated to admit it, Van Denvender appeared to have him cornered.

"Are there any angles that you haven't considered?" Spencer asked.

"None," VanDenvender declared. "I'm holding all of the aces. Today's Wednesday. Come to the law office on Friday night at seven if you want to accept my offer."

"How can I be sure you'll pay me the five million?"

"What? You don't trust me?" he said, acting hurt. "I'll give you one hundred thousand dollars in cash and a plane ticket when you show up Friday. I'll have a private plane fly you to Dulles where you'll board a flight to Frankfurt, Germany. On Monday, I'll announce that you vanished over the weekend. I'll give reporters copies of your signed confession."

"What about the rest of my money?"

"You'll be given a key to a safe deposit box in London. The rest of the five million has already been deposited there. Don't worry, I have a notarized statement from the bank manager who watched the money being put into the box. You'll be given a document that will authorize you to take the money. You'll fly first to Frankfurt and then to London to get your cash. Then you're on your own. I certainly will never wish to see you again!"

VanDenvender blotted his fingers on his napkin. "We're done now, you can go."

But Spencer didn't leave. He addressed Melissa: "I'd like to say that after twenty-three years of marriage, it's been fun, but I guess I won't. I have only one question. Did you ever really love me? Even in the beginning when we first met in school?"

She didn't flinch. Instead, she looked directly into his eyes. "I never loved you as much as you loved me."

Spencer's left palm began to bleed as soon as he pulled away from VanDenvender Hall. He stopped the Jaguar and placed a hand towel that he had brought with him from the Clifton Hideaway over the bandage on his palm. He was bitter. He hadn't stolen the Circus Circus shares. Why was he being punished by the stone? And then he understood.

From the moment that he had learned that Melissa was a VanDenvender, he had insisted that her family's wealth and power had meant nothing to him. He couldn't be bought. He wasn't for sale. He didn't give a damn about her money. But now, sitting in his $85,000 Jaguar sports car, he realized the obvious. He'd always secretly and desperately wanted to be one of them. He'd wanted to be accepted by the Fox Run Country Club crowd. He'd relished the luxuries that Melissa's money had provided them. He'd enjoyed the access that her family had to the highest echelons of political power and social class. Having been reared in a poor family, he'd been both utterly appalled and totally mesmerized by Melissa's opulent world, outwardly hating it, but wanting to be part of it at the same time.

It was the Tenth Commandment that he had broken: *"You shall not covet your neighbor's house; you shall not covet your neighbor's wife, or his manservant, or his maidservant, or his ox, or his ass, or anything that is your neighbor's."* What he had claimed to have despised the most was what he had privately coveted. He had fooled only himself. As much as he hated to admit it, Augustus VanDenvender VI was correct: Evan Spencer had a price tag. And he had no one to blame but himself for what was now happening.

* * *

Late that same afternoon, Patti Delaney received a copy of the videotape that Detective Stuart had made when he interviewed Frank Arnold. At first, she wasn't certain why Taylor Cauldwell was suddenly willing to share investigative information with her. But as she watched the tape, it became clear to her. Even though Frank Arnold had acknowledged staging the crime scene, the Commonwealth still was insisting that Delbert Amil had killed Cassie Arnold. Nothing that Frank Arnold had admitted had changed Cauldwell's mind about proceeding with the trial on Friday.

Delaney honestly couldn't tell who was lying and who was telling the truth about the murder. Delbert Amil, Frank Arnold, and Maxine Arnold each at one time had tried to cover up their actions. Judge Spencer's visions had exposed their lies but had not yet revealed the murderer's face. Sitting in her office, Delaney reviewed each suspect in her mind. A good prosecutor could have made a strong case against any one of them. Amil had been angry at the Arnolds who were kicking him out of their house. He was an ex-con, an L.A. gang member, a snitch who was secretly posing as his own brother, and he'd been having a sexual affair with Maxine Arnold. Meanwhile, Maxine had a hot temper, had beaten Cassie that night after she had wet her bed, and then had lied about it and her affair with Amil. Frank Arnold knew his wife and Amil were having a sexual affair, was jealous, wanted to get rid of Amil, and had admitted to tampering with the crime scene. It was a case of "pick your murderer." And yet, there was still a puzzle piece that didn't fit.

Delaney knew that Spencer had sent her three e-mails. Someone else had sent her a fourth blaming Frank Arnold. Why? Who?

Delaney spread out several police photographs of the murder scene on her desk. *What am I missing?* She picked up an eight-by-ten-inch snapshot of Cassie Arnold with a garrote twisted around her neck. *There has to be some clue left behind. No crime is perfect. Think, think, think.* As she shuffled through the photographs, she saw it. It was like a children's puzzle that you spend hours trying to solve and when you finally discover the answer and see how simple it is, you wonder how you could have missed it.

The police photographs were not pictures of the actual crime scene! Frank Arnold had admitted that he had staged the area. If Arnold were telling the truth, then the garrote, the stun gun, and the duct tape used on Cassie had all been added as props after the actual murder. Delaney had to de-construct the crime scene. She had to make it as it was *before* Arnold had found his daughter's body. Arnold claimed that he had found his daughter lying on newspapers. Only the papers and her. Where had those newspapers come from?

Delaney rummaged through a stack of reports on her desk until she found an inventory compiled by the Commonwealth's forensic team. Item Number 876 was identified as "Newspapers found under victim. Six pages from the *Los Angeles Times,* metropolitan section, dated 1-1-84. Pages 25 to 31. Newspapers taken from tool room." The forensic team had assumed that the killer had taken the newspapers from the basement tool room because that is where he'd also gotten the duct tape and the rope for the garrote. In its report, the forensic team noted that a California moving company had wrapped Frank Arnold's tools in newspapers when they were being crated and shipped to Virginia. The tool room was still filled with crumpled newspapers that had been used to line moving boxes.

What the team hadn't known is that Frank Arnold had staged the murder after he had found Cassie's body *already* lying on the newspapers. Delaney reread the inventory list: the *Los Angeles Times,* metropolitan section, dated 1-1-84. Pages 25 to 31.

She reread the date. The newspaper pages found underneath Cassie were at least *seventeen years old!*

Why would a moving company be using such old newspapers?

It hadn't, she thought. The killer must have brought that specific copy of the *Los Angeles Times* with him. He'd put Cassie's body on top of those specific pages for a reason.

What was it?

Delaney called information and asked to be connected to the *Los Angeles Times*. But the newspaper's in-house operator refused to help her. "I'm sorry," the operator explained, "but our archives are not open to the general public. You may download articles off our Web site for a fee but you can't disrupt our librarians. They're busy helping our reporters."

"Please," Delaney begged, "this is an emergency and the article I need is from 1984. Your Web site only goes back to 1985."

"Then you'll need to write a letter to our library," the operator said. "Do you already have that address?"

Delaney hung up, waited ten minutes, and then called back. "Hi, I need to talk to the city desk please," she said, lowering her voice so she wouldn't be recognized. "I have a news tip."

The operator put her through.

"City desk," a gruff male voice answered. "This is Jack Smith."

"Oh, darn, I'm sorry," Delaney said, sounding disappointed. "This is Doris in the advertising department, the switchboard was supposed to connect me to the library."

"Hang on," he grumbled. "It happens all the time. I'll transfer you."

Delaney crossed her fingers and waited.

"Library," a voice finally said, "this is Edwin Topps, how can I help you?"

"Please don't hang up," Delaney said. "This is an emergency. I'm an attorney in Virginia and I'm searching for a news story from your newspaper that was published in 1984."

"I'm sorry," Topps interrupted, "but you shouldn't have been allowed to call through. We don't answer questions from the public."

"A man's life is at stake here!" Delaney exclaimed. She was afraid he was going to disconnect her before she had a chance to explain. "I'm in the middle of a murder trial and my client's fighting for his life. Please, just five minutes of your time."

The line was silent and for a moment, she thought he'd already disconnected her.

"I can get fired if I help you," he said

"Not if you help save an innocent man," she replied. "I'm desperate, please!"

"What are you trying to find?"

"A story that was published on the front page of your metro section on January 1, 1984. Sorry, but I don't know exactly which story it is."

"That's no problem because we photograph an entire page when we put the newspaper on microfilm. Give me a half hour and I'll fax you a copy of the entire page. Then you can call me back and tell me which specific story you need."

"Oh, God bless you! Thank you, thank you!"

When the bell on her fax machine rang, she rushed over to read the page that was coming through. The metro section's front page had been reduced so much that she needed a magnifying glass to read it. But it didn't take Delaney long to find what she was searching for. She telephoned Topps again on a direct telephone number that he had given her.

"This is perfect!" she gushed. "I need you to fax me a complete copy of the story in the lower right hand of the page under the headline: 'Honeymooners Hit By Drunk Driver Returning From New Year's Eve Bash!'"

Once again she paced until her fax machine finished printing out the sheet.

HONEYMOONERS HIT BY DRUNK DRIVER RETURNING FROM NEW YEAR'S EVE BASH

Adrian Comer and his new bride, Erin, had been married only five short hours when the car they were riding in was struck head-on early this morning by a driver going in the wrong direction on a freeway, police said.

The Comers were traveling north on Highway 110 near South Pasadena when their car was hit by a southbound vehicle whose driver had mistakenly entered an exit ramp.

The newlyweds, both students at UCLA, had just left their wedding reception in the Montecito Heights area. Adrian, age 24, was killed instantly in the car crash. His bride, Erin, age 22, was in critical condition at a local hospital. She suffered severe head injuries.

According to the police, the Comers' compact sedan was hit head-on by a late model sports car being driven by Frank Arnold of Los Angeles. He had just left a New Year's party at the home of a friend, police said. Arnold, who was not injured, refused to take a Breathalyzer test at the accident scene and was taken into custody. At the station, he agreed to take a sobriety test and was charged with driving under the influence after he registered an alcohol level in excess of the state's minimum .08 percent standard.

The rest of the story contained more details about the crash and mentioned several other New Year's Eve car accidents. As soon as she read it, Delaney telephoned Edwin Topps at the newspaper's library.

"I need to know what happened to the Comers: the young couple in the car accident. Let's start with Adrian Comer's obituary."

"I'm busy now," Topps said. "We're getting close to a deadline and reporters are calling us every few seconds asking for clips. Sorry, but you're going to have to wait."

About an hour after Spencer had finished meeting with Melissa and Augustus Van Denvender VI, Taylor Cauldwell telephoned him at the Clifton Hideaway.

"I've just gotten off the telephone with your father-in-law," Cauldwell said. "I'm calling you from a secure phone in my office at the state capitol. I'd like you to call me back on a pay phone." Cauldwell gave him a telephone number. Spencer drove to a nearby gasoline station and dialed it.

"That you?" Cauldwell asked.

"Yes," said Spencer. "Why all the security precautions?"

"Your father-in-law said a half-million shares of Circus Circus stock has turned up missing and you're responsible. He said Boyd, Stackhouse, and Brown is breathing down your neck. What the hell is going on?"

"That's what he said, huh?"

"Listen," Cauldwell said, "we've known each other since college so let's cut through the bullshit. All I know is that old man Van Denvender said this scandal is going to blow up any day now. He was calling me as a favor to warn me. He suggested that I begin distancing myself from you, pronto! He said being identified as a close friend of yours wasn't going to help my chances at being elected governor."

"That was sweet of him."

"I'm scheduled to be interviewed tomorrow morning in Richmond about the kind of judges who I'd like to see eventually get appointed to the state supreme court. I'm sorry, but I wanted you to know that Judge George Minoff will be my choice for the next vacancy—assuming I get elected. I wanted you to hear it from me personally, not on TV."

"I thought I was your next choice!"

"Jesus Christ, Spencer!" Cauldwell protested. "Your own father-in-law just told me you stole a half-million shares of stock!"

"Did it ever occur to you that I was being falsely accused?"

"That doesn't matter and you know it," Cauldwell replied. "My opponent will be all over this. Besides, you haven't been helping me in the Arnold trial. I thought we had a deal and the first thing you did was impose a goddamn gag order! So don't cry to me about loyalty!"

Spencer knew exactly what Augustus VanDenvender VI was doing. He was tightening the noose, spreading word that Spencer was in trouble. He was setting the stage for him to take a fall and flee the country. Taylor Cauldwell was the first of his so-called good friends to abandon him.

Spencer suspected that Cauldwell would not be the last.

24

IT WAS AFTER ELEVEN O'CLOCK THAT NIGHT WHEN PATTI Delaney's fax machine rang. The first page to come out of it was a handwritten message from Edwin Topps, the librarian at the *Los Angeles Times*.

> *You're lucky, I found two clippings in the same file as the New Year's Eve car crash story from 1984. If someone hadn't stuck them in there, I'd never have found them. Good luck saving your client!*

The next two sheets were copies of newspaper obituaries. There was nothing out of the ordinary in Adrian Comer's.

He'd been born and reared in Los Angeles and was majoring in accounting at UCLA. The story noted that his bride, Erin, was still in a coma because of severe head injuries. A week later, the newspaper had printed her obituary. She had never regained consciousness. It wasn't until Delaney reached the final sentence that she understood the importance of her detective work.

Delaney immediately called the Clifton Hideaway and asked to be connected to the Honeymoon Cottage. But Spencer didn't pick up. When the receptionist came back on the line, Delaney asked if she had seen the judge.

"His Jaguar is parked outside in our lot," the receptionist said. "Maybe he just doesn't want to be disturbed this late at night."

Delaney drove from her office to her apartment where she changed into a black jogging suit and slipped on her running shoes. A half hour later, she turned off the main highway and parked her car near a clump of trees. She was about a half mile from the entrance to the Clifton Hideaway. There was sufficient moonlight for her to find her way through the woods as she jogged to the Honeymoon Cottage. It was now well after midnight and she didn't want anyone to see her visiting Spencer. There was a light on inside the cottage but when she rapped on the door, he didn't answer. Delaney tried the knob. The door was unlocked so she pushed it open. Spencer was sprawled face-up on the floor; his left hand was lying in a pool of blood.

Delaney darted inside and dropped to her knees.

"Judge Spencer, can you hear me?"

He forced his eyes open. "Delaney," he mumbled, "sorry, I'm not dressed for company." He was wearing a white T-shirt and gray boxer shorts, both splattered with blood.

"How long have you been lying here?"

"Not sure," he replied groggily.

"I'm calling an ambulance!"

"No! Don't!" he declared. "Call Grasso instead. His number is on that pad."

She dialed it and Kyle Dunham answered on the first ring. Twenty minutes later, he and Grasso arrived. By that time,

Delaney had managed to get Spencer up onto his bed and had stopped the slow bleeding from his palm. She was using a towel to clean the floor.

"He's lost a tremendous amount of blood," she said. "And he's burning up with a fever. He needs to see a doctor! We need to get him to the emergency room!" She fetched a cold towel and held it against his forehead.

"Modern medicine is not going to help him," Grasso said. He examined Spencer's left hand. "Most stigmatics don't emit blood from their wounds, but in the judge's case, it appears to be exactly that." Grasso raised his voice: "Judge Spencer, can you hear me? It's Father Grasso!"

Spencer, whose eyes had been shut, opened them and said: "Yes, Father, sorry I can't get up."

"Did you touch the stone today?"

"No."

"Were you confronted by a new sin?"

"No," he said, lying. A sharp pain shot through his left hand, causing him to grimace, and his left palm began oozing blood again. Spencer did not want to tell Grasso about his meeting with Augustus VanDenvender VI and Melissa. There were no more clean towels, so Delaney took one of Spencer's white undershirts from a drawer and used it to bandage his hand.

"I believe I have found a way to free you from the stone!" Grasso announced.

"I'll do anything. Let's get the stone right now and try it."

"It's not that easy. Do you know what tomorrow is?"

"Yes, it's Thursday," Spencer replied.

"That's correct, but more importantly, it's the Jewish holiday of Yom Kippur. Do you know anything about it?"

Spencer shook his head, indicating that he didn't.

"There's an ancient Jewish ritual that was done before the birth of Jesus at Yom Kippur. It's from the Old Testament book of Leviticus, chapter sixteen, verse seven. God tells a man named Aaron how to make a sacrifice." Grasso repeated the scripture by memory:

"And you shall take two goats, and present them before the Lord at the door of the tabernacle of the congregation. And

Aaron shall cast lots upon the two goats; one lot for the Lord, and the other lot for the scapegoat. And Aaron shall bring the goat upon which the Lord's lot fell, and offer him for a sin of-fering. But the goat, on which the lot fell to be the scapegoat, shall be presented alive before the Lord, to make an atonement with him, and to let him go for a scapegoat into the wilderness."

"Scapegoat?" Spencer asked. "Are you talking about blam-ing someone else?"

"Each year a high priest would release a goat into the wilder-ness after symbolically laying the sins of Israel onto the animal—it was the scapegoat. The goat was released at Yom Kippur because it's the Day of Atonement. This year, Yom Kip-pur begins tomorrow at sundown. I think we can free you from the stone's power if we transfer your sins onto a scapegoat."

"You're going to save me by putting my sins onto a sheep?"

"It's going to be a bit more complicated than that," Grasso replied. "Sundown is at 7:25 P.M. tomorrow. That's when we must perform the ritual. It can't be done before then or after that time. Do you understand?"

"What happens if it doesn't work?" Delaney asked Grasso.

The priest didn't reply. Spencer said: "I need to know."

"If we do nothing, you're going to die—just as Jesus Christ died."

"How much time do I have?"

"I can't be certain. When I was younger, I watched a young girl stigmatic. She was sick, very much like you are now. But after a few hours, she would regain her strength and appear fine, only to lapse into another fit of bleeding and high fevers. They became progressively worse."

"Did you save her?" Delaney asked.

Grasso whispered: "No."

"How exactly did she die?" Spencer asked.

"With Christ!"

"What does that mean?" Spencer asked. "That's the second time you've told me that I'll die like Christ did!"

"Crucified. In the case of the young woman, in her mind, she was crucified alongside him. She felt the same blows, the same pain as he did."

Grasso stepped away from the bed and spoke to Delaney in a hushed tone. "Kyle and I need to prepare for tomorrow but the judge should not be left alone. Can you stay with him tonight?"

"Yes. What can I do to help him?"

"Pray! Try to control the bleeding as best you can."

After Grasso and Dunham left, Spencer asked: "You staying, Counselor?"

"Hey, I've never been one to leave a party early!" she joked. "Besides, I think I've discovered who killed Cassie Arnold and I'm going to need your help to prove it."

"Oh," he replied. He sounded disappointed.

"I also think," she said softly, "that you're a truly amazing man."

Spencer forced a smile. "Stupid might be a more accurate description." He pulled himself upright in the bed. "I have to tell you something in case I die tonight."

"Ssshh," she said. "Just relax. Save your strength."

"This is important and I've got to tell you while I am thinking clearly!" During the next several minutes, he told her about the missing half-million shares of Circus Circus stock and how Augustus VanDenvender VI had framed him.

"This morning, VanDenvender offered me five million dollars if I'd sign a confession taking blame and then run away to Europe. I'm supposed to tell him my decision Friday night at seven P.M. in his office."

"We've got to call the FBI," she said.

"No, Patti, you don't understand! My name is on all of the documents. He's made it look like I stole the shares. If it's just my word against his, I'll lose. You don't know how powerful and evil VanDenvender can be."

Delaney, who was wiping his forehead with a cold cloth, asked, "Are you thinking about taking the cash and running away?"

"Wouldn't you? I don't want to go to prison. If I survive this, if Father Grasso's scapegoat plan works tomorrow night, then I'll have to make my choice—either escaping as a millionaire or being sent to prison for life. I want to ask you a question now: If I take the money, will you go with me?"

"Me? Go with you?"

"We could start over. Both begin new lives. Five million is a small fortune, more than enough for two people. France, the Caribbean, a small villa in Italy! What do either of us have to keep us here—except for bad memories?"

"Spencer, are you serious?"

"Yes, Patti, haven't you ever dreamed of being rich? I've seen the power that comes with money. You can be the dumbest person alive, but if you're rich, people think you're brilliant. They admire you, they envy you, they want to be you. Money can change everything in your life!"

"But money can't buy you happiness."

"Are you so sure? I've always thought that people who said that were simply trying to make themselves feel better because they didn't have any money!"

"What about your wife, your father-in-law, the Frank and Maxine Arnolds of this world—haven't you learned anything by watching them?"

"But we aren't like them! It wouldn't be like that between you and me," he said. "We'd be different!"

"Would we? My father used to tell this really old joke," she said. "You've probably heard it. He'd say: 'A man wanted to have sex with a beautiful woman so he offers her two thousand dollars. She begins thinking about what she can buy with that money. So she agrees to do it and as soon as she does he drops his offer to ten dollars. She's insulted and says, 'What do you think I am, a common whore?' And he replies: 'We've already established that, now we're just haggling over your price.'"

"But my situation is different! Didn't you hear me earlier?" he asked. "I'm going to prison if I don't flee! What good is the truth if you can't prove it and it ends up destroying you?"

She rose from the bed and stepped into the bathroom to rinse off the cloth that she had been using to wipe his brow. When she returned, she said: "This stone, the Bible, your palm—do you remember how Father Grasso said your life would start to emulate that of Christ's life?"

"Yes," he replied. "It's hard to forget when someone says you're going to be crucified."

"Jesus was tempted too. By the devil. He offered him riches in return for his allegiance."

"What are you saying? That if I take the money, I'll be selling my soul?"

"I shouldn't judge you," she said. "It's easy for me to tell you which choice to make because I don't have to live with the consequences." Her voice was beginning to crack with emotion. "I wish I honestly believed that good always triumphs over evil. But I've seen too much, been through too much. I'm not naive. I know horrible things happen to good people and good things happen to horrible people. But I still believe that each of us has to do the right thing. We have to make good moral choices regardless of whether we benefit or suffer because of them. I believe we make moral choices every day. Most of the time, we don't even notice because they're not huge decisions and not dramatic and not as threatening as the choice that you're now facing. They're mundane decisions, simple things, such as telling a waitress when she inadvertently leaves the price of a drink off your check or telling someone little white lies. They seem so harmless. But when you add up these millions of daily choices, they define who you are." She wiped his forehead with the fresh cloth. "There's a good chance you'll go to prison if you don't accept VanDenvender's offer. I understand that. I truly do. But I also know that if I ran away with you to Europe, we'd be settling. I'd be settling for a man I didn't respect. I'd be running away with someone I really couldn't trust. I can't do that! I'm sorry!"

The undershirt that she had wrapped around his left palm had become saturated with blood. She replaced it with another.

"I know the odds are against you," she continued. "I know how powerful Augustus VanDenvender VI is, but I will help you fight him—if you stay."

"I'm freezing," he said suddenly. Moments before, his forehead had been burning hot with a fever. "I feel, it's hard to know . . ." He slipped into unconsciousness.

Delaney wrapped the blankets from the bed around him to keep him warm, but his body began to shake anyway. She crawled up next to him, reached around and pulled him close to her. She whispered: "It's okay, Evan. I'm here. Hang on! Don't die on me! Fight this, fight this for us and the future!"

It was cold and dark. Spencer was rocking back and forth to the motion of the sea on board a small sailboat. He was freezing. But then suddenly, it became hot. A cloudless sapphire sky appeared above him. The sun burned his face. He raised himself up on his elbows and reached over the boat's side to cool his face with water. But as soon as he broke the surface of the clear water, it turned murky green and he could see hideous creatures slithering underneath the boat. They were ghost white and when they spotted his hand on the surface, they raced up toward him as if they wanted to snatch his arm, pull him overboard, and feast on his flesh. He jerked back his hand just in time and hid in the boat, afraid to move, afraid that it might capsize. After several moments, he raised himself up enough to peek over the side. Off in the distance, he saw a figure in white robes walking toward him on the surface of the water. The figure moved slowly, gracefully, with no fear of sinking, no fear of being devoured by the beasts from below. Spencer screamed: "Save me! Please save me!" As the figure came closer, he saw her face. "It's okay. I'm here," she whispered. "I will take care of you. Hang on! Don't die! Fight this for us, fight this for us and the future!" It was Patti Delaney. She had come to rescue him and he felt safe in her arms.

Delaney was still lying next to him when Spencer awoke. It was Thursday morning. The bleeding in his palm had stopped. Considering what he had been through during the night, he felt amazingly well. He tried to scoot out from under the covers without waking her, but she opened her eyes as soon as he moved.

"Go back to sleep," he whispered. "I'm just going to use the bathroom."

"Are you okay?" she asked. "Still bleeding? Is the fever gone? What are you doing getting out of bed?"

"I know I gave you a real scare last night. But, believe it or not, I actually feel fine now. In fact, I'm starving. How about a big stack of blueberry pancakes?"

She was shocked at how easily he moved from the bed to the bathroom, as if he'd just awakened from a restful night. As soon as he entered the bathroom, he stopped. He was looking at the bloody towels and T-shirts that she'd tossed in the tub. "My God!" he uttered. He turned around and faced her. "I'm so sorry," he continued. "I didn't realize how bad it was—how bad it must have been for you."

"What do you remember? Do you remember talking to Grasso about the scapegoat?"

"Yes. Tonight at sunset. The ritual."

"How about the missing Circus Circus shares and the five-million-dollar bribe?"

"Yes and no," he replied. "I remember asking you to run away with me. I'm fairly certain you said no. It was strange. I remember being here alone last night and blacking out on the floor. When I opened my eyes, you were here. I remember you holding me all night, keeping me safe. I remember you rescuing me in my sailboat."

"What sailboat?"

"Maybe that part was a dream, or a vision that was shown to me in the past but didn't occur until last night." He changed subjects: "How did you know to come here—that I needed help?"

"I didn't know. I came because I wanted to tell you that I know who murdered Cassie." She recounted how she had contacted the *Los Angeles Times* and read about the honeymooners who had been killed in a car accident in Los Angeles by Frank Arnold.

"Cassie's murder isn't about any of the things that we thought," she explained. "It's about only one thing: getting revenge! It's about the killer punishing Frank Arnold!"

"How are you going to prove that?" he asked.

"I have an idea but I need to speak with Father Grasso first to see if it's even possible. If he says it is, then I'm going to need your help. But I've got to warn you, it's going to require operating outside the box."

"It sounds like something we need to discuss," he replied, "over breakfast."

25

AT EXACTLY FOUR P.M. ON THURSDAY, MISS ALICE TELEPHONED Frank and Maxine Arnold. "Judge Spencer would like both of you to report to his chambers in one hour," she announced.

At 4:30 P.M., she telephoned Albemarle County Sheriff's Detective Dale Stuart. "The judge wants to see you in his chambers at five o'clock. And he wants you to bring Delbert Amil from the jail with you."

At 4:50 P.M., she telephoned Jacob Wheeler. "Judge Spencer wants to see you in his chambers in ten minutes." Wheeler, who was about to leave his office for the day, asked why. "It's about the Cassie Arnold murder trial and he said you need to be there on time!" she snapped.

"Does the judge know Taylor Cauldwell is in Richmond?" Wheeler asked. "He can't hold a hearing without him. He's the chief prosecutor!"

"And you're the Commonwealth's attorney for Albemarle County," Miss Alice replied. She knew she could bully him and enjoyed doing it. She also knew that Judge Spencer had intentionally timed her calls so that Cauldwell wouldn't learn about the surprise hearing until it was too late for him to attend it. "You've been in court every day of the trial so I'm sure you can represent the Commonwealth at this hearing without bothering the attorney general!" she lectured.

"But this is highly irregular!" Wheeler protested. "Cauldwell is going to be furious! I've got to call him!"

"Do whatever you wish but you've just wasted five minutes, and Judge Spencer said everyone was to be in their places at precisely five P.M., no exceptions!"

Wheeler delayed telephoning Cauldwell and instead scrambled up the courthouse stairs to the third floor. He was panting by the time he arrived. Miss Alice waited a few moments so he could catch his breath and then escorted him inside. The chairs in Spencer's chambers had been arranged to resemble a miniature courtroom. Frank and Maxine Arnold were sitting on one side with Detective Stuart. Patti Delaney and Charles MacDonald were seated along with Delbert Amil on the opposite side. Father Grasso and Kyle Dunham were sitting at the rear of the chamber. Jacob Wheeler slipped into the empty chair next to Stuart.

"Everyone's here now, Judge," Miss Alice announced. She stepped outside and closed the door.

"Ms. Delaney has asked for this special closed session in my chambers," Spencer explained. "It will soon be obvious why." He stopped abruptly, leaned forward, and spoke into an intercom that connected him with Miss Alice. "Please hold all calls and do not let anyone interrupt us."

Wheeler raised his hand like a child in school. "Judge," he said timidly. "I don't mean to interrupt, but I think Attorney General Cauldwell is going to be angry about missing this."

"I'll deal with him and I will take all responsibility for this emergency hearing."

A look of visible relief washed over Wheeler's face.

Spencer held up three sheets of paper for everyone to see. "These are copies of electronic mail that Ms. Delaney has received during this trial. She's just showed them to me. They were written by an unusual source who has provided her with tips about the murder that have proven to be extremely accurate. Because this source gets his information in a most unusual way, I've agreed to let Ms. Delaney question him here tonight without the jury being present. I'll decide afterward whether or not I'll allow any of his testimony to be introduced tomorrow when the trial reconvenes. You may now proceed, Ms. Delaney."

Delaney announced: "I'd like Father Dino Grasso to step forward and take a seat in the witness chair."

Charles MacDonald tugged on Delaney's sleeve and she leaned down so he could whisper to her. "How'd you find this guy? You didn't tell me any of this!"

"I'll explain later," she said.

Grasso hobbled forward and sat in a chair next to Spencer's desk.

"Father Grasso," Delaney began, "do you believe in miracles?"

"Most reported miracles are hoaxes or easily disproved, but, yes, there are genuine miracles, acts of God that can't be explained."

"Would one of these miracles be a rather unusual stone that Jesus once touched?" she asked, "and would a priest, such as you, be able to use that stone to see into the past?"

"Yes, such a stone exists."

Spencer looked around the room. Everyone was watching Grasso.

"One of the e-mails that I received told me that Cassie had wet her bed and her mother had become angry and hit her," Delaney announced. "Another revealed how my client's DNA had gotten onto Cassie's pajamas, and another tipped me off to Frank Arnold and the pen that was used to write the ransom note. All of these events happened exactly how they were described in the e-mails, yet the person who wrote them was not there when they happened. The stone enabled him to see these events in visions."

Delaney had carefully avoided mentioning Spencer as her source. By implication, those watching assumed Grasso had written the messages.

Delaney stepped up to Spencer's desk and lifted a cardboard gift box off of it. She stepped up to Grasso. "Father, were these revelations made possible because of the stone that is in this box?"

"Yes, that's the stone."

Everyone was trying to peer into the box, so Delaney turned and lowered it so they could see the simple white stone.

"We talked earlier about this, Father," Delaney said, "and you told me that you believed you could use this stone today to look into the past and see what actually happened to Cassie Arnold on the night that she was murdered. Do you still think that is possible?"

"With God's help, I do."

She handed him the box and he placed it on his lap. He shut his eyes and said a prayer while touching his rosary. After he finished, he passed his good right hand about an inch over the rock in a clockwise circle three times. He then moved it counterclockwise three more times. As soon as Grasso stopped moving his hand, there was a loud pop, like a single crack of a bullwhip. A razor-thin blue line of electricity shot from the rock into Grasso's right palm. Maxine Arnold screamed! And Delaney stepped backward. Grasso's hand began to tremble and his oversize head fell forward hitting his chest. It looked as if he had been knocked unconscious.

"Father Grasso," Delaney said slowly, "tell us what you see."

"A man is breaking into a house. It's a new house. All white. He's breaking a basement window and climbing through it."

Maxine and Frank Arnold exchanged glances.

"Can you see this man's face?"

"No. He is walking upstairs now, very quietly. He is going into a girl's bedroom. She's sleeping. He is standing beside her bed." Grasso's entire body began to quiver.

"What's wrong, Father?"

"The man is suffocating the girl with a pillow. She's trying to fight him but he's too strong. It's horrible!"

Maxine Arnold was about to burst into tears.

"Is the little girl dead?"

"Yes. He's now carrying her down into the basement."

"Father, can you see this man's face?"

"No, but he's getting something out of his pocket. It's something he brought with him to the house."

"What is it?"

"A folded newspaper. He's spreading the paper on the floor like a blanket for the child to sleep on." Once again Grasso's entire body began to shake.

"What's happened?"

"We're no longer in the basement. The man and I are inside a hospital. The man is standing next to a bed where a young woman is lying. She's in a coma. The man is overwrought. He loves this woman very, very much."

"It's his wife?"

"No, his daughter. Wait. Several days have passed as if they were seconds. The man is still here. He hasn't left his daughter's side. But something has happened. The young woman is dead. Now the man is weeping. His grief is overpowering. He's in agony."

"Can you finally see this man's face?"

"Yes, yes," Grasso declared. "I can see his face."

Delaney carefully removed the box from his lap and put it on the edge of Spencer's desk. Then she placed her palms on each side of Father Grasso's pockmarked face and gently lifted his chin from his chest.

"Father Grasso, can you hear me? Father Grasso, are you there?" she asked. "Father Grasso, I need you to open your eyes and rejoin us."

Grasso opened his eyes. "Water, please?" he stammered. Kyle Dunham filled a glass from Spencer's bathroom faucet and held it to the priest's lips.

Delaney said: "Father, is the man who suffocated Cassie Arnold and then put her body on newspapers in this room right now?

Grasso looked at Frank Arnold and then slowly shifted his eyes to Delbert Amil and then finally settled on Charles MacDonald.

"Why are you staring at me?" MacDonald bristled.

Delaney unfolded a copy of Erin Comer's obituary from the *Los Angeles Times* and began reading it aloud:

> Erin Comer, the young bride who fell into a coma on her wedding night, died this morning in a local hospital. Comer, age 21, was a passenger in a car being driven by her husband on New Year's Eve when their vehicle was struck head-on by a car driven by Frank Arnold. He has been charged with driving under the influence of alcohol.

A stunned Maxine Arnold exclaimed: "You never told me about any car accident! You killed a young girl because you were driving drunk?"

"It happened before we met!" Frank Arnold replied.

Spencer was watching MacDonald's face. He was glaring at Frank Arnold. Delaney continued reading. The next several paragraphs described Erin Comer's background. She had met her husband at UCLA but was not from California. When Delaney reached the final sentence of the obituary, she raised her voice: "Survivors include Erin's parents: Charles and Airelee

MacDonald of Washington, D.C. She was the couple's only child."

"You're that dead girl's father!" Maxine shrieked, pointing a finger at MacDonald who was only a few steps away from her. "Frank killed your daughter?"

MacDonald didn't answer. Delaney picked up a copy of an anonymous e-mail that had been sent to her. "I should've known it was you when I got this e-mail," she declared. "All it says is 'Frank Arnold killed his daughter. His motive was money. Your client is being set up as a patsy.' You wrote this e-mail and you sent it to me on my own computer! It happened that morning when you startled me at work. You'd come into the office early to use my computer without my knowing it. When I came into the building, you dashed down the hall so you could act like you had been in 'the little boys' room.' You're the only one who knew about the other e-mails. You knew I always left my computer connected to the Internet."

MacDonald was still peering at Frank Arnold. "You murdered my little girl!" he declared, his eyes filled with hatred. "Erin was the most beautiful child a parent could want. She was the center of my universe. And you got drunk at a New Year's Eve party and drove your car the wrong way down an expressway. You should have died, but it was Erin and her new husband who were slaughtered!"

Frank Arnold was speechless.

"We'd just gotten back to our hotel room when the police officers called," MacDonald continued. "I prayed and prayed and prayed at that damn hospital, and so did my wife. Can you even imagine what it's like to watch your only child lying there slowly dying, hooked up to all those damn machines, her face turning black-and-blue from the car crash injuries, and all the while, you know there's nothing you can do to save her. Not a damn thing!"

His eyes shifted to Grasso who was still sitting in the impromptu witness chair. "All of my life, Father," MacDonald said, "I've been a good Catholic. I attended mass every week, went to confession, donated my share of money. I believed God stood for love but when my little baby was dying, God turned his back on me. Tell me what good my praying did? Tell me, Father?"

MacDonald didn't give Grasso time to reply. Instead, he glanced back at Frank Arnold. "You should've gone to prison. But you were too rich, too smart, too well connected. You ended up pleading guilty to reckless driving! The judge made you pay a fine! Two people dead and all you had to do was write a check."

In a swift motion honed by working for years as a homicide detective, MacDonald whipped his left hand under his jacket and it emerged holding a short-barreled .38-caliber blue steel revolver. He pointed it directly at Detective Stuart's chest. "Take your gun out," he ordered. Stuart gently removed his handgun from its holster and placed it on the floor. "Now, take out the one in your ankle holster!" Stuart did as he was told. "I've never met a cop yet who didn't carry at least two guns," MacDonald said. "Got any more?"

"No," Stuart said. Then, he added, "What you're doing now isn't going to help anything!"

"If someone slaughtered your child and got away with it, what would you do?" MacDonald turned his pistol so it was aimed at Frank Arnold.

"How's it feel, Frank," he asked, "to have someone kill your daughter?"

Frank Arnold was clearly terrified.

MacDonald continued: "After Erin died, my wife gave up. All of our dreams—destroyed because of you! No grandkids, nothing. You stole our future! People always talk about how powerful love can be. But I learned that hate can be equally strong. My wife should've put up a fight when she was diagnosed with cancer, but she simply didn't care anymore after Erin died. You murdered her too!"

"Why don't you put down the gun?" Spencer said.

"Because that would be really stupid," MacDonald replied with contempt. "Don't you get it, Judge? This is what I've been waiting for. I planned to kill all of them that night. And then kill myself. That's why I brought along the newspaper. I wanted everyone to know why I'd killed them. And then, when I was suffocating Cassie, I decided to change my plan. I wanted you—Frank—to feel how I felt when my daughter was murdered. I figured the cops would suspect you. They always suspect the parents first."

No one said a word, nor moved. MacDonald said: "The next day, the television news said the cops had arrested Lester Amil, some black kid. I didn't even know he lived there. That's when I realized another innocent person was going to have their life ruined because of you! I had to volunteer to help him. I had to make you into the chief suspect."

"Charles," Patti Delaney said tenderly. "You've spent your career helping people, first as a police officer and later as an attorney. Don't do this!"

"None of that matters now. I've already killed Cassie. Now it's Maxine's turn. I want Frank to watch her die!" MacDonald shifted his pistol.

Maxine panicked. "Do something!" she screamed at her husband, but he didn't flinch. She glared at Detective Stuart and then Judge Spencer. "Don't just stand there. You're paid to stop this from happening!"

"Get on your knees!" MacDonald ordered. But Maxine was so terrified that her knees had locked.

"We'll give you anything you want," Frank Arnold offered. "We can establish a college scholarship in your daughter's name! We can get UCLA to name a building after her! There's got to be a way we can fix this!"

MacDonald raised his pistol so it was pointed at Maxine's forehead. "There is," he said. "But it doesn't involve money! You can't just write a check and get out of this!"

"I wasn't in that car!" Maxine shrieked. "I didn't even know him then! I wasn't drunk! Please, please, don't kill me! He's the one who killed your daughter, not me!"

"I said, get down on your knees!"

Detective Stuart started to step toward him but MacDonald was too fast. He swung his gun around and Stuart stopped short. "Don't be a hero," MacDonald warned. "They aren't worth losing your life over!" Stuart stepped back and Mac-Donald aimed his gun at Maxine.

At that moment, Father Grasso pushed himself from his chair and stepped between Maxine and MacDonald.

"There's been enough killing," he said.

"Step clear, Father, or I'll shoot you," MacDonald said. "I gave up on God a long time ago."

"But He hasn't given up on you!"

"Oh yes He did. He let my Erin die!"

Grasso didn't budge so MacDonald said: "I'm going to count to three just like in the movies. That will give you time to step out of the way. If you choose to die, then that's on your conscience, not mine!"

Grasso touched his rosary with his good right hand and closed his eyes in prayer.

MacDonald said: "One, two, three . . ."

The sound of a pistol firing exploded inside the chamber. Spencer's mind tried to make sense of the flash and movements that happened during that deafening boom. He saw Grasso falling to the floor and at that same instant watched MacDonald fly backward off his feet. His body crashed into a wall. Spencer heard a woman scream. He smelled gunpowder. It took him several seconds to sort it out.

Maxine was still cowering next to Frank Arnold. Neither appeared harmed. Detective Stuart, Patti Delaney, Kyle Dunham, Delbert Amil, and Jacob Wheeler were still frozen in place. Grasso was on the floor, but there were no immediate signs of blood, no gaping gunshot wound. Charles MacDonald was a different sight. Blood was spurting from his chest. It was then that Spencer spotted another body on the carpet. It was Miss Alice and she was holding a huge pistol in her hands. It was an antique Civil War revolver.

Detective Stuart hurried over to examine MacDonald. "Call nine-one-one!" he yelled, as he applied direct pressure with both hands over a large hole in MacDonald's chest.

"Did I hit him?" Miss Alice asked. Her eyeglasses were turned lopsided on her nose. The recoil from the pistol shot had knocked her down.

"You sure as hell did!" Stuart replied.

Jacob Wheeler helped Miss Alice onto her feet. "How'd you know what was happening in here?" he asked.

"Judge Spencer flipped on his intercom and I heard that man ordering Detective Stuart to put down his gun. There wasn't time to call the sheriff's deputies so I thought: *Where can I get a pistol?* That's when I grabbed this!" It was her great-great-grandfather's Leech & Rigdon Confederate Army .36-caliber gun. She had taken it from the display case in the hallway. "I wasn't sure if I loaded it right or if that old ammo would work!"

"It did! You knocked a hell of a hole in MacDonald's chest," Stuart said. "He's unconscious. I think he busted his head when the blast knocked him against the wall. How's the priest?"

Dunham was helping Grasso back onto the witness chair.

"Do you need an ambulance too?" Spencer asked.

"No," Grasso replied. "I'm just a bit shaken. I need to catch my breath. I must have fallen down when that thing went off."

By the time a team of paramedics and deputies arrived, the Arnolds had regained their composure and Detective Stuart had taken charge. "I'm going to ride to the hospital with Mac-Donald," he said. "But I'm going to need statements from everyone here." He looked at Jacob Wheeler. "Why don't you take everyone down to the sheriff's office and collect their statements?"

"Okay everyone," said Wheeler, enjoying his newfound authority, "let's go downstairs."

"Just a minute," Spencer said. He walked over to Miss Alice and hugged her. "Thank you for saving our lives." She blushed.

Spencer said: "I'm going to need Ms. Delaney, Father Grasso, and Mr. Dunham to stay here for a few minutes to conclude some business. The rest of you can go ahead. We'll join you shortly."

Wheeler began shepherding the others downstairs. Within five minutes, they were gone. Grasso looked at the wall clock. It was 7:15 P.M.

"We need to hurry!" he said. "We've only got a few minutes before sundown! Quick, hand me the stone so we can perform the ritual!"

Spencer reached for the box sitting on his desk, but Grasso yelled: "Let Ms. Delaney get it. Don't even get close to it or it might kill you! Hurry!" Delaney scrambled over and carefully lifted out the stone. Grasso tried to stand but was too weak to get out of the witness chair. As Dunham and Spencer reached down on either side to help him, Spencer spotted blood on Grasso's left side.

"You've been shot!"

MacDonald had fired his pistol at Grasso but his shot had gone unnoticed because of the blast from the Civil War relic. The bullet had punctured Grasso's abdomen. "We've got to call an ambulance!" Spencer exclaimed.

"No!" Grasso shouted. "There's no time!"

"Why didn't you tell us you were wounded?" Delaney asked.

"If we don't do the ritual right now, Judge Spencer is going to die," Grasso warned.

"Forget the ritual!" Spencer exclaimed. "My car is outside. I'll drive you to the hospital. You're losing blood."

"What about you?" the priest asked.

"If it's a choice between you and me, then I choose you. Let's quit arguing and go!"

Grasso asked: "You'd give up your life to save mine?"

"Stop talking, start moving! We can debate this some other time!"

"No," Grasso said stubbornly, "we must do the scapegoat ritual first, while there's time!"

"Where's the goat?" Delaney screamed. "Where's the scapegoat!"

Grasso said: "Ms. Delaney, I'm the scapegoat."

"What? You? Why?"

"Look at me," he replied, his voice calm, "This is why God created me. Why do you think that after nearly two thousand years, God led me to the *giudicare* stone? There are no coincidences in life. I was born for this moment and I'll not let this cup pass from me."

Spencer and Dunham had already lifted Grasso up from his chair, but Spencer was still gripping Grasso's useless left arm. "I can't let you do this," Spencer said. "You're not going to die to save me!" He started to tug Grasso toward the doorway.

Delaney glanced out the window behind Spencer's desk and yelled: "The sun is setting! It's too late!"

With his good right hand, Grasso reached forward and plucked the stone from Delaney's grasp.

"This is madness!" Spencer shouted. "I'm not letting you die!"

But Grasso was already swinging his right hand and the stone across his chest. He smashed the rock against Spencer's right hand, which was still clutching Grasso's left arm. Spencer screamed as a burst of electricity raced through his body.

A blinding white light flooded the room. It was coming from the stone. Spencer tried to release Grasso and pull away but he was paralyzed. So was Grasso.

"Use the water now!" the priest yelled. Dunham raced to his backpack, pulled out a vial of holy water, and threw it at the men's hands, which had become melded with the stone. When the water hit the stone, a blast of burning air knocked Dunham and Delaney backward, pinning them against the chamber's wall. Unable to free themselves, they could do nothing but watch.

In unison, Spencer and Grasso's bodies began to rise from the floor, slowly defying gravity. Their hands—Grasso's right and Spencer's left—remained joined to the stone, which had started to glow as if it were molten rock. The burning gust caused by the holy water swirled around them, forming a tornado with them rising up within its hollow eye. As they neared the ceiling, both men's legs lifted up behind them so that their feet were now on the same level as their shoulders. They looked as if they were flying. Suddenly, their bodies began spinning clockwise along the whirlwind's rim while the stone remained stationary, floating inside the storm's center with both men anchored to it as they twirled around, like human spokes, gaining speed as they spun faster and faster and faster until it was impossible to see the outline of their individual shapes. To Delaney and Dunham, the two men had become one, a faceless, spinning figure gripping a golden ball of brilliant fire. A high-pitched, piercing scream stung the two onlookers' ears, making them wince in pain.

An explosion erupted from inside the tornado, sending thousands of grains of white sand into the chamber where it peppered Delaney and Dunham like a horde of stinging bees.

The vortex slowed and Spencer came crashing down inside it, hitting the floor with a loud thud. But Grasso remained suspended, even though his body had now stopped moving. He was still clutching the stone but it had turned black, like a lump of coal. The priest could neither speak nor control his own movements. He was frozen. Very slowly, his body turned upright and then his right hand was snapped by unseen fingers straight back from his shoulder. The stone fell to the floor, regaining its white sheen as it landed near Spencer and underneath Grasso. The priest cried in pain as his useless left arm was stretched out. His feet were yanked down and crossed over one another. His body shot upward until his head was only an inch from the ceiling. There was a loud clang, the sound of metal hitting metal, and Grasso's right palm suddenly began gushing blood from a nail hole that had been punched through it. Another bang sounded and blood began flowing from a second wound that appeared in his left palm. A third clang and his feet were pierced and bleeding. Grasso screamed in agony and his side was torn open and began dripping with blood. Tiny droplets appeared on his forehead, as if invisible thorns had been pushed into his scalp.

"He's being crucified!" Dunham hollered.

Grasso gazed down at Delaney and Dunham, who were still pinned against the walls. He looked groggy and spent. He turned his head to his right and it was clear that he was now seeing a vision that only he could see. He tried to speak but no words came out. He began to weep, his face twisted in pain. But the tears were not caused by the physical torture that his body was being forced to endure. Rather they came from an intensity from within him, a feeling of complete and utter shame or unworthiness, of being in the presence of purity and knowing how wanting he was.

"It is finished," Grasso said.

As quickly as the bedlam had begun, it ended. Grasso's body slowly floated to the floor, as if he were a magician's assistant who had been levitated by some trick and now was being returned to earth. Freed at last from the wall, Delaney dashed forward to Spencer while Dunham scrambled to help Grasso.

"Spencer!" Delaney cried. "Can you hear me?"

He opened his eyes. She hugged him and he wrapped his arms firmly around her. Much to his shock, she pushed him away and grabbed his left hand, forcing it open.

"It's gone!" she yelled. The skin was now smooth and unblemished.

"Grasso!" Spencer called.

Dunham was on his knees sobbing next to the old priest's body. He thought Grasso was dead, but as soon as Delaney scooted over and touched his face, the priest gasped and coughed. He was struggling to catch his breath. She moved her ear next to his lips. His sentence came in a puff.

"I was there!" he whispered to her. "I was with Him."

Grasso blacked out.

When Grasso opened his eyes four hours later, he was in a bed at the Charlottesville General Hospital and Delaney, Spencer, and Dunham were at his bedside. Incredibly, he felt fine physically, in fact, his body ached less than it usually did. There was no trace of his ever having been shot by MacDonald. The holes in his hands, feet, side, and cuts on his forehead had disappeared.

"The scapegoat ritual worked," Spencer declared. "The crucifix in my left palm is gone! Father, you saved my life!"

But Grasso seemed confused. "I was supposed to die. I was the scapegoat."

"I know why you both survived," Delaney announced, "and I don't believe it had anything to do with the ritual!"

Spencer, Grasso, and Dunham looked at her, waiting for her explanation. "I'm not much of a Bible expert," Delaney continued, "but one of my favorite verses is something that Jesus said: 'Greater love has no man than this, that a man lay down his life for his friends.' Spencer's sins were wiped away because he was willing to die in order to save your life, Father."

"And me? Why did I survive?" Grasso asked.

"Because you were willing to die to save Judge Spencer's life. Isn't that the entire point of the crucifixion: dying to save someone else?"

Grasso quietly mumbled: "Out of the mouths of children."

"I'm assuming you will be taking the judgment stone back to the Vatican for safekeeping," Spencer said.

"That was originally my plan but it's not anymore."

"Why not?" a surprised Dunham asked. "It's a huge discovery! The stone proves miracles are real! It proves God exists! It's going to make us famous!"

"I thought all of those same things at first," Grasso explained, "but on the night when we left Judge Spencer feverish, I pored over the scriptures and I made a remarkable connection. I was looking for verses about the scapegoat in the Old Testament but I found my mind being drawn to the final book of the Bible: the Revelation to John."

"Isn't that the one that predicts the apocalypse—the end of the world?" Spencer asked.

"Yes, over the years, dozens of self-proclaimed prophets have used passages from it to justify mayhem and, ironically, the verse that kept nagging at me is called the Last Judgment Passage."

Grasso asked Dunham to take his Bible out of his backpack and read aloud verse eleven of chapter twenty.

"Then I saw a great white throne and him who sat upon it: from his presence earth and sky fled away, and no place was found for them. And I saw the dead, great and small, standing before the throne, and books were opened. Also another book was opened, which is the book of life. And the dead were judged by what was written in the books, by what they had done. And the sea gave up the dead in it, Death and Hades gave up the dead in them, and all were judged by what they had done."

Grasso said: "This verse goes on to say that anyone's name who is not found written in the book of life is cast into a lake of fire. Overall, it's terrifying because it's describing the apocalypse, earth's destruction, and the final judgment day. That's when the good receive their reward and the wicked are eternally damned."

"Lovely stuff," Delaney said.

"The first line of that verse is what kept haunting me," Grasso said. He asked Dunham to read it again.

"I saw a great white throne and him who sat upon it."

"For centuries many theologians have assumed that the 'him' in this verse refers to Our Lord Jesus Christ. They have interpreted it to mean that Christ will sit on a white throne and judge humankind. But I now believe this interpretation is completely wrong. If you study the ancient texts, you'll discover that the 'him' is not identified by name. In the earliest translations of the Revelation to John, the 'him' is identified simply as 'the Supreme Judge.' In fact, there's a scroll in the Secret Archives which goes even further. It says a 'Supreme Judge who is yet to be named will sit alone on the judgment seat, not accompanied by the martyrs.' That implies that this person will be a mortal human being."

"Sorry, Father," Spencer said, "but what does this have to do with us or the stone that's locked up in my desk drawer at the courthouse?"

"You'll have to bear with me just a bit longer before I can tie everything together for you," the priest said.

Grasso asked Dunham to read another verse from the Book of Revelation, this time, chapter two, verse seventeen.

"I will give him a white stone, with a new name written on the stone, which no one knows except him who receives it."

"I've never paid much attention to this verse," Grasso explained, "because at the time when John wrote Revelation, there was a popular belief among early Christians that God had created a secret amulet that gave its owner the authority to unlock supernatural portals and mystical seals. I always dismissed such speculation as pure superstition. But now, I understand why this verse is crucial."

"Why?" Dunham asked. "Does such an amulet exist?"

"Yes," Grasso replied, "it's the *giudicare* stone. The stone and the amulet are the same. It's what the early day Christians were trying to find."

"I still don't see how this ties together," Spencer said. "What does the stone, or amulet, have to do with the unknown 'him'—the Supreme Judge sitting judging all human kind?"

"The white stone is on a search," Grasso explained. "It's

being passed from one person to another, judging each of them individually. It's trying to find a human being worthy of becoming the 'Supreme Judge' who will eventually sit on the 'great white throne' on judgment day."

Grasso paused so they could ponder what he had just said.

"Father," Dunham asked, "are you telling us that the stone is trying to find a perfect person, someone completely without sin?"

"Yes, that's exactly what I am saying. And if it ever finds this perfect person, the apocalypse will begin!"

"It's really not a judgment stone then," Dunham said. "It's more like an apocalypse stone. It will cause the destruction of earth."

"The apocalypse stone," Grasso repeated. "I like that."

A nurse interrupted them. She checked Grasso's vital signs and the monitor that was feeding IV solution into his arm. "The doctor will be sending you home tomorrow morning," she said.

"Excellent!" Grasso replied. "I've a class to teach and Mr. Dunham here has a report that is due."

As soon as the nurse was gone, Dunham said: "If this stone is searching for someone who is pure of heart and without sin, then why didn't the apocalypse begin after the stone came into contact with you, Father?" Dunham's question was not said mockingly. He was sincere. "If anyone has never sinned," Dunham continued, "I figured it was you, Father."

Grasso didn't immediately reply. He was thinking of his youth and that morning when he'd been sitting at a sidewalk café in Rome years ago drinking coffee near the Trevi Fountain. That's when he had spotted a beautiful young Italian woman with her fiancé. That's when he had first felt sexual lust.

"No," Grasso said. "I'm far from perfect and God knows this. The stone that Jesus touched—this apocalypse stone—has been passed around for two thousand years and has yet to find a human being worthy of sitting on the great white throne to pass judgment. I suspect it could be a thousand more, or even a thousand thousand more years, before a Supreme Judge finally surfaces. Humankind still has much to learn."

Grasso spoke directly to Spencer: "The apocalypse stone is yours to send. You must let it go so it can continue its search."

"Will it kill the person I send it to?" he asked.

"Probably," Grasso replied, "but this cannot be your concern. None of us can predict the future. All we know is that the stone will humble its owner. If that person seeks forgiveness, repents, and offers to sacrifice his or her own life in order to save someone else's life—then who knows? After all, you and I survived it."

As he scanned their faces, Grasso said: "Do each of you really understand the significance of what you've been part of here? You have either seen or touched a stone that Our Lord Jesus Christ held in his hand. You have encountered a stone that eventually will be held by the Supreme Judge of all humankind. You have encountered a stone that will spark the apocalypse, the end of the world as we know it, and the final judgment of all humankind." Once again, he paused. Then he said: "What you have done is come as close as any mortal ever has come in modern times to actually touching God through a miracle."

26

CHARLOTTESVILLE COURANT REPORTER WALTER CORN splashed another blockbuster across Friday's front page. Under a huge banner headline: ARNOLD CASE SOLVED, MURDERER FATALLY SHOT, Corn identified Charles MacDonald as Cassie Arnold's killer and in breathless prose described how MacDonald had been about to execute Frank and Maxine Arnold when he was shot by Alice Jackson. MacDonald had died from his gunshot wound while riding to the hospital. Corn credited Miss Alice with preventing the slaughter of everyone who had been in Spencer's chambers. It was a completely unsubstantiated claim, but an exciting one. The newspaper printed a photograph of Jacob Wheeler and Detective Stuart standing on each side of a beaming Miss Alice. She was holding her Civil War pistol and was quoted saying: "The last time my great-great-grandfather shot this gun, he killed a Yankee sniper. I know he'd be proud that his pistol prevented a mass murder last night!"

Patti Delaney's name appeared only twice. She was identified as "a local defense attorney" and as "Charles MacDonald's cocounsel." Corn did not give her any credit for solving the case. Instead, he lavished praise on Detective Stuart and Wheeler, who coincidentally were the two main sources for his story. Father Grasso was mentioned in the final paragraphs. Corn wrote that the priest had helped flush out MacDonald by providing authorities with clues based on several psychic experiences caused by a religious relic. But Corn didn't elaborate.

Delaney read Corn's sensational account while drinking her morning coffee. After she had finished both, she telephoned the Clifton Hideway.

"I'm sorry but Judge Spencer checked out this morning," the receptionist said.

"Did he leave a message for me?" Delaney asked, quickly identifying herself.

"No, he paid his bill and then offered to sell his Jaguar to my boss. He was willing to sell it really cheap, but it was still too much. They talked about sports cars for a few minutes and then the judge drove off."

She telephoned the courthouse, but Miss Alice said Spencer wasn't there. "He left me a court order that dismissed all of the criminal charges filed against your client," Miss Alice explained. "He instructed me to telephone the jurors and tell them their services were no longer needed. I assumed we'd wrap up the loose ends in the Arnold case in court today but he canceled the hearing. He's acting very strange."

Delaney could think of only one reason why Spencer would have canceled the hearing and had been trying to sell his much-beloved Jaguar. He'd decided to take the five-million-dollar bribe from Augustus VanDenvender VI and run!

How could he do that after everything that had happened? she thought, and then she answered her own question. The stone was no longer a threat to him. He wasn't going to die!

Why risk prison if you could be rich and free? She was angry. *I'm not going to let you run away like this, Evan Spencer. If nothing else, you're going to have to face me tonight! I'm going to make you look me in the eyes and admit you're a coward!"*

Delaney tried to keep herself occupied for the rest of the day, but it was impossible to think of much else except Spencer. By 6:30 P.M., she couldn't stand it any longer. Spencer had said he was scheduled to meet with VanDenvender at seven o'clock. It was a twenty-minute drive to the Van-Denvender and Wythe law offices. But someone knocked on Delaney's apartment door just as she was about to leave.

It was Delbert Amil. "I wanted to stop by and say thank you." He held out a bouquet of yellow roses. "Thanks for believing in me."

"There were times when I didn't."

"I'm sorry I misled you, but I want you to know this entire experience has changed me. No more gangs or crime. I want people to respect me, not because I'm pretending to be my brother, but because I am me."

"Are you leaving town?"

"Yeah, I'm heading to California with some buddies of mine tonight. We're driving there. Will you tell the judge thanks for me?"

"Why don't you tell him yourself?" she asked. "I'm heading down to see him right now. You can follow me."

"I've got three friends in my car but I guess they won't mind," he replied. "I want to pay him my respects."

After checking out of the Clifton Hideaway early Friday morning, Spencer drove to his bank and withdrew all of the cash in his checking and money market accounts. He also redeemed another $30,000 in savings bonds. That gave him about $65,000. He had more money, but it was salted away in stocks and retirement funds. He didn't have time to liquidate them. From the bank, he drove north on state highway 29 and then turned east onto one of the major arteries that feeds into the nation's capital. He stopped at three different automobile dealerships before he found a salesman willing to cut a deal. In return for his Jaguar, Spencer was paid $25,000 and given the title to a 1984 Ford Escort with 184,000 miles on it and peeling green paint. The Escort reeked of cigarettes but it got Spencer back to Charlottesville by 6 P.M.

Spencer drove to the courthouse where he collected several items that he wanted to take with him. The most important was the apocalypse stone. Although Father Grasso had assured him that he was now safe from its supernatural powers, he picked it up with his fingertips and quickly dropped it inside a Federal Express box. He was ready now for his meeting at VanDenvender and Wythe. Spencer walked down a slight hill to the law office, arriving about five minutes early.

Delaney's unexpected encounter with Delbert Amil and bad luck at a series of red traffic lights caused her to arrive at the law firm ten minutes after Spencer had already gone inside. She correctly assumed that she had missed him, so she parked her Saab directly across the street from the firm's front door and waited. Amil and his friends pulled into the parking spot behind her and also decided to wait. They weren't in any hurry, but they soon became bored and walked down to a nearby convenience store to buy snacks and play video games.

Meanwhile, inside the law firm, Spencer found the first floor deserted. But when the elevator opened on the second floor, he came face-to-face with Ramon "Red" Soleano, who was standing guard outside VanDenvender's office. Soleano, whose nickname referred to his rusty hair, was in his early forties and was listed on the law firm's payroll as a part-time security consultant. But Spencer knew that this title was a euphemism. Red Soleano was VanDenvender's personal thug. He had started out as a wannabe boxer in California and had amassed an impressive record as a teen fighter: twenty-two wins, nineteen with knockouts, and only one defeat. But his boxing career had been short-circuited after he was sent to prison for nearly beating a man to death during a barroom brawl. The fighting had started after Soleano made an obscene sexual request to the man's wife. After he was paroled, Soleano had used his fists to earn a living as a bouncer in a seedy nightclub, as a collections agent for a string of used car dealers, and finally as a security guard in a Nevada casino back in the days when gambling cheats often had their fingers smashed with hammers or were taken on one-way rides into the desert.

VanDenvender had met Soleano during a gambling trip and brought him back to Virginia. Today, Soleano was wearing sharkskin cowboy boots with silver tips on the toes and skintight blue denim jeans held at the waist by a silver cowboy belt buckle with a red, white, and blue rhinestone American flag emblazoned on it. There were four aces embroidered above the pocket on his white cowboy shirt. The top two buttons were undone, exposing several gold chains and a patch of gray and fading red chest hair. He was wearing a black leather jacket and sunglasses even though it was nighttime and he was indoors. Although they had spoken only a few times, Spencer considered Soleano to be one of those psychotic edge-dwellers that some rich people liked to keep around just in case they needed a muscle flexed or wanted to make good on a violent threat. As Spencer stepped from the elevator, Soleano sneered at him. "Hold it, Judge. I need to check you for a gun or a wire." Soleano frisked him and, finding neither, knocked on VanDenvender's door and announced that Spencer had arrived.

Not surprisingly, VanDenvender's office was the largest on the second floor and was decorated in a conservative, masculine, walnut and leather motif. There was a huge, stern oil portrait of VanDenvender hanging behind his desk. The piercing blue eyes in that picture seemed to follow visitors regardless of where they were in the room. It was meant to intimidate— that's the only reason why he'd agreed to pose for it—and it did. Spencer took a seat in one of the high-backed dark leather chairs facing VanDenvender, who was sitting behind his desk and made no effort to stand up or welcome him.

"Here's your confession," VanDenvender said, sliding a single typewritten sheet across the desktop. "Assuming you want to bother, you can read it."

Spencer studied it carefully. VanDenvender was getting full value for his five-million-dollar bribe. The wording had been crafted so that VanDenvender would later be able to argue in court that he and his law firm had been victimized by Spencer and, therefore, shouldn't be held liable in any subsequent civil suits.

"I've decided not to sign," Spencer said, sliding the paper back to VanDenvender.

Much to Spencer's surprise, the old man didn't seem startled. "There are many reasons why I'm rich and you're not," VanDenvender said. "You've just reminded me of two of them. The first is you're an idealistic fool! You apparently think this confession has to do with morality and honor. It doesn't. It has to do with practicality."

Spencer wasn't in the mood for a lecture. "You said there were two reasons. Let's speed this up. What's the second?"

"Unlike you, I always have a contingency plan. Do you really think I'm going to allow you to accuse me in public of stealing those Circus Circus shares?"

Spencer realized that Soleano had stepped behind his chair.

"You're going to break my legs if I don't confess," Spencer said. "*That's* your contingency plan?"

VanDenvender shook his head in disgust. "I don't need your signature on this confession in order to use it."

Spencer suddenly realized that VanDenvender was going to have Soleano murder him. Of course, he'd make it look like a suicide. All Soleano needed to do was leave the confession somewhere the police would find it. End of Evan Spencer, end of missing stock problem.

"I'd like to ask you something," Spencer said, stalling for time. "Is there really a safety deposit box in London with five million dollars in it?"

A toothy grin sauntered across VanDenvender's face. "What do you think?"

"Until a few seconds ago, I thought there was."

VanDenvender reached down by his chair, retrieved a briefcase, and opened it for Spencer to see. It contained a hundred thousand dollars in hundred dollar bills. "If you had signed the confession, I would've given you this and Red would've taken you to Dulles Airport where you would've been put on that flight to Frankfurt—exactly as I had promised," he said. "Only when you had reached Germany, you would've been greeted by some of Red's associates. The plan was to have you disappear in Europe—permanently. The real beauty was that the cash you would've been carrying was what Mr. Soleano's friends were going to be paid for killing you."

"Does Melissa know you're going to kill me?"

VanDenvender mulled over the question. Finally, he said, "I'd love to tell you that she knew and didn't care. But, no, she doesn't have a clue. Had you disappeared overseas, she would have assumed that you had vanished on your own by taking a new identity or some such fantasy. Now, she will no longer be able to believe that illusion."

Spencer tried to bluff. "Aren't you worried that I might have told someone I was coming here tonight?"

"So what?" VanDenvender shrugged. "If anyone asks, I'll tell them that you came to see me because you were ashamed. You admitted to me that you had stolen the Circus Circus stock and wanted me to loan you the money to repay the Worthington estate! Of course, I urged you to give yourself up and confess, but you ran out of my office before I could stop you."

Soleano said: "C'mon Judge, let's go!"

But VanDenvender wasn't through talking. "The truth is," he said, "I'm having mixed feelings about this right now. Not about killing you, but whether or not Red should kick the piss out of you first. I'd love to see that, but I guess it would be easier if your 'suicide' were something simple, such as a drug overdose, rather than having Red toss you off a rooftop to disguise your bruises."

VanDenvender snapped the briefcase shut. "This hundred thousand will be waiting for you, Red, when you return. It's all yours now!"

Spencer rose slowly from his seat, but VanDenvender still had one more parting shot that he wanted to deliver. "When you married my daughter, my friends at the club teased me about how Melissa had married beneath her social class. What they didn't know was that you came with a hefty dowry: all those wonderful shares of Circus Circus stock."

VanDenvender handed the confession to Soleano. "Don't forget to tuck this in his pocket after you're done."

But they weren't finished. Spencer had a little speech of his own that he wanted to say. "You're so smug, so arrogant," he said, "but I know something you don't!"

"Let me guess. You're going to tell me that you wrote all this down and put it in an envelope with instructions that it be opened by the police in case of your untimely death. I've only seen that goofy threat about a dozen times on television!"

"No, if you kill me, God is going to punish you!"

"Is this supposed to be a threat?" VanDenvender asked. "Or are you honestly hoping to scare me with talk of hellfire and damnation? Oh my, my, did you hear that, Red? Maybe we should simply let him go! All this talk of God is really scaring me!"

"Me too," Soleano remarked. "I'm about to wet my pants."

VanDenvender stepped around to the front of his desk. "Hold him!" he said. Soleano grabbed Spencer from behind, pinning his arms. VanDenvender slugged him hard in the abdomen, knocking the breath from his body. He waited for a second and then hit him again and then a third time. Soleano released Spencer and he collapsed to the floor.

"Get up!" Soleano ordered. Spencer slowly raised himself up on one knee. He glanced up at VanDenvender and the old man punched him in the face, flattening him again onto the Persian rug.

"*Now* you can get rid of him," VanDenvender said.

Soleano pulled Spencer to his feet and shoved him into the hallway. They rode the elevator downstairs. Soleano asked: "Is that Jaguar of yours parked out back?"

"No, I walked here from the courthouse."

"Cute, real cute," Soleano said. "Okay, Judge, we're going to exit out the front door and get into my car. You'll drive. Now listen real good. I got a little .22-caliber pistol in my jacket pocket. Its slugs are easy to fish out of a person's skull and I'm positive a headfirst dive off the courthouse roof onto the sidewalk will cover up any evidence that you'd been shot. Are you understanding me here?"

As soon as they stepped out the front door, Delaney saw Spencer and dashed from her Saab across the street.

"Hey, stop right there! I need to talk to you!" she shouted.

Soleano pulled out his pistol. "Who's this?"

Delaney saw the gun and asked, "What's going on?"

"Don't make a scene or I'll shoot you both!" Soleano said.

His car was parked less than ten feet away. "Both of you, walk over to that green car—now!"

Spencer didn't move. "No!" he said. "If you're going to shoot us, you'll have to do it right now, right here!"

Soleano lowered his voice: "I said, *move*. Otherwise I'll shoot her first!"

Just then Delbert Amil shouted Spencer's name. He and his friends had finished at the convenience store and were ambling toward them on the sidewalk.

"An unexpected twist," Spencer said. "Are you really stupid enough to shoot six people right in front of VanDenvender and Wythe? That's a lot of 'suicides' to explain!"

Soleano looked left and right. He didn't know what to do, and he was running out of time. "Maybe you should run back upstairs to your master!" Spencer said.

Soleano slipped the .22 into his jacket and stepped back inside the law firm, clicking the lock on the door behind him.

"Judge Spencer," Amil said. "I want to thank you for what you did for me—letting Ms. Delaney hold that hearing last night."

Spencer shook his hand. "You're welcome! But we've got to run! It's an emergency!" He grabbed Delaney's arm and hustled her toward her Saab.

"Call me from California and I'll explain!" Delaney yelled to Amil. "Good luck!"

Spencer slipped into the passenger's seat. "Drive!" he said. " Now! Fast! Soleano will be coming after us. He's seen your car!"

"Where—to the police station?"

"No, the courthouse!"

She floored the Saab and it lunged forward.

"Who's Soleano?" she asked.

"My father-in-law's chief thug. He was going to help me 'commit suicide' tonight!"

"They were going to kill you?"

"That was their plan."

She gasped. "I thought you were going to sign a confession and flee the country!"

"I refused to sign!"

Now she was even more confused. "Why were you trying to sell your car if you weren't going to run away?"

"Cash," he replied. "I'm going to need cash to fight them in court."

When Delaney reached the courthouse, Spencer said: "We've got to switch cars. Park over there by that Ford Escort!" She did and he leaped out and unlocked the Ford.

"Whose car is this?"

"It's mine!" he replied. "C'mon, let's go!"

She got in. "Yuck! It stinks like cigarettes. Can't we just go to the police?"

"And tell them what? No one will believe me! We've got to find someplace safe to hide and then come up with a plan!"

"But I haven't done anything!" she protested.

"They know you know the truth. That's enough to get you killed!"

As he drove, she thought about where they could hide. "My friends—the owners of Ritchies Restaurant—own a cabin in the Blue Ridge Mountains near Shenandoah National Park. I know where they keep the key."

By the time they had reached the Blue Ridge Mountains, Spencer felt confident that no one was following them. He stopped at a combination service station and food store. Delaney went inside to buy groceries while he pumped his fuel. The cabin was another half-hour ride away, at the end of a narrow and winding rutted road. The key was hidden in a slit between two logs near the front stoop.

Delaney had warned him that the cabin was rustic. It was one large room with worn plank floors. There was an antique potbellied heater in the center of the room and a wood-burning stove alongside one wall. There were no windows. A fire-engine red hand pump next to the kitchen sink was used to suck water up from the well beneath the cabin. There was no electricity or indoor toilet. A double bed on a metal frame, a chrome dinette table with three chairs, and a marred wooden dresser with a mirror attached to it were the only furniture. Spencer found newspapers, kindling, several logs, and an ax on the front porch. It was hardly the Honeymoon Cottage at the Clifton Hideway, but they were too exhausted and emotionally spent to complain. She found a box of matches and lit the oil lamp on the table. He built a fire in the heater.

"I bought spaghetti," she said. Spencer suddenly realized he hadn't eaten all day. She found a pot under the sink, filled it with water from the pump, and placed it on the stove. "You'll have to start a fire in the stove for me," she told him. "I wonder how long it takes water to boil over a wood fire?"

"Obviously, you weren't a Girl Scout," he said.

"Oh," she replied sarcastically, "and I suppose you know?"

"Ten minutes," he said confidently, although he actually didn't have a clue.

"I'll say at least thirty," she replied. "Loser washes the dishes!"

Spencer made a fire in the stove while Delaney unpacked groceries. "I was never a Girl Scout," she said, "but I did follow their motto: 'Be prepared!'" She removed three bottles of wine from a shopping bag. Then she began laughing.

"What's so funny?"

"I didn't buy a corkscrew!"

"I'm not surprised. 'Be prepared' is the Boy Scouts' motto, not the Girl Scouts'. I think theirs has something to do with selling cookies."

"Sexist!" she teased. "Actually, I think 'Be prepared' is both of their mottoes." She found a tub that was filled with flatware and cooking utensils. "Ah, here's a skewer. It'll do!" She used it to pry the cork from one of the bottles.

"You almost got me killed tonight," she said, as she poured a red Cabernet Franc into a bright blue disposable plastic cup.

He toasted her: "Thank you for saving my life. That's two nights in a row we've had guns pointed at us. I can hardly wait until tomorrow evening!"

"Let's drink a toast to Father Grasso," she said suddenly.

They touched their plastic cups together.

Delaney said: "What did you see when you and Father Grasso were twirling around the ceiling?"

"All I could see was a bright light. I know that sounds similar to what people say when they describe an out-of-body death experience, but that's all I could see. At the same time, I felt as if that light were somehow cleansing me, washing over me." He took another sip of wine. "I've never believed in any of that supernatural stuff. Until last night, I wasn't even certain I believed that God was real. And now that I know He is real, I'm actually angry."

"You're angry?"

"Yes. I'm not sure I can explain it but I'll try. Before I touched the apocalypse stone, I had a choice. I could believe in Him or not believe in Him. But now, I don't have a choice."

"You should feel relieved."

"Let me ask you a question. Can you force someone to love you? I mean, if I told you that I was going to kill you unless you loved me, would that make you love me?"

"Absolutely not! But I'd probably say that I loved you—just to stay alive."

"Exactly, and if I told you that I'd give you a hundred million dollars if you loved me, would you love me then?"

"Probably not, but I might say that I loved you so that I could get the cash."

"Right. In both cases, you wouldn't really love me, but you would say that you did, either because you were afraid of being punished or you wanted a reward," he said. "Isn't that what hell and heaven represent? If God really wants me to love him, then I need to choose to love him voluntarily. He can't bribe me with heaven or threaten me with hell or convince me with miracles. If He does any of that then he's tipping the scales."

He topped off her cup with more wine and then refilled his own. Spencer said: "You see, the reasons for your faith—that's what matters! You have to believe in God because of who He is and what He represents. I think Father Grasso understood this after he touched the stone. You shouldn't need a white stone and the end of the world to convince you that God is real!"

"I'm not sure I agree," she replied. "I think you're confusing logical consequences with punishment and rewards."

For the next hour, they debated, drank more wine, and became so embroiled in their conversation that neither remembered to keep track of how much time it took for the water on the stove to boil or even notice it was ready until the lid on the pot began bouncing under the steam.

"My father always put a little olive oil in the water to keep the pasta from sticking together," she said. "I couldn't find any at the store, but maybe this will have the same effect." She poured some wine into the water.

When the pasta was ready, he took a bite and declared it was the best that he had ever eaten. They finished the last of the wine with their meal.

"What are you going to do with the apocalypse stone?" she asked.

"I'm not sure yet," he replied.

"You could mail it to your father-in-law or even Taylor Cauldwell. They've got plenty of sins!" She began giggling. "I've got it, send it to Miss Alice."

"You're drunk," he told her.

"How dare you! It takes more than a few glasses of vino to get a good Irish girl like me liquored up!"

She glanced at his watch. It was after two A.M. "I saw a motel about four miles down the mountain," she said. "But I don't think its owners are going to appreciate me disturbing them at this hour for a room."

"Not to mention you trying to navigate that gravel road. I'm not sure I want to risk loaning you my car. That Ford Escort is a classic!" he said. "Here's the deal. Since you made dinner, you get to sleep in the bed. I'll curl up on the floor by the heater."

The room was more than warm now. The potbellied heater cast a red glow on their faces. The oil lamp sent shadows flickering against the rough-hewn log walls. The smell of burning pine gave the cabin an earthy scent. He started to clear the table but she stopped him. "I don't think the floor looks comfortable," she said. She led him to the bed and they undressed each other. He kissed her softly. After they had made love, slowly as the fire in the heater died, they held one another under the heavy wool blankets, bare flesh pressed against bare flesh. He thought about how long it had been since he had not thought of someone else while having sex. She whispered: "I was afraid you were going to run away."

"I almost did. I'm afraid of going to prison. I'm afraid of what Augustus VanDenvender and Taylor Cauldwell can do to me. Running away with five million dollars seemed like a solution."

"What do you want from this?"

"I want to clear my name. I want to be with someone I can love and who will love me. My life is nearly half over. I want a chance to get it right."

"I've only slept with two other men," she said. "When I was fourteen, I fell in love with a boy who lived on a farm just outside town. We dated all through high school and during our senior year, we decided it was time for us to do it. We were both seventeen and scared but I planned on marrying him, so we went to a motel. We attended different colleges after graduation and I wrote him every day. I could hardly wait to visit him. When I did, he arranged for me to stay in the girls' dorm. He snuck in and we spent the night together in that bed. When I got back to my school, he wrote me a letter and said he'd met someone else. It was the girl whose room I'd stayed in. They'd been having sex almost from the first time they'd met at college. I was so humiliated. I had believed we were truly in love. My mother had given up her life in London to marry my father. I wanted that sort of unconditional love. A few years later, I met Merlin and he asked me to marry him."

"Merlin?"

"Everyone called him Max. We met in law school. I wasn't certain that I loved him, at least not like my first love. But I said yes when he asked me, and we were married, and I was content, and then I caught Max in bed with another man. Crap! I know how to pick 'em, don't I?"

Her head had been resting on his left shoulder, but now she lifted herself up so that she could look directly into his face. "What sort of man are you, Spencer? Will you break my heart too?"

He didn't know what to say and he wasn't really certain that she expected an answer. Her question had been more of a warning, a sad acknowledgment of what might come. She put her head back on his shoulder and soon fell asleep.

He listened to the wind blowing through the trees and the unfamiliar night noises that creatures make outside a mountain cabin. Was he falling in love with Patti Delaney? He barely knew her. He had never been so unsure about his future. Lying there with her in his arms, he also had never felt so alive.

27

THE WHISTLE OF A TEA KETTLE BLACKENED WITH SOOT caused Delaney to stir. For a moment, she forgot where she was and then she remembered and reached over to touch him. Spencer wasn't beside her. He was already out of bed making them coffee. Through half-closed eyes she looked at him. He was naked, the room was chilly, and he was bent over, sticking split logs into the potbelly heater.

"The water is hot enough for coffee," he proudly proclaimed.

"Nice butt! It's freezing in this room," she said. "Bring the coffee and get back in bed!"

Later, after they were dressed, they formulated a plan. She would drive to Washington, D.C., and tell Kevin Michaels, the attorney at Boyd, Stackhouse, and Brown, that Spencer wasn't going to be able to pay the sixty million dollars. She'd explain that the real thief was Augustus VanDenvender VI. Although Spencer didn't have any proof, he was willing to help the law firm go after his father-in-law. It would have a better chance of getting sixty million dollars out of his deep pockets than from Spencer's empty ones. Delaney would then return to Charlottesville and drive directly to the sheriff's office to determine if Spencer had been indicted for stealing the missing shares. If he had been, she would arrange a time on Monday for him to surrender. She'd also notify a bail bondsman so Spencer could be released without having to spend the night in jail.

"There's a way I could prove I'm innocent," Spencer said, "but it's a long shot." When Circus Circus declared its stock split, it would have sent out the extra shares either by registered or certified mail, he explained. The only person authorized to sign for such mail was VanDenvender's private secretary, Belle Patterson.

"Where can I find her?" Delaney asked.

"You can't. She's dead. Cancer. About six years ago. However, Belle was extremely conscientious and meticulous. Her personal office records are probably in storage in the law firm's basement. My father-in-law may have overlooked them when he was doctoring the files. If she signed a receipt for those shares, she also probably made a note about where that stock was sent after it left her hands. The problem is: How are we going to get into the basement to search her old files?"

"Isn't there someone there you can call?"

Spencer thought for a moment. "My former secretary, Traci Sugarman, would know where to look. Even though it's Saturday, she'll be at work until noon."

"We can use my cell phone," Delaney said. "I'll dial the number to keep the receptionist from recognizing your voice." After Sugarman got on the line, Delaney handed him the phone.

"Is this a bad time to talk?" he asked.

"Yes," Sugarman replied.

He gave her Delaney's cell phone number. "Call me back please! It's urgent!"

Ten minutes later, Sugarman called. She had gone into a stall in the women's bathroom at the law firm for privacy. "The cops have been here looking for you," she said. "And that creep, Red Soleano, has been snooping around the office all day. They say you stole money from a client!"

"Traci, there's fifty million dollars of stock missing and I'm getting the blame."

"Hold on!" she whispered. "Someone's just come in." A few seconds later, Sugarman said, "It's okay, one of the other girls spilled something at the copying machine and was washing her hands. I can talk now."

"I need you to go into the basement storeroom and find Belle Patterson's personal files. The Ambrose Worthington estate took two years to get through probate and during that time, the Circus Circus company declared a stock split. See if Belle ever logged anything in her records about the law firm receiving a half-million shares of Circus Circus stock."

"Judge," Sugarman said, her voice trembling. "I've got two kids at home. I need this job! I can't afford to get fired! And Red Soleano scares me! What if they catch me going through Belle's files? I'd like to help, but I'm really, really scared!"

"Listen Traci," he said, "you can do this!" The phone went dead and Spencer felt a sudden sense of dread. But a few moments later, the cell phone rang again.

"Sorry, I dropped the phone," Sugarman said.

"Patti Delaney is my attorney," he explained. "If you find something in Belle's file, give it to the owners of Ritchies Restaurant. They will get it to her. That way, no one will ever know you helped. Please! I'm counting on you!"

The events of the next forty-eight hours happened at whirlwind speed. As Spencer had predicted, Augustus VanDenvender VI had reached out across the state to pull political strings. On Saturday afternoon, Attorney General Taylor Cauldwell held a surprise press conference to announce that Spencer had been indicted for stealing stock from a client. The timing of Cauldwell's news conference guaranteed that the story made a big splash in the Sunday morning papers and on news shows.

"Judge Spencer and I have been close friends since college," Cauldwell told reporters, "and these charges sadden me deeply. But no one is above the law, especially judges who have betrayed the public trust. That's why I have appointed a special independent prosecutor, Willard Dilks, to ensure that this case is handled without any possible favoritism." Dilks was a retired commonwealth's attorney from Richmond who had a reputation for doing dirty jobs for Cauldwell.

All of Spencer's financial accounts were immediately frozen and he was automatically suspended as Albemarle County's Chief Circuit Judge. On Monday, he was also hit with a sixty-million-dollar civil lawsuit filed by Boyd, Stackhouse, and Brown. It named Augustus VanDenvender VI and his law firm as codefendants.

Spencer came out of hiding that same Monday afternoon and surrendered to the police. But even though Delaney had a bondsman standing by, "unexplained complications" kept the county jail from releasing him and he was forced to spend the night in jail. That gave Cauldwell plenty of time to contact the media, and when Delaney arrived on Tuesday morning to pick up Spencer, a mob of reporters and television crews was waiting at the front entrance.

"Cauldwell's turning this into a campaign booster," Delaney warned Spencer. "He's reminding voters every chance he gets that he is the gubernatorial candidate who is so honest that he's willing to prosecute his closest friends if he suspects them of being corrupt!"

Because of the gaggle of reporters outside, they decided to make a run for it out a side door. "Where'd you park my Escort?" he asked.

"You don't have it anymore it was seized by the sheriff last night," she replied. "I drove over in my Saab. You'll have to ride with me."

"What about the two items that I'd hidden in my car trunk—does the sheriff have them?"

"Not a chance. I took out the apocalypse stone and your suitcase of cash."

They made it halfway to the Saab before reporters spotted them and gave chase. Delaney nearly hit a cameraman when she sped out of the lot.

"I've got even more bad news for you," Delaney said as she drove. "You were served divorce papers this morning by Melissa. You've made the front page again!" She handed him a copy of that morning's *Charlottesville Courant*. Walter Corn had conducted an exclusive interview with Melissa at Van-Denvender Hall. Under the headline *WIFE SHATTERED BY THEFT CHARGES: WONDERS IF JUDGE HAD OTHER SECRETS* was a photograph of his obviously distraught wife.

"Do I really want to read this?" he asked.

"Let me give you a quick summary of what Melissa Van-Denvender said," Delaney replied. She paused for a second of unnecessary drama and then said: "She claims you pretty much sucked as a husband!"

"Glad you didn't spare me any of the messy details!"

"Hey, Spencer, lighten up!" she replied. "The good news is I've found you an apartment near the University and since college kids don't ever bother to read the local newspaper, you won't stick out."

"You know," he said sarcastically, "you're absolutely right! I really don't have anything to be depressed about! Still there's one tiny thing that bothers me."

"I'll bite," she said, knowing that he was setting her up for a joke. "I'm guessing that you're upset about Melissa divorcing you—that's it, right?"

"No, I'm really going to miss that Ford Escort."

Delaney groaned.

As a judge, Spencer had always thought three months was adequate time for attorneys to prepare for a trial, but now that he was a defendant, it felt rushed. Some mornings he wanted desperately to get it over with. Other mornings he was terrified about what might happen. His rented attic room near the University reminded him of the first apartment that he and Melissa had shared. The thought weighed on him. Two months after he was arrested, the *Charlottesville Courant*'s society page published another photograph of Melissa, only this time she was beaming as she danced with Taylor Cauldwell at a political fund-raiser attended by the local aristocracy. The gubernatorial race was beginning to pick up steam, and Melissa and Cauldwell had been linked romantically in the press. Delaney also had learned that the VanDenvenders had hired a media consultant from Washington, D.C., to help persuade the public that Melissa had been a victim of an unscrupulous husband. Under state laws, she had to wait six months before her divorce would become final. There was speculation that she would marry Cauldwell as soon as that time requirement ended. Spencer had not spoken to Melissa since their antagonistic exchange on the verandah. What surprised him was how little he missed her even though they had been married more than two decades.

Spencer waived his right to a jury trial. He doubted many Albemarle County jurors would feel much sympathy for: (1) a lawyer, (2) a former judge, (3) a defendant accused of stealing fifty million dollars, (4) a man accused of taking funds from a widow, (5) the estranged husband of an extremely wealthy woman, (6) a man whose wife said he was guilty. Instead, he decided to put his fate into the hands of a fellow circuit court judge. To avoid any possible conflict of interest, it was decided that a judge from Danville, a town that sits on Virginia's border with North Carolina, would hear the criminal case—

although the actual trial would be held in the Albemarle County Courthouse. Officially, Taylor Cauldwell was not involved in prosecuting the case, but on the morning of the trial he arrived with the prosecution team and stopped long enough on the courthouse steps to conduct a short press conference.

"We trust all of our public officials to be honest, but we especially trust members of our judiciary to be above reproach," he declared. "What Judge Evan Spencer did was tantamount to rape—a rape of the public's trust!" The fact that the Circus Circus shares had vanished years before Spencer had become a judge hadn't mattered to Cauldwell or, it seemed, to any of the reporters. They smelled blood.

Danville Judge Jerome J. Peabody was one of only a handful of black judges in Virginia and he had a well-deserved reputation for speaking bluntly. He began Spencer's trial with a lecture.

"Because there are no jurors here for you attorneys to impress," he said dryly, "I'm going to expect both of you to keep the courtroom theatrics and histrionics to a minimum. Let's just stick to questioning the witnesses, presenting evidence, and stating your arguments. The prosecution has told me that it expects this case to take about three or four days, so let's begin."

Special prosecutor Willard Dilks's opening witness was Kevin Michaels, the attorney from Boyd, Stackhouse, and Brown, who explained how the firm had discovered the bonus shares of Circus Circus stock were missing.

"Who was responsible at VanDenvender and Wythe for handling those half-million shares?" Dilks asked.

"Evan Spencer, the defendant," Michaels replied. "All of the court filings and probate records show that he was personally in charge of the Worthington probate."

When it was time for Michaels to be cross-examined, Delaney announced that she didn't have any questions to ask him. Just then, the rear double doors of the courtroom swung open and more than two dozen college students came in. All of the seats were occupied and they didn't know where to sit, so the group fanned out across the back of the room.

"What's going on here?" an obviously irritated Judge Peabody demanded.

"I apologize, Your Honor, for interrupting," Father Dino Grasso replied, as he entered the courtroom trailing behind his students. "We're a class from Catholic University studying ethics. I'm the professor and I had arranged for a bus to drive us here, but it broke down just outside of town, causing us to be delayed. Again, I apologize for the disruption, but we have come a long way to see justice being done."

Peabody sized up the crippled old priest and knew immediately that this had the makings of a public relations disaster. He would look cruel and insensitive if he tossed out Grasso and his entourage. "I don't like interruptions," he announced, "but since your students are eager to learn about our system, you may stay."

"Thank you," Grasso said. "I'm certain these youngsters will give you high marks in their reports!" The spectators in the room laughed. Grasso looked around for somewhere to sit and a man reluctantly surrendered his seat. When Grasso was finally settled in, he waved cheerfully to Delaney and Spencer with his good right hand.

"If you're comfortable now," Judge Peabody said, "we can pick up where we were." He didn't expect Grasso to reply, but the old priest did, completely ignoring the sarcasm that had saturated the judge's voice. "Thank you," he said pleasantly. "I'm sure we're all fine now."

Peabody ordered Dilks to call his next witness. Augustus VanDenvender VI took the witness stand and viciously lashed out at Spencer. "If it hadn't been for my daughter's constant nagging, I'd never have hired him."

"If that were the case, then why did you put him in charge of such an important probate?" Dilks asked.

"Spencer began bugging me about the Worthington probate within hours after Ambrose Worthington's death," VanDenvender testified. "Although I was reluctant, I foolishly agreed to let him handle it because I thought it would be good experience for him and I thought I could keep watch over his shoulder. However, I got involved in other matters and Spencer proved to be very ingenious at hiding things."

"How do you know that he stole the shares?" Dilks asked.

"Not only was it his case, we found a receipt in our files that showed that he had signed for the shares when they were delivered to our office."

Dilks held up a blue slip of paper. "Is this that receipt?"

"Yes, we insert blue slips like that into a file whenever our firm takes control of a financial asset that belongs to someone else."

"What name is signed on this receipt?"

"Evan Spencer's."

Grasso suddenly began coughing so violently that it took several moments for him to catch his breath. By then, he had completely disrupted the proceedings.

"I'm sorry, Judge," Grasso said through a heavy wheeze after he finally got himself under control.

Prosecutor Dilks didn't handle the interruption well. "Ur, ah, let's see, oh, the receipt," he said. But the coughing had not rattled his witness.

"While we were fortunate enough to find the receipt," VanDenvender volunteered, "there's no record that says what he did with that stock after he took it, and our auditors haven't been able to discover how he liquidated those shares."

Spencer whispered to Delaney. "That blue slip is a forgery. I looked through all of those records on the same day that Kevin Michaels contacted me and there wasn't any blue receipt in the Worthington case files!"

Dilks submitted the blue receipt as evidence, asked a few more questions, and then sat down. As before, Delaney said: "I have no questions for this witness."

Dilks had expected Delaney to spend the remainder of the day grilling VanDenvender. In fact, he had already told his next witness, Melissa, that he wouldn't be calling her to testify until tomorrow. He asked for a short recess so he could confer with Taylor Cauldwell.

"The old man's testimony was supposed to guarantee us the top spot on tonight's local news," Dilks complained. "Ms. VanDenvender was supposed to be our big story for tomorrow's newscasts. How do you want to handle this now?"

"See if you can get the judge to adjourn," Cauldwell suggested. "Tell him you need more time to prepare for tomorrow."

Dilks tried, but Peabody saw through their scam. "We

haven't even taken our noon lunch break," the judge noted. "Besides, you've had three months to prepare. Quit stalling and call your next witness."

Spencer was beginning to like this judge.

Melissa VanDenvender wasn't happy about being called early to testify. It wasn't because she hadn't had time to prepare. She was angry because of how she was dressed. The trial was being broadcast live over the local cable channel and on Court TV and her media consultant had picked out a special outfit for her to wear on the witness stand. It was less flashy than the short black skirt and white striped blouse by St. John that she was wearing. Rather than looking sad and sincere, she looked seductive.

"The main reason Spencer married me was because he wanted a job at my father's law firm," she testified. "I didn't know that when I first married him. I was blinded by my love. But I quickly discovered all he cared about was my family's money and social status. He manipulated me."

"Did your husband ever mention specific cases to you?" Dilks asked.

"Never, but one night he brought up the Worthington probate. I can't remember Spencer's exact words now, but I believe he said something about how it was going to be his big break."

"Did he act differently after he had handled the probate?"

"Yes, he did. When we married, Spencer had been dirt poor, so naturally my family insisted on a prenuptial agreement and we kept our finances separate. That made Spencer angry and he was constantly pressuring me for money, so I put him on a weekly allowance. After he handled the Worthington probate, he said he didn't need me giving him handouts anymore. I never knew where he suddenly got his money, but after that case, he seemed to have plenty—even more than me at times!"

Once again, Grasso began coughing.

"Father, are you okay?" Judge Peabody asked. "I'm afraid you're going to have to leave the courtroom if this continues."

"I apologize for my gagging," Grasso said. His face was red and he was still trying to catch his breath. As before, the interruption threw off Dilks.

Like her father before her, Melissa didn't need Dilks to keep her on track. "Let me give you an example of his spending habits," she declared. "Spencer bought an $85,000 Jaguar sports car using cash, and when I told him that was a bit extravagant for a judge, he joked: 'That's why I bought it in black instead of red!' "

Spencer sat stone-faced. He didn't want television viewers or other reporters in the courthouse reading anything into his reactions. But as he listened to Melissa, he silently marveled at her mastery of the semitruth. She understood that the most convincing lies are always hidden by being mixed in with facts. He had bought a Jaguar. That was true. And, yes, he had paid cash for it. And it was also correct that he had switched from buying a red car to buying a black one. But he had earned that money, not stolen it. With Melissa, finding the truth was like peeling an onion. You had to strip away the layers to discover the spin that she was concealing.

Delaney was eager to rip into Melissa when it was time for the cross-examination. But she didn't. She and Spencer had agreed on an unusual trial strategy and she was determined to stick to it. She told the judge that the defense didn't have a single question that it wanted to ask Melissa.

Judge Peabody was so surprised that he asked Delaney if she was certain.

"Judge," she replied, "you said you didn't want us wasting your time." Looking squarely at Melissa, she added, "That's why I am not bothering to question this particular witness."

The judge checked his watch. It was 12:10. "Who's your next witness?" he asked Dilks.

"Actually, Your Honor," he replied. "The Commonwealth is done. I rest my case."

After a lunch break, it was Delaney's turn to put on Spencer's defense. She began by calling him to testify.

"I'd been at the law firm less than one month when my father-in-law summoned me into his office," he recalled. During the next several minutes, Spencer explained how he had signed all of the probate papers in the Worthington case without bothering to read even one of them. "My father-in-law was an experienced attorney and he had prepared them. I trusted him. He was also running late for a golf game and was badgering me to sign them quickly. As long as one of us had read the documents, I figured it was safe to sign them."

"Did you read them sometime later?"

"Yes, that night, and, quite frankly, there was nothing in them that set off alarm bells. The papers gave our firm the right to liquidate stocks and other assets but there wasn't anything unusual about any of that."

Delaney said: "You heard your father-in-law testify that you had signed a blue slip—a receipt for the Circus Circus shares. Did you?"

"I never signed any blue slips the entire time I was at the firm. That blue slip the prosecution has produced is a forgery!"

"Did you steal the missing Circus Circus stock?"

"No!"

"Do you know who did?"

"Yes, my father-in-law, Augustus VanDenvender VI!"

Delaney was finished.

Dilks was so eager to interrogate Spencer that the prosecutor nearly fell as he was hurrying to the courtroom's podium. "Did you graduate from law school?" he asked.

"Yes. UVA, ur, the University here in town."

"And during those years that you were earning your law degree, did anyone ever tell you that as an attorney, you should never sign any document without first reading it?"

"Of course, but I trusted . . ."

Dilks reprimanded him. "A simple yes or no will do."

"I knew better than to sign a document without reading it, but I was young and I didn't want to offend my father-in-law."

"So your defense is that you didn't bother reading these documents because your father-in-law, who is one of the most highly regarded attorneys not only in Charlottesville, but in the entire state of Virginia, had already read them?"

"That's right."

"Now, I've heard rumors that the VanDenvender family is rich?"

Several spectators in the courtroom laughed.

"Yes, that's true."

"Powerful too, right?"

"Yes, the family is well connected, politically."

"Successful?"

"Yes."

"But you expect us to believe that Augustus VanDenvender VI, who already is rich and is highly respected, is the real culprit behind this entire scheme to steal stock? Stock, I might add, that is from the estate of one of his very best friends, Ambrose Worthington, who, testimony shows, never really trusted attorneys but had total faith in your father-in-law?"

As Spencer sat there listening, he suddenly felt afraid. As a judge, he had overseen hundreds of trials in an almost nonchalant manner. But now he was the defendant and he realized how terrifying it was to have another person deciding your future. Part of him wanted to scream: *I'm innocent! I didn't do anything wrong! Please believe me!* But all he could do was play out the role assigned him.

"I didn't steal those shares of stock," he repeated.

"Really?" Dilks replied sarcastically. "Well, let's look at the facts. You were fresh out of school, you were poor, you had married the boss's daughter, who testified this morning that you were obsessed with money, power, and social climbing."

"That's not true!"

"Oh, so she was lying too?"

"Yes!"

"Everyone is lying but you, is that what you're saying? One of the most highly respected men in the state is a liar. So is his daughter. You're the only person telling the truth? Is that right?"

Spencer didn't reply.

"Can you tell us," Dilks continued, "how long were you associated with the law firm of VanDenvender and Wythe?"

"I was there until I became a judge."

"During that time period, do you know of the firm ever hiring a graduate fresh out of college?"

"No."

"What was your GPA at UVA?"

"Before I met Melissa, it was a 3.4 on a 4-point scale. But after we began dating, I had a difficult time balancing a full-time job, my studies, and my social life. It fell to just under 3 points."

"Do you know if VanDenvender and Wythe has ever hired anyone with that low of a GPA?"

"It never has. The firm prides itself on hiring only the best and brightest."

"But it hired you," Cauldwell sneered. "Why? I think that answer is obvious."

Again Spencer didn't reply.

"You found an easy way to get ahead. You married the boss's daughter. Then you found an easy way to get rich! You stole those shares!"

"I object," Delaney said. "He's delivering a sermon here, not asking questions!"

It didn't matter. Dilks was done.

Judge Peabody noted that it was almost four o'clock. He said: "Ms. Delaney, how many more witnesses are you planning on calling?"

"Only one more, and Judge," she announced, "he will only take a few minutes. Then you can make your ruling and we can all go home."

Her comment clearly surprised him. "Ms. Delaney, while I admire your confidence," Judge Peabody said, "I must tell you that your client may not be in as good of a position here as you seem to think he is. Based on what has been said so far, I would strongly advise you to reconsider your obvious strategy of rushing through this trial. At this point, speed is not your friend. Are you reading what I'm telling you?"

"Yes, Your Honor," Delaney replied. "But my client knows what I'm doing and he agrees with it. Now, I'm ready to proceed if you are."

Peabody said: "Go ahead! It's your client's funeral."

Dilks felt smug and so did Melissa, Cauldwell, and Van-Denvender. Spencer was clearly losing.

"The defense," Delaney said, "calls George Anderson, the governor of the Commonwealth of Virginia!"

"You're calling the governor?" a startled Judge Peabody asked.

"Yes, Your Honor."

Two Virginia State Troopers opened the courtroom doors and Governor Anderson walked down the aisle. Miss Alice nervously swore him in. After she was done, he leaned close to her and whispered: "I hear you're one hell of a good shot!" She nearly fainted.

"Governor Anderson," Delaney began, "thank you for taking time to be here this afternoon."

"I can always make time for justice," he replied. He looked directly at Taylor Cauldwell, who was sitting just behind the prosecutor's table. He nodded and smiled. But Cauldwell didn't react.

"Your Honor," prosecutor Dilks said, standing to complain. "I don't know what sort of trick Ms. Delaney is hoping to pull, but I don't think the governor has any connection to this case. Governor Anderson and Attorney General Cauldwell are competing against each other in the current election and this appears to be nothing more than a cheap publicity stunt by Ms. Delaney to embarrass the attorney general by bringing his opponent here today!"

"I don't think the governor would waste his time coming here if he didn't have something important to say," Judge Peabody replied. "Ms. Delaney, you may begin questioning the witness."

Delaney said: "Governor, do you remember me contacting your office several weeks ago?"

"Yes, you met with my top criminal investigator. You claimed you had proof that your client was being framed by a powerful individual in this state. I admit I was skeptical until you showed me several documents."

Delaney opened a brown envelope and removed a blue receipt from it that appeared identical to the one that the Commonwealth had introduced earlier that day. "Do you recognize this blue slip?" she asked.

"Yes, you showed me that receipt when we first met. It shows that a half-million shares of Circus Circus stock were delivered to the firm of VanDenvender and Wythe."

"Do you know where this receipt came from?"

"It came from files in the law firm's basement that had been kept by Belle Patterson, who was Augustus VanDenvender

VI's private secretary for some time. I happened to have known Belle. She was a fine lady."

"Are there any signatures on this blue slip?"

"Yes, the receipt contains Belle Patterson's signature. It indicates that she took responsibility for a half-million shares of Circus Circus stock when they were delivered to the law firm."

"Is my client's name on this receipt?"

"No," Governor Anderson said. "But Belle wrote a bank account number on that blue slip that shows where the shares were later deposited."

"What did you do, if anything, after I showed this blue slip to you?"

"I called the director of the Virginia State Highway Patrol and told him that I needed his very best people to investigate a crime. I wanted this investigation done by the book, so I told him that he was not supposed to be influenced by me nor was he to tell the Commonwealth's attorney general—Taylor Cauldwell—anything about what he was doing."

"What happened next?"

"Two highway patrol investigators and auditors from the state tax commission began tracking down those missing Circus Circus shares. They discovered that within four hours after they were handed over to VanDenvender and Wythe, they were liquidated at a bank in the Cayman Islands. The proceeds from that stock sale were then 'washed' through a series of banks—first in Geneva, then Moscow, then Rome, then a bank in Bogota. Finally, the money ended up right back here in Charlottesville, a little less than fifty million dollars!"

"Governor," Delaney said, "can you tell the court whose account that money was deposited into?"

"Absolutely," he said, clearly enjoying himself. "It was deposited in an account owned by a Virginia company known as the AVD Corporation."

"And who owns that corporation?"

"The AVD stands for Augustus VanDenvender VI. He's also the only person who had access to the corporation's checking accounts."

Judge Peabody rapped his gavel to quiet the crowd. As for

VanDenvender, he sat in his seat staring forward, ignoring everyone around him.

"Were you able to discover how Augustus VanDenvender spent that stolen money?"

"Oh, he still has plenty of it under his control," Anderson said. "Our auditors found that he had invested it extremely well. He'd spent some on new automobiles, overseas trips, and to purchase land and houses for himself and family members. I remember that he specifically bought his daughter, Melissa, several racehorses. But he'd also used a considerable sum as political contributions."

"How much was given to political candidates?"

"More than thirty-million dollars during the past two decades. We're still going through the records, but it was funneled through what appear to be dummy corporations and straw-men contributors."

"Are there any politicians on that list who got this money, whose name we might recognize?"

Dilks jumped to his feet to object: "The governor didn't conduct any of this investigation personally," he said. "All mention of these funds should be stricken from the record and should not be considered. It's based on hearsay!"

"Nice try, Counselor, but I'm allowing it," said Peabody. "This is getting interesting."

Attorney General Cauldwell rose from his seat even though it was in the spectators' gallery. "Judge, you can't do this!" he declared. "Dilks is right! This is hearsay!"

Peabody smacked the bench with his gavel. "You're out of order and unless you want to go to jail for contempt, you'd better sit down!" Turning to Governor Anderson, Peabody said: "Governor, whose names are on that list?"

"Mr. Taylor Cauldwell, my opponent, is one name!"

"Let's make certain I understand this," Peabody said. "You're saying the attorney general of Virginia has accepted campaign contributions that can be tied directly to the missing Circus Circus shares stolen from the Worthington estate?"

"That's right. It's exactly what I am saying. He and a lot of other politicians in this commonwealth have been bankrolled with stolen funds."

Cauldwell couldn't stand it anymore. Despite Peabody's earlier warning, he once again stood up. "This is partisan politics!" he yelled.

Judge Peabody aimed his gavel at Cauldwell. "I told you to be quiet. If you want to protest, you can do it outside to reporters after this hearing ends. Now sit down and shut up!"

Cauldwell looked around the courtroom. His eyes landed on Augustus VanDenvender VI and Melissa. Both looked away from him. He slowly sank into his seat.

Peabody once again spoke directly to the witness. "Governor, do you have evidence that backs up these charges you're making?"

"Yes," he replied. He nodded to one of the state troopers standing in the rear of the courtroom, and the officer brought a two-inch-thick binder forward and handed it to Miss Alice. She, in turn, gave it to the judge. Peabody thumbed through it.

"What you have been given," Anderson volunteered, "is a confidential report by the Virginia Highway Patrol and State Tax Commission that verifies everything that I have just revealed."

"Judge," said Delaney, "may I ask the witness two quick questions?"

"Go ahead," said Peabody, who was still reading the report.

"Did your investigators find any evidence that money from the stolen Circus Circus shares went to my client?"

"Judge Evan Spencer," Anderson said firmly, "did not receive a cent of those stolen funds nor did he ever benefit, directly or indirectly, from them."

"And lastly, on what day did the VanDenvenders begin donating funds to Taylor Cauldwell's campaign?"

"I object!" said Dilks.

"Overruled!" Peabody snapped.

"Attorney General Cauldwell got his first sizeable contribution from them on the very same day that Mr. Cauldwell arranged for your client to be indicted for felony theft!" the governor announced.

That was enough for Peabody. He declared that all criminal charges against the defendant were being dismissed.

Spencer threw his arms around Delaney and hugged her. "You did it!" he cried. "You saved me again!"

"Don't forget Traci Sugarman," she said. "Without that receipt, we would've been sunk!" She noticed that Melissa was watching her, so she hugged Spencer again and kissed his cheek. When she looked back, Melissa and her father were trying to flee from the courtroom but were surrounded by reporters.

Spencer looked for Grasso. The priest was still sitting where he had been earlier, unable to move because of the mob in the room. Spencer forced his way through the crowd.

"Thanks for coming!" he said. "And thank you for the timing of your coughs!"

Grasso shrugged. "It must be allergies!" he said. "I'm allergic to obvious lies!" Grasso asked: "The stone: Do you still have it?"

"Yes, but not for long. I've decided who needs to get it."

Two weeks later, Evan Spencer was sitting on the sidewalk curb outside his apartment reading the morning *Charlottesville Courant* while he waited for Delaney. The newspaper's front page reported that Taylor Cauldwell had dropped out of the gubernatorial race. Several pundits predicted his political career was finished. Another story inside the newspaper revealed that Augustus VanDenvender IV had been forced off the board of VanDenvender and Wythe, and was being investigated by a special grand jury in Charlottesville. Near the end of that story, the newspaper noted that Boyd, Stackhouse, and Brown had reached an out-of-court settlement agreement with former Judge Evan Spencer in its sixty-million-dollar lawsuit. Even though Spencer had been cleared of all criminal wrongdoing, he still had been the attorney of record during the Worthington probate and, as such, he'd been responsible for protecting the estate. His failure to carry out that job had cost him nearly all of his financial assets.

Spencer closed the paper. It was finally over. He thought about how much his life had changed. Less than a year earlier, he had been married, wealthy, and one of Charlottesville's most prominent and successful citizens. He'd anticipated serving on Virginia's Supreme Court. Now he was sitting on a curb with everything he owned crammed inside a single suitcase. He was no longer a judge, had little money, and had been abandoned by his country club friends. Yet, none of that bothered him. If anything, he felt free.

Was he in love with Patti Delaney? He wasn't sure. At one time, he had been deeply in love with Melissa or, at least, he had thought that he was. That marriage had turned into a nightmare. How could he be certain that his feelings about Delaney weren't also going to lead him into another emotional disaster? He found her sexually exciting, intelligent, and fun. He enjoyed spending time with her. But he'd also felt that way about Melissa. Or had he? He did a quick mental comparison of the women and concluded that they were vastly different. Delaney was not self-absorbed nor was she selfish. She was a woman who would love him as much as he loved her, and even more important, more than she loved her own self.

What guarantee did he have that in a month, a year, two years, or even longer they would still be happy together? None! He understood that. There were no guarantees in love. Just like religion, it required a leap of faith.

He finally heard the sputtering of Delaney's Saab as it rounded the corner. She was towing a U-Haul trailer with a woman's bicycle and several boxes lashed to its top. When the Saab stopped in front of him, Spencer popped open the passenger's door and picked up his suitcase. He started to slide it into the Saab's backseat but there wasn't enough room. All of the space was jammed with Delaney's belongings.

"Sorry," she said. "I guess those lamps can be left behind."

He pulled a pair of table lamps from the rear seat. Their bases were made of heavy plaster molded to look like ocean waves. The lamps' necks were in the shape of jumping dolphins. The lightbulbs screwed into the mammals' mouths. They were as ugly as anything that Spencer had ever seen. He placed them on the sidewalk, but his suitcase still wouldn't fit and he had to remove a 3-D photograph of a white poodle in a cheap brown plastic frame. He put the poodle picture next to the lamps, forced his suitcase into the car, and climbed into the passenger seat. He kissed Delaney. She was wearing a sheer top that covered a neon orange bra. It matched her orange Capri pants and orange sandals. There was an orange ribbon in her red hair and on it was a replica of an orange. He'd never seen so much orange on one person.

"What?" she said, noticing his stare. "Too much orange?"

"No," he replied. "You look perfect!" And he meant it.

"How's Santa Fe sound to you?" Delaney asked. "I've heard they've got a good opera company there."

"Opera?" he replied. "I didn't know you liked opera."

"I hate it but it would be nice to know we could go if we ever got the urge."

He laughed as she pulled away from the curb. "We have to make one stop before we leave town," he said, tapping his fingers on a Federal Express package. "There's a drop box at the University bookstore." She kept the Saab running while he went inside and deposited the package into the blue-and-white receptacle.

"It's done," he told her. "I'm finally rid of it."

Minutes later, they crossed Charlottesville's city limits and Spencer noticed that neither of them bothered to look back.

There was no Federal Express office on Tortola, the largest of the British Virgin Islands, but once a week an enterprising islander named Felix Archibald would sail to nearby St. Thomas and collect whatever urgent packages had been left behind at the airport. After he returned, he would telephone the wealthy European and American vacationers who had rented the posh villas on the island during the winter with their grand views of Cane Garden Bay. Archibald would negotiate a delivery fee, and then tie the boxes to his ancient Italian motor bike with coarse string and ride along the narrow roads that rimmed the island's mountainous terrain.

His first delivery on this particular afternoon was to a villa called La Bella, which was surrounded by a twelve-foot-high security fence. The housekeeper who answered at the iron gate offered to take the package from him, but Archibald had learned that his chances for a generous tip were better if he presented the package to the addressee in person. He fell in behind the housekeeper and walked through a courtyard filled with orchids, poinsettias, and philodendrons. He could smell the delicate fragrance of the poisonous but beautiful oleander and the more pungent aroma of night-blooming jasmine. At the rear of the villa, the housekeeper pointed at a single chaise lounge near the edge of a swimming pool. Although there was a white bathrobe nearby, the woman made no effort to reach for it when she saw Archibald coming toward her. She was wearing only a narrow black thong. She looked at him from behind her sunglasses and raised herself up gracefully from the lounge to sign his receipt. He sensed that she was not embarrassed despite her seminudity and he knew why. The woman was not an exhibitionist. Rather, she simply didn't care that her breasts were exposed to him. He was, after all, only a black islander and like the male servants who worked in her villa; she did not think of him as a man, but rather as only a servant.

"Have the maid give you ten dollars on your way out," she said, dismissing him. She did not offer to take the package from his hands, so he leaned it against a waist-high metal-and-glass table that held plastic bottles of tanning lotions and a pitcher of agua de coco. The woman returned to the chaise.

About an hour later, she waded into the cool pool, where she splashed her well-oiled brown skin, and then returned to her seat and picked up the package. She once again read the sender's name and address: Evan Spencer. Charlottesville, Virginia. It seemed so far away from this Caribbean paradise. A world away.

She pulled the tab that ran along the package's spine, which opened the box like a zipper, and peered inside. There was no letter or card, only a round object wrapped in red silk and tied with a bow. A present. She shook the package, causing the gift to tumble out onto the chaise. She undid the ribbon and turned back the silk.

A white stone. A simple, white stone. Nothing else. Why would he send her a stone? She reached down and picked up the rock with her hands so that she could get a better look at it. As she lifted it, Ophelia Elizabeth Victoria VanDenvender, better known as Melissa, felt a weak electrical charge prick the center of her left palm.

"Ouch!" she exclaimed. "That hurt!"

ACKNOWLEDGMENTS

I would like to thank Paul M. Peatross, Jr., presiding judge, Albemarle Circuit Court, Charlottesville, Virginia, and Thomas Fortkort, retired judge, Fairfax Circuit Court, Fairfax, Virginia, for their expert guidance about courtroom procedures. I'm also indebted to Virginia attorneys Charles Anderson, Michael Fortkort, and Jay B. Myerson, who shared wonderful courtroom anecdotes with me. Randy Davis, Deputy Director of Communications for the Virginia Attorney General's Office, helped me interpret Virginia statutes. Marie Deans, founder of Murder Victim Families for Reconciliation, provided me with insights about death penalty cases in Virginia. For questions regarding forensics, I sought guidance from Kathy Reynolds of the American Academy of Forensic Sciences; Ronald Singer, Laboratory Director, Tarrant County Medical Examiner's Office, Fort Worth, Texas; Melinda Carter, Human Osteology Program Director, Illinois State Museum; and Dr. Ed Uthman, pathologist, Houston, Texas.

Stigmata: A Medieval Mystery in a Modern Age, by Ted Harrison, published by Penguin Books, and *The Secret Archives of the Vatican,* by Maria Luisa Ambrosini with Mary Willis, published by Little, Brown and Company, were valuable resources when I was investigating mystical religious happenings and the Vatican.

Thanks also are due to literary agent Robert Gottlieb of Trident Media Group for encouraging me to write novels in addition to my nonfiction books. Robert Gleason, my editor at Tor/Forge Books, was top-rate with his editorial recommendations, and thanks to Sarah Scheffel for copyediting the manuscript. Several friends read early drafts for me. They include: Nelson DeMille, Dianne Francis, Georginia Havill, Walt and Keran Harrington, Barbara Myerson, and Gerald and Miriam

Shur. Each offered me much-appreciated comments that helped improve the text.

As always, my parents, Elmer and Jean Earley, read my first effort and cheered me on. I'd also like to recognize other family members and friends who supported me in my decision to take a new writing path. They include: Gloria Brown, James Brown, Ruey and Ellen Brown, Phillip and Joanne Corn, Donnie and Dana Davis, George and Linda Earley, Marie Heffelfinger, Michelle Holland, Don and Sue Infeld, Reis Kash, Richard and Joan Miles, Lynn and LouAnn Smith, and Elsie and Jay Strine.

I wish to thank my children, who remain my inspiration and keep things real for me: Stephen, Kevin, Tony, Kathy, Kyle, Evan, and Traci. The rap lyrics spoken by Lester Amil in Chapter 4 were written by Kevin, and are much appreciated because I have no ear for rap music.

This novel is dedicated to my loving wife, Patti, who offered me insightful editorial suggestions, was always my biggest booster, and masterfully resolved life's everyday challenges so that I could work undisturbed. She's my best friend, and without her, this novel could not have been written.